PRAISE FOR HEATHER BURCH

"Heather Burch has proven herself to have such an exceptional storytelling range that one might be tempted to call her 'the Mariah Carey of romance fiction.' *One Lavender Ribbon* blew my expectations out of the water and then swept me away on a wave of sweet romance. Don't miss this one."

—Serena Chase, contributor to *USA Today's* Happy Ever After blog and author of *The Seahorse Legacy*

"Burch's latest combines a sweet, nostalgic, poignant tale of a true love of the past with the discovery of true love in the present . . . Burch's lyrical, contemporary storytelling, down-to-earth characters, and intricate plot make this one story that will delight the heart."

—*RT Book Reviews* on *One Lavender Ribbon*, 4.5 Stars

"Heather Burch draws you into the story from page one and captures your attention, your emotions, and your heart strings until the very end. She reaches into your very soul with a story that is so real that it stays with you for weeks after the last page is turned, the last sigh has floated away, the last giggle has played out, and the last tear is shed."

—Carolyn Brown, *New York Times* and *USA Today* bestselling author of *The Wedding Pearls*

Down the Hidden Path

Down the Hidden Path

THE ROADS TO RIVER ROCK SERIES
BOOK 2

Heather Burch

Published by Montlake Romance, Seattle

www.apub.com

Amazon, the Amazon logo, and Montlake Romance are trademarks of Amazon.com, Inc., or its affiliates.

ISBN-13: 9781503949843 (hardcover)
ISBN-10: 1503949842 (hardcover)
ISBN-13: 9781503948099 (paperback)
ISBN-10: 1503948099 (paperback)

Cover design by Laura Klynstra

Printed in the United States of America

For Jake. My firstborn. I've watched you grow into a man and I've never been more proud of you than I am right now. Love you big.

CHAPTER 1

Dear Dad,

It's fall here and the leaves are changing. The colors are unusually vivid this season, the deepest red, the brightest yellow, and the richest orange I've seen. Or maybe it's that I've been gone so long, staring at endless shades of olive drab, I'd forgotten the beauty of autumn.

I drove out to the cemetery yesterday to visit the Havinger family plot where Mom's buried. I wondered if we should contact Grandfather Havinger and see about having your urn placed there by Mom's grave; it just seems wrong that the two of you aren't together.

But I know that's not what you asked for. Your words echo back to me: "We had your mother in life. We can let them have her in death." You were always so strong, so fair—even with those who didn't deserve it. Of everything you taught me about life, three things stand out. How to be a good man, how to be a good soldier, and how to be a good father.

The first, I daily strive for. The second, well, I suppose I've done. The third . . . the third I hope to one day do. And I guess that's what this letter is about.

I've put in my time for Uncle Sam, and though the journey was both long and radically difficult, I find myself missing it and wondering what life would be today had I never signed up. I don't know how to be a civilian, Dad. I'm a little bit scared I'll fail at it. What advice would you give me if you were standing here at the water's edge, enjoying the grand display of colors and life? I imagine you placing your hand on my shoulder and saying, "It'll be fine, son. Truly, it will all be fine." I wish you were here. I wish I could hear your voice one more time.

Though worlds separate us, you're one of the biggest pieces of my heart.

Your son,
Jeremiah

Jeremiah McKinley wadded the letter and dropped it on the last embers of the early morning campfire. Fog rolled off the lake, great billowing clouds that rose and disappeared as the sun trekked over the mountaintop. It had been the pre-dawn hour when he left his house and walked down to the rock-strewn water's edge where he'd started a fire with wood and kindling he'd gathered earlier in the week. There was still a chill in the air and it went straight to his bones as he wondered, for the thousandth time, what he was doing back in River Rock, Missouri.

Jeremiah turned to walk back up the winding path to his house, the place he'd throw his time and attention into until he figured out how to be normal again. When he thought of the road ahead, though he was apprehensive, seedlings of excitement had taken root in his heart. He planned to open a hunting and fishing lodge right here on Table Rock Lake. And instead of carrying a gun to kill insurgents, he'd carry one for hunting deer or turkey, maybe even the occasional bear.

Jeremiah shot a glance in the direction of his sister's land and her ever-odd artists' colony. Charlee'd found happiness, and that was something Miah wanted as well. Happiness. Contentment.

Peace.

An hour later, he headed into town with the weight of all his questions still heavy on his shoulders. When he spotted the breakfast taco truck, he whipped into the Dairy Flip's parking lot.

He counted four people in line and glanced down at his watch. 7:25. Miah chewed the inside corner of his cheek. Since he'd been in River Rock, he'd come to love the breakfast taco truck that showed up wherever and whenever it chose. He hated the fact that you could stand in line and at any given moment, the man inside would say, "Sorry, we're out," and close the little window. Just like that. It had happened to him twice. Miah tapped his foot and waited behind a guy with three kids in tow. Three customers in front of him, a woman with long, ink-black hair stood on the tiptoes of her tennis shoes, arms folded and propped on the counter while she chatted with the guy inside.

Miah had no patience for morning chitchat and was just considering the merits of telling her so when her laugh split the air.

Something shot straight into his gut. The sound from her lips was deep, rumbling, almost smoky, rich as warm butter and sweet as mountain honey. He knew that laugh.

A slender hand reached up and captured some of the silken hair. Jeremiah's mind rushed to catch up. This couldn't be her. But that voice. When the guy in front of him moved and blocked Miah's view, he sidestepped so he could see her fully, if only from behind. He had stepped completely out of the line and a heavyset woman rushed up to take his spot.

Who cared? His eyes trailed over the brunette, assessing the possibility. Right height. But wrong body shape. This woman had long, slender legs, a perfectly shaped rear end, a small waist. No, it wasn't her.

Miah stepped back into line a little surprised at the disappointment rising in his chest.

And that's when she turned around.

———

"Gray?"

Mary Grace Smith almost dropped her tacos. She'd spun from the counter to hurry back to her car when a wide chest stepped out from the line and nearly body-slammed her. Her bottle of Coke teetered on the edge of her makeshift food tray. Choice words shot into her mind. What kind of person jumps in the face of someone carrying food? But then something registered as her gaze slid from the tray between them up over his chest, neckline, chin. He'd said her name. Finally, her eyes found his. And her heart stopped.

"Miah?" It was one word. Just his name. But having it on her lips and looking into that golden gaze caused a flurry of unwanted sensations. *Run. Run, run, run, run, run.*

This was a bad dream; that was all. A bad dream where she'd awaken drenched in sweat. Of course, she'd known the odds of seeing him. She'd heard he was returning to River Rock. And suddenly, with Jeremiah in front of her, blocking her exit, River Rock seemed smaller. Too small.

He was all wide smile and animated eyes as he said, "Wow, I . . . I didn't know you were living here. Are you just visiting?"

Those eyes she'd watched for hundreds, if not thousands, of hours. Eyes that had, at one time in her life, entranced her. Eyes she'd drowned in. Of course, everyone who met Jeremiah was hopelessly trapped in his golden gaze. Add to that the ridiculously chiseled features of a Greek god and that magnetic personality. He was the triple threat. Miah made you feel like you were the only woman on the planet. Even if you were the checker at the Piggly Wiggly and all you were doing was scanning his food. She'd actually seen women swoon. And that right there was why Gray took a full step back.

He didn't seem to notice as he waited—perfect smile in place—for her to answer. Gray mustered her composure. "I just moved back. A few months ago."

"It's great to see you." His brows were riding high, all excitement and anticipation. The sunlight behind him played in the strands of his light brown hair.

Gray steeled herself. "You too." She nearly choked on the words getting them out, and as quickly as she'd run into him, she could run away. "Well, better get going."

When she stepped around his wide shoulders, he caught her arm. *Don't look up. Don't look up.* But her eyes had a mind of their own and trailed to his. The tiniest of frowns creased his forehead. He stood not more than a few inches from her, her shoulder pointing like an arrow at his heart.

"Gray," he whispered, and the sound raced down her body and right into her soul. "We need to catch up."

Gray bit her cheeks hard until she tasted blood on one side. She painted on a wide, cheery smile. "Oh, sure. Yes, you know, I'm so busy these days, Jeremiah. But I'm sure we'll see each other in town now and then." And she blinked, once, and then again. The gentlest tug liberated her from his hand. Her feet fell into motion and before she knew it, she was at her car door.

She fumbled with the keys and the tacos and the cold drink until she managed to get in. Gray slammed the car door shut, closing out everything. Closing out Miah McKinley and his smile that melted hearts. When she shifted to put the keys in the ignition, her hands were trembling. Gray squeezed her eyes closed. The fact that one run-in with Miah could thoroughly wreck her, even after all this time, bit into her pride.

She glanced in the rearview mirror to find him standing in the same spot, one hand lifted to his forehead to block the sun. But from the safety of her car, it resembled a salute, and that shot into Gray's heart and settled there. Miah'd lost his dad not much more than a year ago. And at that time, she hadn't been able to stop her mind from trailing to him. How he was handling the news. Was he okay?

"It doesn't matter," she grumbled to herself as she started the car and backed out of the parking spot. She cast a fleeting glance to him and waved as she drove by. Gray breathed deeply, the scent of tacos a good replacement for the regret she tasted, even now.

She reminded herself that Miah was just a snippet from her past. And as she put her foot on the gas, she let the past go because it was her future she was interested in. Twenty miles down the road, David was waiting for her.

———

Jeremiah took stock of the work he'd completed and gave himself an imaginary pat on the back. Room number two of, oh, twenty was ready for business.

Sweat had gathered across his brow and he brushed at it now, feeling the sting of sawdust as his forearm made contact with his face. Wood shavings peppered his lashes. He needed a shower. After that, he could search out food.

The remodeled bathroom was only a couple doors away in the upstairs hallway of the sprawling lodge. He'd begun to think of it as a lodge. He needed to. Otherwise frightful words came to mind like rattrap, dungeon, impossible money pit. It had been a lodge for parents back in the day when the land he now called home had been a boys-and-girls camp. Before his mother's death, she'd bought the two-hundred-acre camp after it went bankrupt. She'd sectioned it off into forty-acre plots for each of her children: Jeremiah, his three brothers, and his sister, Charlee. Jeremiah's was the best piece of land as far as he was concerned, though Charlee's had the cool little cabins—most of which had been renovated to some degree, and Caleb's section of ground held hot springs that gurgled mineral water up from deep in the Missouri earth. The bubbling geysers were cool, no doubt, but Caleb, with his love for water, was the only logical choice for that hunk of land. It was secluded, too, another plus for Caleb; as a child, they'd barely been able to keep clothes on him. If his baby brother still held an affinity for nakedness, the isolation of the mountain cabin and its surrounding springs would be a perfect refuge. Of course—Miah looked around, catching his reflection in the wide window overlooking the wooded world beyond—everything about the two hundred acres was secluded. He showered quickly even though the new, state-of-the-art rain forest showerhead beckoned a longer visit. It had been an impulse buy. A luxury, since he'd spent most of his time in the last few years showering in open-air tents with the sun overhead and the temperature scorching.

Yes, it was good to be back in the States. But could he make this place feel like a home? Sure, he decided and pulled on a fresh pair of jeans and a T-shirt emblazoned with the words *Army Strong.*

Having his sister on the adjacent property helped. *She'd* made a home there. The Marilee Artists' Retreat made him smile. Thoughts of King Edward and his forever kilt and knobby knees made him smile. The fact his sister had found love made him smile. When he'd first met the motley crew of artists, Miah hadn't been particularly fond of any of them. But they'd grown on him. So had Ian, the soldier who'd stolen his sister's heart.

He paused at the top of the stairs overlooking the vaulted great room below and kitchen doorway beyond. Yeah, he could make this a home. Of course he could. And if Charlee and he had their way, one day their brothers, Isaiah, Gabriel, and Caleb would return from active duty, trade in their fatigues for jeans and work boots, and claim their lands, too. If any wanted to help with the lodge, great. If not, at least they would all be together again. After losing Dad, he'd come to understand just how important that was.

———

Gray bit her lip while she stood at the edge of the auditorium. Heart pounding, palms sweaty. Some things never changed. It was almost as if she were back in middle school. Her gaze flew across David's competition, sizing them up without even meaning to. There were the uninterested ones—and they were no competition at all, really, the kids whose passing grade depended on their participation in the science fair. They sat along the walls or on the bleachers, body language one shade beyond boredom. Then, there were the ones who tried, but just weren't at that top level. They smiled as the judges came by, toyed with their fingers, and scurried to the snack table once the judges had moved on. And then there were the "solemns." That's how she'd come to think of them. So solemn about every grade on every paper, so serious about every test and pop quiz. Right now, they were nervous as cats in a room full of rocking chairs. They shuffled their weight, eyes darting around the room, checking and rechecking their projects, making sure every tiny detail was perfect. And right in the middle of them was David.

Across the expanse, his gaze landed on her and on the inside, her heart did a little flop. The judges were almost to him and he'd sought her out, found her in the crowd, even though his mom and dad were standing right there and were more than enough moral support for a twelve-year-old science enthusiast.

Angie waved Gray over when she caught David's eye on her. A lump swelled in Gray's throat because Angie always did this, sharing the one thing both women loved beyond measure: David.

The judges made it to the table before Gray could get there. David launched into his monologue about the CyberKnife and the research he'd done on its use in radiation therapy for cancer patients.

Gray had heard the spiel multiple times as he'd tweaked and tweaked some more. She'd driven him to the hospital where he'd interviewed a radiation therapist and even got a quote from one of the oncologists.

He'd put his heart and soul into the project. There was no way he could lose. The winner of this year's science fair would win a collector set of DVDs about NASA. It'd be a dream come true for David. From the time he was five and saw the movie *RocketMan*, he'd wanted to know more about space travel.

The judges left and Gray waited her turn patiently. First, a smile from Mom, who told him he'd done great, a chin-chuck from Dad, who said he was a shoo-in. Then David, eyes sparkling with the kind of excitement that only twelve-year-olds and maybe pixies had, reached out for a hug from Gray.

"You sure hugging me won't hurt your street cred?" she said, pulling him into her arms and mashing his silky dark hair against her.

He shook his head, causing the strands to flutter then fall into place. "Nah, all the guys think you're hot."

"David!" Angie's hands went to her hips.

"They do, Mom. Most of them don't know she's my birth mom, so they just think this pretty older woman hangs out with me all the time."

Angie's face read shock. She pointed at him, but looked at Gray. "Can you believe this? He's twelve, talking like this. *Hot* and *older woman* . . .*"

Gray cleared her throat and felt the prickle of embarrassment working its way up to her cheeks. "Oh dear. We may need to clear this up for the boys in your class."

David grinned. "Nope. Let them wonder."

Bill reached over and took his wife's arm. "You should close your mouth, honey."

"I'm appalled at what I'm hearing."

David extended a high five in his dad's direction, but was stopped dead by Angie's sharp voice. "Don't you dare encourage this." She cast a glance heavenward. "Men."

Gray nodded, kept her mouth shut, though conversations like this were common on every subject from what movies to what kind of music was appropriate. Inevitably, they kept Gray included in the discussion, even asked her opinion often, but she volunteered little. She had no claim and no right to offer advice. David was her son by blood only and if she ever lost him, she'd die.

———

An hour later the three adults sat at the ice cream shop with a sullen David picking at a sundae. When his gaze lifted, there was fresh fire in his honey-colored eyes. "Liam Brockman? Seriously? Like no one's ever seen a volcano before." He shoved his sundae away and crossed his arms.

"Sarcasm, David," Angie warned.

He met her gaze squarely. "Sarcasm is a beautiful thing, Mom, when one knows how to wield it properly." His eyes narrowed. "And I can't believe you made me congratulate him. He probably didn't even build the stupid volcano."

Gray concentrated on her chocolate soda, which wasn't as good as the ones Rodney made at the Dairy Flip in River Rock, but it would do. She really needed to stay out of this conversation because she agreed with David. The volcano was stupid even if it did have LED lights and realistic sound. Volcanoes were third grade. And besides, that Liam boy was mean to the bone and probably only won because his dad was a scientist and the teachers were sucking up.

It was a few moments before Gray realized someone was talking to her. She looked up. "I'm sorry. What?"

Bill smiled. "You were mumbling something into your drink."

She blinked. "Was I?"

Three heads bobbed up and down.

Gray tried to swallow her indignation about the injustice of David coming in second to a bully. Of course, Angie didn't know that Liam kid picked on David. Before she could stop herself, words were flying from her mouth. "I was just thinking that Liam didn't really act surprised that he'd won. You know, like he could have thrown anything up there and he'd have the prize."

Angie raised one perfectly arched brow.

Gray's heart nearly stopped. Had she done it? Crossed a line? She tried to swallow, but her throat had gone cotton dry.

Angie's head tilted to the side, her bright eyes sharp as needles. "But don't you agree that David was the bigger person for congratulating him?"

In a perfect world, yes. But this wasn't a perfect world. This was middle school, where acts like that were not only not appreciated, but exploited later. David had already suffered at the hands of bullies. "Honestly, Angie, I was also thinking about what an important project this was." She turned her focus to David. "You brought awareness of a fairly new technology. What if there were people at the science fair today who have cancer? Or may have it in the future. You told them about a treatment they may never have known about. You may have saved a life today. Knowledge really is power. You enlightened people today, and that's worth a heck of a lot more than a blue ribbon and some DVDs."

David studied her for a long time. "Yeah." He pulled his sundae closer and dove in. "I did do that."

Whew. Bullet successfully dodged. That didn't alter the fact that as David got older, it became more and more difficult to tread lightly. Gray didn't always agree with Angie, and that seemed to be more common with the passing years. Bill was a fairly neutral party, but he deferred to his wife.

Gray was—she continually reminded herself—the outsider. Just lucky to have such an open relationship with David and his adoptive parents. Life was funny that way. Giving you for the briefest moment the one thing you desire more than life, then snatching it away. Or out of reach. There, but never yours. Never yours.

As Gray drove the twenty miles from Laver to River Rock, she thought about life and memories. How the things that formed who she was now were the very things that had once nearly destroyed her. Back at home, Gray's thoughts turned to Jeremiah McKinley. She'd seen him earlier in the day and now he haunted the space in her mind she thought she'd cleared. As Gray nuzzled into her bed and tucked under a handmade quilt—fashioned by her grandmother's own hands before the stroke, when Nana could whip together a quilt in record time—Gray tried to force the image of Miah from her head. But when she closed her eyes and the quiet and the darkness took her, she saw him, standing there, his hand in a sort of farewell salute as she'd driven away. The soldier who'd come home. The soldier who'd never been hers.

And never would.

CHAPTER 2

Jeremiah stepped around the side of the building past a giant metal Gerbera daisy and an equally oversize hummingbird perched on one of the petals. He shook his head when the wind kicked up, causing the hummingbird's flat mesh wings—held on by wire—to flutter. Although Charlee's place was only a short walk away, it seemed like a different world. A world of lollipops and metal flowers. A world of color and chaos. He was a soldier, a man who preferred order to impulse and functionality to folly. He was glad he didn't have to look out his windows and see this every day.

He knew Charlee loved this place. She referred to it as her sanctuary of artistry and whimsy. Miah always felt a little out of sorts being surrounded by the gargantuan colorful flowers that seemed to have "grown" in scattered patterns with little thought to their placement. He stopped, sank his hands deep into the pockets of his jeans, and took in the dance floor, complete with outdoor tables all heavy laden with tiny sparkling lights. It was Wonderland. And he was a reluctant Alice.

This was—in all its glory—the Marilee Artists' Retreat, a place where a handful of aging artist types painted and gathered and now lived. Charlee had planned for it to be a short-time thing for the visiting artists, but Mr. Gruber, King Edward, and the sisters had fallen so head over heels for the retreat, they stayed on. And on. And on. Charlee couldn't be happier.

"Charlee's in the kitchen."

Jeremiah turned to face Ian, coming out of the large building where dinners were prepared. Ian was perfect for Charlee—kind, strong, and didn't put up with any crap. He was also the man his sister had chosen from a plethora of potential suitors in town. 'Course, none of them could handle Charlee. So Miah was glad his father had sent Ian. That's how he'd come to think of it. Major Mack had *sent* Ian, along with a journal Ian was supposed to share with Charlee. For the first time in her life, Charlee had gotten to know the poet their father really was. And as a bonus, she'd also gotten the man of her dreams, Ian, who'd been a soldier under Major Mack's leadership.

Miah and his brothers had always known how poetic their father was. He'd instilled in them the importance of writing when in combat. Journaling, jotting down thoughts and feelings, was one way to process, one way to mourn, grow, and move on. Moving on was necessary for men in combat. Moving on was what he was *trying* to do now.

Miah shook Ian's hand over the daisy. "Hope you did the cooking, not her."

Ian smiled. "I got your six."

It was not that Charlee wasn't a good cook, but Ian had been to culinary school—though he didn't finish—and Charlee only knew how to make regular food. Food for the masses. Growing up, it had been Charlee raising her big brothers, cooking dinners, making sure Caleb, the baby, got some food, too. A twelve-year-old when their mom died, Charlee sort of stepped into her shoes. A lot of responsibility for a pre-teen. Now that he thought about it, maybe whimsy was a necessity for her now. The wind kicked up and the hummingbird's wings went into overdrive, spinning in the breeze. Miah chuckled. Maybe he needed a bit more whimsy in his life.

Jeremiah angled to face the kitchen, where warm light seeped from the wide picture window over the stainless steel sink. "What's on the menu?"

"She said meatloaf was your favorite."

Oh. Regular food.

Ian grinned. "Well, I don't do meatloaf, so we're having prime rib with creamy horseradish and au gratin potatoes."

Miah's mouth watered. "Now that you've married my sister, can I come over for dinner every night?"

Ian dropped his hands on his hips. "Sure. By the way, thanks for giving her away at the ceremony. I know we sprung it on you."

"I'm glad I was able to be there. Now that it's been a month, how you holding up?"

"Married life is good." Ian smiled all the way to his eyes. "It's really good."

Miah held his hands up. "Okay, okay. I don't need details."

Ian removed a spiderweb from the daisy. "She still wishes the other brothers could have been there."

"Hey, I'm just glad she got around to planning the wedding."

Ian threw his head back and laughed. "She didn't. My mom and sister had to. I thought girls were supposed to *want* to plan a wedding. Isn't that like some sort of unwritten rule? Some law of being female?"

Miah placed a hand on his shoulder. "Female rules and laws? Dude, you are so talking to the wrong guy if you want answers about females." For a hot instant his underwhelming reunion with Gray at the taco stand flashed through Jeremiah's mind. Women and their laws. Yeah, he was clueless.

"Who needs answers about females?" The voice was old, gruff from years of hard living and too many late nights, but it had a solid ring to it, a sort of granite quality that Miah admired. He turned to face Mr. Gruber, who was stepping onto the dance platform.

Of all the artists, Mr. Gruber was Miah's favorite. The old man's paintings were known the world over, but it was his no-nonsense attitude about life that endeared him to Jeremiah. Gruber just might carry the secrets to life as easily as he carried paintbrushes. And he was always quick with his wit and willing to share his knowledge. Another admirable trait, in Miah's eyes. "Ah. Our modern-day Renaissance man. I bet you have all the answers concerning women," Miah said.

Gruber smiled with his crooked grin. "All the answers. Just don't know the questions."

All three men laughed.

Ian nodded toward the kitchen. "Go on in and say hi to your sister. I'll keep this old coot company."

Gruber closed one eye and pointed an arthritic finger at Ian. "Without witnesses, I'll teach you some manners, Lunchbox."

Miah left the two to duke it out and headed into the kitchen to find a humming Charlee hovered over the stove. Unable to resist, he snuck up behind her and grabbed her waist.

She jolted. Her head of blond curls flew back and barely missed his chest. The spoon in her hand went flying, sending creamy white sauce onto the wall and counter.

"Nice job, sis."

She spun on him and punched him square in the chest. It was a bit like a fly battering a bull. "You jerk!"

Miah only chuckled in response. "You better get used to brotherly abuse. I'm here for good."

Her anger disappeared. She jumped into his arms and hugged his neck. "I know. I'm so glad. If we can just get the others home . . ."

He winked, peeled her arms from his aching neck. "I'm working on it. Isaiah is considering coming home."

Charlee's giant blue eyes widened. "Really?"

He nodded. "Yeah. I've been telling him how much I need his help here working on the lodge." Honestly, he knew Isaiah was getting tired. And tired soldiers were dangerous soldiers. Isaiah had never really been military material, in Miah's mind. He was a profound thinker who experienced the blows of the world a little too intimately. It had always been hard for Isaiah to leave the battlefield on the battlefield. "They call him Preacher, you know?"

Charlee rinsed the spoon under hot water, then tossed it in the sink and selected a new one from the stainless steel drawer. "That's fitting."

"Yeah. I think the only reason he hasn't gotten out yet is because he feels like those young guys in his unit are his flock, and what kind of shepherd leaves his flock?"

Charlee's eyes grew misty. "Just like Dad said in his journal."

Miah'd read the entire thing; some pages he'd read over and over again. He'd dropped more tears than a box of Kleenex could combat, and once he broke down completely, having to close the book and walk away. The words in his father's journal communicated a soldier's most intimate thoughts, fears, hopes, and dreams. And it not only shattered his heart, it rebuilt it anew.

Charlee must have noticed the change in him. She kissed his cheek, having to rise on her tiptoes to do so. "Bring me Isaiah first, then Gabriel, then Caleb. And I'll cook you dinner every night."

He winced. She struck him again, this time on the arm with the kitchen spoon. "Why Caleb last?"

Charlee used her forearm to brush hair from her face. "He's all Army. I don't think he'll give up military life until he's forced to retire. He's got too much of Dad in him."

Miah winked. "If he's going to stay in until retirement, I'd say he's got just enough of Dad in him."

Charlee nodded and turned her attention back to the sauce she was supposed to be tending.

Silence filled the space, a little heavy because Miah wanted to discuss something with her and *needed* to be nonchalant about it. "So, I, uh, saw Gray in town."

Charlee spun to face him. "Gray Smith?"

He nodded, averted his eyes as if to seem casual. "Mm hm."

"Was she visiting? I don't think she lives here."

"She just moved back." Yep. The hem of his shirt was oh so interesting.

"Oh. Is she living at her grandmother's house? It's been empty for years."

He shrugged, pulled a loose thread. "Don't know."

"How did she look?"

"Beautiful." Miah thought back to the sultry body, that deep laugh he'd heard. "I mean, really beautiful. Her hair is longer, ink black and just as straight, lands at the bottom of her waist—which is tiny, by the way, and now she has curves."

"She's a woman now, Miah. She was a girl when you left." Charlee spoke, but the sounds seemed to be coming from far away, as if they were background noise to the memory.

Something cold passed over him, some unnamed ghost stretching its fingers and tickling over his flesh. He met Charlee's gaze and for a long time didn't speak. But the thought of Gray filled his mind. "She's really beautiful."

"She can't be that different. She was always pretty, Miah."

He rubbed the back of his neck. "How did I not notice?"

Charlee rolled her eyes and placed a hand flat on her hip. "Too busy with your cheerleaders. All gloss and glitz." She squared off to face him. "Gray was too good for you."

He laughed without humor. It was true. He'd been all surface and fun. He'd only had an inkling of depth when he was with her; she'd made him more. "I guess you just don't see your best friend like that."

"No, certainly not when cheerleaders are flipping their skirts in your face."

"Hey! I can get this kind of abuse anywhere," Miah said. One thing about Charlee, she didn't mince words.

"Bet she's not too good for you now." Her eyes sparkled. Love looked good on his sister.

"She barely spoke."

Charlee patted the clean spoon against her chin. "Maybe she was just in a hurry."

He shrugged. "Maybe."

"Miah, why didn't you two ever become a couple? You were so close. Always together. Just never *together*."

A hot summer night flashed in his mind. Rain, long hair, wet skin, hot breath. A tiny cabin and a thunderstorm outside. She'd smelled different that night; something primal and delicious had worked its way through the pores of her skin, intoxicating him. Drugging him until all he could do was say yes. And then more.

"Jeremiah McKinley! Are you blushing?"

He blinked, scrubbing the memory from his mind as if it had been right there in front of him for all to see. He couldn't explain the pressure in his chest, the fact that he'd noticed the heat of the kitchen only moments ago and right now, he just wanted out.

"Oooooh. Someone's got a crush. Looks like the tables have turned, my big brother."

"Huh?"

She kissed his cheek again. "Gray was the one in love with you. And you barely noticed her. Now, she doesn't give you the time of day and you're all gawky eyed."

"She was what?"

"Come on. Please tell me you're not that dense."

He shook his head. No, he and Gray had been . . . well, they'd been . . . best buds, that person you share your secret hopes and fears with. They'd been friends. Just friends. Best friends, but still.

And then there was that one night—

Annoying snapping fingers in his face drew his attention. "I'll snoop around a little bit. See what I can find out about her. I always really liked Gray."

"Thanks." It was all he could say because if he voiced any more, it might give away his utter confusion. Gray had never . . . acted like the other girls. He'd never—until that night—suspected that there was any chemistry between them. She was his rock. His anchor in the storm of high school. And even that night had been a rush of teen hormones and a sort of farewell send-off, nothing more. High school was over. She was going away to college and he was going away to follow in his dad's footsteps. They each had plans and a future that didn't include each other. It was their good-bye.

And apparently as far as Gray was concerned, that good-bye was forever.

———

There'd been a variety of mums at the grocery store. Gray planted her hands on her hips, looking over her work after securing the bright flowers at the sides of the leaning mailbox. It didn't always lean. Sometimes, it seemed arrow straight, pointing proudly as if there wasn't rotten wood and a handful of stones holding it in place. She'd found the rocks along the road by her driveway and used her feet to press them into the ground.

The mums were lovely, and Gray continued to stare down at them rather than the house behind the mailbox. How had her Nana's home fallen into such disrepair in the last years? It had sat empty since Nana's stroke, when they up and left town to go live with Gray's aunt in Laver. She'd been three months pregnant then. And everything had changed.

Her nose tingled at the memory, so she dusted her hands together and hoped the neighbors would appreciate her effort to make the house presentable again. Nana's home was little more than a cottage anyway, but the few other homes dotting the road leading south into the town of

River Rock had been meticulously kept, painted frequently, lawns perfected as if a set from *Leave It to Beaver* had barfed right here in the middle of Missouri. The house leaned, too, she realized as she walked back toward the front porch, so she tilted her head to the right. Ah. *That's better.* She was almost inside when she heard the car horn. Gray turned.

A beaming blond woman was waving furiously and for a quick instant, Gray wondered if she'd somehow inadvertently set her jeans on fire—what else would cause such commotion? She glanced down. No flame, no smoke.

The woman sailed into her driveway and threw the old truck into park. A billow of gravel dust rose to envelop the girl as she hopped out wearing jean shorts, a tank, and work boots.

She waved again. "Gray, hi! It's Charlee."

For a second, Gray remained pinned to the sliding front porch, a hand firmly planted on the splintered railing. Then, the words caught up to her at the precise moment the woman caught up to her, and her mind rushed forward, aging the twelve-year-old girl she'd known.

She bounded off the porch. "Charlee!" The two hugged and Gray shook her head. "Oh my gosh. You're beautiful. I can't believe how much you look like your mother."

Charlee hugged her again. "Are you back? For good?"

She cast a labored glance at the house behind her. "For now. I mean, I'm here."

Charlee blinked.

"I planted mums." She pointed to the mailbox.

Charlee glanced at them, then her eyes went back to Gray, probably trying to follow the logic of that comment. It was just that meetings with McKinleys could lead nowhere good. Of this, she was certain.

"Are you fixing it up to sell?"

No. Yes. How was she supposed to answer the woman who didn't need to know her business? Gray bit into her lip hoping for rescue.

Charlee nodded, gathered her shock of curls at the base of her neck. "I understand." Her tone was soft. "We can't bring ourselves to sell Dad's house either."

And all of what the McKinleys had been through rushed unguarded into Gray's mind. Her throat tightened. There was a time she'd felt the McKinleys—*all* the McKinleys—were just as much family as her own nana. But not now. Certainly not now. "I'd invite you in for coffee, but it's really a mess inside. I've just started going through things." Surely, that would end the inquiry.

Charlee beamed. "No problem. I'll take a rain check. Maybe next week."

Uh. That wasn't what she meant.

Charlee sat down on the porch step and waited for Gray to do the same. "Are you working here in town?"

Reluctance causing her fingers to constrict, she sat but remained bone stiff. "Yes, but it's just part time. I'm an occupational therapist."

"Wow. Good for you. Must be rewarding."

"Mm hmm." Her fingers itched to clamp together but she knew that was a telltale sign of tension, so she forced one index finger to trail a crack in the wooden porch floor. The paint was peeling. It scraped against her hand.

"Miah said he saw you at the truck yesterday." Charlee rolled her large, expressive eyes. "I love those tacos! How do they do it? The guy ran out of food that day. Just before Miah could get his. Some lady in front of him bought the last ones."

Gray swallowed, her mind skipping back to the moment she'd left Miah with deeper problems than missed tacos. She'd left him with pain in his eyes about why his best friend from high school didn't even have ten seconds to say hello.

"He's back, you know. For good."

She knew. She didn't care. Couldn't. In fact, if she'd known that a couple months ago, she wouldn't have come home. Laver was only a short drive down the road. But Angie and Bill had talked about sending David to River Rock for high school because of their science department—a glory to be sure for such a small-town school, but when a town produces one of the top scientists in the country, it tends to make a difference. Where other schools were all about the sports or music programs, River Rock prided itself on science.

At the time, it had seemed like a great idea to fix up Nana's house. David would be in high school in a couple years and in the interim, she could get an OT position at the hospital, even prepare a room for him. She knew how busy teenagers were. The reality whispered in her ear, *the older he gets, the less he'll need you, the less he'll want you around.* Age and time would eventually steal him. But maybe she could hold on a bit longer if she had a place for him to hang out during his high school years. Gray glanced down, realized her hands had fisted in an attempt to capture the one thing she had to continually let slide through her fingers.

"The Artists' Retreat." Charlee tapped Gray's leg. "Did you hear me, Gray?"

"Oh, sorry. What?"

"No problem." A hand waved in front of her and a band of gold and a beautiful set of diamonds caught the light.

Gray grabbed her hand. "You're married?"

"Yes." She cast a look skyward. "It was a bit of a debacle at first. Everyone hounding me to plan a wedding. I've discovered I'm not much of a wedding planner. What's the big deal, right? I mean, you're basically on display in a white dress . . . white. Do you know how dirty white gets?"

Gray couldn't help but smile. Charlee was a grown woman, but Gray could easily see the precocious little girl she'd been. "So did you run off to get married? I hear there are weekend wedding packages at Eureka Springs."

Charlee leaned forward. "Ian's mom and sister would have killed me. They're really great people. I didn't want to disappoint them so I turned everything over to them. It was simple and elegant and I didn't spill anything on the dress. We had it at Ian's family's house in Oklahoma a few weeks ago. They couldn't have been happier."

That was the Charlee she'd known. Always pleasing the people she loved. "Sounds lovely." Gray couldn't stop the bits of envy that unfurled in her stomach. A wedding, a marriage. Even dating anyone seriously. Those were all things she'd put on hold so she could devote time to David. And he was more than worth it. Even though she'd been in his life since day one, time was precious. Already, he was twelve. The years had gone by so fast. For her, it was almost like he was aging at record speed and she had no way of slowing the clock.

There'd never been a happier day in her life than when Angie and Bill agreed to an open adoption. Their attorney wrote up the paperwork and Gray was allowed to be involved in the life of the child that she brought into the world. He was a treasure wrapped in flesh.

Besides, once he was grown, she'd have plenty of time to pursue things like relationships and love. Without meaning to, she lifted Charlee's hand and examined her ring. The gold band held an asymmetrical line of diamonds that resembled an ocean wave. "It's really beautiful. I've never seen anything like it."

Charlee moved her hand so it caught the light. "Thanks. Ian had it made for me by a designer in Chicago. She's a girl I grew up with. Younger than you, so you probably don't remember her. So, when will you come see the retreat?"

Huh? She hadn't agreed to that.

"How about Saturday? You could stay for dinner. We bought some new outdoor heaters in case it starts getting nippy. Whenever we can, we eat outside. You'd get to meet the artists."

Dinner under the stars with artists. It sounded tempting. If, of course, this wasn't Charlee *McKinley*. "I can't. But one day I'll drop by if that's okay, and you can show me around."

Charlee smiled, but the cold shoulder she'd received from Gray was evident, flashing through her eyes then disappearing. The moment of sadness turned to determination. "I'll drop by, too, next time I'm in town and we can have that cup of coffee." There was a challenge in the younger woman's voice. One that said, *You might have given my big brother the brush-off, but you won't have as easy a time getting rid of me.*

And with all Gray knew about Charlee, it was likely true.

———

With Charlee gone and the mailbox decorated, Gray couldn't face the interior of the house again quite yet. Her grandmother's imprint was everywhere and sometimes it just became too much. The only bathroom in the turn-of-the-century little cottage smelled like Nana's rosehip perfume, though the bottles had long since been discarded. That warm, floral scent had overtaken her once—a week after moving in—when she'd opened the vanity door to place a cup under the faithful but infrequent drip. With her head beneath the sink, the scent had whooshed out and grabbed her heart, taking her captive.

Hands trembling, she had closed the cabinet while fresh tears had puddled in her eyes. She'd squeezed them tight and imagined Nana standing behind her. Other than physical things like the house and its contents, that scent, now mixed with the hint of rust and mold from aging pipes, was all she had left of the woman. Sometimes she tried to remember her voice, but as Gray got older, the sound faded until she really wasn't certain if she remembered or not. Just echoes. Nothing but shadows.

Gray wrapped herself tighter in her sweater and gave the yard and street beyond a long, slow look. She'd grown up in this house, planting flowers in the springtime and raking leaves in the fall. But the giant oak she'd once climbed had lost its battle with disease and had been removed a decade back.

Beyond the sagging porch ceiling, the sun shone above, peeking through the pine trees lining the drive. It beckoned her. She stepped off the porch and let the sun warm her back. In a few steps, she was headed to her favorite place. The graveyard, three blocks down. As she walked, her mind took her back thirteen years to the one moment, the one night that changed every facet of her world. And even to this day, it continued to rule her life.

———

Thirteen years ago
Gray stood at Jeremiah's side with her heart in her throat. It wasn't strange that he'd asked her to come to the party. It was just a bit out of her league, even though Nana had given her money for a new dress and insisted she look the part.

When Miah glanced over and saw the apprehension no doubt turning her forehead into a piece of corrugated cardboard, he leaned closer and whispered, "What?"

She widened her eyes in an effort to make him realize the stupidity of the question. Inside the ballroom of the nicest hotel in River Rock, an entourage of Hollywood types nibbled on fancy tapas and guzzled expensive champagne. All in celebration of the completion of their movie, *Kissing in the Graveyard*, a movie Jeremiah had been catapulted into when the director discovered him at the Dairy Flip and went ape-crazy over his perfect physique and even more perfect face.

Miah's hand at her back caused a warming sensation, but it wasn't enough to thaw the tension. She didn't care for these people; she'd known that from the first day of shooting, when Miah insisted she come to the set. No, these weren't her people. All the wide, toothy smiles followed by groans of frustration when things didn't go their way. She'd watched an actress throw a temper tantrum when her dress wouldn't lay right. Gray was pretty certain a seamstress had been fired on the spot.

She'd also witnessed too much sugary, disingenuous flattery and affection. Most of it directed at her best friend, Jeremiah.

When he nudged her deeper into the hotel's fancy room, she gave him her steeliest glare. It was met with Jeremiah's infectious smile, complete with twinkling golden eyes a demigoddess would have trouble resisting.

Gray stuck a pointed finger under his nose. "You owe me."

"Undoubtedly," he said, his wide-receiver shoulder tipping up. "For so much more than this."

She blew a long breath into his face. That was the thing with Jeremiah. He could talk a mermaid out of the ocean or a practical girl into a ridiculous Hollywood party.

From across the room Gray noticed someone waving. The crowd parted and a woman in a tight red dress made her way—in an obnoxiously self-impressed manner—toward the two recently graduated high school seniors.

"Miah, you made it!" Jennifer Cransden glided to them as if she'd been born with those five-inch stilettos on her pinched feet.

Gray's skin crawled. She hated that this woman found it appropriate to call him Miah. That was Gray's nickname for him. Sure it had been adopted by half the town, but not strangers. It wasn't for Cransden types or Hollywood types. Or types who gave way too much attention to her best friend. And really, that was the heart of it right there.

Miah always had girlfriends. Of course he did. He was God's gift to River Rock. Too big and perfect for his humble small town. Girlfriends, yes. But they weren't girls who could ever steal him from Gray. Take him away. But Jennifer Cransden with her private jet and home in Malibu, *the Bu*, she called it, had it within her power to whisk away Miah and rob the people who mattered.

Predatory eyes fell on her. "Hello, Gray." The deep red lips smiled, reminding Gray of a vampire in need of her next meal.

"Jennifer, this is quite a party."

She waved a hand through the air, Scarlett O'Hara style, and rolled her eyes. "Well, you can hardly find quality catering out here in the sticks, but we've managed."

Gray swallowed the insult rising in her throat. It was forming there, in the back of her mind, something about how it obviously was difficult for Cransden to find *manners*, too.

Gray felt Jeremiah's hand slide into hers. Oh, he knew her so well. But she didn't need a babysitter. "Tell me, Jennifer. Why do you suppose Hollywood comes to places like River Rock?" She blinked innocently.

The remark was met with Jennifer's confused gaze.

Before the woman could answer, Gray forged on. "You know what I mean, us hillbillies with our dirty four-wheel-drive trucks and loud country music. Hollywood must find something *of worth* here. Though I can't imagine what. With our love for God and country. Our insufferable hospitality and our infectious optimism. Oh, and the fact we have manners."

Jennifer's head tilted, eyes wide.

Miah cleared his throat. When Gray glanced over to him, he'd rocked back on his heels, no doubt enjoying the battle of wits, one-sided as it was. Good. Because she was sick of this group of people insulting her town. At the same time, she didn't want to ruin the night for Miah. It was important to him and that made it important to her.

Jennifer's mind seemed to finally catch up to the insult. A long, slow smile spread on her blood-red mouth. Her hip cocked seductively and she moved to Miah's side and threaded her arm through his. "Hollywood can appreciate what places like River Rock offers." Her free hand slid up and down Miah's arm, crimson nails trickling over his skin. "Let's face it. The views here are to die for." Then she turned Miah's head so that he faced her and planted a kiss on his lips.

Fire shot from Gray's heart to every extremity, leaving her nerves raw and jagged. She'd hoped Miah and this plastic Barbie doll hadn't hooked up, but now she had to wonder.

A man dressed in a white tux stopped near them. "Champagne?"

Jennifer took one and handed it to Miah. Then another to Gray, then one for herself. After a sip, she said, "Now, when you and your little friend are done at the buffet, I need to introduce you to some people. This is an opportunity for you, Miah. Don't blow it."

She sashayed off in the direction of a group of men who hovered near the corner bar.

"I wish you liked her." Jeremiah's voice cut an instant path to Gray's heart.

"Not much to like," she mumbled.

"She's not all bad. She even said she could help us if we end up in Hollywood."

Gray's heart dropped. It had been her dream to go to California and try to make it as an actress. But that had all begun in middle school, and by high school she knew it wouldn't happen. She'd been accepted to a good college within driving distance of home, and Miah would undoubtedly follow his father's footsteps, even though the chatter about going to Hollywood had resurged since Miah's movie part. "That was just a pipe dream, Miah. I'm never going. You know I couldn't leave Nana. Who'd take care of her?"

But during long summer days lying on their backs by the lake's edge waiting for a fish to bite, they'd talked about it—going to LA. It started in junior high, when Gray starred in her first play. Miah had a smaller role, but now, he had a supporting role in a movie. An actual movie. Not that it mattered. She'd never really believed Miah would go to California. He indulged the dream for her sake. It was their go-to conversation when things got tough. And after Miah's mom's illness was diagnosed, things had been tough a lot.

"But what about renting a cheap apartment in Burbank and working as servers in restaurants to make ends meet? What about auditions and counting pennies and stalking directors and writers? What about . . ."

She giggled, drained the champagne glass. "Look at me, Miah."

When his golden gaze halted on her, Gray's heart kicked up. She offered a sad smile. "I couldn't even get a bit part in a movie filmed in my hometown."

He cast a glance over his shoulder. "Not your fault. Jennifer won't allow anyone more beautiful than her on the set. It's in her contract."

Beautiful? Miah thought she was beautiful? With her straight, slick, black hair and weird gray eyes. She'd looked at them in the mirror her whole life, but when she looked at everyone else, she had to admit—they were weird. In all the conversations she and Miah'd had, he'd failed to mention he thought her beautiful. She took the champagne from him and downed his glass. She didn't drink, normally. But feeling out of place and now with Miah thinking she was beautiful and all, Gray worked her way through three more glasses while they chatted with the crew that would be leaving within a few days.

A couple hours later, Miah found her sitting alone at a table. Two of the guys from the crew had just left her.

"You were flirting," he said as he pulled out a chair and sat next to her, where his powerful legs created a perfect frame for her to lean on.

Gray tossed her hair. "Was I?"

"Mm hmm."

"You know what they said?" She didn't wait for an answer. "They said I could make it easy in Hollywood. Said I had a unique look. Exotic." She pointed into the air as if she'd unraveled the mysteries of the world. "No wait, intoxicating."

"They're right." Something solid hit Gray's floating heart, causing it to stop. Though the room had been dreamlike and whimsical moments ago, it was suddenly rock hard. Jeremiah was close enough that she could feel every breath he exhaled. Her hand was flat on his thigh, her face inches from his.

"You've never told me I'm intoxicating." Heat rose through his pant leg and if it didn't feel so good, she'd snatch her hand away. A war entered his golden eyes. Did Jeremiah really think of her as intoxicating?

Fingertips, warm and smooth, touched her cheek. "You're more than that, Gray."

And that's when she realized he was only now seeing her. Maybe it had taken him a long time, but Miah was finally seeing more than the girl he'd grown up with. Their time together was ending; high school was over. "Why? Why now?" She didn't need to explain her question. Miah knew her like no one else did.

He leaned back. "I didn't like seeing those guys volleying for you."

Her gaze narrowed on him. "I've watched girls fighting over you my whole life."

He turned away. "That's different."

"Why?"

He didn't answer, so she cupped his face with her hand and forced him to look at her. There really was a battle going on inside him. Golden eyes caught the light of the chandelier above, bouncing little sparks into the space between them.

But the silence gave Gray courage, and all the things she'd wanted to say to Miah for so long were rising to the surface on champagne bubbles. "Why should you get to have a steady stream of girlfriends traipsing through your life, but I can't have one movie crew member taking an interest?"

"It's just different, Gray." His teeth were gritted, the muscle in his jaw tight.

She tilted closer to him, her hand still clamped on his thigh. "Why? Because I'm a girl?"

Jeremiah blew a breath of frustration into her face. "No. Because you deserve better than a guy like him. Better than . . ."

Suddenly, the room felt smaller, all the pretty decorations eaten up by the intensity that was Jeremiah. "What?" She'd leaned closer and when he stood, she nearly fell to the ground. But strong hands clamped on her arms and pulled her to her feet.

"Come on, I'm taking you home."

———

Outside, the air was cool and crisp, unusual for early summer in River Rock, but a nice reprieve from the stuffy party and stupid Jennifer Cransden. Gray stood at the edge of the sidewalk overlooking the downtown street, now empty of the bustle of noise and traffic it normally held. It was late. Later than she usually stayed out, but Nana had taken some ibuprofen and wouldn't be up until dawn, so it hardly mattered. Miah strolled to his car, but Gray stayed on the sidewalk, enjoying the quiet, the night, the dreamy way she felt.

When the wind kicked up, she tilted her head, closed her eyes, and let the breeze play through the strands of her hair. Miah was parked nearby, but she felt warm and powerful on the inside and if she kept him waiting there by his car door, so what? The hem of her thin silk dress flittered against her legs. She'd never realized how amazing silk felt against her skin. Soft and smooth and cool. Like touching heaven. Her fingers slid over the garment from her stomach to her hips, relishing the slick, glossy material and the way it pressed, just so, to her body.

Something trickled across the back of her neck, leaving a trail of gooseflesh. She opened her eyes to find Miah leaning against his car, one foot cocked in front of the other. He'd look perfectly at ease if it wasn't for the intensity in his gaze.

Realization dawned for her. He was looking at her, noticing her stance, feet apart, wind pressing the dress to her body, hair flying behind her. She felt the power of being female, like a mermaid, or one of those women on the front of a ship with the breeze against her and the world as her audience, forging her own way, taking no prisoners.

For how many years had she been desperate for Miah to see her? How many times had he missed opportunities? And now, now that he *wanted* to see her, she didn't want to be seen, at least not by him.

Around her the wind died, and with it, her moment of pretend immortal power. It left her empty. Now, she just wanted to go home and go to bed. Tomorrow was a new day. She'd wake up with this night behind her because to know that she could attract Miah meant she could maybe in some strange alternate universe *have* Miah.

And that meant she could lose Miah.

Her stature became lax as she corralled her hair, then dragged the length of it over her shoulder and hid behind it the best she could.

Jeremiah dropped his keys and bent to pick them up. When he righted himself, she saw the concern in his eyes.

"What's wrong?"

"I don't think I should drive."

Her chin jutted forward. "Were you drinking?"

"No. I mean, I had several glasses of the punch. Jennifer gave them to me. I told her I had to drive home."

Gray cut a glare to the door of the party. "You can't trust people like Jennifer."

"I can have Gabriel come pick us up."

Gray touched his arm. "Gabriel is singing at the Neon Moon, right? We don't want to cut his night short. If we sneak through the graveyard, it's only four blocks. Let's just walk."

Miah's face split into a grin. "You and your graveyards." His eyes were a little glassy.

Gray took him by the hand and drew him in the direction of the cemetery where half the founders of River Rock were buried. She loved the place, the tilting headstones, the solitude. She hated the fact that a Hollywood scout was the only other being on the planet who had found value in the aged cemetery. He'd said it was the perfect spot for their movie, and suddenly, everyone in River Rock was talking about how wonderful and quaint their graveyard was. Gray felt a bit protective of it. Like she was its guardian. Or perhaps it was hers. She'd even done battle with a girl in seventh grade who'd called her *freak* and *zombie* for hanging out at the cemetery. A bunch of those girls had walked by once when she was placing wildflowers on a woman's stone. She hadn't known the woman, but her stone had looked lonely and Gray understood that. The girls had busted out laughing and now that she was older, Gray supposed it had looked weird, putting flowers on a gravestone of someone who'd been dead longer than she'd been alive. After that, she'd been pronounced the town freak, middle-school freak, high school freak. No, she couldn't say that. In high school she just didn't have any friends. Except Jeremiah. Which by design meant people tolerated her, but no one really liked her. It was okay. Life was bigger than high school. At least, she hoped it would be.

The breeze was a constant companion for their silence as she and Miah walked. Wind blew first at their sides, then into their faces after only a nominal pause at the car. Gray's hands came up and cupped her elbows.

Miah moved closer. "You cold?"

"A little chilly." She cast a glance over the slip of her dress. "Thin material."

"I don't have a jacket, but you can take my shirt if you want."

One brow cocked. "That's okay."

They ducked under the section of wrought iron fence and the cemetery opened up before them. Gray's attention moved over the moonlit tombstones. They seemed to glow with unnatural light, their long shadows cast beside them opposite a full moon that peeked from the gathering clouds, brightening the area.

"Why do you like graveyards?" Miah leaned into the wind. It was steady now, sending stray leaves and debris along the dirt paths of the cemetery.

She turned to face him. "I don't know."

His golden eyes searched her.

"I guess a cemetery is a place of honor. It marks life and life is precious. I think cemeteries don't get the honor they deserve."

Miah chuckled. "So, you probably don't appreciate the fact that the production company of the movie built a set right at the edge." He nodded toward the wooden cottage that had been constructed.

Gray's shoulder tipped up. "They said it would be suitable for a caretaker. Since they made it look old, part of the property, I guess I don't mind it. In their own way, they've improved the area. That building will be there long after we're dead and gone."

They walked on, taking the dirt path that would lead them beyond the cottage and out to the street. Just as they reached the corner, the sky crackled and lit up with jagged strips of lightning.

"Come on." Miah took Gray's hand and pulled her beneath the small awning at the front door of the movie-set cottage.

Gray scanned the sky. "I didn't see that coming." Of course, that's how it was in the Ozark Mountains. Storms rose without warning.

When the wind shifted and caused giant drops of water to pelt their sides, Miah used his body as a shield. Warmth rose from where he stood, his back to the storm, his chest facing Gray. And for the longest time, she stood right there, thinking about the future, how she knew in her heart Miah and she were on vastly different paths. She knew this might be one of the last nights they spent together like this. Best friends, but just a little bit more. When rain began to run in rivulets down his arms, she reached out and dragged him closer.

Miah planted his hands on the wall behind her, closing her into a safe half circle. She let her hands trail down his arms to remove some of the rain.

She shook off the excess and watched as the water speckled the last bits of dryness on the porch floor at her feet. When her eyes came up to Miah with an apology on her lips, she halted. His gaze had changed to molten lava. His breathing, ragged. A new kind of heat flew off him in waves and before Gray could stop herself, she was trapped in it. The heat rose, swirling around them, and now her breathing matched his.

Miah licked his lips and somewhere deep inside, she knew a war was going on. But she didn't care. She'd loved Miah since junior high, when he'd seen the invisible girl who everyone called Gray.

In an instant, all their time together rushed into her mind. It was like people who say their life flashes before their eyes right before death. Swimming in the river, long walks in the woods, late-night study sessions when she fell asleep with her head against his chest. And quite suddenly, a new sensation skated through Gray's being. A territorial sensation.

Miah was hers.

So many times, she'd hoped he'd ditch the friendship card and play the boyfriend card, but he never had. And she'd certainly never go there if he didn't. Except. Except right now, Miah was looking at her with eyes filled with desire, and suddenly Gray realized for the first time ever, she was in control of the relationship.

Her hands, still wet, came up to rest against his chest. *Tell me what you want,* her gaze said to him, and when her hands fisted into the cloth of his shirt, Miah's groan answered her question.

It fueled her. Gray reached up behind her and gripped one of his hands. When she placed it on her hip, another groan slipped from Miah's lips. Gray captured the other hand. He came willingly now, putty in her grasp. Fire rose around them and they might as well have been standing in an inferno. Gripping his wrist tighter, she used his fingertips to trace the line of her breastbone, down, down, over her flat stomach and finally rested them on her other hip.

And then the world became a blur. He dragged her closer, so close they touched everywhere from chest to thighs. Miah had never kissed her. But she knew, she knew he was going to, and it would likely ruin her, devastate her, but it didn't matter. Right now, Miah McKinley was hers, and she wouldn't feel anything but joy.

His lips came down on hers hard, as if the whole of their relationship needed to be summed up in that one deep kiss. Or maybe it was to wreck the relationship they'd had and build a new one. Nothing was ever gained without loss. Gray had saved up her whole life for this kiss, and as his moist lips and tongue danced over her, she realized it was all worth the wait. He crowded around her more tightly, fitting her into him as if she'd always been there. As if it was her home. Miah couldn't seem to get enough of her, and as his mouth trailed to the edge of her jaw and he whispered, "What are we doing?" into her ear, maybe it should have stopped her. Reminded her she was a practical kind of girl and Miah was a guy who'd had a lot of girlfriends. He was schooled at all this. She was new, and yet that wasn't how it felt at all. She felt in control of her destiny for the first time. It was good and reckless and perfect.

Lightning struck just above the building, causing Miah to jolt. It broke the moment. He blew out a breath and started to take a step back. But she trapped him, her hands clasping around his neck, her eyes staring deep into him.

"Is this door unlocked?" she whispered.

A quick frown, then understanding lit his gaze. "Gray." It was an answer and a question all rolled into one.

"Tell me you don't want this and we'll walk away." Her touch became a caress. His body instantly responded. "Tell me you don't want me, Jeremiah."

He squeezed his eyes shut and pulled several breaths. "I . . . I don't . . ." Then, his eyes popped open and he was touching her everywhere. Lips on her mouth, fingers sliding over her bare shoulders. He growled into her ear, "I don't think I can do that."

"Then stop pushing me away and take me inside."

CHAPTER 3

Jeremiah woke with a start and sat straight up in bed. He tried to shake the grogginess from his being, but in the short months he'd been out of the army, he'd gone soft. He scanned the room with his powerful night vision. There was nothing there. He closed his eyes and quieted his breathing, listening, tuning in to the most acutely trained of his five senses. A light wind outside, the hum of his clock, a ceiling fan, no other sounds penetrated his mind. And that's when he knew he hadn't heard anything. He'd sensed something. At the realization, Miah threw off the covers, his feet hitting the hardwood floor. Without the help of a light, he grabbed the jeans he'd shrugged out of just before dropping into bed and tugged them on over his hips. He wasn't cold, but that didn't stop the gooseflesh from rising along his neck and shoulders. Miah made his way downstairs, a curse and a prayer vying for dominance on his mouth.

Something was wrong. Tragically wrong, and if he had to guess, it involved one of his brothers. He clutched his cell phone and paced the floor while trying to make contact. It took him two hours to get any information at all, but once he did, he went straight to Charlee's house.

He pounded on the door until Charlee answered. Her curly hair was a fright and she tugged a robe around her midsection and blinked away the sleep while flipping on the porch light. It was the middle of the night and as soon as she saw him, she sucked a deep breath. Instantly, she knew something was wrong, just like he'd known.

A desperate look crossed her face and he could tell her teeth were clinched together as if the motion could shore her up for what Miah was about to say.

And how exactly was he supposed to explain? His mouth opened, but nothing came out. Worry had stolen the color from her face and he knew he had to tell her *something*. But for a man who'd dealt with his fair share of pain, words failed him.

The tension in the air was stealing the oxygen, making everything worse, and it was at that moment Miah remembered Ian was out of town. He needed to get a grip. Needed to be strong for her.

"Miah, *what* has happened?"

His eyes blinked and then filled with tears.

Charlee grabbed the doorframe, her thin fingers locking on the wood to help hold her upright. "Miah! What?"

"It's . . ." He started to take a step in, but stopped. "It's Caleb. He's been in an accident. Charlee, they said he might not make it through the night."

He watched as she absorbed the words. She paled, a black veil appearing to float over her eyes. Charlee was about to faint. He grabbed her up just as her knees buckled.

The motion helped clear Miah's addled mind. He had to hold it together for her. She was lax in his arms, and he led her to the couch where she could sit.

Without invitation, a vision of a younger Caleb entered Miah's mind. His baby brother was seven and had found a mud hole where he'd proceeded to slather himself. It was Sunday morning and they were supposed to be going to church when a mud-covered Caleb rounded the edge of the house, his white eyes and bright smile the only things that distinguished him as a human.

More memories of baby Caleb rushed into his thoughts. Miah'd been at his side when he took off his training wheels, when he'd skinned his knee climbing the off-limits cherry tree in Farmer Roger's yard. Six years younger than him and a year younger than Charlee, Caleb was the baby. And now . . . now he was . . .

"What happened?"

Miah clutched his cell phone. "I don't know exactly. He was in a caravan. Not sure if it was an IED or if they were attacked." His hands threaded together and released around the device that would bring news of their brother. "Anyway, he's in transit right now. I don't know where he'll end up."

"We need to be there. We can fly—"

"Charlee, we could be chasing him for days before we'd catch up. As much as I hate to say it, we have to wait until they let us know what's going on." He'd run the scenarios in his mind already. Waiting. That's what they had to do. Neither of them was good at it.

She tugged him down on the couch beside her. "But Miah, he's all alone. What if . . . what if—"

He shook his head. "He won't. Okay? Don't even think that. He's going to pull through. He's a fighter." But as he gave her his strongest, most stern look, he hoped she couldn't see the doubt. Sometimes soldiers died. And there was nothing they could do to change that.

She made tea while they waited for word on Caleb. Neither of them talked. Charlee had dragged a throw blanket over her legs and Miah sat soldier straight on the edge of her couch. The tea finally got cold sitting on the coffee table between them. Miah'd been there over an hour, clutching his phone and staring at it, willing information about their little brother. "When will Ian be back?"

"Tomorrow."

"Good." Miah rubbed his hands through his hair. "He needs to be here."

"How do you know someone will call tonight?"

Miah sat the phone on the table. "Called in some favors from some of the higher-ups."

Charlee nodded. "They're doing this because of Dad, aren't they?"

He nodded. "Yeah. Dad's still taking care of all of us, even though he's gone." Miah choked a little on the last word because they'd lost enough already. First their mom, then their dad. It wouldn't be fair . . . couldn't be right to lose Caleb, too. Surely the two of them wouldn't have to plan their baby brother's funeral.

When he could take the quiet no more, Miah went out front and got an armload of firewood. Fall was still in full swing in the Ozarks, meaning comfortable days and chilly nights. The leaves were turning brown and falling from the trees and it really wasn't cold enough for a fire, but he chose to make one anyway. Charlee followed him, grabbing up the smaller pieces of timber and opening the front door.

It wasn't long until the fire was blazing and Charlee was opening the windows to balance the warmth of the cabin. Two hours later, the call came in. Caleb was alive. And that's all the good news they were given.

———

Eighty-seven days after Caleb's accident, Miah was informed he could make preparations to bring Caleb home. He knew it wouldn't be easy, but what in life ever was? Miah focused his attention on the lake, fog rolling off the water, low clouds surrounding the top of McKinley Mountain. He'd hiked it multiple times. All the McKinley boys had, including Caleb. At the hospital in Tampa where Caleb had spent the last three months, they'd talked about hiking it again one day. Miah had no idea if Caleb would ever be able to do it, and that thought alone brought the tears he'd kept at bay until now. He swiped the back of his hand over his eyes and looked down at the letter in his grasp. Clearing his throat, he began to read.

> *Dear Dad,*
>
> *I should have been keeping you up to date on what's going on here. Caleb is doing better, but still not a hundred percent. Christmas came and went and Charlee and I spent more time in hospital waiting rooms than we did at home. Caleb's still at Tampa. He has therapy daily. Multiple times throughout the day, in fact. And for being in a hospital, they sure keep him occupied.*
>
> *He's had a brain injury, Dad. The first time I saw him, I felt my chest caving in on me. And it made me realize how hard it must be to be a father and watch your child hurting. But don't worry, Dad. I'm going to take care of Caleb. No matter what. I'm splitting my time between Tampa and the lodge right now. When I'm there, I sit for long hours and think about all the things that need to be done at the lodge. When I'm home, I work around the clock making a safe place for Caleb. We'll be okay, Dad. I swear.*
>
> *Love, Jeremiah*

Miah folded the page and dropped it onto the fire. He could feel the gravel in his eyes from a late night after too little sleep and a long drive from Tampa. But in a week, he'd bring Caleb home. The edge of his letter caught after a billow of smoke slithered over the page. Miah rubbed his hands on his face, trying to wake up. In a couple hours, he had an important meeting.

The hospital in River Rock was a small facility compared to the center in Tampa. Jeremiah'd come here after a shower and shot of coffee. A fresh wave of anxiety hit as he waited for the nurse. He'd scheduled an appointment with her once he knew he could bring Caleb home.

Between his fingers, he rolled the pamphlet on traumatic brain injuries, nerves—a constant companion for him these days—getting the better of him. He'd read a thousand of these little leaflets and could probably write one himself now. After three months, he'd have thought he'd be used to this. But one never really got used to planning and executing things one should never have to for his baby brother. He thought back over the months. Seeing Caleb for the first time, head half shaved, swollen, bruised. Miah choked back the tightness in his throat and curled the paper a little tighter.

The woman sitting across from him was a kind head nurse named Jamille. She ran the physical and occupational therapy departments of the facility. Smiles, looks of sympathy and sorrow crossed her face at specific times as he'd explained Caleb's situation to her and the reason for his visit.

She spoke. "I think at-home care would be in order. The problem will be finding someone qualified for the therapy he'll need."

There was someone qualified, and he'd learned that little tidbit of information from his sister. "I was hoping maybe an occupational therapist working here might be interested in picking up some extra work."

She leaned her forearms on the desk, her left getting stuck on a manila folder. There were a few dozen more like it littering her desk. She shook loose from the file. "They told us automated was the way to go for our records. All on computer, it'll be so much easier, they said. Now I have twice the paperwork and none of the help doing it."

Miah offered as much of a smile as he could muster. "Has anyone asked about extra work?"

Gray worked part time here, from what Charlee had told him, so his inquiry wasn't completely without some foreknowledge. He even felt a little bad about not going directly to the source, but the way Gray had acted when they'd run into one another didn't really suggest a desire to reconnect. But things were different now. He needed her. He needed someone. She fit the bill and whether she wanted to admit it or not, making a living on a part-time wage couldn't be easy.

Jamille shook her head. "I can't think of anyone here at the hospital who's looking for more work. Have you tried an agency in Laver?"

"No, ma'am. I was really hoping you might know of someone local." He leaned forward in the stiff chair and shot her his best smile. "Please. If you can think of anyone. Anyone at all." One blink. Two.

The older woman stopped breathing, brows rising, eyes widening just a slight bit.

Oh yeah. He had her.

Then all the air left her lungs and she leaned out of his trajectory and shrugged. "Wish to heaven I could help you, but . . ." The shrug again.

Huh. He must be losing his touch. "Sorry for wasting your time." Miah stood and even he could sense the desperation he oozed. He stepped to the door, fighting that sense of hopelessness that continually threatened to take him. He dropped his head. "It's just that it's my baby brother." He practically whispered the words because even now, it was hard, no, nearly impossible, to talk about this stuff.

"How long has he been at Tampa?"

She came around the desk and took hold of Miah's arm as he was preparing to open the door to leave. This had been a mistake. "Three months."

She motioned for him to sit back down. When he did, she propped her weight on the edge of her desk, a half grin on her face. "I've got one girl."

Miah's gaze shot up from the pamphlet about therapy to meet her eyes.

"She's PRN, meaning she works here as needed, which sadly hasn't been that much. But I'm fairly certain she won't be interested. She's putting her house up for sale and . . ."

Her house? Nana's house? Charlee had told him she'd been working on it and he'd driven by several times when he'd stuck his head up out of his own renovation project, but for sale? "She's leaving?"

"Seems like. Said she'd planned to stay, but things hadn't gone too well. There are OT jobs in every bigger city around here, just not here."

"Would it be okay to contact her?"

She moved around the desk. "I can't give you any information, but . . ." She looked him up and down. "Let me see what I can do."

Within moments she'd clicked away on the computer and had the desk phone at her ear.

This was even better than he'd hoped. He knew he needed a professional recommendation to get past whatever roadblock Gray was hauling around with her.

"I have a gentleman in my office who needs to hire an OT. Wondered if you may be interested?"

She winked at Miah and nodded.

"It's local. No, it wouldn't affect your PRN status. He's assured me he will work with your hospital schedule." Her brows rose high on her head in question.

Miah nodded with vigor and mouthed, "Absolutely."

"Great. Maybe full time, maybe part time. But days only. No nights, no weekends. I know that's important to you." She placed her hand over the receiver and lowered it from her ear. "She sounds very enthusiastic. Even mumbled the word *miracle*."

Nurse Jamille went back to the conversation. "No, honey. I haven't given him any of your information. Hospital policy. But he needs you to come see if his home is ready to receive the patient. That might be a good time for the two of you to meet and have a little interview."

Jeremiah's heart was beating harder than it should, and most of it . . . *most* of it was because he'd have a qualified caregiver available for Caleb. Part of it was the fact that the caregiver was Gray. Then a thought struck him. What if it wasn't Gray? What if it was someone else working PRN?

The nurse laughed. "Okay, Mary Grace. I'll let him know. I'll text you the address. He said tomorrow at ten a.m. would work if that's okay for you." A pause. "You're welcome. Oh, his name is McKinley. Jeremiah McKinley."

———

Gray's hands were sweaty as she pulled to a stop at the end of Miah's long driveway. She stared at her phone as if, magically, it would answer all her questions about this potentially disastrous situation. The phone was silent, giving her no answers since yesterday when Jamille had called and let her know about the job. Her stomach was as twisted as towels in a locker room and just like those terry weapons, she was about to snap.

Breakfast threatened to revisit as two thoughts fought for dominance in her head. Number one, she couldn't take this job. And number two, was it possible it was for Caleb?

The second thought wrenched her gut because she'd heard around town that Caleb had been injured on the battlefield. And her heart had wanted to know the details but her mind forced her thoughts and questions away whenever the subject came up. She'd also become a master ninja avoiding anyone and everyone connected to the McKinleys, even hiding behind the door three times when Charlee had dropped by for that promised cup of coffee. Incognito was not too easy in River Rock.

Now, here she sat in Miah's driveway. Gray closed her eyes, drew a deep breath of courage, and stepped out of her car.

By the time she had the door shut, she knew he was watching her. His gaze crawled over her skin like a hot breeze and she hadn't even looked up at the house to see him yet. But she knew he was there, standing in a window and looking out at her. Growing up, she'd always known when Miah's eyes were on her. They'd given her strength, courage, stability. Then later, as the two of them had gotten older, those eyes had given her hot flashes that ran from her spine into the deepest part of her stomach; they'd given her sleepless nights and the kinds of dreams teenage girls lived for. But now, they only gave her fear.

The click of his front door caused her steps to falter. *Get a grip. You can do this.*

He stepped out of the house. Gray painted on her best practiced smile and reached a hand out to shake his as she neared.

He took two steps down off the front porch and still towered over her, golden eyes dancing in the morning light. He was dressed in jeans that fit him far too well and a pair of scuffed work boots. A red T-shirt stretched over his chest, and, oh Lord, it was hard not to trace the muscles beneath.

His gaze narrowed playfully as he inspected the outstretched hand. Then he reached for her hand and even that somehow had a sensual sensation as his fingers slid over hers and interlocked.

"Gray." His voice was velvet. Did he have to say her name? It was too intimate, too personal.

"Jeremiah—" She had a plan. A plan to explain that she could certainly check out the lodge to see if it was set up in a manner suitable for the patient. She'd brought booklets and paperwork and would explain how an occupational therapist worked and what could be expected. As she opened her mouth to dive in, his hand tightened on hers. A tremor passed from him to her and when Gray's eyes again met his, she found him fighting tears.

And suddenly the world had no oxygen. Her own throat closed. "Is it Caleb?"

Massive shoulders quaked once, then again. His strong chin quivered, eyes filling with so many tears they seemed as if they'd float away. He swallowed and she knew he was battling to keep his composure. Everything in Gray's mind about keeping things professional began to drain from her. He didn't need to answer her question. Of course it was Caleb. And apparently, things were a lot worse than she'd anticipated.

When he pressed his lips together in an attempt to regain control, she squeezed his hand.

Miah sniffed, blinked, tried to smile.

And she saw the boy she'd loved. All those years ago. She'd seen him do this very thing when his mom died. Trying to be strong, but Miah's love ran deeper than most. He brushed his free hand over his face. "I'm sorry. I've been really committed to not doing that."

He hadn't allowed himself to crumble yet. Probably staying strong for Charlee and the other brothers while not allowing himself to cope with his own emotions about Caleb's injury. "Jeremiah, you have to do this. Allow yourself to process."

He sniffed again, drawing strength from the world around. "Can't. He'll be here in a few days. Too much work to do."

She squeezed tighter. He was like a ticking time bomb. If he didn't deal with this, at least to some degree, it'd fester and eventually he'd explode. "Miah." She released him long enough to drop her stack of papers and brochures on the porch floor.

He started to turn, but with both hands free, Gray gripped his arm, turned him to face her. "Look at me," she whispered. He'd closed his eyes and she knew it was because Miah couldn't ever look at her and not tell the truth.

Haunted eyes opened slowly and such a hard war was being waged there, it made her want to turn away. But she held him firmly. He had to break. He'd need to if he was going to be able to do any good for his brother. "How bad is it?"

A sound that was neither a cry nor a groan caught in his throat.

"How bad, Miah?"

"It's bad, Gray." And then he broke, silent sobs racking his shoulders. Face contorted, body curled forward.

She didn't speak. She didn't need to. Gray had once known Jeremiah better than anyone in the world. And though he'd gone away to be a strong soldier, she knew instinctively what he needed. She pulled him into her arms, wrapping herself around him as much as she possibly could. Gray held him so tightly it made her muscles ache, and there, standing on his front porch, Jeremiah cried.

CHAPTER 4

Of everything he'd planned to do to convince Gray to take the job, his display on the front porch hadn't been part of the equation. But when he'd seen her there, all of his emotions surged up from that place where he'd put them. This was Gray. She'd been with him when his mom died. She'd known everything there was to know about him and had loved him anyway. That's what best friends did. And when she'd stepped out of her car and headed toward him, she was no longer the occupational therapist he needed to hire. She was his best friend, and the years had melted away. She was there for him, just like she'd always promised she would be.

After giving her the folder on Caleb's injury and the recovery plan, he brought her a cup of hot chocolate because she was a terrible choco-holic and no one made cocoa like he did. He'd purchased real whipped cream for the top. She cradled the mug in her hands and sat down on his couch. "Tell me about it."

He knew she wanted to know the information that wasn't in Caleb's chart. But not just that, she wanted to know Miah's plans where his brother was concerned. He sat his own cup down on the coffee table and looked out over the mountains beyond the picture window. Gray'd made no mention of the lodge or the amazing view. None of that mattered to her. Gray was all about people. Not creature comforts.

"He suffered the traumatic brain injury in a Humvee accident. They were traveling along a ridge and hit an IED. The Humvee went off an embankment. He was trapped. They got him out, but there was a lot of damage."

"Tampa has one of the best TBI facilities in the country." She took a sip of the hot cocoa.

"Good?" He nodded to the mug.

Her silver eyes dropped to it. "Incredible. I'd forgotten you're a hot-cocoa master."

He had become one. Because of her. In all the time they'd spent together, it seemed she was always the one helping him. He'd wanted to give back. Cocoa was her favorite. "I still remembered my recipe."

"You should patent it."

It was good to see her smile. Finally, she almost seemed relaxed.

"So, with the extent of his injuries, he'll need to relearn certain things." She watched Miah over her mug. "How long has Caleb been in Tampa?"

"Three months. They have a step-down program where he could stay another three, but he just wants to come home."

She placed the mug on the table in front of them. "Are you sure he's ready? That last three months would help give him the skill set he needs for living life. I've read up on their program. It's done amazing things for our soldiers returning home with traumatic brain injuries. You need to understand, certain parts of his brain aren't functioning normally. Things could get very challenging for him as well as you."

Miah threaded his fingers together on his lap. "I know, I know. I tried to encourage him to stay, but . . ." He shrugged. "You know Caleb."

She rolled her eyes. "Yes. McKinley stubborn."

"He's made great progress already."

"Will they even let you bring him home this soon?" Gray's brow furrowed.

"Yes. He's completed the necessary rehabilitation. They'd like him to stay, of course, but—"

She waved a hand through the air. "I know. McKinley stubbornness."

"I need a professional to sign off on the lodge. The paperwork states that it will be a safe environment for him. I've leveled all the floors down here, have got a bathroom working on this level, and made a ramp outside in case the few stairs to the front porch are an issue."

Gray smiled over at him. "You're a good big brother."

There was a catch in his throat. No, if he'd been a good big brother, he'd have talked Caleb into leaving the military before this happened.

"Reading over his limitations, I think you've covered the basics here. He can get to the kitchen, restroom, bedroom; you've removed tripping hazards and have dedicated spaces for furniture. That will all make an easier transition for him, but, Miah, there's so much more to brain injuries than the physical things."

He knew that. Had already been warned about it. But where some of the soldiers were embracing the next level of therapy, for Caleb it was beginning to take a toll. A soldier was only as strong as his mental state.

"Caleb has some behavioral issues, am I right?"

"Frustration, mostly."

Gray leaned forward. "For you it may seem like frustration, but for him it feels like the world is falling apart. Throwing him into society before he's ready could pose a huge threat to his progress. Plus, what are your goals? Caleb needs goals. Something he's working toward."

"Getting well."

She pressed her hand firmly against the folder. "Getting well for what? A goal, Miah. Not just a destination. Didn't they walk you through all of this? I seem to remember them offering classes to family members. Caregiving classes."

"Yes. They did. I got through the first few hours, then got a call that my pipes had busted. I had to leave."

He watched her closely as she weighed his words against what she'd read in the file. His hold on the situation was slipping. In another moment, Gray would stand and tell him she wouldn't sign off. He had to make her understand.

"Gray, that's why I need you. Obviously, Caleb needs daily therapy. That's what he'd get if he stayed in Tampa."

"That's right. They simulate living in society, but it's in a controlled environment. So much safer for the soldiers." She sat the folder on the coffee table by her cocoa.

"Caleb has had about all of the *controlled environment* he can handle." Miah reached over, placed his hand on hers. "Please, Gray. I need you to sign off on the paper. Then, I need to hire you to help rehabilitate him."

She pulled a deep breath. "Do you have any contact with your grandfather? Grandfather Havinger? You know I see him in Laver now and then."

Miah blinked, trying to catch up to the change of subject. "Uh, no. None of us have spoken to him."

She tugged her bottom lip into her mouth and bit down. "The kind of care you're talking about will be expensive, Miah. Your grandfather could—"

Miah stood. "No. He couldn't. He wanted to take our mom away from us, Gray. When she was dying, he wanted to send her off to Europe. Or have you forgotten?"

"For an experimental treatment." There was a pleading tone to her voice.

"A treatment that had shown zero results." His own voice rose in frustration, so Miah corralled it as best he could. "Listen, Mom set up trusts for each of us. The money isn't an issue."

He could plainly see her doubt. Of course, Gray didn't know how much money they had, just that the treatment and care could be exhaustive.

"Tell me about the building alongside the lodge."

Another quick change. Somehow this all fit together, even if it was only Gray who knew how. "It's an indoor pool. Drained. So, I guess it's a giant hole in the ground. Why?"

"Does Caleb still love the water?"

"Yes."

"How expensive would it be to fix? It could be a really great form of therapy for him."

Miah rubbed a hand over his face. "More than I want to spend right now, but if it's necessary . . ."

"It's not. We're near the lake. When summer rolls around, it will be useful. Caleb can fish, swim. All of that just seems like normal activities, but for him, everything is now therapy. Do you understand?"

"Yeah." He could run the numbers. See if the pool could be worked into the budget. He'd just been bragging that the money wasn't an issue. And now here he was, counting dollars to see if he could rebuild an indoor pool. Of course, the lodge had taken a hefty chunk, and he'd done his homework on what therapy could cost.

"I really appreciate you coming, Gray. Jamille told me the going rate for an OT. I'm willing to pay that and more if that's what it takes. I could use you full-time to start, then maybe after a few months, part-time. Can I count on you?" He just wanted to close the deal so they could move on to making a rehab plan for Caleb.

"I'd be happy to sign off on your paper, Miah. I already have, in fact. But I'm afraid you'll have to find another therapist. I have to turn down the job. I'm really sorry."

And she stood up and strode to the front door, leaving him with his mouth hanging open. The click of the latch snapped his attention. "Wait."

She paused, standing in the doorway with the sun slipping in around her.

"Why?" His heart was sinking.

"I'm just not the person for the job. Run an ad in the Laver Community Hospital's employee newsletter. I bet you'll have five therapists fighting for the position." She smiled. But it was that same detached grin she'd offered at the taco stand.

"I'd always thought you were really fond of Caleb."

Her chin rose a degree and that's when he saw the truth. There was a big part of her that wanted to take the job. It just wasn't the part that was in control. "I always thought of him as the little brother I never had. Caleb was really special to me, Miah. More than I could ever say."

"Just not now that he needs you." He hadn't meant to say that and he hadn't meant for all the bitterness to accompany his words, but this didn't make any sense. When she hadn't known it was being offered by Miah, she'd mumbled the word *miracle* in reference to the job. She needed a job. He had a job perfect for her.

Gray swallowed and he watched as a carefully placed veil slipped over her features. "I'm sure it's difficult to understand."

His gaze narrowed on her. What was that? That cool, collected attitude? As if she'd spent the last several years covering her real feelings. Fear, quick and sharp, shot into his heart. "Gray? Are you in some kind of trouble?"

Her eyes fluttered. She tried to hide it. But he'd seen the crack in the marble shell. "No." She smiled and it was almost convincing. It *would* be convincing to someone who didn't know her so well. "Quite the opposite, Jeremiah. Thanks for thinking of me. Give Caleb my love."

The door clicked closed behind her.

Gray scrutinized her reflection after changing her clothes yet again and traipsing to the living room, where the ancient full-length mirror clung to a wall by the front door. "Other than you, David, guys are a great big pain in the butt."

He'd been reading a manga book, sitting cross-legged on the couch when she passed him. Nana's house was warm with the fire blazing in the cute little square fireplace. Cozy. But inside, Gray was all ice chips and frozen organs. Winter had settled into River Rock with all its chilly glory and for the first time, her town felt cold outside and internally. It made no sense whatsoever, things were the same as they'd always been, but knowing more and more McKinleys were in town made the space feel small. And frigid.

David dropped the book on his lap and pivoted to watch her inspect the angles of her reflection.

"I hate this one," she said.

"It's a nice dress, Gray."

She turned to face him, arms outstretched. "Even the bat wings part?"

He bit his cheeks when she fluttered her arms, causing the material to dance. He laughed. "Maybe not that part. Can you tuck them in somewhere?" His face scrunched.

"What was I thinking?"

David went back to his manga book. "It's just a date, Gray. No big deal."

Oh, it was a big deal. Too big. Which made it even worse. She was a thirty-one-year-old woman who typically didn't date. "It's been a while."

"I know. You're like a dinosaur. Date-less-a-saurus."

She reached over the couch, grabbed his sides, and trickled her fingers over his ribs. He jumped, laughed, wriggled free, then grabbed her wrists and held her away from him.

"You're really getting strong, David."

His honey eyes glistened. "Stronger than you." The front of his button-down shirt was wrinkled from lying on the floor in front of the fire. He'd stoked up the blaze earlier and now had a soot smear on his cheek.

"That's not saying much; after all, I'm practically extinct. Now, since I don't have time to sew up these stupid bat wings, please tell me what to wear on this cursed date." She snapped her fingers. "And be quick about it. I want to be changed before your mom gets here to pick you up."

"She's coming in this time, you know. You can't keep her on the front porch forever."

Oh Lord. That was all she needed. "I just wanted to have more of the interior done before she saw it. Your house is so nice, pristine, pretty."

"Like a museum."

Gray sighed. "Yeah." When Angie had started volunteering at the senior center, she agreed to let Gray pick David up at school three days a week and drive to River Rock, where they'd work on algebra and other subjects Angie referred to as "above her own pay grade." That suited Gray fine. She loved being the first one to hear about his day.

David stood and strode into her bedroom, where the closet door hung open and outfits littered the bed. "This is a nice place, Gray. Feels warm and homey. Plus, I can ride my skateboard in the kitchen down the slope in the floor."

Gray covered her face with her hands.

David stood at the closet inspecting the choices. He spun to face her and shrugged. "I got nothing." Then his eyes landed on her jeans and sweater in the corner. She'd discarded them after throwing them on earlier in the day to run to the store. He pointed to them. "Wear those."

A black turtleneck and True Religion jeans. She could add her tall black leather boots. "Really?" she asked him.

"Sure. You look great in that."

Oh. Huh. She hadn't thought about wearing jeans. They did fit her nicely and made her feel sort of svelte and powerful. Like the perfect cross between a big-city girl and the hillbilly she really was. She closed one eye and pointed at him. "Good choice."

Gray shooed him out and changed quickly. She was just tugging on her boots when the doorbell rang. Oh no. "I'll get it."

But it was too late. David had run to the front door and threw it open. Angie stood on the other side and pushed her way in as David stepped aside. "It's about time I see this place." She gave him a quick hug.

"I'll get my stuff." David tromped off to the far bedroom and Gray watched from the safety of her room as Angie's eyes scanned the space. First the cracked walls, the spot of missing ceiling tiles, the peeling wallpaper. Her face said it all. Disgusted. But probably too sweet to say so.

Gray emerged from her room, hoping Angie would also notice the lovely fire in the fireplace, the pictures of David, sitting on the mantel, the warm quilts and how she'd tried to make it feel like a home. "It's a work in progress."

Angie blinked. "Yes, I can see that. It is safe, though, right? You've had the wiring checked?"

"Oh yes. Of course. That's the first thing I did. The whole house has been rewired. It was built in 1903. Sort of historical." Stop it. Stop trying to justify the mess that it was. She'd had no idea how much work would be involved in renovating.

Angie moved to take a step and the floor creaked. "Is this—" She shifted her weight from side to side.

"Unlevel, yes. Eventually, they'll have to jack up the floor."

Angie nodded, hands folded in front of her. "Are you still thinking of moving back to Laver?"

Gray chewed on her cheek. She didn't know why the image of Jeremiah skated across her mind at the question. "Yes. I really wanted to finish the place and try to make it a home, but I'm not getting many hours at the hospital and this is—" she waved her hands around the room, "—a huge undertaking."

"Well, Bill checked with his friend who owns the apartment complex downtown in Laver. He has a cute studio apartment he can let you have. You could save some money. Get back on at the community hospital."

A studio. Meant no room for David. Also, no outside space. Not that it was her job to provide those things, it certainly wasn't, but she'd just hoped . . . she'd hoped . . . well, as her nana used to say, "Spit in one hand and hope in the other and see which one fills up fastest." Plus, she'd left the Laver Community Hospital a few months ago. It was a nice enough facility but only offered nights. Of course, work was work, and right now she barely had enough to make ends meet.

Angie dusted imaginary lint from her coat. "Gray, I was wondering if the two of us could get together for coffee soon."

Something about the way Angie said that caused a thread of apprehension to skitter over Gray. "Yes. Is everything okay?"

She brushed a hand through the air. "Yes. Just . . . well, with Bill expanding the business, we've taken a bit of a monetary hit."

When Gray frowned, Angie painted on a bright smile. "It will be worth it. Just growing pains. But . . . I just need to talk to you."

"Anything I can do to help."

Maybe Angie was worried about David's college fund. Maybe they were thinking of borrowing from it. Not that that was any of Gray's business, but still. She'd been involved with the plans from the beginning. Or maybe Angie just needed a shoulder to lean on. Gray could do that. Angie and Bill had done so much for her, she'd be honored to return even a tiny bit of their kindness.

David popped his head out of his room. "Gray, you can't sell this place. It's too awesome. Mom, there's a graveyard just a few blocks down. A *graveyard*. We went for a walk there the other night. It's totally creepy and cool."

A wide-eyed smile was frozen on Angie's face but her eyes skittered to Gray.

"I was telling him about the history of the town."

This brought a sharp frown to Angie's brow. And Gray realized the error of her words. Her heart raced to undo the damage. "Just boring dates and events. Anyway, the graveyard has become somewhat iconic." *Don't worry,* she wanted to say, *no mention of David's biological father or his family's history.*

David came out of the room with his coat on and a backpack across his shoulders. "Gray has a date with a cat doctor."

Really, did he have to tell everything? "He's a veterinarian. We went to school together."

Angie clasped her hands in front of her. "You look very nice, Gray. Classy and comfortable. Perfect for a first date."

Angie was trying to be nice, but comfortable? Like an old flannel shirt? Or comfortable like a worn-out recliner?

"I told her what to wear." David beamed. "She was going to dress like a bat."

"That would be unfortunate." Angie's brows rose. "Good thing you were here."

Gray nodded. "Yes, he rescued me from myself." If he'd only rescued her when she'd run into Vince Evers at the hardware store. Why had she accepted his dinner invitation? He asked, and stupid Miah McKinley ricocheted through her mind, and her mouth opened and said yes before she could even think about it.

"Have a fabulous date, Gray." Angie crossed the room to her and planted a kiss on her cheek. "You deserve it. Bill and I are still planning to be gone for a week at the end of the month. Can you stay at the house with David?"

"Been planning to."

David hooked his thumbs on his backpack straps. "I told them I was old enough to stay alone."

Angie turned a sharp stare on him. "I don't think so."

"When can I then?"

"When you're thirty."

David raised his hands and dropped them. "That's ancient."

Gray gave him a mock-glare. "Watch it, bud."

"*Ancient.* Dinosaur old."

Gray rolled her eyes. "Come here, you." She pulled him into a hug. "Don't neglect your math. We just got through those equations. You need to practice them or we'll have to start over."

He groaned.

Angie slipped her gloves on. "I'm just glad you can help him with it. They lost me when they added letters."

David looked up at her. He was almost as tall as Gray, but Angie was another three or four inches taller. "I could teach you algebra, Mom. It's not that hard."

From a few steps away, Gray smiled, but it was bittersweet. He was growing up. Now there was hair on his legs and his voice was deepening. David was going from boy to young man right before her eyes.

He turned to face her. "Have a good date, Gray. See you next week."

They left. She listened as they backed out of her driveway. Already, the house felt emptier, colder. Lonely.

Gray huffed. "Cat doctor." She grabbed her coat and headed to the Neon Moon, where she'd meet her date. But the only guy who really mattered had just driven away. With his mom.

———

"You sure you're up to this?" Jeremiah asked Caleb as he threw the truck into park. It had only been a day since Caleb had arrived and a week since Gray had turned down the job offer. The Neon Moon's new LED sign flashed like a beacon behind them, lighting the side of Caleb's face. His hair had grown and practically covered the scar that ran along one side.

Sometimes it took Caleb a few extra seconds to answer, as if the words had gone in jumbled and were having to be sorted. He nodded.

"Charlee's with us. I'm hungry." From the time they'd spent at the rehab center in Tampa, Miah had learned that sometimes with brain injuries, details were left out. What Caleb probably meant was, "We've had this planned all day. I don't want to disappoint Charlee"—who was in the Jeep parked beside them—"and I'm hungry."

"Yeah, me too," Miah answered and wished the Neon Moon wasn't quite so busy. It was a hopping Friday night and Caleb's first real outing.

Caleb fumbled with the door handle, his right hand working to clamp down. They'd taught him to try using his right hand and not letting his left do all the work. It was his right side that had been affected. His right side and his mind—which sometimes had lapses.

Jeremiah waited patiently, busying himself by knocking the dirt off his boot.

Caleb stepped out. "Ready." He fell into step beside Charlee, who instantly threaded her arm through Caleb's.

Ian and Miah walked behind them. "How's he seem?" Ian whispered.

Miah tilted his head back and forth. "If you just looked at him, you'd never know what he's been through. Other than walking a little slower and the limp."

Ian nodded. "Charlee's so stoked he's home. She floats around the house like a fairy."

Miah's grinned. "Driving you nuts yet?"

"Nah. I'm just thankful Caleb is okay."

Miah stopped. "He's not okay, Ian. There's still a long road ahead."

Ian nodded. "I know. That's not what I meant. The guys in my unit, we all talked about this. So many of us going home with missing limbs or brain injuries. Real scary stuff you're dealing with, Jeremiah. Whatever I can do to help . . ."

Miah nodded. "Charlee needs you. I'm really glad Dad sent you to her."

Ian's smile faded at the mention of the man who Miah knew had been more of a dad to Ian than his own father. "We don't want you to feel like you're alone in this, Miah."

Oh, but he was alone. His one chance of having someone . . . someone he could really count on to be there with him, had been Gray. And she'd walked right out of his lodge and his life with nothing but a smile and weak apology.

They stepped inside to find the place throbbing with people, country music, and all the sounds of a busy restaurant. Glasses and plates clanged as tables were served and cleared, noise from a din of voices and the scent of fresh, hot food made Miah's mouth water.

Caleb half turned to get Miah's attention then pointed to a booth on the far right. Miah nodded and together they made their way to the only empty table.

Just before Miah could sit down, two guys slid past Caleb and Charlee and dropped into the booth. Charlee turned and shrugged. Miah's gaze moved to Ian. He knew Ian didn't much like Charlee being dissed and the last thing he needed was an indignant Ian on his hands.

Miah watched as his brother-in-law swallowed the insult—out of character for the aggressive soldier—and turned to scope out another spot to sit.

But it was Caleb's hand smacking the tabletop that drew Miah's attention. "This is our table." His words were level, filled with anger, but controlled.

Miah took Caleb's arm. Shock registered on both guys' faces and Miah knew this could spiral out of control quickly. "It's all good, Caleb. We'll find another one."

Caleb jerked free. "No. This is ours and they knew we were headed to it." He leaned his weight on the Formica tabletop, planting his palms and looking the guys in the face. "Get up."

One swallowed, obviously nervous. "You should have gotten here faster."

Miah's hands fisted. Outrage shot a trail into his stomach, but beating the crap out of a couple of idiots probably wasn't the best prescription for a first outing. "You're a real piece of work, jerk." He took Caleb's arm, this time gently.

Again, Caleb pulled free. "I'm not leaving."

The other guy leaned back in the seat. "Fine, stand there. We're not going anywhere."

Caleb hit the table again, this time drawing attention from half the restaurant. From the corner of his eye, Miah watched someone leave the bar and make his or her way over.

He turned when he heard a husky female voice say, "Do we have a problem here?"

One of the guys at the table pointed at Caleb. "This reject says it's his table, but we were obviously here first."

Raina Hayes turned to face Caleb. Dark eyes and dark hair a perfect contrast for the Neon Moon white apron she wore. Her gaze trailed to Miah, then Charlee, then back to Caleb.

She turned and placed her hands flat on the table in the same manner Caleb had. "Get up."

Indignation landed on both faces. One mumbled, "What?"

Raina leaned forward and took ahold of one of them by the collar. "I said get up."

They were both too stunned to move.

She straightened, folding her hands over her chest. "If Caleb McKinley says it's his table, then it's his table. And I don't care if you've been sitting at it for an hour. Understand?"

The two men slid out, cursing under their breath. They headed straight for the front door. "Better burgers down the road at Carol's."

"Good," Raina hollered after them. "You should have no trouble getting a booth there."

When she turned, there were tears in her eyes. "Caleb!" She opened her arms and he moved into the hug she offered, his left arm squeezing tightly, his right doing the best it could do.

Raina was a big fan of the McKinley boys. Especially Gabriel and Caleb. She was a good six years older than Gabe, but the two of them used to sing together on the Neon Moon's stage on Friday and Saturday nights when the boys were in high school. Although Miah didn't pay much attention to romance-y-type things, there'd been a powerful connection between Raina and Gabe at that time. Especially when they sang together. Caleb had always been the hang-around little brother, sitting on a barstool and eating giant bowls of ice cream.

She squeezed his cheeks. "You look good. Miah told me you were coming home, but I didn't know it would be this soon."

Caleb's smile lit the room. He'd always had a young look about him. Of course he was the baby, but even so, he *looked* young, angelic even. Everyone in town loved Caleb. When their mom had died, the town sort of took it on their shoulders to watch out for him. And Caleb had learned to milk that for all it was worth. He had Charlee's blond hair and stormy blue eyes. They both looked like their mom. Isaiah and Gabriel looked like their dad. And people told Miah he did, too but he didn't see the resemblance.

"Caleb was anxious to get a Neon Moon burger," Miah said.

Raina clasped her hands together. "I can certainly manage that. You all have a seat. I'll have Sandy come get your drink orders. Anything you want. On the house."

Miah took a step to her. "You don't have to do that, Raina."

"Don't have to. Want to."

But Miah didn't want pity for Caleb. That wouldn't help him recover. "Really, it's not necessary."

Her hands went back to her hips. "Did you see me throw those guys out? Don't make me get rough with you, McKinley. It's *my* place. I can do what I want."

"Leave her alone, Miah. She wants to give us burgers." Caleb grinned, boyish and sweet, and it made Miah's anger at the whole thing intensify.

"Stay out of this, Caleb." Miah faced him, blocking Raina, and placed a hand flat on Caleb's chest. Caleb had always used that smile to get things for free. The poor kid whose mom died. He could turn on the charm and get whatever he wanted. But Miah knew that falling back into that pattern would only hurt his progress.

That's when something warm slid over Miah's skin. A scent, dark and delicious, entered his nose. He turned to find Gray standing behind him.

"Caleb," she said and stepped past Miah, leaving the sultry ring of her voice to trail into his gut and wrap around the lowest part of his belly.

"Gray." Caleb pulled her into an embrace and Miah couldn't help but notice the way he drew her name out as if sampling a delicacy. He also noticed Caleb's inability to let her go.

Miah worked the muscle in his jaw and counted to ten. Still hugging. His hands fisted at his sides for an entirely different reason than before. Now, he just wanted to peel Gray off of his brother. That's what it would take, from the looks of things. Chest to chest, hips to thighs, her head firmly against his pecs. Miah's hand clamped on her shoulder in an attempt to turn her. Rather than come willingly, she tucked herself under Caleb's arm as if they were on a date.

The goofy grin on Caleb's face reminded Miah of when his baby brother had passed into manhood and found his first pubic hair. He'd grinned for a week about that one.

She looked up at Caleb. "You look great, Caleb. They take good care of you at Tampa?"

Miah's heart sputtered. Should she bring up his rehab? Honestly, he didn't know.

"Food was good, but the weather wore me down."

She tipped her head and a stream of that night-black hair tumbled over her shoulder, feathering Caleb's arm as it trailed. "It's the tropics."

"I know. I'm a four-seasons kind of guy."

Finally, she stepped away from him. "Well, we're all glad to see you back home."

Miah let out the breath he'd been holding.

"Join us," Charlee added. Until she spoke, Miah had all but forgotten his sister and Ian were there.

Raina motioned for the server. "We can bring another chair over."

"Oh, no. I'm here on a . . ." Her words stopped, eyes flashed to the other side of the restaurant.

Miah's gaze followed to find a blond guy, about their age, staring at the spectacle that had become the McKinleys' first outing. "A date?" he mumbled.

Gray's gaze dropped to the ground. "Yes. Anyway, it was great to see you."

Caleb's smile was all for her. "You too, Gray. You look incredible." Another hug.

No. Stop it. Miah tried to quiet his mind, which had gone all kinds of vile places in the last few minutes. You'd think a veteran soldier would handle things better.

Gray angled to face him. "Jeremiah, if you have a couple minutes, I'd really like to speak to you."

When he didn't know what to say, she continued. "About the paperwork you showed me the other day. Please. Five minutes. My car is right outside."

Confusion forced his legs to move, though his mind hadn't caught up. If Gray was going to try to rescind her decision to sign off on the lodge, she could forget it. He'd already sent the paper to Tampa.

He matched her step for step until they'd passed through the front door. When they got outside, Gray stopped at her car and turned to face him. "What was that?"

"What?" There was silver fire in her gaze, accompanied by specs of blue from the neon sign above.

She cocked her head and her hip. "Miah, you can't handle Caleb like that. He needs you."

Miah pointed behind him to the front door. "Are you kidding me? What do you think I'm doing? What Caleb *doesn't* need is pity."

She met him toe-to-toe. "No, what Caleb doesn't need is his brother *assuming* everyone is giving him pity just because they are trying to do something nice." Tenacity looked good on her.

"Well, if I had a therapist on board, I'd know that, wouldn't I?"

"If you'd stayed in the class for home care, you'd know that."

His anger boiled, second only to the thought that maybe on some level, she was right.

"Look," she said, and he could see her trying to rein in her own frustration. "When you told Caleb to stay out of it, you were shutting him out. Like he's not capable of making his own decisions."

"Oh, like the decision to physically drag two guys out of a booth because Caleb laid claim to it?"

She moved closer, head tipped and not backing down. "You told him it wasn't any big deal."

Miah leaned forward, close enough to see the dark liner around her eyes. "It's a booth."

"No. To him, it was a challenge. He's a soldier, Miah. He's a warrior. But you just brushed it off like it didn't matter. They insulted him."

"What was I supposed to do? Call them out? Beat the snot out of them?" A car pulled into the parking lot and several teenagers piled out.

She huffed. "Look, this isn't something I can explain in a five-minute conversation."

"No." Sarcasm was thick and full on his tongue. It tasted good. "Not with your *date* waiting."

Gray clamped her teeth together hard as the wind kicked up. "I'll take it."

Two cars zipped past them on the road, throwing dust. It was cold outside, but Miah didn't notice the chill until Gray wrapped her arms around herself and hugged. "Take what?"

She cast a glance heavenward. "The job. If it's still available."

That brought the world to a sudden stop. So, she wanted the job. Well, too bad, sweetheart.

When he didn't answer, her face clouded, full mouth tipping into a bow shape. "Or is it filled?"

He shrugged. "I followed your advice and put an ad in the newsletter yesterday."

She sent a long look to the front door of the Neon Moon and Miah almost felt bad, because on the other side of that door was a soldier who had to learn to do life all over again. It made Miah feel bad because Gray knew that too and seeing Caleb made her want to be part of the process.

"I see," she mumbled. "Sorry for butting in."

He grunted. "I'm sure you thought you were doing the right thing."

She attempted a smile but it died on her face. "Good-bye, Jeremiah." Gray headed for the door just as her date was coming outside. His face was a wash of confusion, his hands holding her outstretched coat.

Instantly, Jeremiah detested him. Too polished. Too perfect. Hollywood-white-capped teeth and a tanning-bed tan. Not the kind of man a woman like Gray needed. He was all plastic and fluff. She'd eat him alive.

Pretty Boy smiled, but it was forced. "Everything okay out here?"

Miah enjoyed the quiver in his voice. He obviously didn't want to go toe-to-toe with a towering soldier. "Oh yeah. We're having a great time."

Gray cut him with her eyes, then turned to face her date. "I'm really sorry, Vince. It's just that this is—"

Miah thrust a hand out. "Her boss."

Surprise flickered on Pretty Boy's face and Miah realized he recognized this man. Couldn't place a name, but Miah was certain he knew him from way back.

"My boss," Gray echoed.

They shook hands, Pretty Boy reluctantly.

Miah's gaze narrowed. "Do I know you?"

He smiled, all dazzling and toothy. "We went to school together. I was a couple years younger."

"Oh yeah." Miah turned away from him to address Gray. "So, Monday morning? Or did you want to get started tomorrow since Caleb's here?"

She smiled, but it was forced. "No weekends, per our agreement, remember?"

"Right. Just didn't want to do too much damage to him in the interim."

She swallowed the insult that was no doubt on her tongue. "You'll manage until Monday."

"Great. It's a date." Miah wiggled his brows, looked at her date, and winked. "You two have fun."

As he went inside, her voice drifted on the breeze. Pretty Boy was saying good-bye. Miah had likely ruined her night. In fact, he hoped he'd scuttled that whole disaster of a relationship. Come Monday morning, Mary Grace Smith was his.

CHAPTER 5

Jeremiah tried to stay out of her way for the first few days. He'd brush past her in the hall or catch her in the kitchen while she'd watch Caleb make them lunch. It was always Caleb's job to do the fixing as Gray assured them it was therapy. Today, she was sitting on the barstool overlooking the oversized country kitchen the lodge was equipped with. Counters framed the hardwood floors and a massive butcher-block island anchored the space. Copper accents had been placed here and there, some original, some Miah had added after finding a sale at the hardware store. But what drew his attention was how well she fit right there in his kitchen, elbows propped and feet swinging gently beneath the barstool. "Coffee?" Miah asked.

Gray nodded then hopped off the seat and moved to the stove's copper backsplash. "This is really pretty."

Jeremiah turned from the coffee pot. He'd snuck down from the upstairs room he was remodeling when he heard Caleb turn on the shower. "You noticed." He stepped behind her and heard her breath catch. Heat slid into his stomach, warming him from the inside out.

"Sorry I hadn't noticed it before. When I'm working, I tend to have tunnel vision." There was the tiniest quiver in her voice and he willed himself to move away. Lest she *run* away.

Miah leaned against the counter, a motion that offered a bit of space between them. "It's okay. I'd prefer for your mind to be on your patient rather than on my projects. Where is he, by the way?" He knew, but didn't want to be too obvious about keeping her company while Caleb showered.

"We walked to the lake this morning, worked up a sweat." She reached out to take the coffee he offered.

Miah took a tiny step closer to her and sniffed. "Him or you?"

She bit back a smile. "Him. Insisted on taking a shower before making lunch. Honestly, I think he's just stalling."

Miah helped himself to a cup and had to admit it tasted better with the company of Gray than it did when he was alone. "Caleb always knew how to get out of work."

She gave him a mock frown. "Not with me, he won't. I don't give up."

Something about hearing her say that caused a spike of tension to work its way through Jeremiah. "I'm counting on that. How is he doing?"

Her hand went to her neck, where she kneaded the muscles on one side. He'd like to do that for her, work his hands over the creamy skin of her neck, over the gentle curve of her shoulders.

Gray seemed not to notice his interest in how her fingertips moved beneath her hair, squeezing and rubbing what must be stiff muscles. "He's doing great. Good attitude, too. Makes all the difference."

Yeah, Caleb lit up like a dang Christmas tree every time Gray entered the room. "Prognosis, Dr. Gray?"

She threw her head back and laughed, the sound like dark velvet curling around his bare skin. "Within a year, I think Caleb could be virtually on his own."

Miah dropped his cup on the counter. "What?"

She blinked. "No reason he couldn't. I mean, there will always be things that are a bit more of a challenge for him, but people live on their own with far greater disabilities. Miah? Are you all right?"

No. No, he wasn't. And yet, he was more than all right because he'd assumed Caleb would need to live with him for the rest of their lives. And he was okay with that. Great with it.

"Miah?" Concern edged her words.

He ran a hand over his face. "I just, I . . ." What to say? "This is good. I mean, it's great for him. I didn't know that would become an option. But will he want to live alone?"

She shrugged. "I don't know. We haven't talked about it. It's just the first week. I'm still learning him, you know?"

No, he didn't really know. And she quickly picked up on that. "Miah, I don't want to give him expectations that he's not ready for. At the same time, he needs goals."

"Yeah, you mentioned that before."

"Right now we're taking baby steps, but if I know Caleb, pretty soon, he'll be serious about determining what he wants to accomplish."

Her eyes sparked with an excitement and intensity that only came from loving what you do. Gray Smith, the girl he'd known. The girl he'd cut school with and TPed the principal's house with . . . all grown up. "You're good at this, aren't you?"

"I'd like to think so."

He needed to leave. Now, while things were pleasant and not quite so extreme between them. "Gray, can I ask you something?" His mouth did tend to overload his better judgment.

"Sure." But a wariness entered her eyes.

"Are you . . . involved with someone? I mean, I know it's none of my business and I know I saw you with the shiny veterinarian the other night, but you're obviously not *with* him. I was thinking maybe you were involved with someone else and I don't know, had a fight or something." There. He'd said it.

Her gaze narrowed, but more honest suspicion than anger. "You've done a bit of thinking about my love life, McKinley."

That much was true. Miah had spent the better part of the last several days processing what Charlee had told him about Gray having been in love with him all those years ago. At first, he'd thought it ridiculous. But judging her actions and reactions at seeing him again, well. Maybe. Just maybe. At the taco stand, she couldn't seem to get away from him fast enough. So either she wasn't interested in running into a past love or he reeked like dead fish. Since he hadn't been fishing in weeks, he had to assume she was involved with someone and didn't want Jeremiah messing anything up or confusing her emotions. The two of them had always had an unnatural bond, an inexplicable connection.

For some strange reason, the thought of her, of what could be, had kept him up at night. And then there was the look on her face—disgust, was it?—when the good doctor had brought her coat to her in the parking lot. He figured she must be in a serious relationship that had recently taken a nosedive. Maybe the doc was her boomerang guy. Miah would have liked to have fit that bill. "So, are you?"

For a long time, Gray's attention stayed on her coffee. On the wall, the clock ticked; above them, water rushed through pipes, sending a soft white noise to fill the silence. Gray blinked. "Yes, I am." She lifted the pottery mug to her ample lips and took a drink as if it held the power to create a wall between them.

"Tell me about him."

She coughed into the mug. "Excuse me?"

"Tell me, Gray." His words were soft, a request from a long-ago friend, not the kind of question an employer uttered.

Her eyes widened, rimmed with a hint of red from choking on her coffee. She stepped away from him, toward the sink, where a window

overlooked Table Rock Lake. "He's . . ." Her voice drifted away, drawn
by some unnamable power. "He's incredible. I've never met anyone like
him and I'm fairly certain I never will again." Her mug found its way
to the counter beside the sink and her hands came together in front
of her while the trees beyond the window swayed in the wintery, late-
morning breeze.

"Why were you with the animal doctor?"

She chuckled. "It was an experiment. One that failed, by the way."

Miah rubbed the back of his neck. "You can probably thank me
for that."

He'd moved closer to her, not too close, just close enough.

"No. It was a doomed proposition. I shouldn't have accepted his
invitation. But, you know, we went to school together and all." Then
her eyes met his and Miah watched as an apology of sorts entered first
her gaze, then the rest of her body, causing each motion, each breath,
to soften. It was as plain to see as if she'd said it. She was feeling bad
about the way she'd treated him at their first reunion.

He should rescue her from this, but he couldn't find the words to
do it. Not with her so close and looking at him, actually looking at him
instead of trying to look at everything else. There was a long strand of
dark hair partially covering one of her silvery eyes. His fingers itched
to reach up and touch it. Instead, he sank his hands deep in his pockets, where they couldn't lash out and damage what little progress he was
making with her.

"Miah, I'm sorry about the taco stand."

His heart lurched, but he opted to keep things playful. "Yeah, it's a
beast when they run out."

"That's not what I meant. Anyway. I didn't handle seeing you very
well. I'm sorry, it's just—"

And then his body did what his mind knew he shouldn't. He
stepped closer, trapping her between himself and the sink. "It's just
what, Gray?" He could feel heat rising up between them, heat like the

stove was on, heat like a sauna, heat like . . . like there'd been on another night when he'd trapped her against a door.

A blood vessel in her throat throbbed, and Miah wanted to place a hand there, feel the force pulsing through her.

She smiled, leaned away. "It's just that we were such good friends in high school." One shoulder tipped up. "And since I'm in this relationship, I got scared. It would be inappropriate to pick up where we left off."

Pick up where they left off? That would be at her doorstep, where he'd once again kissed his best friend after the rainstorm and the Graystorm and the graveyard. It had been a night he'd never forget. And it was the last time he'd seen her. "We should talk about the graveyard."

Panic entered her features, eyes first, then settling around her mouth. "No. We shouldn't."

"But—"

"Miah, it was a long time ago. A lifetime ago. Let's just drop it, okay?"

"Is that why you didn't want to take this job? Your guy, knowing about us, wouldn't like you working for me?"

She threw out a long breath. "There was no us, Miah, there never was. It was one night. A—"

"A mistake?"

At that, her gaze softened, features filling with something beautiful, an emotion he'd never seen on her, a look that was morning sunlight after a long winter's night. "No. Not a mistake. Definitely not a mistake. Just something that needs to, *has to* stay in the past. Can you respect that?" She was pleading now, her body language neither guarded nor careful, just hopeful.

"How can a guy be okay with you out on a date, but wouldn't be okay with you working for a past friend?" He was just trying to make sense of it.

Gray focused on the wall behind him. "It's complicated. We were . . . taking a break." Her mouth twitched. A telltale sign. Gray was lying.

"And now?" He didn't like where this was going.

"And now we are together. Permanently."

Those words cut a slice out of Miah's heart. "I see." He needed to rally. Needed to at least attempt to handle this with some dignity. "So, what's his name?"

Her mouth opened then closed.

Miah wondered when silence had gotten so loud.

She looked blank for a few moments. Gray smiled. "His name is David."

Her eyes were full of adoration. Either this David was practically a saint or he had her completely snowed. Miah had a strong feeling it was the latter. Gray wasn't herself when she talked about this guy and it reminded him of stories of women who were abused, women who wanted, *needed*, to get out of a bad relationship but couldn't. Miah would keep his eyes open. Because at the end of it all, Gray had once been his best friend. If she needed him, he'd be there. And maybe, just maybe, in time, he could carve a place in Gray's heart for himself. David might have her right now, but she and Miah had something that was difficult to match. They had their entire life's history together.

———

Miah woke to the sound of a freight train in his front yard. Since there wasn't a train around for miles, he leapt out of bed, grabbed his jeans, and didn't bother with shoes; he had some boots by the front door. He tugged on a shirt as he headed downstairs.

Caleb stood in the kitchen doorway with Gray peeking around his shoulder. Caleb's face twisted into a look that displayed all the confusion Miah felt. "What's going on?"

Miah rushed to the door. "I have no idea." He pulled the boots on to his bare feet and threw the door open to find a large yellow tractor and two truckloads of men just arriving. "What is this?" he mumbled, wondering if he'd somehow slipped into a weird dream.

But then he saw it. The champagne-colored Bentley pulling up in his driveway. Cold, then dread, passed from his heart to every extremity of his body as he watched the man behind the wheel pull to a stop. In a moment the car was parked and the seventy-something, designer-clothed man stepped out, long wool coat and scarf flowing in the winter wind as he pointed at the pool house with a leather-gloved hand. Without so much as a greeting, he started barking instructions.

Miah flew out of the house and stomped to his grandfather. "What do you think you're doing?"

At that moment, the tractor barreled into the side of the pool house.

"Good to see you, too, Jeremiah." He was tall and had thick white hair on his head like a halo. But Grandfather Havinger was no angel.

"This is private property."

He scoffed, the lines around his mouth deepening. "Yes. Property I purchased."

Fury settled deep in Miah's gut. "My mother bought this property for us. You have no right to be here."

"Yes, she did. With my money." His red scarf caught the breeze and danced between them playfully, but it wasn't enough to soften the stone-hard edge of the aging businessman. Instead, it gave the appearance that even the elements were subject to his orders.

Miah wanted to grab each end of the scarf, cross them, and jerk. "If you think I won't call the sheriff and have you removed, you're wrong."

"Call him. Ask how his wife, Betsy, is doing. We had dinner a few nights ago. She wasn't feeling well." And then he smiled that broad, thick Havinger smile that had ruined men and built empires.

"You just think the whole world caters to you, don't you?"

The man, dignified and arrogant, raised his arms. "Yes. I can see how rebuilding your pool benefits me greatly." Grandfather Havinger leaned closer and used his politician voice. "Let's not make this about us, Jeremiah. This is for Caleb. He needs a swimming pool for therapy."

Miah's heart burned because the only way Havinger could know that was from Gray. He threw a look to the front porch were she stood beside Caleb. When his gaze landed on her, she shrunk away. Smart girl.

Havinger noticed. He clucked his teeth. "Now, don't blame the girl. I ran into her in Laver two days ago. Asked if she'd seen any of you."

"You are not doing this." Miah refocused his fury back on his grandfather. "If Caleb needs a pool, I'm capable of providing it."

"Just as stubborn as your father." Havinger stepped to his car and reached inside.

Miah didn't want to beat the snot out of an old man, but right now he was tempted. Havinger returned to him and shoved a folder into his hand. "Get your pride out of the way and see that Caleb is more important than your hatred of me. You won't find any pool company in the area willing to take on this task at this time of the year. I'm paying them double and pulled them off my hotel job in Branson to get this expedited."

Miah stared at the page, a blueprint for a perfectly beautiful indoor pool. Caleb would love it. His heart melted just the smallest bit.

"The point is, Jeremiah, Caleb needs that pool for therapy. Are you going to stand in his way?"

Miah closed his eyes. Already, Caleb was tiring of the daily ritual and its level of *boring*. Though his brother hadn't complained. The pool would give him something to enjoy, to look forward to. Still, the last thing Miah wanted was Havinger insinuating himself into their lives in any way. "Only this. Nothing else. And I promise you, this doesn't change anything between us."

Havinger saddened, the lines around his eyes seeming to deepen. Had that statement actually hurt the marble-cold patriarch? He swallowed, and, for the first time in Miah's life, the man looked almost frail. "They'll be done in a few weeks." He turned from Miah and waved a leather-gloved hand in Caleb's direction. He also treated the younger McKinley to a rare smile.

Caleb remained stoic.

"Good-bye, Jeremiah."

Something rushed over Miah, forcing him to take a step forward. "Charlee and I went to visit grandmother before she died."

Havinger paused, one foot in the car. His blue eyes sought Miah. "Did she know you?" There was real pain there, and Miah thought back to the frail woman at the luxury nursing home. Tiny on the white bed, scared from the disease that had stolen her memories and filled her with apprehension.

"She thought Charlee was Mom. She didn't know me at all. It was a couple weeks before she passed."

Havinger's tough outer shell cracked a bit and Miah could see the weight of losing his wife on his powerful shoulders. "Thank you."

Miah jerked a nod.

Without another word, Havinger got in his Bentley and drove away, kicking up dust and leaving a crew of workers in Miah's front yard.

Dear Dad,

Caleb is doing well. Wish you could see him. It's been three weeks now and he seems to be getting stronger every day. He's tenacious about his progress and Gray is tenacious about pushing him even further than he wants to go. I never thought about what it must be like for the soldiers who come home with debilitating injuries. Ian said the guys in his unit talked about it. We never did. How does a warrior become a patient? How does a man who months ago held an automatic weapon feel when he has to relearn how to hold a pencil? In Tampa, I watched so many of our boys—your kids, you used to call them—relearning the smallest of tasks. They are even greater heroes to me now. On the battlefield, there's an unwritten rule about having the other guy's back. It was no different at the hospital. Sure, sometimes one or more of them would have a bad day, but they were never alone. Their brothers in arms were right there to lend a hand or share a hug. It was the thing we know from war, but it came home with them. It was amazing to see, Dad. They're still an army. They're just fighting a new enemy now.

I wish you were here.

Jeremiah

Miah wadded the paper and tossed it onto the bonfire he'd built in the early morning hours. It was burning down now and the sun was rising over the frostbitten trees. A voice behind him drew his attention. He angled to find Gray trekking toward him, hands slid into her jacket pockets.

"Morning," he said, ignoring the little jump in his heart rate. She wore snug-fitting jeans and cowboy boots, a fleece jacket, and a red V-neck beneath. She looked good enough to eat.

"So, you're the one who leaves these campfires burning. What would Yogi say?"

He let out a laugh. "The bear? Don't you mean Smokey?"

She scrunched her face. "Oh yeah. I always get those two mixed up."

The wind worked invisible fingers into her hair and she fought to maintain control of the locks. He'd like to help. "To what do I owe the pleasure of your company?"

She grinned. "Aww. Has your male ego taken a hit because the only girl who comes here does so for your brother, not for you?"

After a few weeks, they'd fallen into a nice routine of banter, a tad bit of innocent flirting, even a moment or two of tender appreciation. Mary Grace was slowly coming around. She bent to choose a smooth rock and lobbed it into the lake. It skipped twice and went under. "Good job," Miah said and moved behind her. "Do another one."

She bent and grabbed a flat stone. Miah enjoyed the view.

"Went farther." Then she turned to face him. "Did you even see it?"

"Mm hmm. It was fine."

Silver eyes sparked. "I need to ask you a favor."

"Name it." He took a stone and tossed it into the lake. It bounced three times then sank.

"I need a few days off. At the end of the week. Would that be any problem? I can leave a list of daily exercises and things for Caleb. You can walk him through them if you'd like." She shrugged. "Of course, he's capable of doing them himself, but sometimes he thinks the therapy is silly. I don't want him slacking off while I'm gone."

"No problem. So where you going?"

She was midstoop to retrieve a new rock, this time bending at the knees rather than the waist so as not to give him such an obvious view of her rear. Her hand stalled over the stone for a few moments. When she leaned up, she saw that he'd moved in. "Going on a trip or something?"

"Um." She obviously hadn't expected questions. That was intriguing. "I'll be out of town."

He waited.

She dusted the rock.

He smiled.

"I'll be with David."

Of course she would. He just wanted to know why it took her so long to answer every question about her mystery man. Why her lips twitched like she was lying, why she had to rub her hands on her thighs as if they'd become instantly sweaty. She painted on a bright smile and tossed the rock. It fell with a thud and disappeared at the water's edge.

"Listen, I've been wanting to talk to you about the pool," Miah said. She'd been so embarrassed that she'd avoided him for two days after Havinger showed up.

"Miah, I'm still so sorry. I had no idea he'd just arrive and take over. I ran into him in Laver and, I don't know, he somehow got a lot of information out of me in a three-minute conversation."

"Well, that's what Havingers do." Miah had lost interest in skipping rocks. "That and take over."

"But not when they go head-to-head with a McKinley." Her chin tilted back in a motion that suggested pride. Proud of what? Him? The McKinley name? Maybe Gray was proud of being part of the family. She was, whether she wanted to admit it or not. She was once again, just like before.

He nodded. "McKinleys and Havingers. Might as well be Hatfields and McCoys."

She put a hand on his arm. "I was really impressed with your decision to let him do the pool. It took a big man to be able to do that. I know it wasn't easy."

"He just wanted to do the right thing for Caleb. So do I. So did you when you spoke to Grandfather. We're all on the same team here."

"Yeah, team Caleb."

Miah laughed. "Don't tell him that. He has enough of an ego. He doesn't need to know he's got a whole team behind him."

"My lips are sealed." At the mention of her lips, Miah's gaze went there and held. She had beautiful lips, full but not too big, a perfect frame for her even teeth and those sassy words she'd been volleying in his direction for the last few weeks. A half smile or smirk was her almost-constant companion when dealing with Miah. Caleb, of course, got the benefit of her full smile. Frequently. Miah only got half, at best, and it was usually accompanied by some snide little remark. He loved it.

Gray reached for another stone, but jolted. "Ouch!"

Miah moved in. "What happened?"

"Something stuck me." She turned her hand over to see a small brown splinter jutting from the meaty part of her palm.

"Here, let me." He closed his hand around her wrist and inspected the damage. "Not so deep. I think it will come out easily." His voice was soft, barely mumbling, as he used his index finger and thumbnail to try to grasp the splinter.

When his fingers closed around it, she jerked, but he could tell she'd tried not to.

"You're going to have to hold still, okay?" His gaze sought hers. But when their eyes met, he saw it. And it was everything she'd been denying between them. It was pressure and pain and excitement at his touch, and the very thought that his hand on hers could bring about such a complete and yet desperate look caused his own heartbeat to shift. Her eyes were filled with hunger, unrequited desire; it was raw and pure and honest.

And it was for him.

In that moment, it didn't matter what kind of relationship she was in. It didn't matter what kind of man was waiting for her down the road. It was Miah she wanted; the truth was clearly written on her face no matter how much she denied it. The night they were together rushed like wildfire into his mind. It took no prisoners and left no survivors. As a teenager, he'd not been able to process what had happened as he'd held her in his arms. How she'd felt, so warm, so sated. She'd been like a drug for him, and now, in this moment, he was returning the favor.

He spread his legs a bit, shifting his weight so that there was more room for her to get closer. With each breath, she warred—and he could see it—fighting her desire and whatever unnamable obstacle that lay between them. But the obstacle had a name. It was David.

Painfully slowly, Miah lifted her hand closer to his face.

Her breath froze, chest filling with both anticipation and apprehension; this, he saw as plainly as neon signs flashing every emotion she felt.

A half smile curved his lips and instead of grasping the splinter with his fingers, Miah closed his mouth over her flesh and used his teeth.

A tremble ran over her and a sound that wasn't exactly like the previous ones slipped from between her lips. He plucked the splinter from between his teeth and held it out to show her. "See it?" He made no motion to let her go.

"Uh-huh," she uttered, face flushed, chest rising and falling with a few labored breaths.

"Better?" His thumb made tight little circles around the wound.

"Yep." Her gaze had gone wide, frightened and excited all at once. The eyes of a doe getting ready to either become a hunter's prey or to bolt into the nearby woods. "All better," she said and took a complete step back.

Miah let her, but the satisfaction was sweet, and no matter what Mary Grace wanted to claim about her mystery man, old flames died hard. And maybe sometimes, they were unable to die at all.

She walked away from him and paused so close to the water's edge, the tips of her boots got wet. Across the way, McKinley Mountain watched over them. "Okay, so I can count on you two boys to take care of things while I'm gone?" Her brows rose high on her forehead and Miah realized she needed to redirect the conversation, so he'd let her.

"You can absolutely count on us."

Her hands landed on her hips. "I mean it. I expect you two to get all of your work done."

He had to chuckle. She sounded like a *mom* scolding . . . not scolding exactly, but certainly *warning* her boys to toe the mark while she was away.

Her chin rose. "I need to hear it from you." She'd oh-so-quickly left their moment behind. But that was okay. Miah knew it had happened. And he also knew what it meant.

"Yes, ma'am. We will do our homework and keep the house clean and we won't have any wild parties or anything."

Her face split into a grin, a full one this time, and Miah relished it.

"Lord help me, but I'm going to trust you."

"Two soldiers with no supervision." He shrugged. "What could go wrong?"

She pointed a finger under his nose. "You take care of my patient."

He gave her a mock salute. "Yes, Dr. Gray."

"I'm not kidding, Miah. He's made great progress." When she angled toward the house, she fell into step beside him.

"Good Lord, woman. What do you think we're going to do? Go skydiving?"

She laughed. "You're right. I'm sorry. Things are just going so well right now and I've found that sometimes when things are going well . . ." The wind caught her hair and threw it into her face.

She tried unsuccessfully to corral the strands. Her head dropped, but it didn't stop Miah from seeing what lay inside. Fear, in her eyes, flashing from her being.

He turned her to face him. "When things are good, what?"

She tipped her head back and examined the sky. "Something always seems to mess it up."

He used his hands to help her corral the hair. "That doesn't sound like the Gray I know."

She nodded. "Used to know."

"She's still in there."

"No, Miah. I'm a different person now." It almost seemed as though she were pleading with him to understand.

"We change, we grow. We don't turn into someone else."

She drew a breath. "I did."

"Yeah, a mom."

Horror shot into her gaze; her face paled.

"Gray, I just meant that you sounded like a mom warning her kids earlier. I didn't mean anything by it." *What the heck was that?*

She swallowed, mouth a straight line. "No. It just surprised me. You know, I'm not the motherly type."

Well, that was debatable. But he'd obviously said the wrong thing. Maybe Gray had lost a child. He didn't know; she was so mysterious about the past several years. He'd try to find out more once she got home from her little trip with David. Until then, he'd just have to wonder.

Gray gazed out the kitchen window of the lovely four-bedroom house. It sat in a gated community in Laver, where the sky above had started dropping beautiful, fat snowflakes. The scent of fresh cookies filled the kitchen while the oven timer counted down the minutes to hot snickerdoodles.

David glanced up from the table. "Do you think it's too early to start looking at colleges?"

Gray stopped at his chair and peered over his shoulder. "You're twelve."

"So that's a yes?"

"David, you're going to get a full ride from whatever school you choose. You're super smart. But a lot of factors can change between now and then." Colleges? Really?

"Like what?"

"Your interests."

"Gray," he deadpanned. "I've loved science and space travel since I was a kid."

She bit her cheek. He was still a kid, but she saw no reason to mention the fact. "I think you'll always love it, but you may like other things as well."

He shrugged. "Maybe. Hey, I ordered a charm bracelet for Mom for her birthday next week."

"Great idea. She's been dropping hints for months." They were planning a small party to mark the occasion. Gray and Bill were handling the arrangements.

"Yeah. She's all about subtle." He popped a hunk of cookie dough in his mouth.

"Raw eggs, David. Don't make me hide the dough from you."

"Don't make me wait so long for cookies."

"These are for your folks. Remember?"

His grin was quick and sly. "Of course. It was my idea to make cookies. *All* for them."

She pointed the spatula at him and closed one eye. "You know, the older you get, the more devious you seem to become."

A knock at the front door ended the conversation. Gray hurried to put the spatula on the counter. "Must be them."

"Nah. They wouldn't knock. They'd just come in."

She was getting ready to argue that perhaps they'd lost their house key when David pulled the door open to find a police officer standing on the other side. He smiled, but Gray froze in place. When the officer removed his hat from his head, Gray took a firm hold on the doorframe. Her heart pounded in her ears and cold wind rushed in, slamming her in the face. Her hand instinctively came around David's shoulder.

He peered at the officer, then asked, "Is this about the kids down the road? My mom called you guys last week. They were drag racing in front of our house, but I didn't think it was any big deal."

The officer smiled. "No, son." His eyes trailed to Gray. "Is this the Olson residence?"

"Yes."

He was holding something in his hand. It looked like a driver's license. When he tapped it against his other hand, Gray saw that it was Bill's. Oh no.

"May I come in?"

She moved out of the way and wasn't sure if it was better for David to be there with her or not. But her fingers were in a vise grip on his shoulder. "Has something happened?"

"Yes, ma'am. There's been an accident."

The contents of Gray's stomach began to churn. She looked at David.

His face clouded, the heaviness of the moment settling in. "Did someone get hurt?" David asked. His eyes, now filling with fear, shot from Gray to the officer and back again. "Are my mom and dad okay?"

"Your mother is in the hospital, son."

"My dad?"

Words were useless when the officer's demeanor said everything he wasn't. "I'm very sorry. As a result of his injuries, your dad died at the scene."

CHAPTER 6

"My dad's . . . dead?"

Gray sucked a sharp breath. This . . . *this* was how tragic news was delivered to a twelve-year-old? David's face turned white, ghost white, and Gray was scared to touch him for fear he might shatter.

But the horror of what the police officer had said caused her to reach out and capture David in a hug. He didn't hug her back; he felt stiff, in shock, not even breathing.

The officer pointed to his car. "I'd be glad to drive you to the hospital. Mrs. Olson was asking for David. I think it'd be good for him to be there. Also, she said you have a temporary guardianship document? Please bring it if you don't want CPS involved."

As he spoke, she had to decipher each word, break them down syllable by syllable as if English were a second language. "Yes. Of course." She stumbled to the small table to the right of the front door, her gaze narrowing to a tiny tunnel before her. Temporary Guardianship. It was a paper they were never supposed to have to use. The wooden drawer groaned as she pulled it open and retrieved the paper that gave her guardianship of David in an emergency. She stared at it blankly. This wasn't supposed to happen. It was for a worst-case scenario. She sucked a full breath when she realized this was exactly that. Gray tried to focus. There were other things she'd need. A purse, keys. For some reason, all of that escaped her as she attempted to pull things together enough to get David to his mother. It was a good thing the officer was there. She'd never be able to drive right now. "I just need . . ." She glanced around the room as if it would anchor her and tell her what to do.

David moved to the officer's side. His eyes were wide, an unnatural line drawing his mouth tight.

The officer pointed down. "You'll want your shoes, ma'am."

Gray looked at her feet. Socks, no shoes. She had shoes. Where were they?

As if she were a robot, she gathered her things.

"I smell something cooking. Is the oven on?" The officer was patient, but the strength of his voice helped power her, her body having gone on complete shutdown.

"Yes," she answered.

David absently tugged his coat from the hall closet and the officer wrapped it around him. "We're making cookies for my parents."

Tears began to flow unbidden down Gray's cheeks. The streams of moisture created a sort of cocoon, refining her scattered thoughts. Basic necessities flashed through her mind. She needed to turn the oven off. Gray disappeared into the kitchen and returned with the oven mitt still on her hand. David removed it for her and placed it by the door. With the policeman at their sides, they walked to the squad car. When David was tucked inside the back of the patrol car, Gray caught the officer's arm as she closed the car door. "What happened?" she whispered.

The officer glanced inside the car where David sat staring straight ahead. "A furniture truck struck Mr. Olson's car."

Gray kept David tucked under her arm as the nurses and doctors made their way in and out of Angie's room. Gray couldn't see inside from their vantage point, but the rush of people and the intense concern on each face let her know the battle was just beginning for Angie.

"We're getting her cleaned up," a nurse told Gray in a half whisper, as if David wouldn't hear. She tilted her head to look David in the eye. "Your mom keeps asking for you. We'll let you in soon, okay?"

He jerked his head in a nod and found a seat in the corner to wait.

The nurse turned her attention back to Gray and the officer who was still with her. "Officer Cummings."

"Ms. Bartlett." He shook the woman's hand as Gray realized they knew each other. From here, perhaps. Similar situations? What a horrifying thing to be unified by.

"Officer, Mrs. Olson isn't in any condition to talk to you right now, if that's why you're staying."

Gray just wanted to know Angie was going to be okay. "How is she?"

"It's very touch and go. She has a lot of internal damage. We're taking her into surgery as soon as the radiologist has seen the rest of the X-rays. I'd like for David to get the chance to see her for a few minutes before we take her down. Do you think he'd be able to handle that?"

Gray's hesitation seemed to concern the nurse. How could anyone know the answer to a question like that? "He's very strong, emotionally, but . . ." Her words trailed off.

"Mrs. Olson has got a lot of bruising. She doesn't look good."

"I want to see my mom." It was David's voice, strong at first, but breaking as he finished. His hands fidgeted at his sides, shoulders rising and falling and eyes straight ahead, as if they alone held the power to keep him upright.

The nurse nodded and motioned for them to follow her. As they walked, with Officer Cummings in tow, David slipped his hand into Gray's.

They entered the room and the nurse slowly drew the curtain aside. For a few moments, Gray had to look away. David's hand became tighter in hers and trembled. Angie lay on a bed with hair matted against her head on one side. They'd done what they could to clean up the blood, but its remnants were everywhere. Smears along the bedrail, a trail half mopped on the floor. Gray reached with her free hand to cradle David's in both hers until she realized he was pulling away from her.

The din of hospital noises, various beeps and hums, filled the silence as the nurses and hospital techs left, giving David time with his mother.

He shuffled to the bed, started to rest a hand on the railing, but stopped just short of touching it. "Momma?" His voice was soft, barely a whisper, and sounded like it belonged to a much younger child.

Swollen and bruised eyes opened and found David.

David pulled a deep breath and in a moment's time both mother and son were crying silent tears. "My baby," she whispered, and the motion opened a cut along the edge of her mouth.

He choked on a sob.

"Shhh." Angie placed an IV-laden hand on his. "It's all right. It's all right, David."

"Mom . . ." he said, between tears. "Are you gonna be okay?"

Angie's eyes fell on Gray, who'd grabbed the officer's arm for stability. "I want you to listen to me, David. You're the best thing that ever happened to us. You're the miracle we prayed for and the joy we didn't deserve." Her quivering hand came up to touch his cheek.

But David was folding forward, reaching over the railing as if his mom could take him in her arms and hold him until everything was better. With David's head against the cold metal, Angie's eyes fell on Gray. "You take care of him, Gray. Promise me."

Gray wanted to speak, but there were no words.

Angie frowned, the motion drawing her brows together sternly. "Promise me."

This couldn't be happening. David shouldn't be seeing this. This was wrong. They were supposed to be eating cookies and drinking milk. But the request caught up to Gray and she nodded. "I will. I swear."

Angie's hand fell away from her son and the tiniest hint of a smile touched her face. Her eyes closed and the machine monitoring her heart—the steady beep beside her—flatlined.

"Mom?" David's voice was high, panicked. Gray rushed forward and took him by the shoulders as people flew past them into the room, hospital shoes squeaking on the tile floor.

"Call the code team," someone yelled as the officer who'd been standing by ushered Gray and David from Angie's side.

In the hallway, she held David in her arms while he cried. It seemed forever that she watched people rushing in and out of the room. Finally, she moved David deeper into the waiting area, where the noise of people trying to save his mother's life wasn't quite so loud.

They worked with Angie for over thirty-five minutes but were unsuccessful at resuscitation. She was gone. Bill was gone. And David had curled up in a hospital chair, his gangly, preteen legs hanging awkwardly off the cushion.

Officer Cummings held a steaming cup out to Gray.

She took it. "This can't be real."

"I'm sorry about the Olsons. Is David their only child?"

Her eyes, now burning from too many tears, found his. "Yes. I'm his birth mother. They adopted him as an infant."

Officer Cummings nodded, a frown creasing his smooth forehead. He was about Gray's age, she realized. Handsome with dark hair and sharp eyes.

Gray continued. "It was an open adoption. I've been involved in his life since the day he was born." And for the nine months before that, but it didn't seem necessary to say so.

"I see. I can't believe Mrs. Olson had the capacity to have you bring the temporary custody documents."

"That's Angela." Or was, Gray realized. Angie was gone.

"Would you like me to take the two of you back to the Olsons' house?"

Gray nodded. Never again would Bill and Angie enter their own house. Never again would they use the plates in the cupboards or the clothes in the closets. Fresh tears found a home in the corners of her eyes.

They tried to rouse David but he'd all but passed out from exhaustion. Finally, the officer pulled him up into his arms and carried him like a baby. "I've got two of my own at home."

Twelve-year-old David didn't care. He'd lost his whole world tonight. He dropped his head against the officer's shoulder and pretended to sleep.

———

Gray paced the master bedroom of the Olsons' house and tried to sort all that had happened in the last few hours. She'd tucked David in, turned on his nightlight—something he'd stuck in the drawer to pull out only for emergencies—and left him to sleep. The digital clock read 1:45 a.m. and sleep was somewhere on a distant shore even though her body screamed from fatigue.

Everywhere she looked, she saw Bill and Angie, and how . . . how on earth was David ever going to be okay after this? How could he wake to know they weren't coming home? She needed to be strong for him and even for herself because Bill and Angie had been the closest thing to family she'd had for a long time. All those years ago, when she'd considered raising David on her own—even though she'd known that would be impossible—they were there. But she had *wanted* to raise David, a dream that dissipated once her grandmother had the stroke. It was after finding out Gray was pregnant. At eighteen, there was no way she could have cared for Nana and the baby. Even though she and Nana had moved in with Gray's aunt in Laver when Gray was three months along. Aunt Sharon had a tiny house. There was no space, no money. And Gray had been a single young girl with a disabled grandmother to take care of.

There'd been another couple who'd wanted David. But they hadn't been agreeable with the idea of an open adoption, and Gray had been selfish not wanting to lose her child entirely.

Bill and Angie were—had been—wonderful parents. Now, it was up to her. She curled onto the master bed and tugged a throw blanket over her. The guest room was downstairs, but she didn't want to be that far from David in case he needed her.

A sound at the bedroom door caused her to look up. He stood there, hands at his sides, something dangling from one. For a twelve-year-old, he looked small. He lifted his hand and Gray could see it was a Ninja Turtle. "My dad bought me this when he took Mom to Vegas."

Gray leaned up on her elbow. "I remember. You were nine or ten."

He took a step inside. "Yeah. He said he would bring me a stuffed animal from Circus Circus. I said I was too old for stuffed animals."

When he moved into the room, the light caught the sheen of tears on his face. "He brought me this. Said it was okay to have stuffed toys if they were ninjas."

Gray bit into her cheeks to keep the tears at bay.

David hugged the turtle. "I wasn't really too old. I loved it. I wasn't too old, Gray. Do you think he knew I liked it? I did. I swear I did."

"David, your mom and dad knew everything about you. And they *loved* everything about you. Your dad knew you loved it. Your mom knew you hated peas. She told me she only put them on your plate so she could watch you think of creative ways to make them disappear."

He stood straighter. "She did?"

"Her favorite was the night you dropped them one by one in the flower vase."

"She knew that?"

"Your dad told me you loved that Ninja Turtle and when the side ripped out, he stitched it himself."

"I didn't know that."

"Sewed the thing to his pant leg in the process. Had to redo the whole thing. Your mom and dad were the smartest people I've ever known so please, please don't ever wonder if they knew how you felt about them." Because that's what this was really about. Gray knew. She understood. In the last couple years as David had gone from being a kid to being a preteen, he'd been trying to test the boundaries of his independence. He'd even planned to put the stuffed animal in a garage sale, but Angie had pulled it out, saying, *he'll be sorry if he gets rid of it.*

How had they been so smart? They'd never raised a child before, yet seemed to instinctively know what David needed. How was Gray going to fill those shoes?

"Do you need a glass of water?" she asked, wanting to help, not having a clue how. What would Angie do?

He shook his head.

"Shall I come tuck you back in?"

Moonlight seeped through the slats in the window, slashing his face. "Can I lie down with you?"

Her heart nearly burst. "Sure." Gray patted the bed and readjusted the throw so she could cover them both.

David moved onto his parents' king-size mattress. He snuggled into the pillow with the Ninja Turtle tucked beneath his arm. "It smells like them," he whispered.

Gray fought tears because David was trying to capture the scent of his mom and dad just like she'd tried to capture the scent of her nana. She placed a hand on his head and the smooth hair he'd gotten from her. It was black as coal and straight. She might as well be touching her own head. Just as she thought he'd drifted off to sleep, his giant honey eyes opened.

She smiled.

He didn't smile back, his demeanor serious. Then he blinked and she watched his chin quiver. "I love you, Gray."

"I love you, too, David." And her heart melted because she'd hoped and prayed for the last twelve years she'd hear those words, and now that she had, she wished she could change everything in the last several hours if it would mean bringing back his parents, even if that meant never hearing those words from her son's mouth.

———

Miah had been gracious about letting her stay home from work without peppering her with questions. She'd told him only what was necessary. The friends she'd been babysitting for died on their way home. She'd be taking care of their son for a bit.

Thursday after the funeral, Gray sat in Wilson Granger's office. He'd been the Olsons' attorney for years and had even handled the adoption. For the first few days, she'd stayed at the house with David, but when the quiet seemed to be taking a toll, she'd brought him to her house in River Rock. He'd needed a change of scenery and she'd needed to think. If she'd figured right, she could possibly have her place done in the next six months. It was January now and the weather had been unusually warm, but if a cold snap came, Nana's house was nothing if not drafty with the wind whistling right under the doors and in around the windows. But they could manage. David loved it there and she wasn't sure how smart it was for him to be home with his parents gone.

"You look tired, Mary Grace." Wilson smiled over his half-glasses. He was a kind man who'd aged gracefully in the twelve years she'd known him. "How's David?"

She was here at his request. Gray had been with Angie and Bill when they assigned Gray as not only the temporary guardian, but as permanent guardian as well in two separate documents that would give her custody in the event of their untimely passing. Now all that was left were the details and that was undoubtedly why Wilson had called. "David's holding up. Not ready for school yet, of course. In fact, I wanted to ask you about that because Angie and Bill had planned for him to transfer to River Rock when he went into high school. Since I already live there, do you think it would be wise to transfer him now?"

Wilson pulled the glasses from his face.

"I mean, I know he's been through a lot, and, believe me, I don't mind driving him to Laver Middle School each day; it's no trouble. I just wondered what you thought? If a fresh start might be good?"

"Do you remember coming in with the Olsons to set up the guardianship papers?"

"Of course. It was over three years ago. Bill and Angie set up the Temporary Guardianship Document and the Permanent Guardianship Document along with the Instructions to Caregiver and Instructions to Guardian."

"Yes, that's right, the Child's Protective Plan, the directives in case something happens to one or both parents." Wilson rubbed a hand over the bridge of his nose. "Mary Grace, did the Olsons speak with you about their financial situation?"

What did that have to do with David? Their corporate dealings were none of her business. "I know Bill had expanded his company. Angie mentioned that they were having some difficulties in their finances, but just growing pains."

Wilson leaned back in his leather chair and stared at the ceiling. "There couldn't have been a worse time for this to happen. Not that there's ever a good time, but the Olsons had refinanced their home, essentially liquidating everything to sink into the company."

Was he saying there was no inheritance for David? That didn't matter, not really. He was smart, would get a full scholarship to the college of his choice and, in the meantime, Gray was capable of taking care of him. An inheritance didn't matter.

Wilson went on. "They'd even cut their life insurance policies. The accident was most likely their fault; eyewitnesses said Bill swerved to miss a dog running across the road."

"I'm sorry, Wilson. What does this have to do with me?"

His chest expanded with the breath he drew, causing the buttons on his dress shirt to groan under the pressure. "I just need you to understand." He frowned. "Angela didn't discuss anything with you recently?"

Gray was tiring of this. "She asked me a few weeks ago if we could get coffee, but we never did."

He frowned. "And that struck you as odd?"

"Only because she had the same look on her face as you do now." Gray's heart was pounding. Something wasn't right about this whole meeting. Wilson had been too formal, too professional, shaking her hand when she arrived when usually he gave her a hug. "Wilson, what's going on?"

But then the secretary knocked and swung his door open and there . . .

Gray stood from her seat because in the splash of sunlight that slipped through the front door and right into Wilson's office, she saw something that wasn't possible. Couldn't be possible. There, standing on the other side of Wilson's secretary, was Jeremiah McKinley.

CHAPTER 7

There was more than a little confusion in Miah's golden eyes as they trailed from Wilson to Gray and back again. His brow furrowed, his shoulders filling the doorway.

"Mr. McKinley, thank you for coming." Wilson smiled.

And the whole of what might be happening right now began a slow drip through Gray's system. The secretary disappeared and closed the door behind her.

"Please, have a seat." Wilson used his attorney voice, the one that was friendly but edged with control.

Miah stepped in, reached out toward Gray. "Did you ask him to call me?"

A shake of her head caused Miah to look to Wilson for answers.

"Before we go any further, I need to ask you if it's all right for Mary Grace to remain in the room while we discuss the matter concerning Bill and Angela Olson."

"Wha—Yes, of course it's okay for Gray to be in here. She's the one who knew them." Miah crossed his hands over his chest to wait. He obviously wasn't enjoying the red tape and half answers.

"Mr. McKinley, Bill and Angela Olson were—and still are—my clients. Do you know who they are?"

Gray's eyes closed. No. This couldn't be happening.

"Yes, sir. Friends of Gray—er, Mary Grace—she said they'd died in a car accident and she was keeping their son for a time."

"And I understand that Mary Grace works for you? Is that why she informed you of the situation?"

"Yes, sir. She'd taken off a couple days to keep their son, and that's when they had the car accident. She's been off since, of course."

"And she didn't explain anything unique about this situation?"

His gaze landed on her. "No, sir."

If Gray could sink into the marble floor and disappear, she would. She'd worked so hard to stay away from Miah, worked so hard to maintain the promise she'd made to Angela when Angela had found out the truth.

"Mr. Granger, I don't mean to be rude, sir, but I spent the last twelve years in the Army and I've found that when people need to say something, it's best to say it and not beat around the bush."

Wilson rested his forearms on the desk. "All right, Mr. McKinley. The Olsons were also dear friends of mine. I'd like to speak frankly as their attorney, but also as their friend."

"I'd appreciate that." Miah clasped his hands in front of him and waited.

"Twelve years ago, I handled an adoption for Mr. and Mrs. Olson. They adopted a son, named David. It was an open adoption, allowing the birth mother to be part of the boy's life. Mary Grace, would you like to interject anything here?"

Miah looked at her.

Tension wound her body so tightly, she couldn't move. In her periphery, she knew Miah was putting the pieces together.

He stood from the chair. "Gray, is David your son?"

She attempted a nod.

He took a step closer to her. "Why didn't you tell me?"

But she couldn't look at him, she couldn't even breathe because her carefully constructed house of cards was getting ready to crumble.

Wilson continued. "This meeting isn't about Mary Grace's relationship to the boy. It's about yours."

For a few moments, the world went black around Gray. Beside her, Miah stumbled two steps away and fell back into his chair. Gray dropped her head in her hands and cried.

———

Miah had been in a firefight once where everything seemed to happen in slow motion. Only once. Usually, time sped up. But there was that single day when he could hear every snap of a twig, every pant of the guys beside him; he could smell the blood rising from a fresh wound on his arm, could taste the sweat as it slid between his lips, could even taste the gun residue in the air.

That paled compared to this. The attorney sat across from him, eyebrows high on his head, fingers tapping the desk as if counting off the seconds until Miah exploded. But he was a trained soldier; explosions weren't part of his MO. Access, redirect.

The attorney's information was wrong. Plain and simple. "Mr.—" He had to look at his gold plate to get the name right. It had slipped right out of Miah's mind. "Mr. Granger, that's impossible."

How could the guy have gotten his information so messed up? "Gray." It was a question and a command and caused her head to snap to look at him. "Tell him. He's got it wrong."

That's when he saw the haunted look in her eyes. And the meeting at the taco stand filtered through his mind—how quickly she'd wanted to get away from him. Then he thought about her resistance to take the job, her lack of willingness to reunite with the man who'd been her best friend. Suddenly, he felt nauseous. Miah leaned forward, planting his hands on his knees, and pulled several deep breaths.

"Miah, I . . . couldn't tell you." Gray's voice, weak, small.

No. This couldn't be happening. Then he remembered how she spoke of the mystery man in her life and how Miah feared her heart already belonged to someone else, leaving little room for him. "David," he scoffed.

"I'm sorry." She looked over at him, but could only hold his gaze for a moment. "When Angela found out it was you, she made me swear never to tell you. If I did, she'd take David away."

"Why? I never even knew them." Miah gripped the arms of the chair with such force, he thought they might disintegrate in his hands. "How long have you known he was mine?" he ground out.

"If I may interject," Wilson said, raising a finger. "Mary Grace told us she didn't know who the father was at the time of the adoption. That made our . . . situation easier. The Olsons wanted a clean adoption. They didn't want to run any risk of being challenged by a birth parent down the road. Since Gray requested an open adoption—and since there was no father in the picture—they felt certain it would all be fine."

"Fine?" Miah choked on the word.

"I think Mary Grace was trying to do the right thing. There was another child the Olsons could have adopted. They may have gone that way if we'd had to track and get the okay of an absent father."

Gray stared at the floor. "But when Angela got to know me, she said there was no way I'd have a child not knowing who the father was. David was two. I admitted the truth."

Wilson raised his index finger as if to make a point. "I had no foreknowledge of this. But from what I understand, Angela made Gray promise not to tell you about the boy."

Miah could feel the adrenaline running through his veins. He turned his fury on Gray. "Do you know how crazy that sounds?"

"Mr. McKinley, I can advise you to get a paternity test." Wilson leaned back in his leather chair.

Miah tried to wrap his head around all of this. Gray. At eighteen. She hadn't been dating anyone, spent every free moment with Miah. And there was that one night. He corralled his anger, walked to where she sat and kneeled in front of her. "Is it true? Is David my son?"

She looked as if her world was crumbling. Maybe it was. And in her eyes, he knew. She didn't even need to say it, but he wouldn't let her off the hook.

"Yes," she whispered. "He even has your eyes."

Miah's eyes drifted shut.

Wilson kept talking. "You're still welcome to do a paternity test."

Miah shoved to his feet and spun. "Not necessary. If Gray says he's my son then he is."

Wilson folded his hands in front of him. "Now, if we've established that, let's move on to the next—"

Miah raised both hands. "Stop. Just stop. I need a minute." He walked to a small window that overlooked the street. Outside, a small child was being chased by his mother in the park that anchored the square of downtown River Rock. "I have a son." The toddler in the park opened his mouth wide when his mother grabbed him up in her arms. "I have a son." And the whole of all he'd missed, all he'd not gotten to experience, overwhelmed him.

He spun toward Gray. "How could you? How could you watch him live and grow and not tell me?" The oxygen was too thin in Wilson's office and Miah suddenly felt light-headed. "How, Gray?"

She stood, looking only slightly more in control than she had moments ago. "You'd run off to Hollywood, Miah." Her voice was flat.

"And this was to somehow punish me?"

"It's not all about *you*. I was trying to do what was right for David."

He took a step toward her, pulling Wilson up out of his chair again. "By keeping him from his father?"

"You were a kid, Miah. One who ran off with a starlet."

"And what were you?"

"Smart enough to know that a couple like the Olsons could give David a good life." Her hands were fisted at her sides, a motion he'd seen her do whenever she talked about things that were slipping through her fingers.

He smacked his chest with an open hand. "We could have given him a good life. Together."

"We weren't *together*, Miah. You made that clear that night when you took me home. You called it a 'good-bye send-off.' Remember?" There were tears on her cheeks now.

"I was . . ." He shook his head. "I was just trying to make sense of what happened between us."

She squared her shoulders. "Well, you seemed to reconcile it all pretty well."

For an instant, he hated himself for having said those words to her. It was wrong. He'd even known it at the time. "No." Miah shook his head and stepped out of the regret. "That doesn't justify this."

"I was three months along and Nana had a stroke. We left River Rock and went to live with my aunt in Laver. From that moment on, everything I did was so David could have a good life. With two parents who loved him and loved each other."

And then once again, it hit him. "I have a son." His eyes trailed the room, looking for something to bring equilibrium, but there wasn't anything. A wall clock on the mantel of a fake fireplace, a palm tree in the corner, but it all looked rubbery and unreal; even the walls seemed to be melting before him.

Wilson's voice interrupted him. "If we could move on with these proceedings, it would be helpful."

Miah looked at him as if he were an alien, newly landed, searching for the man in charge. Silently, he passed Gray and dropped into the seat.

"The Olsons have granted you Permanent Guardianship of their son, Mr. McKinley."

Gray sprang out of her chair. "What? That's impossible. I was with them when you set up the documents—" And then, Gray swayed, grasping, reaching out, but finding nothing but air. Miah grabbed her and lowered her into her seat.

Wilson continued. "Recently, Angela and Bill amended those documents. Yes, for years, Gray was to have sole custody of David. But because of their recent financial decisions, their business was going under. They felt as though it would be in the child's best interest to be in a stable situation." Wilson leaned forward, his leather chair squeaking with the movement. He offered a friendly smile. "Whether we'd like to admit it or not, money is a vital concern when one is considering the long-term care of his or her child. Once you returned from the war, a decorated soldier, owning your own home, and, of course, the fact that your family is the Havingers, well." He raised his hands as if the name *Havinger* solved all the money issues of the world.

"Because I'm a Havinger?"

Wilson put on his game face and glanced through the documents in front of him. He handed a small stack of pages to Jeremiah. "Because you have a stable home situation. No one ever expects something like this to happen, but the Olsons were very proactive in their wishes."

There was ragged breathing coming from the seat beside him, but Miah didn't care.

"Wilson." Gray was trying to gather her composure. She was failing miserably. "I have a home."

He scoffed. "Mary Grace, Angela didn't feel it was suitable for raising a child."

She wrapped her hands around the chair and leaned forward. "I was making it suitable for David. I started working on my grandmother's house so I could have a place for him if he attended River Rock high."

"Angela was also concerned about your work situation. You left a full-time position at Laver Community to take an as-needed job at River Rock."

Miah saw the panic on her face, in her eyes, but it didn't matter. For weeks she'd worked at his house without bothering to mention the fact they had a son together. "For—"

"For David?" Wilson repeated, almost mockingly so.

Her head dropped. "The job at Laver was nights. I never got to see him."

"Mary Grace, you know Angela was only trying to do what was right for David. Look at this as an opportunity." He pointed at Miah. "David will get to know his biological father. This could help give him back a little bit of what he's lost. If, of course, Mr. McKinley is interested in having the boy."

Her gaze shot to Miah, pleading, fearful, bloodshot.

His focus went to the first document in his hand. It was titled "Nomination of Guardian" and outlined that he was to serve as guardian in the event that neither William nor Angela were able to. He read on to see Gray's name near the bottom. In the event Jeremiah was unwilling or unable to serve as guardian, the task fell to Mary Grace Smith.

Somehow, seeing the terms *guardianship* and *parent* on the pages brought the whole thing home for Jeremiah. This was his child, his blood. A boy he'd never met. Shock slapped him once again when he thought of raising, nurturing, helping this child grow into a man. He cleared his throat. "Oh yes, Mr. McKinley wants the boy."

There was a moment when Gray's face froze as if time itself had stopped, but then her brow furrowed and her mouth became an O shape and the saddest sound he'd ever heard clawed from her lips. "No. No, Miah. You can't."

Oh, but he could. "I've got twelve years to make up for."

He was so focused on Gray he'd forgotten Wilson until the man spoke. "Of course, Mary Grace is an important part of David's life. If you will look at document six, you'll see specific instruction concerning her."

Miah flipped through pages until he found a document titled "Instructions to Guardian of Minor Children of William and Angela Olson." It outlined their wishes about Mary Grace being consulted regarding the manner in which David would be raised.

Wilson lowered the paper in his hands. "It's also important for David's well-being that she be involved. She's been the most important part of his life aside from his mother and father."

Miah hated that he liked the feeling rising in him; it was something akin to revenge. That wasn't typically in his nature, but this was unconscionable. "Sure. She can come visit." He sniffed. "We'll work out a schedule or something."

She shook her head, her face a wash of fear. "Please, Miah. Don't do this."

He stood. "Do what, Gray? Take the opportunity to get to know my son?"

"Please," but the word was lost in a sob.

His heart squeezed. In his lifetime, he'd never caused any woman the kind of emotional torment Gray was displaying. Her eyes were swollen and red, fear and shame volleying in the depths of her silver gaze. Her face was a tear-slick mask that read absolute devastation. In a word, she was shattered. His fingers itched to reach out, but reality bit at his consciousness, reminding him that for the past twelve years, he's had a son. And no one bothered to tell him. He turned away from her, clearing the vision of her pain from his mind.

Miah swallowed the lump lodged in his throat. He directed his attention to Wilson. "How soon can I pick him up?"

———

David made a point to eat all of the bacon cheeseburger, even the lettuce. His appetite hadn't been great since the accident and he knew Gray was watching him to make sure he didn't get too skinny. Something else was wrong with Gray. Something besides everything they were already going through. As he'd gotten older, he'd learned to see it. She fidgeted, just like he did when a teacher was getting ready to hand back a graded test and he wasn't sure how he'd done. There was a time he would have just brushed it off. But things were different now. He was different now. With his dad gone, David was the man of the house. "What's up, Gray?"

From the sink, she spun to look at him. A smile first, but it faded, and David could tell she wasn't looking forward to whatever she had to say. But it was okay because he could be there for her. He could help her. He was practically a grown-up and had been dealing with grown-up problems since the moment he'd jerked the door open and found a policeman on the other side.

The kitchen chair scraped against the hardwood floor as she pulled it out to sit. David liked sitting on the other side of the table because the floor was crooked and he could shimmy his weight back and forth and rock the chair all the way to the kitchen door. It was cool.

Gray took a deep breath. "I have some news for you. You're going to get to meet your biological father."

His biological father. That couldn't be right. His mom had told him the birth father wasn't in the picture and never would be. "But Gray—"

She held up a hand. "Let me explain everything and then you can ask every question you have, okay?"

He closed his mouth, but there was a sick feeling in the pit of his stomach. "He can't be a good person. I don't want to meet him."

Gray threaded her fingers together on the tabletop. "He *is* a good person, David."

David stood up. "He can't be. Or I would have met him already. My mom swore to me that he was never, *ever* going to be around." His teeth clenched; his skin felt hot but also cold and he shouldn't be yelling at Gray, but he couldn't help it.

"That wasn't his choice, David. He didn't know about you. He didn't know he had a son until today. That's why I was called to Mr. Granger's office."

"Why didn't he know about me?" David clamped his hands on the edge of the table.

"Because I never told him. I should have. I wish I had because maybe—" And then Gray dropped her head. It was a long time before she spoke, and when she looked up to meet his gaze, there was a new strength there. "David, Jeremiah is a good man. And you will be fortunate to have him in your life."

David chewed his lip for a moment. He wanted to believe her. Even if he was mad at her. Even if she should have told his birth dad and hadn't. He moved to her and placed a hand on her shoulder. "It's okay, Gray." It nearly broke him to say it because he didn't think he could deal with any more changes. But right there, with a tummy full of his favorite dinner, he made a decision. If he was going to be the man of the house, he needed to act like it. And that meant being strong like Gray. No matter what.

——

Gray pulled it together, if only marginally, as she packed Bill's largest suitcase with David's clothes. Yet again, she was getting ready to let go of the only thing in the entire world that mattered. Slipping through her fingers, like dust on a windy day. Once more, she'd say good-bye to her child so he could go live with someone else. Both their hearts had broken anew when she told him what had happened at Wilson's office. Not only would David be meeting Miah for the first time, he'd be moving in with him.

When David rounded the corner by grabbing the doorjamb and sliding into the room, she painted on the smile she'd been practicing for two days since the meeting with Wilson. "Get your books?"

He dropped his weight against the doorjamb. "I don't want to go, Gray."

Her heart squeezed because she knew he was trying to be strong. But this was all so unjust, uprooting him again. She moved to David and took his face in her hands. "I know. But it's time for you to get to know him."

He pulled from her and crossed the room to drop in front of his bookcase. "I don't need him. I have you."

"But I'll be there the first night, maybe the second." She'd begged Miah to let her stay a day or two until David had acclimated. He'd reluctantly agreed. He'd also agreed to let her stay on as Caleb's therapist as long as she was gone before school got out so he and David could have time to bond. But he'd also promised her access to her son. It had been Bill and Angie's wishes and Miah was willing to respect that. Miah wasn't a cruel person, and he must have realized her depth of commitment to David.

"You're going to like Jeremiah. He's a really good guy."

"If he's so great, why didn't you ever tell me about him? Why didn't you want him to know about me?" David pulled the manga books from his low shelf.

"I knew Bill and Angie were going to be great parents for you. Jeremiah and I were just kids back then. I was scared that telling him might mess up your future. It was stupid, but that's the only excuse I have." She swallowed hard.

"But after I was born? Why didn't you tell him?"

Well, she couldn't really divulge to a twelve-year-old that his adoptive mother threatened to deny Gray access to her child if Gray let Jeremiah know about David. Angie had been furious when she realized the birth father was a Havinger, a family with lots of money and access to high-dollar attorneys that could fight for rights to a potential heir. "You didn't need him then. You had a dad. A great dad."

"I had a mom, too, but that didn't stop you from hanging around."

"Nothing will keep me away from you. Ever. From the first moment I felt you kick inside my belly, I knew I loved you." And it felt so amazingly good to be able to tell him that. Just say what was in her heart and on her mind. So often she'd bitten her tongue so she didn't overstep her bounds. Now, she could tell him everything.

He gave her a sad smile. "Will I get to see you much?"

"Yes. We're working out a schedule. But also, you need some time to get to know him. You won't do that if I'm *hanging around* all the time." She ruffled his ink-black hair. "I know this is hard, but will you try?"

He sighed. "I guess."

She glanced around the room; already it felt emptier. "Ready?"

He nodded and stood, then moved slowly to the door, a prisoner making that final march to execution.

———

A light dusting of January snow made the lodge look even bigger than it was. From the outside, Miah glanced up at the chimney. He'd built a fire in the large great room fireplace, but the flue had made a strange clunking noise when he opened it so he went outside to inspect it.

Caleb stood beside him. "I told you it was fine." There was a slight pause between each of Caleb's words. But all in all, speech seemed to be coming easier for him.

Miah stared at the smoke billowing into the sky. "Yeah," he grumbled.

"You're nervous as a pig in a bacon factory."

Miah threw an arm around his little brother. "Well, you keep my feet on the ground." As they walked back toward the lodge, he slowed his steps to make the trek easier for Caleb. "Do I look okay?"

Caleb rested his hand on the railing as they mounted the porch steps. "No. Dude, you look awful."

Miah ignored the intended insult. "I should change into that blue shirt, right?"

Caleb scoffed. "Gonna look bad no matter what you put on."

The joke finally caught up to Miah. "Great. Thanks."

"Just keeping your feet on the ground."

"So, they'll get here. I'll show him his room, drink some hot chocolate, then we can go over to the retreat for dinner. Do you think that's a good idea? Or should I just make some sandwiches here?" Miah refolded the collar of his shirt.

"It's not rocket science, Miah. He's a kid. He'll think the lodge is awesome. He'll love Charlee's retreat. All good."

"Yeah, but—" Caleb clamped his hand over Miah's mouth before he could finish. "I don't want to overwhelm him," he mouthed around Caleb's fingers.

Caleb shook his head and walked away. He dropped into a seat in the living room where he could watch the fire. "If you don't want to overwhelm him, turn down the intensity a few degrees. You're like Tigger."

Miah planted his hands on his hips, spread his legs apart, and tried to calm his racing heart.

Caleb pointed at him. "Dude. You're gonna stroke out."

Miah opened his eyes, stared down his little brother. "I'm not having a stroke."

Caleb chuckled. "That throbbing blood vessel on the side of your head would disagree." It might take Caleb a few extra seconds to sort his words, but his mind was sharp and quick with the good-natured insults.

"Oh crap! I forgot something." Miah threw the front door open and sailed out to his pickup truck. There in the front seat was the football he'd bought earlier in the day. The day before, he'd purchased a baseball, two gloves, and a bat. Then, he'd found Frisbees and a soccer ball. No easy task in the middle of winter.

He'd also discovered the electronics. The newest game system was now littering the floor in front of his TV with cordless controllers and three of the "top games for teenagers," per the electronics guru at Walmart. They were all first-person-shooter games and Caleb had already launched a campaign on each.

He pulled the football from the bag. "Do you hear a car? I think I hear a car."

Caleb reached for a controller, only to be quelled by Miah. "No. No games until later. And we need to let David play. Not you. This is for him."

Caleb crossed his arms over his chest to sulk. "Who died and made him God?"

Miah was fairly certain Caleb was joking. "He's a kid, Caleb. One who just lost his parents."

"Yeah." Caleb chewed the inside of his cheek, causing his mouth to quirk. "So did we, but we lived."

Really? Was Caleb actually being this petty? "We had each other. He's got no one."

"He's got Gray. Or he did until you took him away from her."

So that's what this was about. Well, he shouldn't be too surprised that Caleb would land on her side of the argument. After all, the two of them seemed thick as thieves. He didn't need this right now. He was still trying to assimilate the fact that his whole world was getting ready to change. He was a dad. And having had a great dad himself, he knew the task wasn't an easy one. At least he'd had younger brothers. That experience was bound to help him. Wasn't it? This was the question that kept him up nights even though he was bone tired and full of uncertainty about this entire situation.

Caleb leaned forward as if to reclaim Miah's attention. "You just took him away from her. It was cruel, dude."

"Like she took him away from me all those years ago."

Caleb's blue eyes turned stormy. "You were kids then. This is totally different. You should know better." And with that he stood up and headed toward the stairs.

Miah's indignation burned. "Come back, Caleb. I want us to both be down here when they arrive."

Caleb's hand landed on the stair railing. He turned. "Well, you don't always get what you want." He continued up the stairs and slammed his bedroom door.

A knock drew Miah's attention. He'd wanted to greet them before they got to the door. This was going all wrong. When he turned the knob and tugged, he noticed his body was trembling. He needed to get a grip or he was going to scare the kid to death.

It had started to snow again, and the two people standing on his front porch wore the remnants of little white flecks in their hair and on their shoulders. Standing a few inches shorter than Gray was David. Same black hair, same pale skin, but where Gray's eyes were that strange color of silver and magic, David's were golden, shaped like almonds. Miah's eyes.

"Hey," he said, pulling the door fully open. Wind whooshed inside and carried snowflakes with it. His heart was in his throat and though he just wanted to reach out and grab the kid that he'd been denied for so long, Miah had thought this through. To David, he was a stranger, and first impressions were paramount. He opened his mouth to say all the things he'd practiced, but fear had stolen his words.

So, he stood there, his mouth hanging open, his heart stopped and his eyes bugging out of his head.

"Hello, Mr. McKinley." The boy held his hand out. "My name is David Olson."

Something surged in Miah's heart. "Hello," he forced through a throat so tight, he could barely breathe. He shook David's hand. "It's really nice to meet you."

David's eyes trailed to Gray as if to say, *Satisfied?*

She gave him a smile and an almost imperceptible nod.

For some reason, that tiny motion threw Miah into hyperdrive. "I bought you a football."

Gray's brows rose. She nodded inside the house.

Miah frowned. What had he forgotten? "Oh, come in!"

They stepped in and he took the suitcase from Gray and deposited it by the stairs. "I also bought baseball stuff, but that's only fun if it's not slick outside, and I'm not sure how much snow they're calling for."

David was holding a stack of books, so Miah slipped them from him and sat them on the coffee table. He handed over the football. David stared at it.

"Frisbee too. And a soccer ball. I didn't know what you liked, so I bought what I could find."

David's mouth twitched. "I'm not really into sports."

Huh? Miah shook off the remark. "Okay. Well, I bought the new Xbox and some games." He waved David and Gray over to the TV.

David touched the edge of the system. "Any RPGs?"

Oh man. "No. All first-person shooters."

David's gaze dropped to the floor. "Oh."

Gray picked up the cases and examined them. Her look of indignation fell on Miah. "These are all rated T for Teen."

"Yeah?"

"Did you happen to notice why?" She held one of the cases to his face.

"No. The guy at Walmart said it's what all the teens are playing."

Her mouth pursed in that way it always did when she was frustrated.

David took the case, rescuing Miah. "Yeah, I might like to try this one."

"Uh, no. You won't." Gray's tone left no room for discussion. From either of them.

She placed the game cases a little too hard on the coffee table and walked back toward the front door.

When she was out of earshot and when he knew David was looking at him, he whispered, "Oops."

David bit back a smile. "Do you have PlayStation?"

"No." Miah looked at the covers of the games. They looked fine to him. "But we can go get one tomorrow if you want."

The sharp turn of Gray's head quelled him. If her eyes were daggers, he'd be full of holes right now.

"My sister is cooking us dinner at her property. My brother is upstairs. Are you hungry?"

"Yeah." David pulled his coat off and looked around the room.

"Just toss it anywhere."

David's eyes finally fell on the coat closet by the front door. He walked to it, pulled the door open, and hung his coat.

Wow. Just wow. Miah watched, wondering where this miniature businessman was hiding his kid. "We're pretty informal, here." Needed to establish that quickly. "You can help yourself to whatever's in the kitchen. Or if you want something and don't want to deal with it, just let me know. I'll get it for you."

David nodded slowly and looked around. "Big place."

"It grows on you. I'm remodeling it right now. If you ever want to help out, you can. I'll pick you up your own tool belt in town."

David chewed on his index fingernail. "I'm pretty sure there are labor laws concerning minors in this country."

Miah chuckled, but stopped laughing quickly. He wasn't sure if David was joking.

"The lake runs behind the lodge. Want to go check it out? I'll walk down with you."

"It's cold." He threw a rescue-me look to Gray, just returning from the car.

Miah nodded. "Well, yeah, it is. Missouri in the winter. That goes with the territory."

Gray stomped the snow off her boots and came back inside hauling a much smaller suitcase, and Miah hated, *hated* the fact that it gave him the slightest thrill to see her standing in his doorway with an overnight bag in her hands.

She smiled across the room at her son. "You should go check out the lake, David. It's cool. You'll love it."

"Okay," he mumbled and dragged himself up off the couch.

She grabbed his coat from the closet and held it as he shrugged it on.

"There's hot chocolate on the stove. Keep it stirred while we're gone?" he asked Gray.

"Sure." But her voice sounded dead. And for a hot instant, Miah actually felt bad for her, for the situation. But, he reminded himself, it was her own fault things were like this.

———

Through the kitchen window, she watched father and son walk to the water's edge while snowflakes danced on the current of light wind. The world below was magical, icicles and pixie dust, and she was inside stirring the cocoa. They looked good together, Miah and David. Like father and son should. Both tall, built the same, only David hadn't fully grown into his gangly legs yet, but you could easily see the man he'd become as he walked with his father. Same stride. Same manner of nonchalance. Wow. Until this very instant, she'd never thought of them being that much alike. But there they were. And here she was, and if she wasn't careful, she'd burn the cocoa.

"Need a hand?"

The voice came from behind, causing her to start. She turned to see Caleb in the doorway. He leaned against it, wide shoulders framing the entire space, and a half smile on his mouth that could light up a girl's heart. "Hey there." She brushed at her face hoping he wouldn't notice the tear.

Caleb moved in behind her, took a hold of the end of the spatula and let his hand slide down until his was over hers. "From the bottom," he whispered in her ear. "Like this." And his hand began a motion that shouldn't have seemed seductive, but did.

Gray stepped back. "Got it. Okay. How about you do the choco-late and I'll get the cups?"

"You know, I told him not to do this."

At that, Gray stopped with one hand reaching into the cupboard. "Do what?"

"Take David away from you. You're his mom."

A giant load seemed to drift right off of Gray's shoulders at those words. She'd assumed she'd be the pariah at the house, assumed the entire McKinley clan would be against her. "Caleb, I know he doesn't understand what happened all those years ago."

Caleb shrugged. "Who cares? It's not like you had a choice. He'd gone to LA with Jennifer Cransden."

Gray swallowed; hearing that—even after all this time—hurt. "Yes, but he was back when I found out I was pregnant but I just . . . I blamed him for—"

Caleb spun and moved to trap her by the sink. "For what? For what he did? You had every right, Gray."

She couldn't bear to look him in the eye, so she studied the floor.

He continued. "Miah has always gotten whatever he wanted and never thought about the destruction in his wake."

It donned on Gray that though this might have to do with her, there was plenty of sibling rivalry bubbling to the surface, too. "Are you and your brother fighting?"

He chuckled. "There's no point in fighting with Jeremiah. Right or wrong, he gets what he wants."

She was angry with Miah, too, but he'd taken the care of Caleb on his shoulders and was willing to spend every last dime he had getting him the therapy he needed. He didn't have to do that. "He's trying to do what's right. I know that in my heart."

Caleb laughed without humor. "And you're defending him."

"No." Gray brushed her hair away from her face, wishing Caleb would step back. The kitchen—though massive—was too small to be crowded by a hulking soldier.

Caleb caught her hand in his as she lowered it. "It must have been terrifying. All alone."

In the last few days, she'd relived that time over and over. "Nana had a stroke. I was three months along. Miah was preparing to leave for boot camp, but I knew I was pregnant. I'd known for a month. He'd tried to come and see me before he left, but I wouldn't see him."

"Darn right."

"Caleb, that night wasn't Miah's fault. I pushed for it. I pushed him right over the edge."

Caleb stiffened. "Guys are guys, Gray. No one in their right mind would turn you down. I don't blame him for that. It's how he handled it after. Not okay under any circumstances."

That much was true. He'd deposited her at her door, kissed her like he meant it, and pronounced that it was a great good-bye send-off. Her stomach still soured at the memory. Here she thought she'd finally become what Miah wanted, was finally the girl he'd walk away from the others to have. He'd certainly acted like that when they were in the cottage together. He'd made her feel like the only girl on the planet, like the only light in his world.

And just like that, the light went out. When he'd returned from his little stint in LA, she'd refused to see him.

"Hey," Caleb whispered, catching her chin with his thumb and index finger. "It's gonna be all right. You're not in this alone."

Her nose tingled and a fat tear trickled from her eye, down her cheek. Sweet blue eyes trailed the tear until his hand reached to swipe it away. And she was so tired of wiping her own tears, anyway. She was so tired of crying alone with no one to hear and no one to understand or care. Caleb opened his arms and pulled Gray to him. She didn't fight. She didn't try to be strong; for once, she could just melt into something more powerful than her sorrow. She could melt into his friendship.

———

Two stories below, Jeremiah walked back up the hill with his son beside him. "If it warms up in a couple days, we can go fishing. You like to fish?" But his eyes were on the kitchen window and his heart was pounding because there, standing at the sink, were Gray and Caleb. Too close. Too intimate. Not okay.

"Never been."

Miah stopped. "What?"

David stopped, too, turned to face him, raised and lowered his hands as if to say, "What's the big deal?"

"You've never been fishing?"

"Nope." David kicked at the smattering of good Missouri rock at his feet.

"Well, we'll break you in."

David's shoulders went up then down in a shrug. "'Kay."

How could his kid have never been fishing? They lived in the Ozarks, for heaven's sake. Doesn't like sports. Doesn't play video games. Hangs his coat in the closet. *Dear Lord, I spawned Donald Trump.*

His gaze trailed back to the window where Gray and Caleb were— he squinted to make out the silhouettes in the onslaught of snow-flakes—in each other's arms. Fire rushed up over his head and down his spine. Miah quickened his pace.

"Can we build a snowman tomorrow?"

A request. Finally. "What? Sure. Yeah. A whole family of them if you want."

David's face fell and Miah's heart dropped into his stomach. Wrong word choice. Crap. He was really bad at this.

David studied the sky for a few short seconds, his thick lashes blinking back the flakes that sought to land in his eyes. "The weather-man said it wouldn't be much of an accumulation anyway. No more than a couple inches."

"Weatherman, huh? You watch the news?"

David nodded and met his gaze. "Every night."

"Okay. Let's get inside. We've got hot cocoa waiting for us." As they closed the distance to the back door, the words *in over your head* kept ringing through Miah's mind. So far, he'd found nothing, not one thing for the two of them to connect over. This parental thing wasn't going to be easy. He just hoped it wouldn't prove impossible.

CHAPTER 8

Gray and Caleb had burned the cocoa. Of course they had, with their arms all tangled around each other's bodies. Miah wanted to curse under his breath at the scent of scalded milk and burnt chocolate—that was sacrilege. Rather than point out their stupidity, he passed them in the kitchen, went straight to the stove, and dumped the cocoa down the sink.

He shot Caleb a warning look, but his little brother only smiled smugly.

"Let me show you guys your rooms."

David stopped just inside the kitchen door. "We usually know when Gray is cooking. The fire alarm goes off at some point." A smile toyed at the corner of David's mouth.

"It does not." Gray squared her shoulders, but had to fight a grin of her own.

Miah was going to have a long talk with Caleb about Gray and propriety and keeping his hungry little fingers to himself. But he didn't have time for that conversation now. Instead, he took David's large suit-case and headed up the stairs. He opened the door to the first room on the right and stood back so Gray and David could enter.

"Miah, when did you have time to do this?" Gray's amazement sent little sparks over his skin. He ignored them. She angled to face him. "I saw this room not long ago; it was a wreck."

"Yeah. Pretty much worked 'round the clock to get it done." It was a room with a great view of the lake and McKinley Mountain beyond. It had one of the best views in the whole lodge and Miah had thought about fixing it up as his own, eventually. That was before.

David moved to the window and looked out at the white world. "Wow. Take a look, Gray. You can see Canada from here."

She laughed and moved to the window, where mother and son stared out at the world beyond. Something caught in Miah's throat. "Make yourself at home, champ. I'm gonna show your mom where she's sleeping. She'll be close if you need anything. Right across the hall."

Gray spun from the window, her hair flowing in an arc around her. "Across the hall? That's your room."

He rubbed a hand over the back of his neck. "Yes. I didn't have time to get another one done."

Hands fisted at her sides, she stormed past him. "I'm not putting you out of your room."

"It's just for a night."

She stopped to look at him once they were in the hall, eyes plead-ing and voice low so David wouldn't hear. "Two nights. You said I could possibly stay two nights, maybe even three if David wasn't feel-ing comfortable."

Miah bit back a smile and led the way into his master suite. "You don't want to put me out of my own bed for one night but for two or three it would be okay?"

Gray bit into her bottom lip. "It's a lodge. I know there are other rooms."

He slid his hands firmly into his pockets, letting her know this was a battle she had no hope of winning. "Would you like to see where I'm sleeping?"

"Yes."

He shrugged and ushered her down the hall and into the far bedroom. As soon as he opened the door, she sucked a breath at the cold draft coming in around the window. Her eyes scanned the space. Mattress on the floor, open rafters. Dust carefully swept to the corners of the room.

"I can sleep here," she said, but her voice cracked, betraying her.

"Yeah, and get pneumonia. No."

"Are you immune to pneumonia?" She cocked her head and her hip and, Lord help him, he found it attractive. She was a woman he'd once been intimate with, and she'd be sleeping in his own bed. For a night. The whole of that realization caused the image of her in a flimsy nightgown to flash through his mind, to rake over his flesh and drag his thoughts into a deep pit of both potential pleasure and pain.

He watched her huff. "Pneumonia, Miah? I asked if you were immune."

"I'm a soldier, Gray. Used to adapting."

The room was quiet and cold as they stood nose to chest, a silent tug-of-war raging between them. The tough outer shell he'd seen on her since they'd first run into each other seemed fragile tonight, like it had gone through the fire but hadn't survived. Her eyes softened for the briefest of instants. When he started to reach up and touch her, she turned away from him.

Gray took a throw blanket he'd dropped at the foot of the bed and walked to the window. "I can see you're trying with David. I appreciate that." She tucked the blanket around the bottom of the window, balancing it on the sill.

"He's different than I imagined." He didn't know what he'd expected, but news watching and weather reports weren't it.

"What did you think, Miah? He'd be a carbon copy of you? He's been raised by a couple who are white collar. They took him to museums, not ballgames. He's seen the ballet, not monster trucks."

Miah stared at the rafters. Far above, a fat spider made a web in one corner. "I'm sure there's an insult in there somewhere; maybe if I wasn't such a hillbilly, I'd get it."

She rolled her eyes. "Don't even go there, McKinley. I know you too well. You're as smart as you are handsome and though most women find you irresistible, I just find you irritating."

One side of his face split into a smile. "At least that hasn't changed. I'll try to not ruin David's pedigree."

"Oh, Miah. He's an amazing young man. You couldn't ruin him if you tried." And with that, Gray walked back to him, patted his cheek and left him in his slightly less drafty room. He crossed to the window and examined her handiwork. Things were warming up between the two of them and though Miah's heart—as well as his libido—liked that, his mind assured him that was one danger zone he should avoid. He grabbed the blanket from its spot and tossed it on the floor with a scowl. He didn't want to admit it, but he couldn't easily stay angry with Gray. Even though he knew he should.

———

David leaned over to Gray. "We're not seriously going to eat outside, are we?"

She gave him her best "I don't know" look. They were tromping over to Charlee's place when Gray noticed the warm glow over the treetops. "Look," she said. It was a soft yellowy hue that brightened the nearby section of sky. When she stepped into the clearing, her breath caught. It was magical. Four outdoor heaters had flames shooting up from them and disappearing into the starlit night above. Tables were ready with plates and cutlery and tablecloths of giant turquoise swirls.

At each setting was a steaming cup. Gray rubbed her eyes. Looked again, thinking it would change.

"Neat, huh?" Jeremiah was right in her ear and though she'd like to swat him like a pesky fly, the heat of his breath sent a visceral reminder down her back that this was in fact real.

David's mouth hung open. "Whoa," he muttered. "Okay. I'll eat out here." They passed some giant metal flowers on the way to the tables just as Charlee and two older women appeared carrying trays of food.

"Helloooooooo," one of them said, waving with her elbow because her hands weren't free. Brightly colored spikes topped her head, making her seem younger, but as they approached, Gray could tell the woman must be in her sixties.

"David, don't stare."

"She's an old lady, Gray, with liberty spikes."

Miah pointed. "The spiky-haired one is Wilma. She paints. The other one is Wynona. She was a dancer back in her glory days."

Wynona sidestepped around Jeremiah and spun the tray in her hands. "My boy, these *are* my glory days." And then her hips and her skirt were swaying to some imaginary music that must have been lovely, if the look on her face was any indication. Her stream of long hair moved in rhythm to the make-believe tune.

David took a step back.

Gray instantly liked her, liked them both, in fact.

Wynona's eyes fell on Miah. "And I'm quite sure I could teach you a few moves, young man." She hip-bumped him.

He held his hands out in surrender. "No. Please. I've heard about what you did to my brother-in-law."

"Oh, pish-posh. I gave him grace and helped him get in touch with his inner Fred Astaire. This *must* be David." She placed the tray on the table behind her and took David's hand in both hers. "It's absolutely divine to meet you, David. I've heard some fascinating stories about your birth parents when they were your age." She winked and leaned closer. "And I'll tell you some of them when they're not around."

Gray's heart warmed. Already, they were making David feel welcomed.

Wynona motioned behind her. "This is my sister, Wilma. But as you get to know us, you'll realize I'm the fun one. Even though she has the youthful hairdo."

Wilma moved to shake David's hand.

"Is that colored gel in your hair? I saw some once when I had to go with my mom to her stylist." Twelve-year-old excitement threaded his words.

Gray cleared her throat. Manners weren't usually difficult for him, but he'd been through a lot lately.

Wilma tilted her head down for David. "Here, touch them. They're dyed, but I do use that hair product called quick-cement. You could spear a hog with these things."

David reached up and laid his hand flat against the spikes. "Man. Like a porcupine."

Gray swallowed. If Angela were here, she'd be saying his name right now in that motherly way one should when her child was calling an elderly woman a porcupine. But David was being assimilated into the herd, and Gray needed to stay out of the initiation ritual as much as possible. Introductions were hard enough on awkward preteens. Not so much here, though, she realized as they all sat down to the steaming cups of hot apple cider and homemade steak chili. As the conversations went on, and Gray became slightly more comfortable, her thoughts turned to the night ahead. She'd sleep in Miah's bed. He'd left little room for discussion or compromise. Gray realized her hand had fallen to her lower stomach, because there, right there in the pit of her being was the ache she'd felt for so long. It was wrapped up in Jeremiah and all that could have been if only . . .

If only he'd loved her like she had loved him. And now, her worst fears were realized because *now* she had to share David with the one man who'd devastated her. She wasn't sure her heart could take sleeping in his bed. In his home. With him right down the hall.

But it was more than just their past that scared her. It was the way Miah looked at her, even after finding out about David. It was just fleeting moments, but they burned into her consciousness, his gaze fiery hot on her skin. And worse than his glances was how her flesh reacted. Scorched and yet hungry, as if it not only welcomed the flame, but begged for more. When she realized how far her thoughts had trailed, she forced herself to rearrange them, to focus on the dinner. When others laughed at some comment she'd missed, Gray laughed, too, but her eyes betrayed her by trailing to Miah. There, sitting at another table with his hands folded over his taut stomach muscles, he watched her. A sizzle passed over her exposed flesh, lighting a trail as those eyes, golden and flashing in the firelight, crinkled lightly at the corners. She was trapped. And he was smiling.

Gray pivoted her seat so that Miah was gone even from her periphery. Over the course of the evening she'd discovered David liked Mr. Gruber. Actually, he seemed to like all of them, even King Edward and his turned-up nose and pretentious attitude. Everyone had taken them in, no questions asked. Everyone except Charlee. There was enough commotion going on that no one noticed, but Gray could see, Charlee was still dealing with this news. She'd been gracious to David, thank goodness. But her eyes had skated across the room and found Gray, and from the inside out, Gray had gotten a little chillier. She needed to do what damage control was possible. Friction wouldn't help David. When Charlee stood and announced she'd clear the plates, Gray stood to help her.

"That's not necessary," Charlee said, stacking plates with a little too much force.

Gray was as tenacious as the tiny blond, and where David was concerned, she'd toss her manners right out the door if necessary. "Really, I insist," she said.

Charlee finally relented. She carried the dishes inside, but the motion was accompanied by an annoyance that was unmistakable.

Once in the kitchen, Gray sat the dirty cups and silverware on the long stainless counter. "Charlee, I know what you must be thinking, but please . . ."

Charlee threw three wooden spoons in the large sink and gripped the edge. Tension tightened the muscles in her back, one that had become bone straight at Gray's words. "No, I don't think you do."

"If you'll let me explain."

Charlee spun on her, blue eyes stormy in the glaring kitchen light. "He was half a world away fighting a war and could have died."

She took a couple murderous steps toward Gray. "He could have died and never known he had a child. How do you explain that?"

Gray pressed her lips together. "I can't. In fact, it's unfair for you to even have to listen to me try, so I won't. You're right."

Charlee's smooth brow split into a frown.

Gray shook her head. "You're absolutely right about all of it. But please don't take it out on David. He's innocent. He's done nothing wrong."

Charlee's hand came to cover her heart. "I would never do that."

"Charlee, I have no right to ask you, but Jeremiah and David and well, me, because I'm in this with them up to my eyeballs—we need you. Miah needs you now more than ever. Please find it in your heart to set your hatred for me aside."

Charlee blinked, thick lashes hooding her blue eyes. "I don't hate you, Gray."

Inside, Gray's stomach was sour. "You'd have every right. It's my fault your dad never met his grandson."

Charlee reeled back and drew a deep lungful of air. Both her hands came up in a stop gesture, blocking Gray, blocking the pain she'd just inflicted. Confusion stole her features for a few long seconds until she shook her head as if trying to settle the comment, make it something *not quite* as bad as it was. "Are you nuts? You're asking me to forgive you and move forward, and in the next breath you're reminding me what you've cost my family?"

Gray raised her hands in the same manner, but on her it meant surrender. "There's no sense trying to sugarcoat it."

"Well, you certainly didn't do that." Charlee shook her head again as if she had no possible hope of understanding Gray. Or her motivation.

"Look, Charlee, I didn't say anything you haven't thought about, probably a hundred times since you all found out about David. I just want you to know, you have every right to feel that way. And I'm asking you, no, I'm *begging* you to lay down your right for his sake."

Charlee turned to face her again, but there seemed no more fire in her eyes, just sadness. The sink was filling with soapy water even though there was a commercial-grade dishwasher in the corner. Charlee shut the water off. "I'll try. For David's sake. And Jeremiah's."

"Thank you." It was more than she could have hoped. And far more than she deserved.

———

Gray sat straight up in bed, breathing hard. Something woke her. She smelled the residue of a long-gone fire in the fireplace downstairs and Miah's blasted cologne. It was everywhere in this room, putrefying the sheets, absorbing into her clothes. She'd have to wash them for a week to get the stench out. At least it was only her T-shirt and underwear. She'd left her sweatpants on the foot of the bed. She'd started to get in with them on because the room had been chilly. But she kept thinking of Miah in that cold, half-gutted room down the hall and it seemed wrong to be in his bed and be cozy while he was probably shivering. So instead of wearing the sweats, she'd slid under the blanket, her legs bare and her feet instantly turning into ice blocks. In no time, the warmth of the down comforter had taken her sacrifice to a whole new level as she let her exposed skin move beneath the satiny cotton cloth. This was Miah's bed. Had he changed the sheets? Probably not; with that, she'd snuggled in deeper, then proceeded to scold herself for doing so.

Being there was worse than she'd imagined. She'd even dreamed he lay beside her, brushing his hand over her head, whispering in her ear. When she'd turned to nuzzle deeper into him, he was gone. She closed her eyes and tried to remove every fragment of Miah. Impossible. Utterly impossible.

When a noise in the room across the hall grabbed her attention, she leapt up, out of the bed, grabbing her sweats on the way.

She slung the door open to find Jeremiah standing just outside David's door. She hid as best she could behind the door, peeking around it. "Nightmare," she said. "He's been having them since the accident."

Jeremiah raced into the room while Gray fought with her sweats. She pulled them on and flew into David's room, where Miah was gently trying to wake him. When Miah saw her, he moved out of the way.

She sat on the edge of the bed. "David?" Her hands cupped his shoulders and her heart ached. His face was twisted into a frown, his smooth brow furrowed and sweat matted strands of hair on his forehead.

"No," he said, voice rough with sleep and the obvious tension of the dream. "No. Don't get in the car. Please. Don't." His hands reached out as if he could grab the ghosts haunting him.

Gray's heart broke because she knew this dream, knew what was happening inside the head of the twelve-year-old boy who was trying to deal with the loss of his parents. Her voice waxed stern this time. "David. Wake up, honey."

But he was still reaching for the unseen, and Gray thrust her hands into his while he mumbled, "Don't go. Don't." And then he woke. Scared eyes darting around the room, landing on Gray. All of the fear and all of the pain of the whole world was summed up in that one troubled look, and Gray had seen it over and over again.

"I had them this time." His voice was small, broken.

"I know, sweetie." His flesh was clammy and his face pale in the slash of light coming from the hall. Gray wanted to scream. To stand up and just scream at the injustice of this whole thing.

"I had them." And in one great quake of his shoulders, the dam of tears burst forth. Gray dragged him up into her arms and rocked him as he cried.

She was only vaguely aware of Miah slipping out of the room.

———

Gray noticed the lights on downstairs in the kitchen and followed the fresh scent of hot cocoa. It had taken close to an hour to get David calmed enough to go back to sleep. She brushed the hair from her face as she entered the room. A single overhead light illuminated the space. "He's been having them for days."

Miah tapped the spatula against the pan, but she figured it was more out of frustration than necessity. "I'm glad you were here."

"About that—" This was her opportunity to explain why David needed to be with her. For now, at least. Her heart quickened.

His eyes were fire when they landed on her. "He's not leaving."

Same stupid, pigheaded McKinley. "Then next time, you're up to bat."

His gaze dropped to the swirling brown liquid. "I'm no stranger to nightmares." Miah shrugged one of his wide shoulders. They were bare, his shirt off. A scar marred one pectoral muscle, and the remains of a summer tan created a barely visible line that cut his ample biceps into two equally large sections. Had he been shirtless earlier? She supposed, but hadn't noticed. Now, it seemed the only thing in her vision and that irritated her.

"How did you know? You're clear down the hall." She chose that as a topic for discussion rather than his reluctance to cover his half nakedness.

"Heating vent runs from his room to mine. Besides, I wasn't asleep."

"Really?" And what was he doing awake in the middle of the night?

"An hour ago you were sawing logs like a lumberjack." His golden eyes caught the light as he glanced up at her. Mischief and mystery danced there.

Her heart did a little flop and she steadied a hand there to equalize it. "And you'd know this from experience due to all the lumberjacks you've slept with?"

He chuckled, took a mug in one hand and poured cocoa into it with expertise that only came from years of practice. Right out of the pan and didn't spill a drop.

"I see you haven't lost your touch," Gray conceded.

"I see you've kept you sense of humor intact, just well hidden under all that stuffiness."

"Hey!" She pointed at him, puffed her chest a little, and then quickly realized what an error that motion was as Miah's gaze dropped to the front of her T-shirt. Gray caved her shoulders and took the offered mug from his hands. To keep from allowing him to see the heat crawling across her face, she cradled the mug and turned to the window.

Miah stepped beside her and the scent that had invaded her night, her dreams, was right there, permeating the air between them. "I need you to stay on a few extra days. He needs you here."

Her heart lifted as if she'd won the lottery and become the queen all in one fell swoop. Outside, snow still fell silently; small flakes had clustered and were larger now, beautiful as they fluttered to the ground and collected at the lake's edge. Already the evergreens were thickening with an icing of snow. She didn't trust her voice to talk about David or her elation about staying on for a bit longer, so she turned to a safer subject. "It wasn't supposed to accumulate."

Miah moved a little closer. "No. Two inches, no more, according to the weatherman and the news."

She glanced over, confused at the wryness of his tone. "Right."

He took a drink and made a face.

"What? You don't like your own cocoa?" But she had a suspicion he'd made it for her, the scent having threaded its way to the stairwell after she'd gotten David settled. She was useless to resist.

"Guess not. I'm in the mood for root beer." He stirred the chocolate concoction while staring into his cup. "Gray, what kind of kid watches the news every night?"

She stared at him, dead-on, though with Miah towering over her, it wasn't a nose-to-nose moment. "A kid like David."

"You know him so well, don't you?"

"Yeah." Gray gripped the mug tighter. "I want you to get to know him, too, Miah. Just . . . just do it the right way."

His mug hit the counter and sloshed. "The right way? What's right about any of this, Gray? We've got a twelve-year-old upstairs trying to rescue his dead parents."

She didn't answer. How could she? Miah's eyes were filled with the same confusion and pain she saw on a daily basis in David's golden gaze. When she only shook her head, he said, "How's that right?"

The words bit, scalded, even, as she drew them in and tried to absorb them. On a long exhale, she said, "It's not. I'm doing the best I can here."

And then his hand, warm from the mug moments ago, landed on her shoulder. "I know you are," he whispered, and Gray could smell the cocoa on his breath. "But I'm not the enemy."

She squared her shoulders and pulled away. "Anyone who tries to take him from me is the enemy, Jeremiah." Though she hated to admit it, even Bill and Angela had become the enemy. How could they have chosen Miah as David's guardian instead of her? She'd gone over and over it in her head. To them, money was important. Having the finances to give David everything he could ever want, but what about love? She'd loved him since the day he was born. How could they just snatch him away? Then again, Wilson had explained more than once that the Olsons really believed they were doing the right thing. David would want for nothing, and she'd maintain the same relationship with him she'd always had. But they couldn't have known that she'd wanted more. That seeing her son grow each and every day was wonderful, but also left a hole in her heart. They'd betrayed her. There was no one she could trust. "I don't want any more cocoa." She placed the cup in the sink and walked out of the kitchen.

———

Miah stayed in the kitchen for a time, just listening to the silence of a house asleep. Gray had long since gone back to bed when Caleb entered and started digging things out to make a sandwich. He didn't bother to speak to Miah. "You're hungry? It's the middle of the night."

"My appetite is at its peak these days."

Miah patted his shoulder as he walked past to get a can of pop out of the fridge. He opened the door and searched. "Are we out of root beer?"

"Yep." The sound of a pop-top sliced the air and Miah's mouth watered. Behind him, he heard Caleb guzzling the drink. "Oh, sorry. I took the last one."

Miah shut the refrigerator door. "You got something to say, little brother, just say it."

Caleb smirked, his blue eyes shooting sparks. "At least you gave her your room."

Miah knew what this was about, but it wasn't Caleb's business and he needed to establish that. At the same time, Gray had warned him about the way he handled Caleb. Geez. Why did this have to be so hard? He scrubbed at the day-old scruff on his jaw. "I just can't . . ." Miah shook his head and pointed at the door as if Gray were standing just beyond it. "How could she come here day after day and look me in the eye knowing, *knowing* she'd lied to me all this time?"

Caleb looked less than interested.

But if Miah could make him understand, make him see, this would be one less disaster he'd have to deal with. "She spent her days here, Caleb, then went home to him. How does someone do that?"

Caleb sniffed. "Don't know. I've never been a scared, alone, eighteen-year-old pregnant girl."

"The sarcasm really helps, Caleb."

He took a bite of his sandwich. "How's the drama helping?"

Miah curled his hands into fists. No one got under his skin like his little brother. "You call this drama?"

"She did what she thought she had to do. It's not like you were there for her." Caleb's open hands rested on the counter.

"You were a kid. You don't know anything about it."

At that, Caleb threw the half-empty can of pop at the trash. He spun to face Miah. "Really? I know what it did to Dad when he realized you were gone."

Fire shot from Caleb's eyes and Miah knew he'd gone too far.

"You ran off. Just like that. Supposed to be getting ready for basic, and bam! You're gone. It was three days before we knew you were in LA. Dad went through hell in that time and I was right there with him. So, don't tell me I don't know anything about it. It hadn't even been a year since we'd lost Mom."

Miah swallowed. The fury in his brother's voice, the pain he must have felt, stole a little of the anger from Miah. He opened his mouth, but didn't have words. "Gray left first. She was gone the day after—"

"The day after you what, Miah? The day after she gave herself to you?"

He was trying to sort it, but it was a long time ago. "She left that next day." And honestly, he'd felt relieved she was going to be gone for a while.

Caleb ran a hand over his right arm. Miah knew he did this because it sometimes felt numb.

"I asked her about it," Caleb said. "She told me you knew she was leaving for a week. Counseling at that camp in Laver. You slept with her, but you couldn't wait for her to get back before running away with Cransden?"

"I shouldn't have. It was really stupid. I should have been there when she got home. But what happened between Gray and me spooked me. I was a kid." It didn't excuse his actions. Nothing did. He'd hurt his best friend so badly she had never wanted to see him again.

"She was a kid, too, Miah."

Caleb was right. Still, this was between Gray and him and Caleb needed to keep a distance from it. Whether Miah's actions were right or wrong, nothing excused twelve years of secrecy. "You don't have to tell me I messed up, okay? I get it. I didn't do everything right."

"No, bro." Caleb tossed the rest of his sandwich in the trash. "You didn't do anything right."

CHAPTER 9

A ray of sun split the room into two parts as Gray squinted against the glare. It was morning. She stretched, tried to muster, but the bed was warm, the air was chilly, and she was in Miah's private space.

Reality settled over her like a frozen slushie and she slithered out and made her way to the master bath. Inside was a claw-foot tub that beckoned her, but she ignored it. She needed to check on David.

She found them all downstairs in the kitchen. Miah stood over the stove, David at the sink, and Caleb was sitting at the counter on a barstool. They all looked up when she came in. She grunted and David giggled. "She's not a morning person."

Caleb leaned forward. "You're *always* perky and chipper when you arrive in the mornings. What happened?"

David laughed. "That's *after* coffee. Before coffee, she's a bear. And not like a little panda bear; like a grizzly, all showing her teeth and growling. It's scary." He looked good. Seemed well, even a bit of color to his cheeks and a smile still firmly planted on his face.

She gave him a mock glare. But this was good. He was feeling more comfortable in his surroundings. Oh. This was *bad*.

"Do I mix the batter like this, Jeremiah?" Innocent golden eyes searched out his father's face, and Gray's heart sputtered in her chest. It was such a normal and average thing for a son to ask his father, yet Miah really had been denied little inquisitions like this one. For twelve years. Because of her.

Miah had on a sweatshirt and jeans. He looked fine. He leaned over from the stove and stared into the bowl of batter David stirred at the sink. "Great. Skillet's ready; you want to drop them on?"

Gray took a seat beside Caleb and stretched to look in the bowl. Oh. Pancake batter. Miah poured a cup of coffee and shoved it across the counter to her.

David shrugged. "Sure. Gray burns the pancakes. Always leaves them in the pan too long. They get black on one side."

She dropped her head to the butcher block. Nothing was sacred. She tilted slightly and peered at David. "You don't have to tell everything, you know."

David grinned at her and moved to the electric skillet beside the stove. She hadn't seen him smiling for days. Maybe this was all going to be okay.

Miah moved closer to him as David hovered over the cooktop. "Stick your finger in the batter and let one drop land on the skillet."

David shrugged and did as instructed. When his hand got a little too close, Miah took hold of it and raised it a few inches higher. The tiny ball of batter sizzled, danced, and cooked quickly. Miah used the corner of the spatula to lift it and drop it in the sink. "That's how you know it's ready."

The batter bowl had a pour spout, so David tilted it above the skillet and watched as the pancake began to form. "Just one at a time?" David asked.

"You can fit another on there."

"Will I have room to flip them?"

"Yep."

He poured another as the first continued to sizzle.

Miah pointed. "When it fills with bubbles that means it's ready. Pancakes should only be turned over once or they get tough."

David's gaze snagged on Gray. "Hey, maybe that's what's wrong with yours."

Again, she gave him a warning look, but had to admit, it was great to see him teasing. Even if she was the butt of the joke.

As David kept a close watch on the sizzling pancakes, he launched into a story. "One time, Gray thought she'd put a cookie in the microwave for twenty seconds, but she hit twenty minutes and walked out of the kitchen."

Miah's eyes grew wide as he split his glances between David and Gray. "What happened?"

"She found it after a couple minutes. Said she smelled something burning."

Miah laughed. "I bet she did." His shirt stretched across his taut chest muscles and Gray willed herself to look away. She should be happy. David was talking, joking, almost seemed like a normal boy again. But seeing Miah and David navigating life and pancakes and their newly found relationship just made her feel further away.

David's honey eyes were filled with sparks of gold and mischief. "Tell them what you told me, Gray."

She sighed, resolved to her morning of torture. "The cookie was on fire."

Miah's brows rose. "What?"

She nodded. "Yeah. Who knew? Right there in the middle of the microwave, flames. The neighbors called the fire department. It was quite a spectacle."

"I love that story," David said. He used the spatula to point at the pancake. "Is it ready?"

"You tell me."

He nodded and slid the spatula under the pancake. Miah stepped behind him and cupped his hand around David's. "All in the wrist. We're gonna slide it over, then flip it right into the same spot. Go."

David did, and when the pancake dropped onto the skillet, it was a perfect circle with just a bit of splatter around the edge.

"Good job." Miah went back to his scrambled eggs and left David cooking pancakes.

When breakfast was finished, and Gray's stomach full, she leaned back in the wooden chair at the farm table, the big country kitchen and all its wonderful smells surrounding her. "Great pancakes, David."

"Sorry I didn't burn them the way you like."

She placed her fork on her plate. "You know, there are things I *can* cook."

David grew somber. "She's right. I'm just giving her a hard time. Gray's a great cook. She can do salad, fruit, cereal, granola bars."

Caleb made a gagging sound. "That's not food."

Gray tucked her hair behind her ear. "I can cook."

Miah's gaze landed on her. His fork dangled between his hands where he'd propped his elbows on the table. "Is that so?"

"Yes."

"Then you can prove it tonight. I'm grilling steaks. You can make the sides."

David frowned. "Steaks? Outside? There's like five inches of snow."

Miah's wide shoulder tipped up. "So?"

"Whatever." David took a bite of his pancakes.

"You want to go play in the snow after breakfast?"

David nodded.

And Gray had to smile because he and Miah were finding some common ground. Only one problem; it was becoming more and more clear, there'd be little room for her.

She'd offered to clean up since the men had done the cooking. After the kitchen was back in order, she went upstairs, changed into warmer clothes and her heavy coat, and stepped outside. Miah had already cleared the back porch and the telltale signs of snow play marred the yard. "Where are they?" she asked Caleb as he came around the side of the house.

"Taking the snowmobile out."

She didn't know Miah had a snowmobile. And she wasn't sure David should be out on one anyway. Then, she remembered. He was with his father. Still, she would have liked the opportunity to offer her opinion.

Caleb pulled a lawn chair from the edge of the house and sat it beside her, then got another one for himself. "They'll be fine. You know Miah and I grew up on those things."

Yes, when Missouri was gracious enough to offer snow. Some years there just wasn't any and some years, there was more than the road crews could handle. "Do they clear your road?"

"Who? MoDOT? They do the road, but not the driveway. Miah's got a small tractor with a shovel on the front. He'll get to it eventually. Until then, you're stuck with us." And Caleb flashed one of those electrifying smiles. She needed to establish some boundaries with him.

"Since I'm here, we can get back to your therapy if you'd like."

He scowled. "Nah. I'm enjoying the time off. Just be here, Gray. Stop feeling like you have to work or babysit everyone."

He didn't understand. "I don't want you backsliding. We've made good progress. Are you keeping up with your exercises?"

"Yeah, yeah." That wasn't an answer, but it placed a bit of much-needed space between them.

She looked out over the yard and realized something was missing. "Where's the snowman? I thought they were going to build a snowman."

"Started it. Had a fairly good-size body until I wrecked it."

She shot an angry look at him.

He scoffed. "Lighten up, Gray. David's a kid. It ended in a massive snowball fight and I lost. Face-planted in the snow with David standing on me, so stop acting like he's this frail little porcelain doll."

It was hard to know the boundaries of protecting someone and smother-mothering them. She caught her hair in the wind. "Face-planted, huh?"

"Yeah. You'd think they'd be more careful with a cripple, but nope."

"Two against one? That's hardly fair." But she had to bite her cheeks to keep from laughing.

"I asked for it."

"Did you learn your lesson?"

He raised his hands. "Do I ever?"

Gray stood. "I think I hear them coming back." She walked to the edge of the porch where she could see the long, winding trail through the trees and deep into the forest. Her eyes were adjusting to the shimmering glare of the sun on the snow when down at the far left edge of the property, the snowmobile came into view with a beaming David on the back and Miah hitting the freshly plowed snow with vigor.

David waved as they sailed right on past, headed toward the lake.

A hand pressed to her heart. How could anyone have such a rush of competing emotions? First, there was joy at the genuine smile on David's face, especially since he'd walked the earth like a corpse since the funeral, where he'd stood at their graves in a suit that he would soon outgrow. Right along with the elation of seeing him happy now was the very real and tangible fear at seeing him on the snowmobile. When had she turned into such a fuddy-duddy? That's what her grandmother called people who never took risks. Then again, Gray knew. She'd entered full fuddy-duddy status when she learned there was a child growing in her belly.

Miah had taken her out on snowmobiles plenty of times when they were in high school. It was good, clean fun. And David seemed to be loving it. This was a brave new world for him and she'd have to get used to it. Plain and simple. David was staying with a soldier now. A man who spent the biggest part of his life carrying an automatic weapon and dodging gunfire.

She'd be a good balancer. But she'd also have to let David experience the life she denied him. It was only fair.

———

David's eyes were sparkling like melted gold; his cheeks were bright red apples. Miah had stopped the snowmobile to show him one of his favorite winter things. He hooked an arm around David's shoulder and pointed across the lake. "Look at those icicles." They were at least ten feet long and latched to a rock embankment that overhung the lake.

"Those are cool."

"Yeah." Miah slipped off the snowmobile, but David stayed on, resting his gloved hands on the handlebars. Miah gave him a smile. "My friends and I used to come down here and watch as they melted. Sometimes one would drop into the water. It was awesome."

"You grew up at the lodge?"

Miah dusted the snow from David's shoulders. "No. Had a friend who lived down there." He pointed to a trail running along the lake. "I'd stay with him whenever we thought there'd be a snow day. Some of my other friends would meet up with us."

David chewed the inside of his cheek. "I don't really have a lot of friends at school."

"No?"

David shook his head. "They're all so immature."

Miah threw his head back and laughed. "Is that so?"

David shrugged. "Yeah."

"The key to having a friend is being there for him when he needs you most. Know who taught me that?"

David shook his head.

"Your mom."

David frowned. "You knew Angela?"

"I meant Gray."

"Oh. She's my *birth* mom."

Miah didn't really see the need for the distinction, but okay. "Your birth mom taught me that."

David chewed his cheek. "But she said she didn't really have many friends growing up."

"Let me tell you something about your birth mom, David. She was the best friend I ever had. She was with me during some of the hardest times of my life. She may not have had a lot of friends, but the ones she had, she was fiercely devoted to."

He watched as David gnawed on that for a while. "Like she's devoted to me?"

Miah winked. "Exactly. You want to drive home?"

His eyes turned to saucers. "Seriously?"

"Sure."

A smile curved his face. "Okay."

Miah gave him a quick lesson.

David tugged his stocking hat over his ears. "What's down that way?"

"We used to call that the Hidden Path. If you follow it along the lake, you'll pass a log cabin and if you keep going, there's a cove. At the edge of the cove is a small graveyard from I don't know how far back. We always joked that it was haunted."

"Cool. Can we go there?"

Miah pointed at him. "You're driving."

He knew David was still mustering his courage to take the wheel, so he launched into another story. "One winter we had a really hard freeze and a deep snow. My friends and I were all out on the snowmobiles and we'd missed like two weeks of school. One of them got the bright idea to try to take the snowmobile across the cove."

"Did he sink it?"

"No. He floored it and went straight across. Then, he decided that if the rest of us were real men, we'd follow him. Stupidest thing I've ever done."

"Did you fall in?"

"Nope. The water is shallow there, twenty feet, maybe. It was frozen solid. But that was a really dumb thing for us to do. Of course, it made us feel like men. Like we'd conquered the elements or something."

"So, who's in the graveyard?"

Miah turned to look down the path. "I don't know. There are only eight stones. Some of them are hard to read."

David grinned. "Haunted, huh?"

Miah shrugged. "So we thought. Once we were standing in the center making up stories about who was buried there and a tree branch fell right behind us."

David laughed. "What did you do?"

"Went running and screaming like little girls."

"That's really funny, Jeremiah."

Miah rubbed a hand over his face. "Yeah. It is. Keep it to yourself."

"No promises." David wrapped his fingers around the handlebars. "Ready?"

"Let's ride."

———

It seemed like they were gone forever when Gray finally saw them coming back down the trail toward the lodge. Her nose was starting to run and her hands tingled, frozen Popsicles at the ends of her arms. As the gleaming tan snowmobile angled toward her, Gray's heart caught in her throat. David was driving.

She opened her mouth to yell for him to slow down, that he was going too fast. She quickly judged the distance between the snowmobile and the edge of the house. Too fast. Way too fast. They bounced and jostled as they drew near and the smile she'd seen on David's face was now turning into horror. His eyes were fitted on the woodpile they were getting closer and closer to.

Jeremiah's voice caught up to her first. He was telling David to slow down. He repeated it twice, but David was as frozen as Gray's heart. Miah reached around him and grabbed the handlebars, but it was too late. There was no time to slow. Miah jerked the handlebars, but the snowmobile kept barreling forward. Cold fear shot down Gray's spine, leaving her too weak to scream.

Miah grabbed David around the middle, shielding him as much as possible, and bailed off the snowmobile. They rolled and came to a stop, covered in white and both breathing hard as the snowmobile made contact with the corner of the woodpile.

Gray knew she'd screamed David's name because she'd heard it, heard the terror in her own voice and was running to them before they stopped rolling.

She dove into the snow and found a down coat. She grabbed David's shoulders, pulling him to a seated position. He coughed out a bit of snow. The two guys were a tangled mess of arms and legs, but Gray's hands roamed freely, feeling for breaks as she went along.

David's hand clamped on to hers. "I'm fine. Gray! I'm okay." A gloved hand shoved her away.

Her fingers tightened on David's shoulders just as Jeremiah was untangling his long legs.

"Sure you're all right?" he said, dusting snow from both of them. He didn't even sound upset.

Gray's worry quickly morphed into fury. She turned to Miah. "What in the world were you thinking?"

Miah didn't seem to have an answer, but his face tensed as he looked over his shoulder to find the snowmobile crashed against the woodpile.

Seeing it there, Gray realized just how close this was to a serious accident. She'd already learned how quickly an accident could turn into a tragedy. Fire shot into the pit of her stomach. "This isn't the army, Jeremiah. He isn't one of your new recruits. He's a child. Barely twelve years old."

She pulled David up from the snow so that he stood beside her. When his hand went to his head to remove his stocking hat, she saw the blood. "Oh no." Gray gripped the sides of his face as he tugged the hat from his head. The blood had smeared, but she could see the inch-long cut above his brow.

"Come on, let's get him inside." Miah took David by the arm.

David's hand went to his head. He turned a little pale when he looked down to find his glove smeared with blood. "Did I ruin your snowmobile?"

Miah barely gave it a glance. "Nah. Just clipped the edge. She's had worse."

"I'm never driving it again," David mumbled as the three of them made their way to the back door.

Miah stopped and tilted David's chin to get a better look at the cut. "Sure you are. You gotta get back on the horse, kid. Maybe just don't open the throttle quite so much next time."

Next time? Gray gave him a cold glare. If Miah actually thought there was going to be a next time, he was delusional.

As soon as the roads were clear and she could dig her car out, she was going back to Mr. Granger's office to see what she could do about this whole thing. Miah wasn't ready for this kind of responsibility. And since he wasn't, that put David in danger here.

Miah still stood at the door, his fingers cupped around David's chin. She wanted to hurry him along, but something made her stop. Jeremiah's face softened as he looked into the eyes of his child. "Don't be afraid of the snowmobile, okay, David?"

Gray's eyes closed because she didn't want to see this. Didn't need to see this. It was a father instructing his son. It was a soldier giving advice to someone younger and with less experience. And under different circumstances, she could appreciate the gesture.

Miah used his hand to swipe away the remaining trickle of blood that had started to congeal. "In fact, don't be afraid of anything."

Oh good grief.

Just as they were stepping inside, none of them bothering to knock the snow from their feet, Caleb met them at the door. He took one look at David, then Miah, then angled to look out back. "Are you kidding me? You wrecked the snowmobile?"

"Shut up, Caleb," Miah said as he shoved past him.

"Just great. Way to go, kid." Caleb slammed the back door. "And they're calling for more snow."

———

Gray sat on the corner of Jeremiah's bed. If more snow was in the forecast, she needed to reach out to Mr. Granger by phone. She cradled her cell and hoped the heating duct didn't carry her voice. She dialed his number and when he answered, she launched into an explanation of the situation.

For a few moments, Granger was silent. "Mary Grace, I know this has to be difficult for you."

She squeezed her eyes shut at the condescension in his tone. "This isn't about me, Wilson. It's about David's safety."

Was that a chuckle on the other end of the phone line? "So, you're telling me father and son were out on a snowmobile and he got a bump on his head?"

Bile rose in her throat. "He could have died." Why was no one understanding this? Bill and Angie had died just driving home from the airport. Was it really necessary for her to explain the parallels? Did no one get it? Life was precious. And fleeting. And where David was concerned, she wasn't interested in taking risks.

"You're being a bit dramatic, dear. I'd say that Miah's interest in the boy shows his determination to become a good father, a good role model. Already they're bonding. I think you should see this as a positive thing."

"A positive thing?"

"Yes. Jeremiah is obviously trying to bond with his son." There was a long pause. "Mary Grace, kids get hurt. It's a natural part of life. Now if you'd told me Jeremiah had been drinking or there were . . . I don't know . . . drugs involved, that'd be a different story. But right now all you're telling me is David got hurt doing something any normal, red-blooded American boy might be doing."

Tears filled her eyes. "Are you telling me I'm just supposed to stand by and watch as Jeremiah uses trial and error to figure out how to be a father—with David and his safety hanging in the balance?"

Granger sighed. "I'm pretty certain that's what all mothers have to do."

She hung up the phone, swiped the angry tears, and barely noticed the light tap on her door. "Come in." When her voice cracked on the last word, she pooled her strength and painted on a smile.

David opened the door, but didn't enter. "I bled through the other Band-Aid, so Jeremiah put this one on." His voice was weak, and she was fairly certain the day's events had taken what little spark she'd seen earlier and turned it into a wasteland. David fingered the wound. "He called it a butterfly bandage. He's good at doing these."

"Years in the military and helping raise three younger brothers." Gray motioned for him to come in. She took his hand and pulled him onto the bed with her. "You doin' okay?"

"I want to go home." His fingers twisted on the down comforter.

Gray's heart broke. "I know, sweetie."

He pulled a deep breath and let it hiss through his lips. His cheeks were still rosy from the cold outside, maybe even a little windburned. He dropped his head on Gray's shoulder. "But I don't have a home anymore, do I?"

She tucked him beneath her arm. "You've always got a home with me."

"Yeah," he mumbled. And it sounded like such a hopeless sound, it made Gray tighten her grip on him a little more. "I'm never riding a snowmobile again."

"Well, that's good because, honestly, I don't think my heart could take it."

"Is he going to make me?" He tilted out to look at her and Gray saw the little boy he still was.

"I don't think so. He'll have to get through me." She offered a mock frown and her best mean look.

David's face split into a smile, causing the gold of his eyes to dance. "Like that would be hard; you weigh about seven pounds and he weighs like five hundred."

"Oh? This morning I thought I was a grizzly."

"A skinny little emaciated grizzly." He tapped the bandage, testing it.

She huffed. "Emaciated? Where exactly did we pick up that word?"

"Science class. Now he's taking me fishing tomorrow because it's supposed to be sunny in the afternoon."

She tilted to look at David's face. "There's five inches of snow on the ground and they're calling for more."

David threw his hands up. "I know. There's a winter storm warning. Another cold front is coming through and we're going to get hammered by it tomorrow night."

David did talk like a grown man sometimes; she had to smile. "Did you tell Miah?"

His eyes widened and he made a show of nodding his head.

"What'd he say?"

David rolled his eyes. "He pounded on his chest and grunted something about real men."

Oh. "Fishing is pretty fun. I'm sure Miah will take hot cocoa and make sure you don't get too cold. On another note, don't worry about the snowmobile. I'll talk to Jeremiah about it. I used to be pretty persuasive where he was concerned."

"In high school when you two were friends?"

"Yes." It seemed a lifetime ago. It *was* another lifetime. In that one, Gray and Miah had a connection the whole town recognized. If there was any shred of it left, if he still cared for her on any level, maybe she could convince him to take things slower with David. However, she knew Miah. And slow wasn't something he was accustomed to. Where he was concerned, there was full throttle and hyperdrive. But somehow, she had to get through to him. After all, David was all that mattered.

———

Jeremiah dropped a match on the kindling and watched as ribbons of smoke turned to glowing embers. He knelt on one knee and blew across the fire. Flames, bright and hot, coerced by the press of oxygen, rose from the rock-encircled campfire. He brushed the snow from a nearby tree stump for sitting and warmed his hands, holding them above the flame. He'd shoveled several inches of snow to light the fire and now that it was glowing, he wondered what in the world he was doing. His gaze trailed to the lakeside where, a few hours ago, he and David had sat on the pier fishing. If raising kids was as easy as lighting a fire, maybe he could do this. The fishing, much like the snowmobile ride and the videogames, had been a disaster. Miah looked heavenward. He clasped his hands in his lap, fingers cold, but with the warmth of the fire, it was manageable. Night had fallen and, usually, he reserved early mornings for these moments of quiet contemplation. But the fishing excursion had driven him out here. First, David had tossed the fishing pole into the water while trying to cast. Miah had fished it out, but soaked his coat to the shoulder to do it. Then, David had jerked as the worm went onto the hook, and the hook had gone through the meaty part of Miah's hand. Finally, David had given up entirely.

Miah stared at the heavens. The sky above was a star-bright navy blue blanket. He cleared his throat. "If you've got some advice for me, I could really use it right now."

Wind blew across the valley, curling the flames and making the smoke dance. When it hit his eyes, he closed them tightly, surprised to find moisture already settling there. When no other answer came, he planted his hands on his knees. "It's just that I'm a soldier. I'm accustomed to taking orders. Going in blind doesn't scare me half as much as the possibility that there's no one in charge of this mission. Failure isn't really an option here. If you could just give me . . . I don't know . . . a sign or something."

The night sky remained silent. But footsteps behind him drew his attention. He listened. A wide gait, one foot slightly dragging before each step. Caleb. Miah steeled himself, eyes drifting closed. The last thing he needed right now was a smart-mouthed little brother telling him everything he's doing wrong.

"How'd the fishing go?"

"Not good."

Caleb crowded onto the stump beside him. "So no bass for dinner tomorrow night?"

Miah gave him a flat stare.

"I'm just kidding. I already gave the kid a hard time about impaling you and not catching anything."

Miah bit his tongue because he didn't need to say what he was thinking.

"Hey! Look at that." Caleb stretched back.

When Miah followed Caleb's fingers, pointed at a spot in the winter sky, he saw nothing.

"A shooting star. Ya see it?"

Miah stared blankly. "No." Was that his sign? Had he missed it because of his inconsiderate brother? "Did you need something, Caleb? I kind of came down here to get a few minutes alone."

Caleb remained, but didn't speak, his hands finding the warmth of the fire. He made no attempt to leave, and that irritated Miah beyond belief. "Nah. I don't need anything."

Miah used a stick to poke at the fire.

Caleb kept his eyes on the cloudless sky. "Look."

Miah didn't bother. If it was another shooting star, he didn't want the disappointment.

"That's Isaiah's star, right?" Caleb stretched again, this time pointing to a section of sky just above McKinley Mountain where a single brilliant star outshined the others.

Miah began to grin. He'd all but forgotten his brother Isaiah's lesson. "The Eye of God," Miah whispered.

"Yep. I swear, seeing that thing has kept me going on more than one occasion. Oh, by the way, we're out of root beer again." Caleb shoved off the stump and towered over Miah. "Guess I did have a reason for coming down here."

Miah smiled up at his brother, then let his gaze trail to the star. The Eye of God. The star that Isaiah claimed watched over you in your darkest hours. "Hey, Caleb, thanks for coming to check on me."

Caleb half grinned and loped back up to the lodge.

CHAPTER 10

David walked the edge of the lake, thinking. That's what his dad used to do when he was under stress. Of course, he'd walk the neighborhood, not the lake. Hands sunk deeply into his pockets and sort of strolling along. David thought there must be something to it or his dad wouldn't have done it. His dad was nothing if not prudent with his time, and he certainly wouldn't have strolled if it offered no benefits.

David thought over the days he'd been living with Jeremiah. Over a week now and Gray was still there. The snow kept the driveway a mess, but he liked her there and he thought Jeremiah did, too, though they tended to fight like the puppies he'd watched at the pet store in the mall.

David stopped at the edge of the water. He didn't know what his dad used to think about, so that gave him a disadvantage in this whole walking-and-thinking thing. His dad had done quite a lot of walking in the weeks leading up to the accident. David knew his mom and dad had been worried about money. They had hoped to make the business bigger, but David guessed they hadn't done it right.

He kicked a rock into the lake. None of the business stuff mattered now because his mom and dad were gone. *When one door closes, another opens,* his dad used to tell him. David tilted his head back and stared up at the sky. "I don't see another door, Dad." When there was no answer from the sky, he sank his hands deeper and kept walking. Before long, he'd rounded a curve and the tracks from the earlier trip on the snowmobile disappeared. Up ahead, something moved at the lake's edge. His first instinct was to turn and run—word had it there was a bigfoot in the Ozarks—but curiosity pulled him forward. The snow was silent as he continued to take slow steps. There. A flash of red. David squinted.

The sun was lower in the sky now, shining off the water and making it look like melted gold. He raised a hand to shield his eyes, and he saw it again. And then it yelled at him.

"Hi!"

For a second he was frozen, but as he continued closer and the trees and brush gave way to a clearing, he saw the girl, waving, smiling, with two pigtails hung on either shoulder, and she held a fishing pole in her hand. As he neared, he could see her nose was bright red and her hair was blond. "Hi," he said back.

"Did you get lost?" she said, and flipped the pole, casting it far into the water.

How'd she do that? "No. Just . . . you know, walking and thinking."

She frowned, her cheek ticking on one side, then she smiled again. "Yeah, I know, I do that a lot, too." She started reeling, then stopped and looked over at him. "Actually, I don't. What are you thinking about?"

Well, that was the question. His shoulder tipped up. "I hadn't decided yet."

David kicked at the snow until he found a smooth rock. He held it like he'd seen Jeremiah hold one and skipped it out over the water. To his surprise, it bounced twice before falling.

The girl laughed. "I'm fishing here."

"Yeah."

She took a few steps closer and he could see her eyes were green. Easy to tell because she had them open wide in exaggeration. "I'm *fishing*."

He could see that.

She rolled her eyes. "You'll scare off the fish."

Oh. David wanted out of there. He turned. "See ya." He started walking back in the direction of the lodge. "Good luck fishing." She really made it look easy. But he knew it wasn't.

"Wait. What's your name?" He half turned to find the girl coming toward him. She'd dropped her pole at the water's edge. Didn't she know how dangerous that was? Fishing poles could sink.

"David."

She stopped at his feet. "What grade are you in?"

"Eighth."

"I'm in seventh." She cast a look behind him. "Are you visiting someone here?"

"Yeah." He pointed behind him to the snow-crusted lodge that was easily seen from their vantage point. From here, it looked really cool, like a postcard or something with the snow on the roof and the dark brown walls. "I live in that big brown place."

"Oh. The lodge. It looks cool. Can I come see it sometime?"

His mouth was dry. He should have brought a bottle of water with him. He tipped his shoulder. "I don't care."

Her eyes narrowed. "Do you homeschool?"

"No."

She reached out and gripped the shoulder of his coat and tugged until he was leaned out over the water. Then she pointed at the sky. "See that line of smoke?"

David swallowed.

"That's my house. Lived here for six months and the lake is my favorite part." Her eyes narrowed. "I've never seen you at school."

"I go to school in Laver." Or he did. Before. It seemed every part of his life was dissected into before the accident and after. He was a science project gone wrong.

"Laver has a big deal about basketball, don't they? My older brother plays. Says he wants to transfer there."

He nodded. "But River Rock has science. I might even go there when I'm in high school."

She smiled again and David's heart did a little flop. "You like science, too?"

His hands were sweaty but he didn't know why. "Uh-huh."

She kept looking at him and he wasn't sure if it meant he was supposed to say more or what. David chewed the inside of his cheek. "Did you catch a fish?"

"Not today, but I usually do."

He nodded, kicked at the snow.

"You fish?"

"Uh." He could just say yes. "I'm really not good at it."

She shrugged and turned to face her gear, and when she did, one of the braids sailed over her shoulder. "So, I could teach you. I mean, first, you shouldn't throw rocks in the water."

He blinked.

Her chin jutted out. "That's a joke."

"Oh."

"I have to get home, but if you want, we can meet down here tomorrow. School's already cancelled. Woo-hoo." She pumped her fist when she said the last part and David realized he was smiling.

"Okay. What time?"

Her eyes narrowed and she tapped her finger against her chin. "Hmm. Late morning maybe. I'd say early, but it's too cold then. Let's meet around ten. Okay?"

"Okay." He didn't know what else to do, so he turned and headed home. A few feet away from her he stopped. "What's your name?"

She was still watching him. Was she going to watch him walk all the way down the water's edge?

"I'm Anastasia, but everyone calls me Stacey. Or Stace. My grandmother calls me Stasia. But she's the only one."

He frowned. "What do you like to be called?"

Her head tilted, curiosity on her face. "I don't know. I've never been asked that. I'll think about it and tell you tomorrow."

David nodded and turned away from her. Girls were weird. Hands in his pockets, he started strolling back to the lodge. He had a lot to think about.

———

The light knock on his door pulled Jeremiah's attention from the guardianship paperwork in front of him. The documents were pretty straightforward and simple—in fact, the most easily read documents he'd ever seen from an attorney's office. Still, he stared at each of them for extended stretches of time, as if more instructions would magically appear before his eyes. He'd done this for all of the sixteen days since he'd met with Wilson and Gray in Granger's office. Another winter storm had dumped a ton of snow and marooned them at the lodge. Not that he was complaining. He let Gray have her space and plenty of time with David. Meanwhile, his own relationship with David was coming along. His relationship with Gray was another story.

"Can I come in?" Gray leaned her weight on the doorjamb, putting up a nonchalant front. He didn't buy it; she was ready to bring out the claws and draw blood on a moment's notice, but hey, he'd give her props for trying. They were civil to one another. She'd gone back to working with Caleb in the daytime hours and helping to burn dinners in the evenings. But there was always an underlying something that suggested she could grab David and run off. Or maybe snap. He'd remodeled the room he stayed in, replacing the drafty window with one he'd previously purchased, making it more livable since Gray didn't seem to be in any hurry to go. And honestly, he wasn't in a huge hurry to get rid of her. But this wasn't normal life. And he knew normal life was only a snowplow's work away. That scared him, but they couldn't remain forever playing "dysfunctional house" with Gray staying on and David ditching school. The whole county had been out of school for the last several days, so that was a plus, but sooner or later, David would have to return to a regular schedule. And Miah didn't really know how he'd handle being a regular dad with a regular routine.

She knocked again.

"Oh, sorry. I got lost in my thoughts for a second." He motioned for her to come in. She wore jeans ripped at the knees, a total turn-on for him. He tried to ignore how good she looked. "Where's David?"

"With Stacey. Those two have been joined at the hip for days, ever since he met her. It's great, though. I love seeing him with a friend."

"Yeah, they robbed all the carrots from the fridge to use as snowman noses. But I think they are leaving them outside for the animals. We saw some deer the other day and David was concerned about how they find enough to eat."

She pulled a chair over so it sat straight across from him. "You look like a man with a lot of questions."

"I guess I am. Gabriel and Isaiah have the opportunity to come visit us for a few days. Do you think that would be okay?"

"That's great. They're your family, Miah. Of course they should come." Her full-moon eyes stayed firmly on his. "Why would you ask?"

"David. He's doing well right now and I don't want to throw another wrench in the machine."

She touched a hand to his arm. "David will get the chance to meet his uncles. I think it's great."

He nodded. "They'll love him. He's such an incredible kid. Plus, I'm planning an all-day fishing trip and he can keep me posted on the weather."

She smiled. "I'm sure he will."

"Still, I don't know how—"

Gray leaned closer.

He tapped the document on his lap and stared at the words *Instruction to Guardian of Minor Children of William and Angela Olson*. "How are we supposed to raise our child by someone else's set of rules?"

He saw the spark in her eye, even though she tried to hide it. Miah leaned forward and snagged her with his gaze. "Before this discussion goes any further, let me make one thing crystal clear. I won't give up custody of my child. I'm not looking for a way out, Gray. I'm just still searching for some of the answers."

She practically deflated before him. "What about joint custody?"

"Gray, he's twelve. I have maybe six years to make up for the time I lost. He's living with me. It's not up for debate. I'm just not sure I know how to do that according to someone else's set of rules."

"I've spent twelve years helping raise him by someone else's rules."

"Which is why I need your help now."

"Or you could consider letting him live with me. Use the time you have when you visit to just have fun with him. Not have to carry all this responsibility. It's all so new to you."

"Did you miss that whole statement a few seconds ago? *Never* gonna happen." In another six years David would be eighteen, an adult going off to college. There was so much Miah'd missed already. But not anymore. He'd cherish every day.

She clenched her teeth, leaned back, and tried to calm down; it was evident in the tilt of her head, the gleam in those silvery eyes. Gray reached out with a slender hand and slipped the paper from his grasp. For the longest time, she stared at it silently. He couldn't even hear her breathing.

But the words must have become blurry because she batted her eyes, lips quivering, and if Miah wasn't careful, he'd feel bad, horrible for what she was going through. And if he felt too bad about it, he'd do whatever he could to make her pain stop.

"I know this hurts." It was all he could say.

She brushed the back of her hand against her left eye. "Like they betrayed me."

Yeah, he got that. Gray had apparently spent a lifetime having people betray her. Him included.

Suddenly, his hand was on her knee. Denim and the silk of her skin just beneath his touch. "We'll get through this, Gray. We have to for David."

She laughed without humor. "He's all that matters." She met Miah's gaze squarely and what he saw there, in her eyes, looking right into the depth of her soul was the question. *But can't I matter just a little bit too?*

Without realizing what he was doing, Miah gripped the front legs of the chair and drew them to him, pulling Gray closer. She came along easily—beings with no fight left in them were that way. Deep inside her, there was a hopelessness. It reached toward him through the veil of pain, tangible enough it could grow legs and walk around. He hadn't wanted that. He just wanted to get to know his son.

The chair stopped when their knees bumped. He spread his to allow more room and the ability to drag her just a little closer. She looked so lost, so fragile, like a strong wind could lift her and carry her away. Sliding her toward him, Miah was reminded of that thing, that magnetism that had ultimately drawn the two of them together during high school. Gray was the battery and Miah, the jumper cable. They'd been united then and had weathered every storm side by side. It used to make Miah's girlfriends crazy. "They were all jealous of you," he mumbled.

"What are you talking about?" Until she asked, he hadn't realized he'd said that out loud.

"Different girlfriends I had. They didn't want you around me."

She rolled her eyes. "That was high school."

His hands clamped down on her knees. Didn't she realize that thing was still there? Maybe he'd not known it then, but now it was screaming like a banshee, bright as a dang neon sign. Like the LED lights at the Neon Moon. She had to sense it. Feel it. "Gray, did you ever think about what might have happened if . . . if you'd told me and if we'd—"

She flew out of the chair. "How many times do you think my mind shot down that path? But it's a dead-end road, Jeremiah. I could never be with someone who doesn't love me." She brushed her hair back, tilted her jaw defiantly. "I deserve better."

And that's when the night at the party entered his mind, wrecking his intentions. He'd watched two dirtbags from the movie crew hit on Gray. And he hadn't liked it. He'd even admitted it to her, saying she deserved better. She also deserved better than him. Still did. Because he had been too stupid back then to see what they had. And now, with David in the middle of their relationship, he didn't know if he'd be able to navigate any better. After all, he was still the same person. Older, hopefully wiser, but who knew? And she seemed so fragile. Still, he'd like to try. "Maybe it's not a dead-end road, just a hidden path. Sometimes you have to explore a little to know what you're dealing with."

She moved across the room, away from him, out of reach from the possibility he offered. She stopped at the window. "Sure. If it was just us. Maybe that could happen. But we have to consider David. I won't take any chances on him getting hurt by us sending mixed signals. I'm sorry."

He hated the fact that she was right. If things worked out between them, great. But if they didn't, David would be hurt again. Miah stood from the bed and walked to the window to stand beside her. Outside, the snow was beginning to melt. It had been a beautiful snow. Perfect, almost. But now there were real-world decisions to make and none of them were going to be easy. "How soon do you think David should return to school?"

"I want to go back next week." They both turned to find him at the bedroom door.

Gray painted on her happy face that almost masked the concern. "That's soon."

He nodded. "I know."

Miah split his glances between mother and son. This was out of his league.

"Are you sure you wouldn't rather take another week?"

"It's been almost three. Also, I don't want to go to Laver. I want to transfer to River Rock." With that, he turned from the door and left. Footsteps on the stairs confirmed he was out of earshot.

Miah looked at Gray. She shrugged. "I don't know."

"In the 'Instructions to Guardian,' it talks about River Rock for high school."

Gray nodded. "Yes. There's a really great science department." She hugged herself. "I mean, I asked Wilson what he thought of transferring David now. You know, fresh start and all, but I didn't know if it was a good idea or a terrible idea."

"What did Wilson say?"

She bit back a bitter smile. "That you'd be making that call." Her mouth twitched and Miah knew something about that wasn't exactly true.

She forced out a breath. "He never answered because he was trying to let me down easy about you being given guardianship."

"Why don't we go talk to the counselor at his school?" Miah stacked the documents together because it seemed more efficient to do that than leave them spread all over his room.

"At Laver? I can already tell you what they're going to say. They won't want to lose him. Laver detests the idea of kids leaving there for the science program at River Rock."

His mouth dropped open. "It's a school. She's the counselor. Shouldn't the child's best interest be at heart?"

"It is, to a degree. Welcome to middle-school politics, Miah. The counselor will absolutely believe it's best for him to stay right there. I guarantee it."

"She won't be an unbiased professional, is that what you're telling me?"

"She's a woman who has poured her heart and soul into the care of the kids at Laver. You can't expect her to think it would be better for him to be uprooted when we could just make the thirty-minute drive each day."

"This is so hard."

Gray nodded.

"Fine. Tomorrow morning, we go to River Rock. Talk to the counselor there. If we're not satisfied, we drive to Springfield or even over to Branson. We get perspectives from as many professionals as we feel we need to make a solid, informed decision."

Gray crossed her hands over her chest. "Are you going to handle every situation this thoroughly?"

Of course he would. He was a good soldier. When he didn't answer, she tilted her head back and laughed. "We are in for one interesting ride."

As she stepped past him to leave the room, she reached over and brushed a hand across his arm. It was the most contact she'd instigated and it sent tremors down his spine. "Don't worry, McKinley. You're doing okay."

Was he? He didn't really think so. The snowmobile had given David a scar he might have for life, and the fishing was . . . well, it was a fiasco. For a guy who prided himself on doing things well, Miah was lacking in this area.

"Hey, did you hear me?" Gray reached up and gave his arm a little shake.

"Back in high school when I messed up, you were always there to smooth it out. I never—" The words caught in his throat, but he needed to say this, had to say it. Right now. "I never thanked you."

His hand came up, slowly made its way to her cheek. Her skin was dewy soft and smooth, cool like the granite that held her together. For the quickest instant, she nuzzled into his touch. "You're welcome." And there in the depths of her eyes he saw the desire to take another path, a path with him. A road that might lead nowhere or might lead to the very thing they each desperately wanted. But before he could act, she steeled herself and stepped away from him.

"Gray?" He hated the alarm in his voice.

She half turned and threw him a look over her shoulder, long black hair catching the light. "Yes?" Her hand was planted on the doorjamb. Maybe to keep herself from rushing back.

"We gonna be able to do this?"

Something flashed across her features. Something that both stopped his heart and kick-started it again. "Of course." But her mouth twitched when she said it and Jeremiah knew she wasn't convinced, and that, in fact, this whole thing could blow up in their faces and the one who would really suffer was David. For the first time since he'd gotten the news that he was a father, Jeremiah understood all Gray had gone through to keep David a secure, happy kid. For the first time, he understood her sacrifice. And for the first time, he was distinctly aware, a large part of his heart loved Gray.

Miah's chest hurt, a dull aching he wasn't accustomed to, so he dropped his gaze to it. His hand followed and rubbed against his T-shirt where a traitorous heart beat just beneath the thin cotton material. In another time, in another life, he could have had her. Could have had every ounce of her to call his, but he'd blown that opportunity without even knowing it was before him. His chest burned. His hand fisted into the material of his shirt. "She's still too good for you," he said to himself, because there was no one left to hear. Gray was gone.

CHAPTER 11

Gray had to admit it. She was impressed. Jeremiah had called the school in River Rock and discovered the counselor would be in for a few hours the following day even though school was canceled. He cleared the drive with a big yellow tractor David decided to name Buttercup, and had dressed in his best jeans and a nice shirt. He was nervous as a cat, and when she wondered if he might claw through the chair arms in the school office waiting area, Gray reached over and placed a hand on his. "Relax, tiger."

He hooked a thumb at the office behind them. "I didn't know she'd want to talk to David. I mean, what if she says the wrong thing? He's doing well right now. No nightmares for days, I just . . ."

Gray squeezed his hand, then let go. "She's a counselor, Miah. She's trained for this. Relaaaaaax. You made the right call to come here, to get this counselor's opinion. If we aren't convinced it's all for David's best interest, we'll talk to another."

His eyes met hers and held. And right there in the molten gold of his irises, everything shifted. His voice became a whisper as he raised her hand to his lips. "I couldn't do this without you." And there on her knuckles, he placed a kiss so lightly she had to fight the urge to reach over and capture the sensation. Suddenly, the tension about David was gone and a new tension was there, bright and hot and rising to the surface on the heat she'd inadvertently created.

Gray tried to lean out of the trajectory of his gaze, but Miah was Miah and he was so darn sexy, even the Greek gods would be jealous. The feel of his lips on her hand remained even though the touch was long gone. Before her, the wide glass window separated the offices from the extensive hall. She placed her focus there, hoping it would slow her racing heart. But she was inundated with memories of a past life when Miah would pick her up in the mornings and together they'd drive to school while talking about their nights and making plans for the weekends. This was their old high school. The middle school had taken it over when the new high school was built a few years back. And it didn't help that these were the corridors where she first fell in love with Jeremiah McKinley. "We sure spent some time walking these halls, didn't we?"

"Yeah." He reached over and grabbed her hand for a quick second. "It's kind of comforting to know David will be here. Feels familiar, you know?"

"Comforting for you. You were the demigod of River Rock High. For all of us peasants, it might have been a bit different."

His face troubled. "Do you think he'll have a hard time adjusting?"

She sighed and took a peek over her shoulder to make sure David was still in the counselor's office. "He's a unique kid. He'd have a hard time adjusting anywhere."

"Should we leave him at Laver?"

She shook her head. "He didn't really have any friends there. At least here he has Stacey."

"Yeah. What's up with those two? Running off almost every day since he met her."

"They formed a bond quickly, that's for sure." She smiled. "Don't you see it? They're us, Miah. Way back when."

"But we don't know what they're doing, and that bothers me."

She laughed. "If David were a year or two older, it'd worry me, too."

"Do you think she's the reason he wants to attend River Rock?"

She'd thought about it quite a bit, actually. "Partially, yes. But he was having a hard time at Laver."

Miah pivoted in the too-small chair. "What do you mean?"

Gray ran a hand into her hair and scrubbed at her scalp because every time she thought of it, she got angry. "There was this kid, really popular, and he took a dislike to David. Anyway, the bullying escalated until one day when I showed up and saw three other guys around him."

Miah went from zero to furious in less than a second.

"They weren't being physical or anything, just . . . I could see it in his eyes, in their body language."

"This is good then."

Gray offered a smile. It was good if the same thing didn't happen here.

———

"Mr. McKinley, Ms. Smith, please come in." The counselor at River Rock turned to David. "While I visit with your birth parents, David, you can go check out the library I told you about. Miss Carpenter is in there moving some things around; she's our media specialist."

He reached out and shook her hand. "It was nice meeting you, Ms. Forrester."

She blinked, gave him a smile, trying to hide her surprise. "You too, David."

He headed down the hall and Miah and Gray went in her office.

"He's quite a remarkable young man." Ms. Forrester sat down behind her desk, but her general body language seemed friendly. She wore a silk blouse that was tucked into jeans, probably casual because of the snow day.

Gray fought the urge to slip her hand into Miah's. Instead, she threaded her fingers together and kept them on her lap.

"I wanted to speak with David because sometimes adults can go around and around the heart of a subject without ever really getting to it, when all they need to do is ask the child."

Miah leaned forward. "What is the heart of the subject, Ms. Forrester?"

Gray shot him a quelling look. Maybe that's how a soldier handled men in his charge, but his directness with Ms. Forrester might not be appreciated. They needed an ally, not an enemy.

She rolled a pencil over and over between her fingers. "I like your candor, Mr. McKinley."

Gray watched him as he shot Ms. Forrester one of those skin-melting smiles. "Please, call me Jeremiah." *Oh, you've got to be kidding me.* Gray's eyes trailed to Ms. Forrester. Putty.

She needed to intervene. "Ms. Forrester, what do you feel is the best decision for David?"

She blinked, leaned back, and placed the pencil in a holder on the edge of her desk. "Most counselors would suggest waiting until the end of the school year. David lives in River Rock now, correct?"

Jeremiah scooted forward to the edge of his seat. "Yes. With me. Gray owns a home here, too, at the edge of town."

Her heart lurched. *Don't tell her the address. The house still looks like a demolition site.* Her silent prayer was answered.

"So, River Rock is inevitable. He lives here. Right now, we need to look at the pros and cons of waiting until the end of the school year to uproot him."

Jeremiah rubbed a hand over his face. "Yes, ma'am. That's exactly what we've been trying to figure out."

"Having spoken to David, I think he would do fine changing schools now. He seems to be very intelligent, self-aware. Decisions like these all come down to the individual child." She offered them a smile. "And I think he'd be very happy here. He's already made a friend, Anastasia."

"She lives down the lake from us," Miah said.

"Anastasia is a good girl, a jewel. Her older brother is on the basketball team and is a natural leader. He's in David's class. It might be nice for the two of them to become friends. Could make an easier transition for David."

In her heart, Gray had known this was the right decision. But her heart had been wrong so many times, she no longer trusted it. Her elation must have been obvious.

"My recommendation agrees with you, Ms. Smith?"

"Very much. I think David needs a fresh start." Something squeezed her hand. She looked down; there, fingers interlocked with hers. Miah's hand. Her gaze trailed to him in question. He only smiled in answer and squeezed again.

Ms. Forrester took turns looking at one, then the other. There were questions in her eyes, but she must have decided to shelve them.

It took a moment for Miah and Gray to realize it was time to go; they were too busy grinning like fools at one another.

Ms. Forrester cleared her throat. "David can start school on Monday, if that's agreeable to you. We are just launching into a major fund-raiser. Most of the kids get involved, and I think it would be a great opportunity for David to get to know some of his classmates." She thought a moment. "Do you know anything about bees, Mr. McKinley?"

He shot her another Oscar-winning smile. "No, ma'am, and it's none of my business, but bees may not be the best fund-raiser."

She laughed. "Agreed. No, that's not what I meant. When two separate colonies of bees need to be put together, the beekeeper dusts them all with powder. You see, the bees are so busy cleaning the powder off themselves and others they don't even realize strangers have been introduced to the colony. By the time the hive is clean, they're all one big happy family."

And Ms. Forrester leaned back in her chair with her mouth pursed and waited for one of them to give the moral of the story. Gray shot a blank look over to Jeremiah, who sat beside her, a thoughtful expression on his face. His chin dipped. "I get it."

Huh? Gray's hand squeezed his. If he thought he could bluff his way through this, he was wrong. Ms. Forrester was an educator. She could probably sniff out a bluff from a mile away. But then Miah continued.

"You see this fund-raiser as a way for David to be introduced to the hive. Everyone is busy, all working toward the same goal. Everyone's on the same team."

Forrester winked. "Exactly. This is our biggest event to raise money for the basketball team. It would be great for David to get involved."

"Yes. Absolutely. Anything we can do." Miah reached out and shook her hand.

"Also, his attendance and yours at afterschool events . . . helps kids acclimate. I realize David isn't a sports kid, but if he supports them, they'll support him."

Miah was still shaking her hand. "Anything we can do. Anything at all. Please. Just keep me informed. I'd be glad to help out."

———

Gray stood at her car door, a sinking feeling in the pit of her stomach. *You need to do this*, she reminded herself. It had been ten days since they'd met Ms. Forester. Gray had run out of excuses to continue staying at the lodge. All she needed now was a strong enough shot of courage to propel her into the driver's seat and down the road.

She'd already loaded her suitcase into the trunk and said goodbye to David. She had to be strong now, but her hand trembled as she reached for the handle. All her planning to make a clean break crumbled when she heard the front door open. She closed her eyes and knew the exact moment Miah stepped behind her.

The heat and warmth of his body near hers was unhinging. Already she'd begun to feel cold, like a person roaming the earth utterly alone. The heat he offered, she drank in, letting it saturate her soul and all those icy rooms in her heart. The chill had nothing to do with the weather; it was not because of the lack of sunshine, but because in a few minutes, she'd be home in an empty cottage where even her grandmother's imprint continued to fade. What hope did she have of David's imprint being there and being enough to keep her company?

Miah's hands closed on her shoulders and tilted her back so that her spine rested against his chest. For a few moments, she allowed herself to enjoy it, the strength he provided, the wall behind her.

His breathing was deep, long, and for a stretch of time he did nothing but hold her, shore her up. Because that's what she needed and he was Miah, the one able to take the shaky ground and make it solid. He'd always had that power where she was concerned.

He kissed the top of her head. "You don't have to go."

Her eyes closed, shutting out the words because she did, *she absolutely did* have to go. Because staying meant risk. And she was so tired and so frightened of once again losing him, there was no fight left in her soul.

His cheek nuzzled against the hair on top of her head. "You could stay." He wasn't being pushy, but there was an intensity to the words that told her they were headed down a path that could end up destroying everything they were trying to build.

She forced strength into her body and turned to face him. "And what, Miah? I can't just keep finding excuses to spend the night here. Especially now that the driveway's clear and David's back in school. I have a home. And you and me . . ."

There was a smoldering look in his eyes and she knew he was considering the possibilities.

"I wake up . . . in your bed . . . and there's a big part of me that just wants to come find you." She shouldn't be admitting this to him, but Gray knew she was a terrible liar, so the truth would have to do.

The smolder lit, blazing a fresh fire in his gaze. She watched the thought play out in his mind.

"But, Miah. David. He's the most important thing right now and we're—"

"We're making progress with him. He's doing great. He's had his first week of school and is thriving."

Relief flooded her. He understood. "He has to be our focus right now."

He ran a hand through his hair. "I agree." Then Miah surprised her. He pulled her into a hug and held her against him for a long time. "I don't have to like it, though. I really enjoy you being here."

She squeezed her eyes shut because she enjoyed being there, too, but they couldn't play house and not have repercussions later.

He cupped his hands around her face. "I'll miss you, sunshine."

She half smiled. "Not sunshine—Gray."

"Not to me. Not anymore. You're more like sunshine." He tilted down and gently pressed a kiss to her lips.

Soft. Cold from the chill outside. Moist. Lips that could search out every secret place on her body and feel new at each brush and at the same time feel as familiar as her favorite quilt she kept on her bed. They were comfort. They were home.

It took every ounce of fortitude she had to get in the car and drive away. Before she even made it to the main road, her cheeks were wet with tears. "Take good care of my baby," she whispered as she cast a glance at the lodge behind her. Before her, a cold, empty house waited.

———

The lodge was growing on him, but David hadn't attempted another ride on the snowmobile. The best part of his day was seeing Stacey, but he also liked it when Gray burned the vegetables and Miah laughed at her and told her not to worry, there was plenty of meat. Who needed vegetables, anyway? Not him. He didn't mind carrying firewood into the lodge, and Miah had taught him how to build an awesome fire, how to stack the wood just so, and he'd told Miah the science behind oxygen and flame. Caleb was a jerk sometimes, pointing out things when David did them wrong, but other than that, the lodge was pretty cool. But he missed Gray being there late at night. He'd gotten used to her sticking her head in his room to say good night after they'd all watched the news. At least she was still there in the mornings to work with Caleb, so he got to see her before he left for school, and she still usually stayed for dinner, but no more sleeping over.

David watched Jeremiah's fishing line sail out over the water in a perfect arc. The chubby worm disappeared beneath the surface. On the dock beside him sat a tackle box and Styrofoam containers of worms. There was still a lot of snow on the ground, but they'd shoveled most of it off the pier a few days earlier. The sun was shining today, making it feel warmer.

"You sure you don't want to drop a line in? The fish are biting."

David focused on the goal. He needed to ask Jeremiah about the fund-raiser. "No, thanks. So, Ms. Forrester told me you were all gung ho—her word, not mine—to help out at the school."

"It's hooray, not gung ho." Miah winked at him. "And yeah, I'm all in."

"So, there's this fund-raiser." David sat down beside Jeremiah on the dock where his feet could dangle a couple feet above the water. There, in a reflection below them was an image of him . . . and his birth dad. The image made him smile.

Miah reeled. "She mentioned it when we went in to talk to her."

"Will you do it?"

He reached over and ruffled David's hair. David scowled and pulled away, but secretly, he liked it.

"Great. I'll put you down as my pledge."

Miah stopped reeling. "What's that mean?"

"Well, everyone at the school has to get an adult to be their pledge, then you'll have to be present at the fund-raiser and . . . you know . . . do what they tell you to earn the pledge money."

"Like a race or something? Like when you pledge to give so much money and the person has to run a marathon?"

"Yes. Something like that."

"No problem."

That was easier than David had figured. "Great! One down," he mumbled.

"What'd you say, champ?"

"Huh? Oh, nothing." He stood from the dock. "Do you mind if I go find Gray? I need to ask her about the fund-raiser, too."

David left Jeremiah fishing. He sneaked around the edge of the house to find Stacey waiting for him. "How'd it go?" she whispered, though there was no one in earshot.

"Good." He looked from side to side—just to make sure. "He didn't suspect anything. Come on, let's go find Gray."

They rounded the corner to find Gray and Caleb sitting on the side of the indoor pool. The walls of the new pool house were glass or Plexiglas or something.

"Hey there," Gray yelled through the wall and waved them in.

Stacey's eyes widened. "This is the coolest thing I've ever seen. I don't know anyone with an indoor pool at their house." David held the door open for her and they stepped inside. The air was wet and the room smelled like chlorine.

Caleb rested his foot on the edge. "The water is still chilly, but we're supposed to be able to get in today."

David turned to Stacey. "When it warms up more, maybe you can come over and try it out."

Stacey clasped her hands together. "That'd be great. I haven't been swimming since the lake started getting colder."

Caleb frowned. "This isn't going to become some juvenile hangout, David. So don't get your hopes up."

Gray gave Caleb a dirty look.

David squared his stance. "Since it's *my birth dad* who owns the pool, I guess he'll be the one to decide that."

Caleb chuckled and gave a reluctant nod.

Gray smiled at David, and he almost felt bad for what they were doing, but the sensation faded quickly. "You know about the fund-raiser, Gray?" he asked, sinking his hands in his pockets because he'd decided men looked more intelligent when they frowned a little and their hands were in their pockets.

"Yes."

David fidgeted. "Well, Stacey needs an adult to be her pledge for the fund-raiser. Would you do it?"

He saw the questions across her features and hoped she wouldn't ask why Stacey's parents weren't doing it. "Um, yes. Sure. What will you need me to do?"

This was the part they'd practiced. Stacey was up. She stepped forward and an angelic smile lit her face. "It's really easy for the pledges. You just show up the night of the banquet. All the work is up to us. David and I are going to start collecting pledge money around town."

And then her smile broadened and her green eyes blinked and David chewed the inside of his cheek.

"Anything you need from me, David. You know that."

I'm counting on it.

The two left Gray and Caleb at the edge of the pool. "Thanks," David hollered over his shoulder.

"Need me to help?" Caleb asked. "I'd be glad to come and *babysit* your little friends."

David turned to face him, choosing to ignore the insult. "Nope. Don't need you at all."

And then they left and gave each other a high five once they were around the corner of the house, where the Plexiglas wouldn't give away their excitement.

When he'd walked Stacey back to her house, she stopped on her front porch. "You don't think your birth mom and dad will be mad, do you?"

Stacey called them his birth parents because he called them his birth parents. And that made his heart proud because it mattered to her what he thought and what he wanted. "Nah." He kicked at a clump of dirt and snow. "They'll be cool."

He hoped he was right.

————

Gray sighed. This animosity between Caleb and David really needed to come to an end. On the one hand, Caleb was her patient, and she understood that with traumatic brain injuries, there were often little lapses in judgment . . . things like picking on a twelve-year-old when you're twenty-five. On the other hand, David was her son and she did tend to have momma-bear syndrome where he was concerned. *It'll get better,* she told herself. *They'll find a balance.*

She had to admit David was learning to stick up for himself. He didn't let Caleb bully him, he was quick with the retorts . . . a la *Nope, don't need you at all.* Angela would have gotten onto him for that little remark, but Gray let it slide because it showed some backbone, some grit. He wasn't going to let a big soldier push him around. And if he wasn't going to let Caleb push him around, he certainly wouldn't let someone at school.

This was why it was good to have older siblings, she realized. She was an only child. David was an only child. No one to prepare you for the world out there. Well, she didn't like the way Caleb wouldn't cut David any slack, but she also wouldn't interfere with it. Growing pains came in all shapes and sizes.

Her feet dangled in the water, but it was still too cold, so Gray stood up. She was in shorts and a T-shirt, but Caleb had changed into his swim trunks at the mention of water possibly, maybe, not likely, but *possibly* being warm enough for swimming.

"Let's let the heater work its magic for one more night before we dive in. It's still freezing."

"Do whatever you want, Powder Puff, but I'm going swimming." He stood, pulled off his shirt, took a couple steps back, and cannon-balled in.

Icy water splashed up onto her legs and arms.

Caleb came up sputtering, arms flailing.

"Nice try, soldier." Water went in arcs around his wide shoulders, his feet were kicking frantically, and in a rushed moment Gray caught on to what was happening. The look of horror on his face snapped her into motion. Caleb was drowning. His head went under.

"Caleb!" she screamed and dived in, trying to come up beside him. His thigh connected with her head, causing it to whip to one side, but she ignored the pain, groping to get a grip on him before he went under again. He reached for the side of the pool, but was too far in the center. Gray came up out of the water and threw her arm over his wide shoulder. She'd had lifeguard training in high school, but they never used a tank as a victim. Her whole lifeguarding career she'd spent pulling kids out, not bulls. Her hand slipped off him and his head ducked under. She altered her grip, knowing her nails were likely digging into the meaty part of his triceps muscle. With him in position, locked beneath her arm, she swam toward the side of the pool. It was twelve feet deep at its core and that was more than enough to drown in. Even as she got him to the edge and he started to calm, coughing out all the water he'd inhaled, Gray knew this had been a close call. What if he'd jumped in when no one was around?

Her hands came around him in a hug and for a long time, she held him right there.

An hour later, Jeremiah brought her a steaming cup of hot cocoa. She sipped it and scooted a little closer to the fire. She was chilled to the bone and no amount of heat was going to correct that. They were calling for snow again, and Gray was still too rattled about Caleb to drive home. Miah had suggested she go ahead and spend the night. She'd agreed.

"What do you think happened?" Miah sat down on the area rug beside her, his foot catching on the handmade quilt he'd tucked around her shoulders.

"I've been asking myself that for an hour. Miah, this is Caleb. He could swim circles around the whole swim team."

Miah stared into the flame. "I know. Is it neurological? At the rehab center in Tampa, they talked about how the mind can shut off certain things, skills, even."

Her hand rubbed her neck. It was stiff from slashing around in the pool trying to haul a Mack truck. "This was different. It must be psychological. Miah, he looked terrified."

"Drowning, scary business."

"I know, but he's a soldier. He's accustomed to adapting. This was . . . this was real terror." She chilled at the thought and pulled the blanket closer.

He placed an arm around her. "I'm so glad you were there."

She smiled over at him. "Me too."

"What are we going to do now?"

She shook her head. "I don't know. I'll talk to Jamille. Maybe put in a call to Tampa. See what they think. I'm not sure if I should ease him into the pool or give this time to blow over before we start any kind of water therapy. I just want to do what's right for him."

Jeremiah caught her chin in his hand. "That's all you ever want, isn't it?" His voice was velvet soft and tender, and the fire danced on the side of his face making him look unearthly, ethereal and perfect. Miah was beauty and danger all wrapped up in a package that was becoming harder and harder to resist. And she was just getting so tired of pulling away from that magnetic force drawing her. His fingertips grazed her jaw and tiny little bells went off as those fingers moved gently but with precision. He dusted her cheek, index finger stopping at the chicken pox indention. He scrubbed at it. "We both had chicken pox at the same time, remember?"

"How could I forget? You called me every hour to complain."

He smiled. "You did your share of complaining, too."

She nodded. "I guess I did."

"Remember that trip to the lake when we skipped school and got lost trying to find the waterfall?"

"Fourteen of us went. Twelve came back covered with poison oak. But not you and me. Not sure how we dodged that bullet."

"Yeah. Lucky, I guess. Hey, do you remember—"

She cut him off, gripping his hand tightly where it held her cheek. "I remember all of it, Miah. Every. Single. Moment." And she closed her eyes because if she didn't, he'd be eighteen again and she'd be seventeen and in love with the only boy who had the power to break her heart. But instead of moving away, she felt his body shift, coming closer, moving in, and when she pulled a breath it was filled with him, his scent, the very thing that made Jeremiah just a little bit beyond human. Her eyes opened to find his. Miah's hand slid with delicious slowness from her cheek to cup her neck. She knew that on his lips was the question only she could answer. He wouldn't do this, she realized. He wouldn't complicate things just to satisfy his own flesh. But he wanted to, that was clear in the ragged breath he drew, in the way his tongue slipped over his lips as if preparing to taste her . . . or perhaps remembering what she tasted like from all those years ago.

When Gray could stand the pressure no longer, she closed the distance to his mouth to find a new kind of heat waiting to consume her. He was warm from the fire and some internal blaze and all of it shot from her lips down. His hand kneaded the muscles at the back of her neck and it felt like . . . it felt like being stroked by the wings of an angel. His head tilted and she moved in response, giving him full access to her mouth. A tiny groan slipped from him, then a shudder ran the length of his body and she felt it in every part of her being from her mouth to her soul.

She knew. She knew right then that Jeremiah McKinley had not only ruined her once, but quite possibly twice, and there was nothing— not a thing—she could do about it.

When he finally broke the kiss, his lips left hers with such reluctance, it almost seemed the intensity might pull them right back together. "That was long overdue." His voice was smoke and sin.

And she wanted more. Gray tried to clear her throat, but it was bone dry. No moisture in the room; Miah had consumed it all. She wouldn't be surprised to look around and find nothing left but a barren wasteland, all of life absorbed by him. But when she blinked, there was still a fire, a mantel, a lovely grandfather clock ticking away the minutes. There was still an area rug beneath her rear end and a hardwood floor beneath that. She glanced around, trying to find something to anchor herself to.

And there it was. Standing behind them was David.

Miah and Gray split apart like two rockets flying in opposite directions.

David's brows were high on his head. He pointed at the kitchen. "I just came down for a bottle of water."

Miah launched into a spiel about there being water in the fridge and some in the pantry if he didn't want it cold and something about going to the store earlier in the day. Good heavens, he sounded like a teenager who'd gotten caught out with the wrong girl. Er . . . well, other than the teenager part, that was sort of close to the truth.

"Miah," Gray whispered, in an attempt to calm him down. "Not helping."

Miah clasped his hands at his waist and they both watched as a pajamaed David slipped into the kitchen like nothing had ever happened. The hems of his sleep pants made a whooshing sound as he moved. Once gone, Miah slapped a hand to his forehead. "Oh no."

Gray wanted to chuckle, but she wouldn't. "Settle down. I'll follow him up and talk to him."

The very thought must have horrified Miah because he turned white first, then a lovely shade of embarrassment-pink. She gripped his shoulders. "Calm down. You're only making it worse."

"I just don't want to confuse him."

"Miah, I'll handle it."

She felt the tension leave his muscle groups. And loved the fact that she could calm the beast with just a few words. "I'll go talk to David. You go check on Caleb. I thought he said he'd be down here after his shower."

Miah's face fell. "You don't suppose he . . ."

"What? That he saw us, too? Probably. What else could go wrong?"

"We're a bit like gas and a fire, aren't we?"

She had to agree. They went off, two rockets in two directions with one destination. Try to smooth the waves.

———

"Are you and Jeremiah dating now?" David sipped his water bottle then replaced the lid.

"No." Gray stood at the head of his bed and drew the flannel covers back so he could climb in.

"But you kissed him." David placed the bottle of water on the nightstand by his manga book.

She fluffed the pillow. "Yes, I did."

"So you like him." He climbed in and let her pull the covers up around him.

Gray drew a breath and wondered how to tiptoe around such direct questions. There wasn't any way, so she'd have to just give David what he deserved. The truth. "I like Jeremiah. I have for a long time." She sat on the edge of his bed and it squeaked under the pressure.

"Since you and him conceived me?"

Gray cleared her throat. Angela had always insisted on David being told the "grown-up" version of things. No code words, no euphemisms, just the facts, ma'am. "Even before that. We were friends for a long time."

"And you *liked* him back then?"

"Yep." That was a nice, delicate answer. Oh, she was soooo smooth.

"And now you're kissing him."

"I know it sounds fairly simple, but there's a lot more to relationships than liking and kissing. Sometimes, you have to . . . you have to . . ." And something Jeremiah told her skated through her mind. "You have to walk a path to know if it's a dead end or a hidden place, a treasure waiting to be discovered."

"And that's what you're doing with Jeremiah?" David settled into his bed.

"You're so smart. I was testing the waters a little bit tonight."

David yawned. "You should, Gray." He rolled onto his side and tucked his hands against his cheek. Practically angelic.

David was one perceptive young man. He hadn't been coddled, hadn't been so sheltered that he had an unrealistic idea of life. He was grounded—even with all he'd been through. He was strong, maybe strong enough to understand that things like love and relationships didn't always work out. And if so, maybe she and Miah could give this thing between them a chance. Carefully, slowly.

David's eyes were heavy and each blink became longer and longer. "He's a good guy," he said on a yawn. And as all the air left him and sleep was claiming him, he added, "He's a good dad."

CHAPTER 12

The house was busy in preparation for company, but David ignored everyone rushing around. He and Stacey were stretched out by the fire, foreheads getting hot, feet pointing at the front door. Stacey had a pillow tucked under her, but David was tough. He could take the hardwood floor with only the rug for cushioning. "My uncles are coming."

Stacey put down the fifth volume of his favorite manga series. Typically, he didn't loan his books out, but this was Stacey and that made it okay. Plus, it was fun to have someone to talk to who knew the story. "What uncles?"

"Isaiah and Gabriel. I've never met them. My dad said they're both planning to get out of the army in the next few months."

She wrinkled her nose. "Do you think you'll like them?"

He rolled onto his side. "If they're like Jeremiah, yes. If they are like Caleb, no."

She brushed blond hair from her face. "I think Caleb's okay."

Something fiery hot shot right into David's chest. "He's not okay."

She tilted her shoulder. "I feel kind of bad for him. His right hand doesn't work as well as his left. And he limps."

"So? It's not like he can't *live*. He plays video games and everything."

"Did he really almost drown in the pool?"

David chewed his cheek. "Yeah. He hasn't been back in. Won't even wade in the shallow end."

"I hope your uncles are like Jeremiah, too." Stacey propped her head on her hand and smiled.

"They'll be here in a couple days. Dad's planning a big fishing trip. Think I'll be ready?" They'd spent almost every day at the lake's edge with Stacey teaching him the tricks to casting, reeling, how to put a worm on a hook. He could do it now. Without jumping out of his skin or planting a hook in someone's flesh.

"Does your dad know we've been working on your skills?"

"No, he keeps asking me to fish with him, but I keep telling him no and acting totally uninterested. I'm going to surprise him when we go on the fishing trip."

Stacey's smooth brow tilted into a frown. "Will you be lakeside?"

"No. He's renting a big boat."

She sat straight up. "Don't forget what I told you about snags. They'll be worse out on a boat, even though you may be close to the shoreline."

He sat up, too. "Why is it that people go out on a boat, then fish in places they could reach from the shore? Doesn't make any sense."

Stacey rolled her giant green eyes. "David. Stop trying to dissect it."

He pointed at her. "You're not answering because you don't know."

She huffed, but a smile caught the edge of her mouth. "Maybe. All I know is that you go where the fish are. He's going to be so excited when he sees your new fishing skills."

"I hope so." David chewed on his bottom lip. "I want to make him proud."

"Gray calls this therapy. I call it free labor." Caleb carried the toolbox to Jeremiah, who was straddling the snowmobile.

"You're the one who wanted this thing running again." The sun had chosen to peek out from its hiding place behind layers and layers of winter clouds. Both men stopped to push the sleeves of their sweat-shirts up to their elbows.

"It'll be great if this weather holds while Isaiah and Gabe are here." Caleb inspected the sky.

Miah nodded and pointed to the toolbox, so Caleb opened it and handed him a wrench. "It's supposed to. If the weatherman has half a brain. Should be warmer all week."

Caleb knelt beside him. "You're kind of getting into this whole 'watch the news' thing."

Miah leaned back. Already, his back was aching, but that had less to do with working on the snowmobile and more to do with busting his butt to get a couple more rooms ready for his brothers. Of course, the room he'd stayed in while Gray was there was complete, but he wanted two more done and an extra open in case . . . in case . . . He torqued the wrench until it slipped off and his knuckles came in contact with the side of the machine. Who was he kidding? There was no need for an available room for Gray because she was at her own house and David was at the lodge, doing well, adjusting like a champ, and though they both seemed to look for excuses for Gray to hang around long after work hours, once dinner was done and David's homework was com-plete, she left. And every night, Miah hated to see her go.

Miah would watch the clock, counting away the minutes until she was home. He'd made her promise to call every night once she was there. Which was silly, he knew. But it was winter in Missouri and the hilly, curvy roads could be deadly. And she had a decent car, but not a new one. And what if she got a flat on the way home? And . . . and he liked to hear her voice as he climbed into bed. He'd close his eyes and imagine her crawling into her bed, dressed in a long-sleeve T-shirt and socks. Just like she'd been the night David had his first nightmare. He'd come down the hall and she'd thrown the door open while dragging on a pair of sweats. She'd looked beautiful. Messy hair, torso covered, and legs disappearing into those stretchy pants. The image was still so fresh in his mind, it could have happened five minutes ago. That image sent him off into dreamworld each night. Yeah. He had it bad.

"You gonna finish fixing this thing or just sit there and nurse your bloody knuckles?"

Huh? Miah looked at his hand. His knuckles were bleeding. Well, that's what he got for trying to fix the snowmobile. "You can take over anytime, little brother."

"Much more fun to watch you work."

Miah winked at him. "Work was never your strong suit."

Caleb sat down on the ground beside Miah. "Well, some of us get brawn and some of us get brains."

Miah retrieved the wrench from where he'd dropped it. "Yeah, what did you get?" This was good. Normal. Not like a few weeks ago when Caleb was still adjusting to his new life and had his sights set on Gray. There'd been a lot of anger in his little brother then, but now it seemed to be melting. He had even backed off where Gray was concerned. At the same time, Miah knew Caleb was embarrassed about the whole swimming-pool fiasco. Maybe his ego had taken too much of a hit to recover.

Caleb pulled a shop towel from the box and lobbed it at him. "Here, clean yourself up." Caleb took the wrench in his right hand, using his left as a guide.

Miah fought the urge to tear up, which was stupid, but when he saw Caleb pushing himself, this pride in his little brother almost overwhelmed him. "You're doing great with your therapy, Caleb."

The sunlight caught his blond hair, creating a halo around him. Blue eyes looked over, a smile on his face. "Thanks."

"I'm really proud of you." Miah placed a hand on his shoulder and squeezed.

They didn't have a lot of moments like this. But the ones they did have were important.

Caleb rolled the wrench over and over in his hands. "When I woke up and they told me about my injuries, I thought I'd rather be dead. But life's worth living, you know? Even if you can't live it as fully as you'd like."

"It would have killed me to lose you."

There was a tear in Caleb's eye. "I can't remember the accident. I don't remember anything about it, and even the things that happened after, the hospital and all, they're hazy. Like a dream."

"That's probably normal."

Then, Caleb's gaze found him, and Miah saw more tears swimming in his eyes. "But I remember thinking I couldn't die because I couldn't let you down. You kept me alive, Miah."

Miah choked back a sob. "I need you, little brother. Life wouldn't be the same if you were gone." And they'd already lost so much. Their mother died young, their father in combat. The siblings only had each other and since the boys had all joined up at a young age, they'd missed out on so many things. Holidays, Christmas mornings, Easter, cook-outs, and fishing trips.

Caleb sniffed. "I think I blamed you. I kept thinking it would have been easier if I died. And you were the reason I was still alive. When I got here I had a major chip on my shoulder. But, I've been watching you and I've seen that everything you do is for others. For me, for David. You're a rare kind of person, Miah. I'm sorry for how I treated you."

Miah slung his arm around his brother. "Don't apologize. I'm just glad you're okay. I'm also glad you've kept clothes on. As a kid, you ran around naked all the time."

"Just wait until the weather breaks. You won't be able to keep clothes on me."

"Please. You're making my lunch come up."

Caleb used his right arm to thread around Miah's neck. He squeezed with all his might.

"Hey, you're getting stronger."

Caleb nodded. "Gray is a tyrant. She's impossible. Good luck with her. You're gonna have your hands full."

Miah wasn't sure how to answer that.

Caleb chucked his shoulder. "This thing between you and her. It's good. It's right."

"You're okay with it?" Not that he had to be. Miah was going after Gray with every fiber of his being. No matter what his baby brother thought of it. But, it would be nice to have him on board.

"Yeah. She's really special. Don't screw it up, bro."

"I thought she was a tyrant."

"She is. You deserve her."

Something caught in Miah's throat because he'd maybe always known that Gray was so much more than he deserved. She made the sun brighter. And a bright sun could guide you and keep you no matter how dark the path. "I think I love her."

Caleb laughed. "No, really? There's a shocker."

Warmth settled in Miah's gut. "Yeah. I really think so."

"Well, Captain Oblivious. What now?"

He shrugged, unwound from his brother, and took the wrench. "Don't know. See what happens, I guess."

"Gabe and Isaiah will be here tomorrow. After they leave, you can make your kill shot."

"My kill shot, huh?" Miah laughed. "Spoken like a true sniper."

"Yeah."

Miah needed a change of subject. He wasn't so comfortable with this *kill shot* idea. "Hey, I wanted to tell you thanks for going a little easier on David the last few weeks."

Caleb squinted up at the sun. "Is that what I've done? I'll have to up my game."

Miah shook his head. "I know you didn't like him that much at first. I can see you two are beginning to acclimate."

"He's a good kid. Always was, just soft as warm donuts, you know? Way too soft. He needed to be toughened up. I volunteered."

Miah wanted to launch into the spiel about how it wasn't his job, or his business, but he had to admit, the two of them seemed to be doing better. David didn't really seem like he liked Caleb any more than he ever did, but he also wasn't letting Caleb push him around. It was a moment before he realized Caleb was talking again.

"I learned from the best."

Miah scrunched his face. "What?"

"I just treat him like a little brother."

Okay. He couldn't argue with that.

———

Gray and Miah put the finishing touches on the brothers' rooms while Ian and Charlee went to the airport to pick up Gabriel and Isaiah. Yesterday, she'd watched through the upstairs window while Miah and Caleb fixed the snowmobile. And from the safety and quiet of the fresh, new room, she'd allowed herself to dream. What would it be like if this was her home? Today, she kept her wanderings in check. Mostly.

Gray turned to face Miah, a pillow in her hand and a throbbing question in her heart. Miah had been busy the last few days preparing for his brothers' visit, but still, he made time to gaze at her from across the dinner table, a longing so deep in him, it was practically screaming at her. And that, she understood. Every night she drove home and lay in bed thinking about the man she'd just left. Thinking about the life that might be available to her . . . if only she could stop being scared.

She forced her thoughts in another direction. "Is Charlee angry all the brothers are staying here instead of with her at the retreat?"

Miah hammered the last piece of replacement wood in the back of Isaiah's closet. "No. She knows us. We tend to be fairly difficult to separate when we only have a few days together. Plus, they want to get to know David." Gray had just shoved an overstuffed pillow into a blue pillowcase. They wanted to get to know David. That warmed her heart.

She met Miah in the middle of the room to admire their handiwork. "Thanks for your help with all this." When he said it, his hand slid down the length of her arm. A tool belt still hung from his hips, making him look like one of those posters where hot guys decorated the months of the year. He could be Mr. January. The perfect way to start the year.

"My pleasure." But the words were husky and came from so deep in her throat, she cleared it to remove the obvious signs her mind had strayed somewhere dark.

"It's a nice room. We did good." His voice dropped low to match hers. "Bed looks incredibly comfortable." Miah removed the tool belt and sat it on the small table by the door. In an instant he was back, grazing his knuckles over her arm again.

Her heart stammered. How could such a gentle touch set off so many nerve endings? All of them skittering and scattering throughout her body until she wanted to scream for him to stop. Or touch her more.

Mischief danced in his eyes, so Gray swatted at him. "You're impossible, you know that?"

"Yes, ma'am. Good thing for you I'm irritating, not irresistible." He took a step toward her, which made her take a step back. The freshly painted, freshly decorated room surrounded the two of them like a calm sea waiting for a good, long storm.

"You're a little bit of both," she whispered, dropping her head.

Another step, this one accompanied by both his hands finding their way to her arms, blocking her from stepping away from him again. "Is someone tired of running? Tired of fighting this?"

She wanted to melt into those words. She was tired. But she was also scared. And not just for David. Scared for herself. "I . . . I . . ."

He used his thumb and finger to lift her chin. "Gray, it's okay. I can give you whatever you need. Even if it's more time."

His hands were on her, touching, caressing her. How long had it been since a man had held her in his arms? So long. So very long. And she needed that, but not from anyone but Miah. Her heart told her to go ahead and jump, and she wanted to, wanted to with every ounce of her being. Every ounce except her mind. And for so long, her mind had ruled her, made her decisions, told her what to do. She needed Miah to know it wasn't *him* that was the problem. He was . . . well, he was almost perfect. She opened her mouth expecting words to flood the space around them, expecting to be able to explain why she was the way she was. But all that slipped from between her lips was, "Slow."

He moved so gently, it was barely perceptible. He nodded, a hint of a smile appearing on his face. "Slow," he repeated and she knew that he understood.

"But not stopped," he said, head tilting to make sure *she* understood.

His body pressed against her and she relished it, the very feel of him, the scent, the sound of his breath and heartbeat. *Slow but not stopped*, she repeated in her mind.

Although warning thoughts tried to shoot through her head, they were all absorbed when his mouth touched hers. Warm, sweet. Home. Gray wound her hands around his neck and gave in to the man she'd loved for most of her lifetime. His hands skimmed her back, tangling into her hair, his touch the fire that made Miah everything he was. And made Gray want to disappear into it. She wanted to be fully saturated in the gold that was Miah. A fever skittered through her veins, a rush, like lava heating, melting, changing her.

And in that moment, she didn't want to be safe. She didn't want to be careful. She wanted to be a reckless girl whose actions mirrored her bravery. She wanted him.

He must have realized she wasn't backing away, was even pressing forward, kissing him with more fervency, the kind that could barely be contained. Miah broke the kiss, his breath ragged. In his gaze she saw the flame and the question. "Are we doing this?"

It was an honest inquiry. Direct. Like Miah. And right now, she was weak. "If you'd asked me that five minutes ago, I'd have said no, but . . ."

His hand dropped with a clop and she watched the war raging within him.

Embarrassment tried to take root in her, but she wouldn't allow it. She and Miah, they were beyond petty things like embarrassment. But he'd just made her a promise that they'd move slowly. And here they were, both ready to ditch that commitment.

"We're not," he said. It was hard for her to hear, even if it was the right choice. Judging by his reaction, it must have been difficult to say. He looked like a man being ripped in two. "I messed this up once before. I don't want to do that again, Gray." And his hands came up to touch her in such a soft embrace, such a tender caress, she had no choice but to disappear into it. To become everything he needed. "I can't run the risk of messing us up again."

A tear slid down her cheek, half from the fact that she'd waited for this man her whole life and half from the fact that she'd have to wait a little longer. In her moment of weakness, he'd been strong. And that was the kind of thing that built enduring relationships.

He dropped his forehead to hers and the sound that left his mouth was a deeper sorrow than sadness. "Even if we're ready, David's not. This is inevitably going to change things for us." He thrust his hands into her hair and squeezed his eyes shut. "God, I want to do this right." It was a prayer. And a plea.

And it settled the matter.

She dropped a peck on his lips. "We're going to move slow. Period." She stepped away from him to find her legs barely able to carry her weight. "It's the right thing."

"Come on. Isaiah and Gabriel will be here in less than an hour." Hand in hand, they left the room and went downstairs for cold drinks. No hot cocoa today, they were already scorched inside. Ice-cold root beer. And it barely helped.

———

Gray knew David was nervous about meeting his uncles, but he tried to keep from fidgeting. He stood arrow straight, on the porch beside Gray, his shoulder brushing her upper arm—it was for support. She'd come to learn that David was a kid who liked the touch of another human being. Angela had always discouraged too much touching. Once he was old enough to listen and obey, she didn't hold his hand. Gray leaned a little closer so their arms were pressed together. Some of Angela's ideas about childrearing were just a tad misguided. She'd read the "less touch is better" mantra from a book that compared raising kids to the dynamics of wolf packs. "Raising the Alpha Male in a Dominating World." Utter trash. Why hadn't Gray ever questioned her on it? She'd had no right to, that was why. But it was all different now and she had as much say-so in David's upbringing as Jeremiah did. And that was an incredible gift. If the situation upstairs earlier in the day was any indication, they were both willing to put David's well-being far above their own.

Ian whipped the raised Jeep into the gravel parking spot beside Miah's truck, and Charlee, Isaiah, and Gabriel piled out. Both young men looking fresh from the military with short hair and cut muscles.

Jeremiah hugged each of his brothers, then had them follow him up onto the porch where David and Gray waited. "This is David," he said, with so much pride it caused Gray's nose to tingle and she felt a tremor run David's arm. He thrust a hand out to them, Gabriel first. "Nice to meet you."

Gabriel shook his hand. "You look like your dad." When Gabriel smiled, the whole world lit up around him. How had one family spawned such good-looking boys? All four of them, standing around Gray now, each with his own individual look, but each one no less striking. Both Gabriel and Isaiah's ultra short hair drew attention to their expressive eyes. All eyes and smiles, these McKinleys, and Gray could only hope they'd be warm to her for David's sake. Charlee had thawed, but who knew what kind of reception she'd get from these two brothers?

David took care of it. "This is my birth mom, Gray Smith."

Gabriel stepped in front of her, stared for a fraction of a second, then grabbed her up in a bear hug. "Gray! You don't weigh a pound more than you did in high school." Gabriel was two years younger, but super smart. He and Gray had been fairly close, the two of them sharing some AP classes.

"My scale would disagree," she grunted, dangling midair, her tensions dissipating.

Miah used both hands to separate them. "Okay, that's enough manhandling David's mom." He stepped fully between them, turning to face Gray. "And how does my brother know what you weighed in high school?"

She shrugged, rolled her eyes. "I can't recall."

Next Miah introduced Isaiah. "I'm really happy to meet you, David. I think you can probably keep Miah in line." He shook his hand then leaned in a little closer. "He needs someone to keep him in line."

David nodded knowingly, and just like that, they'd taken him in and made him part of the pack. No lack of touching required.

———

Dinner was ready when they got to Charlee's. She'd cooked spaghetti with Ian's homemade marinara and fresh Parmesan cheese. There was a Caesar salad that disappeared as quickly as it hit the table and baskets of homemade bread. Charlee beamed. "I have to be honest, I knew this would be an easy dinner to clean up and I wanted all the time I could get with my brothers since Miah is stealing all of you tomorrow." She gave him a mock glare, but it held little animosity. With all her brothers there, she was floating around like a Disney princess.

"So what's the plan for tomorrow?" Gabriel asked and leaned back to rub his stomach.

"Get up early; the boat's already tied at my dock and ready. Grab the gear and go. Supposed to be warm tomorrow. We should get in a full day."

"Caleb made sandwiches for everyone."

"Ah, Caleb," Gabriel oozed. "Such a sweet thing to do."

Caleb grunted and pointed at Gray. "You try telling her no. She's a dictator."

Miah reached for another piece of garlic bread. "I thought you told me she was a tyrant."

David stood up. "She's both."

The group busted up laughing at that, and Gray even had to chuckle. It was true.

David started clearing plates so Gray joined him. She knew he was tired, school all day, and he'd want a good night's sleep before the big fishing trip tomorrow.

Charlee stood to help, but Gray waved a hand for her to sit. "Let us. You need to visit."

Charlee gave her an appreciative smile and didn't argue. She sat back down.

Gray and David loaded the dishwasher. She handed him a plate and said, "So, Miah wants me to stay at the house tonight. He said the fishing trip would be over by about one and he wanted to see if I'd help him with an early dinner."

"That's nice."

"I told him no. That I'd just come over tomorrow at one, but I was thinking that I'm pretty tired and maybe you and I could head back to his house. Get a good night's sleep. You have a big day tomorrow. Who knows how long these guys will be up."

David rolled his eyes. "I'm capable of going back and going to bed myself."

They put the last of the dirty dishes in the dishwasher and Gray turned it on. "You know Miah would insist on going with you."

David huffed. "True. Okay."

"Did everything go okay at school today?"

He bent to put the dishwasher soap under the counter. "Sure, why?"

She brushed black hair from his eyes. "You just seem a little . . . off tonight."

His head dropped, lashes too thick for a boy hooding his eyes. "I just want tomorrow to be a good day."

Ah. The fishing trip. He'd be on display in front of his uncles and his last fishing adventure had ended with a flesh wound to his father. She leaned forward for emphasis. "Miah will be right beside you."

His mouth twitched. "I know. He makes me feel . . . safe. Does that sound stupid?"

"No." She dragged him into a hug. "He makes me feel safe, too."

They joined the group, and Gray told them she was tired and planning to stay at the lodge. No one asked, and she chose to ignore the upturned brows. This was for David. He'd be a bear in the morning if he had to stay up half the night listening to war stories. Besides, the others didn't know that when David first came there and there'd been snowstorm after snowstorm, she'd stayed quite a lot. It was none of their business, but she was aware of the loud silence after her announcement and the sets of eyes trailing to Miah. He stood. "I'll walk you back."

Gray shook her head. "Stay here and visit with your family, Miah. Moments like these are rare."

He gave her arm a squeeze, then turned to David. "See you tomorrow, champ."

———

"Gray! Gray, wake up!"

She shook the sleep from her as the panic in David's voice settled in. He'd pushed her bedroom door open with such force, it slammed against the wall. The noise helped rouse her. She sprung from the bed, trying to assimilate her surroundings. "David, what's wrong?"

"I—I can't find Jeremiah."

Her eyes leveled on the clock by her bed, but the numbers were blurry. Finally, she saw it was seven in the morning.

"Daylight. He wanted to leave at daylight. But he didn't wake me up." He stood in her doorway, fishing clothes already on and she realized he must have slept in them.

She grabbed her robe, a sinking feeling souring her stomach.

Downstairs, they found no sign of the McKinley men. The house was deathly quiet and empty. David turned to her, such a sad, confused look on his face, it broke her heart.

"Did he have to go to the bait store this morning?" David asked. Hope, so much hope in his tone.

She pulled a breath. No. He didn't. He'd been to the bait store the day before. She moved away from David so she could look into the backyard where the dock had anchored the boat last night. She said silent prayers as she moved in an effort to unblock the view. But when she stopped at the window, it confirmed every fear she had.

The boat was gone.

David stepped beside her, searching the east end of the lake, then the west. His breath made an oblong fog mark on the window. It was a long time before he spoke. "They went without me?"

Her heart shattered. How could Miah have done this?

Innocent, golden eyes looked to hers for answers. "Jeremiah went without me?"

She opened her mouth, but had no words.

David dropped his head and mumbled, "I've been practicing with Stacey. I wanted to surprise him."

A dart of pain settled in Gray's chest. She shook her head. "I don't know what happened, David. I don't think he would do that, intentionally leave you behind."

Stiffness entered his muscles. "But he did."

David tried to turn and walk away, but Gray wouldn't let him. Gripping his shoulders, she drew him in. And for a good half hour, she held him while he cried.

CHAPTER 13

Six hours after they'd left, the McKinley men returned. Gray knew the moment the boat pulled in. She steeled herself for whatever excuse Miah could hope to give about leaving his son behind. She'd tried to call his cell phone as soon as she realized they were gone. It rang inside the house and that's when she knew she'd have to wait until he returned to get an explanation.

The others were still outside when Miah came in the house calling Gray and David's names. She waited in the kitchen at the sink. "Hey, where's David? I want to show him what we caught."

She spun, gripping the butcher knife in her hand more tightly. "Why didn't you take your cell phone?"

But his focus was on the weapon. "Whoa." He raised his hands in surrender. "No reception on the lake. Uh, everything okay?"

"Is it okay?" No. Nothing was okay and she'd been fooling herself to think it would be. Miah was Miah and all through high school, he'd picked other girls over her. Now, he was picking his brothers over his son and though she knew he likely had some reason for leaving David out, the fact remained that David's heart was broken. "You tell me. I spent the morning consoling a twelve-year-old."

Concern for David caused him to step forward. "Why? What happened to him?"

As he moved closer, she realized she'd been holding the knife like a weapon. She discarded it on the counter. "You, Jeremiah. You're what happened to him." She so knew that feeling. The feeling of being overlooked. She didn't want to bring it up, didn't even want to admit it still cut her heart like a dull blade, but it did. All these years later, it did.

He shook his head to clear it. "I don't know what's going on."

She pointed at the back door. "You didn't take him. Had you planned on him staying home alone all day?"

"Well, yeah. When you said you weren't staying the night, I thought it must be fine for him to be alone for a few hours. Is that what this is about?"

She leaned forward. "You went without him, Miah. You ditched him for your brothers. He was heartbroken."

She watched the realization rise like a morning sun on Miah's face. "David wanted to go fishing? That can't be right. He never wants to go. I've asked him a dozen times. He *hates* fishing."

"Well, right now he hates you more, so congratulations." She cocked her hip and crossed her arms. She knew she was being hard on him, too hard, probably, but it hurt so deeply to be shoved aside like yesterday's trash. All David wanted was for his dad to be proud of him. All she'd ever wanted was Miah's attention. And when she finally got it, finally believed she was able to have him, he'd kissed her on the top of the head and said their night together was a great send-off. "I should have known this would happen sooner or later."

"Because you're always so ready for me to fail. Look, I didn't think he'd want to go."

She took a step toward him. "Well, he did. And even if he hadn't wanted to fish, Miah, this was your bonding guy time and you completely alienated him. You treated him like an outsider, like he didn't belong. He's your son."

All of it, all the feelings David must have experienced were running like wild horses through Miah's mind and she could see the horror. He hadn't meant for it to happen like this; of course he hadn't. But it still had. They'd worked so hard to build a firm foundation for Miah to crush it all due to carelessness. He gripped her arms. "I have to fix this. Where is he?"

"He's upstairs. But I don't think he's going to be very excited about talking to you. He's embarrassed now."

"I have to try." Miah ran a hand through his hair. "I'm sorry, Gray. The parenting thing is still new. Please don't give up on me." He walked through the doorway that would lead him past the living room and up the stairs.

She stopped him halfway there. "Miah, you know how you've been wondering what he and Stacey were doing all the time?"

"Yeah?"

"She was teaching him how to fish."

His face crumbled into a deep frown, lines around his mouth tilting down. It was so painful to look at, Gray focused on the wall beside him as he turned and rushed up the stairs. *Don't give up on me*, he'd requested. She didn't want to. But trusting him proved dangerous, for both her and David. And Gray had spent so many years alone, it seemed best to back away and not mess up her perfect record.

———

He found David on his bed, lying on his stomach reading a book. "Can I come in?"

David angled to look at him, but his face was stoic, the only signs of his hurt the red rims around his eyes. "If you want."

The bed sank as Miah perched himself on the edge of it. "I really screwed up today."

"No big deal." Too disconnected. Too detached.

He started to put a hand on David's shoulder, but opted not to. It hovered there until Miah finally dropped it back to his side. "It's a really big deal to me, David. I should have asked if you wanted to go."

"You didn't want me to go. Like I said, it's no big deal."

Miah's chest tightened. "No, that wasn't it. I didn't think you'd want to and I didn't want you to feel like you had to."

"Had to what? Spend the day with my dad on a boat? Yeah, every kid hates that." There was sarcasm in his tone, just enough to almost mask the pain. Beside his bed, a stuffed Ninja Turtle sat at the ready, bo staff in his hands.

"I'm sorry. I should have asked you."

David whirled on him and threw the book at the wall. "No. You should have told me to go. You're my *dad*, right? Aren't we supposed to do things like go fishing together? Or is that only when your brothers aren't around? Is that when I'm important to you?"

"You're the most important thing to me in the whole world." Miah had to fist his hands to keep from grabbing him and holding him. And though that might make him feel better, he knew it wouldn't help David yet.

David started to get up, but Miah caught him. Hands clamped on his arms, he pleaded. "David, listen to me. I thought you hated fishing. I didn't know. I was trying to . . . I don't know, I was trying to handle the situation the way I thought Bill and Angela would."

The tiniest spark of understanding flickered in David's eyes and Miah took it as a sign to plunge forward. "I feel so bad for not being everything you need."

David frowned. "What do you mean?"

"I mean, I'm a pretty simple kind of guy, David. I wouldn't know a museum from an art gallery. I wouldn't have a clue how to act at the symphony and I don't own a suit. Your parents gave you so many things I can never give you. I've felt like I've been pushing you to be something you're not."

David chewed the inside of his cheek.

"And the fishing . . . you didn't like it the time I took you."

Anger settled back over his features. "Just because I wasn't good at it doesn't mean I don't want to try."

If there were any remaining pieces of Miah's heart that weren't shattered, those words completed the task. Miah nodded, kneaded his son's shoulders. "I know. I know that now."

David picked at his fingernail, head down. "I like the stuff we do here." It was an olive branch, and Miah gladly took it.

"Can we go fishing?" Miah said, his throat tight.

David frowned. "When?"

Miah shrugged. "Right now."

"But you just got back."

Miah stood. "So? Come on, there's still gas in the boat and plenty of daylight left."

David stood up, too, slowly, testing the idea. "Will your brothers want to go again?"

Miah winked. "They're not invited. Come on." He pulled a heavy jacket from the closet and helped David shrug into it. Within a few minutes, they were downstairs and headed for the back door.

Caleb stopped them. "What are you doing? We've got fish to clean."

Miah pulled from the grip Caleb had on him. "Clean 'em. David and I are taking the boat back out." The warning look he gave Caleb stalled the conversation.

"Okay. Leave us all the work."

"We'll be back in a couple hours." As he left the house, his gaze landed on Gray. She didn't look angry. But she also didn't look happy. Distant. With her head tipped back and her stance squared. David had forgiven him, but he had to wonder if Gray would be able to. David was the only thing that mattered to her. Miah'd made a monumental mistake in assuming David wouldn't want to go. How many more mistakes could he make before Gray shut him out? She could do that. She had once before. Completely shut him out of her life. He couldn't blame her for being skittish, but he wouldn't let her run away. Not ever again.

———

Gray kept a cool distance from Jeremiah for the next few days. Caleb refused to do his therapy while his brothers were there, so Gray had been scarce around the house, only stopping by to help David with homework or to drop him off after school. Miah was giving her free rein with David—that's how it needed to be. She was amazing with him, and, without her, Miah would be utterly lost. He wouldn't make another stupid mistake like the fishing again. Watching Gray with David was so rewarding, he'd begun to really understand the depths and levels of a parent's love. Her love. Back when he'd learned he had a son, his intention had been to make her suffer. That had gone desperately wrong and somehow desperately right. But now, Gray had backed away. Not from David, but certainly from Miah. On the outside, she seemed cool, calm, detached from him, but he knew her. Knew her secrets and her fears. And he was determined to fix it. She was spooked.

His brothers had left the day before and today would be yet another first and another new parent adventure. It was the day of the banquet—the big fund-raiser he'd volunteered for—and David had insisted he and his dad go to Laver to shop. They parked the truck and were passing boutique store windows decorated for spring.

"Do I really need a suit for this thing?" He thought of the tight neck, constricted arms. A shiver ran the length of his body.

David just grinned at him. "Okay, we're here. Now, the people inside are really nice, but don't spill chocolate milk on that rug in the center of the room or their smiles sort of morph into the Joker's while they clean it up."

Miah ran his sweaty hands over his pants. They had no chocolate milk. "How do you know all this?"

David shrugged. "I used to come here with my dad. He was always getting new suits or shirts or ties."

Miah groaned. "Will I have to wear a tie, too?"

David thought a moment. "Probably."

As David grabbed him by the wrist and dragged him toward his unfair destiny, a little piece of Miah's heart erupted. David was in his element doing this. And that was a beautiful thing. Miah had expected him to try dozens of new things, and he'd done it like the champ he was. This was poetic justice. And in a way, having David telling him what to do and all the excitement rising from the boy was, well, it was pretty great. But a thought brought him to an abrupt stop at the men's haberdashery door. "David, what kind of fund-raiser is this?"

His laugh was high, happy, and a bit sadistic.

———

David sank his hands in his pockets and looked Jeremiah up and down. The two scarecrow women—that's what David liked to call them because they were skinny as bones—stood just behind David, eyes inspecting their work.

Miah tested the shoulders by lifting his arms and bringing his elbows together. "These are more comfortable than I expected."

The redheaded scarecrow grinned. David decided she always looked like the Joker. "They're cut for men with wider shoulders and muscular arms and chests. Is the neck too tight?"

Miah stuck his index finger beneath the collar and tugged. "No. I think it's good. Time to settle up, I guess."

The older woman motioned to the younger saleslady. "Rose, why don't you show David the new books we stocked in the kids' corner? I'll take Mr. McKinley to the register."

David followed the Joker, even though he'd already seen the books.

When a man entered and asked about designer suits, the Joker got right to work, so David decided to head back and find Jeremiah. He stopped just short of the register behind a tall shoe display when he heard his name.

It was the older scarecrow, and she'd always been nice to David and interested in the manga books he'd bring along, fascinated by the fact that they were read from back cover to front. She spoke in a hushed tone. "We were all so sorry to hear about Bill and Angela. Heartbroken for David."

"Thank you, ma'am."

"We're very fond of him. We've watched him grow up." David heard her clicking away on the register.

"He's an incredible kid. I'm . . . I'm really lucky to have him."

There were a few seconds of silence while David dissected those words. Did Jeremiah feel lucky? David had thought maybe he was just a burden to him.

Jeremiah continued. "He's so brave."

David pressed his lips together. Jeremiah thought he was brave. Even though Miah'd seen him after nightmares and even though he slept with a Ninja Turtle and the nightlight on.

The scarecrow spoke, her voice soft. "We were surprised he wanted to bring you here."

Jeremiah released a long breath. "I know. It has to be hard on him, but he's the bravest young man I've ever known, and, ma'am, that's saying something."

It wasn't hard until now. David brushed at his face. His eyes had watered a little bit.

Scarecrow spoke. "Oh, yes, David told me you were in the military. Well, we always give a military discount, but Mr. McKinley, if you wouldn't be offended, we'd like to do a little better than that."

"Offended, no."

"Well," she said, but seemed to be gathering her professionalism. "Today, everything is half off."

Wow. They'd never given his dad a discount like that.

And then she added, "For David."

And the discount was because of him. That was kind of cool. He figured he could join them now, so he popped out from behind the shoes as if he'd just walked back. Oh yeah, he could totally be a ninja. "All set?" David smiled big and hoped they didn't notice he'd cried a couple tears a minute ago.

"Just have to change back into my street clothes."

David lifted Miah's wrist and tapped his watch. "No time, Cinderella. We gotta get you to the castle."

"Yes, sir." Miah thanked the scarecrow for the suit and they rushed to the truck.

———

It was a nice evening with a fresh layer of snow that MoDOT had moved to the edges of the road. This day was different than any other day they'd spent together so far, and Miah's heart was bursting with happiness. David had gotten to take the reins. Miah glanced over. "Hey, champ."

David's hair flew as he looked over. "Yeah?"

"Thanks for this."

A grin that held more pride than happiness spread on David's face.

Miah tapped the steering wheel. "Maybe one day you could show me around a museum?"

David's gaze left him and focused on the road. "Okay. Yeah. I'd like to do that."

Miah reached over and gave his leg a squeeze.

David yelped.

Miah removed his hand until he realized what the reaction meant. "You ticklish?" Instantly, he reached over again and clamped his fingers around David's knee. The boy jolted, foot flying out and hitting the underside of the glove box. His laugh was hearty and the best thing Miah had ever heard. Finally, Miah relented.

Yes, things were great with him and his son. Gray, on the other hand, had stayed resistant to Miah since the fishing trip. She was scared. Scared to death, that much was obvious, but he didn't fully understand why. After all, they were both going to be in David's life for the duration.

"Give me your phone. I'll tell Gray to be ready when we get to her house." David barked orders like a drill sergeant. Guess his McKinley side was starting to shine through.

He listened as David argued with his mother. "No. You can't just meet us there . . . Because." He paused and rolled his eyes. "Gray. We're coming to pick you up. Be ready." And he hit the disconnect button.

"Does she know about the dress code?"

"She went shopping yesterday." When Miah started to ask another question, David reached to the stereo, found a hip-hop station, and cranked it loud.

⸻

Jeremiah's mind completely stalled when he put the truck in park and watched Gray step out of her house. A coat covered her torso, but a deep green dress peeked from beneath. It landed midcalf and had a slit in the front that highlighted her gorgeous legs when she moved. Even with the coat, she looked incredible.

Before Gray could get in, David hopped out, and motioned for her to slide into the middle beside Jeremiah. She gave him a quick glare and pointed to the snug skirt. "You gotta be kidding."

With a huff and an eye roll, she shimmied into the truck. And Miah enjoyed watching her.

The middle school was only a few miles away, but the silence was deafening. Finally, Gray spoke. "David, please tell us about this fund-raiser. I know it's a banquet. Are Jeremiah and I serving dinner at the banquet?"

"Nope." He busied himself playing with the window button.

"So, what are we going to be doing tonight? You've been secretive about it and I think it's time we know what to expect."

David glanced over, thoughtful, careful. "I got people to pledge money. They can either make a donation or pay outright for a dance."

"A *dance*?" Gray repeated.

He shrugged. "Yes. That's why Stacey needed you to be her pledge. Her mom and dad are still married and who wants to dance with an old married woman?"

Miah found it the slightest bit amusing. Gray, not so. She went from a shade of red to a deep sickly green. "Are you telling me you went around town selling dances with me?"

"You signed up."

"David."

There was the mom voice. Miah bit back a smile. What was the big deal? So, the middle school was renting them out for the evening. All for a good cause.

Gray shook her head. "No. You . . . should have told us."

"Mom!"

The one word caused Gray's heart to melt a little, it was obvious. To Miah's knowledge, he'd never called her Mom before this moment. She drew a breath, shoulders rising, and practically beamed. Joy spread across her features, making her look even more beautiful.

David raised an upturned hand in explanation. "This is a great way to make money for the basketball team. They need new equipment, and you know how River Rock is all about the science. Well, the jocks have to suffer for it."

Miah leaned closer to her. "You don't want the jocks to suffer, do you?"

She stiffened beside Miah. "You're telling me other people signed up for this? Willingly?"

"Yeah. No big deal."

Though Miah was having fun watching her squirm, he opted to be the voice of reason. "I suppose it wouldn't seem like such a bad thing if we'd known ahead."

David continued on, his political voice in full force. "Every student participating had to find a single relative or neighbor to be their pledge."

Gray dropped her head in her hands. "This is mortifying. It's like high school all over again."

David just grinned.

"How many dances?" She peered through her freshly painted fingertips.

"Ten. And your *whole* card is filled up."

She gave Miah a scorching glance. "I suppose you were in on this."

"Nah. I just found out. Just like you. But hey, if I have to dance with some little old lady to help the basketball team, it's worth it." He winked.

"David, how do you know you didn't give dances to some psychopath?"

"Gray." His chin tilted down. "It's River Rock. Everybody knows everybody."

It was a small town and maybe that's why ideas like this could work. Miah supposed they had to get more and more creative with the fundraising. All the money came from a very small pool.

"So, how will this go?" She was trying, Miah could tell, to mentally prepare herself for the night, for being on display, for being the center of attention. Gray never made a big deal out of the fact she was pretty; she just was herself and didn't care who noticed her. In fact, she likely preferred not to be noticed, not to be in the limelight. But she deserved the spotlight. She deserved her own moon to revolve around her. And quite suddenly, Jeremiah wished he'd known about the details. He'd have pledged money for a dance with Gray. Then, the thought of her spinning around all evening in other men's arms shot like fire through his mind. And the fun of the evening took a quick right turn and out the truck window.

Her nervousness found its way to her fingertips. They clicked together, something he'd noticed she did when she was uncomfortable.

He reached over and gave her hands a quick squeeze. He parked the truck and opened the passenger door. David bailed out, but Gray remained motionless, her giant eyes glassy and focused on something directly in front of them. "Come on, princess," he urged.

Reluctantly, she slid out of the truck, giving him a great view of those legs again and, side by side, they walked toward the gymnasium. David was a few steps ahead. Miah leaned over and gripped her hand. "You gonna be okay?" he whispered in her ear.

"Not much choice. Welcome to Parenthood 101. Always get details where fund-raisers are concerned."

Miah watched their son walking in front of him. "It's weird that he was so secretive about it."

"He knows me. I'd have never agreed."

Miah stopped her. With gentle pressure on her arm, he turned her to face him.

"Not true. You're just like me. You'd rope the moon if he asked. You can do this, Smith. You're so much stronger than you know." And she was beautiful. She'd put on makeup to enhance her formal attire. Her hair was down, long, lush, and waiting for his fingers to rummage through it, but he wouldn't be doing that because they both had a card filled with names.

"I'd have bought a dance with you." Miah didn't pull her closer, though her body moved in, if only slightly, and he had the suspicion that he could thaw that ice queen if he only had the time and if he didn't mess everything up again in the process.

"Come on, you guys." David tugged the gym door and the banquet and dance lay just beyond.

———

Gray hadn't been able to eat during the banquet because her stomach was a ball of nerves that felt like barbed wire unraveling in her gut. The gym had been modestly enhanced with cardboard and tissue from what was likely a decade of collected Valentine decorations. Red and white and a million balloons. If the decorating committee's goal was *middle school romance*, they'd nailed it. David and Stacey came over. "Okay, inside the envelope is your card. Each card has lines. On each line is the name of the person you dance with. There are ten dances."

Gray's fingers bit into the envelope and she hoped for . . . well, she didn't know what to hope for. Empty. That's what she hoped for. She stared at the page, then hollered for David, who had already started sneaking away. He and Stacey made their way back to her.

"There's a mistake here. My card just says Jeremiah McKinley."

At that moment, as if summoned by her words, Jeremiah came toward them with the same look on his face that she was experiencing. He held the card up in front of David. "What's this?"

Gray tilted on her high heels to see, but couldn't read what was on his card.

David grinned. Stacey grinned. Finally, David raised one hand in explanation. "I told you, we could either sell dances or get people to pledge money *toward* a dance."

"So?" Jeremiah's head tilted down and Gray realized he was finally tiring of this tug-of-war surprise, too.

"So, you're pledged to dance with Gray."

Miah nodded toward her. "But how can I dance with her when she already has a full—" He snagged her card from her hands and stared at it. She watched his eyes skitter across the page that read *Jeremiah McKinley* on every line.

Miah blinked and for what was likely the first time in his life, he seemed to have nothing to say.

"David." Gray's tone was low, cautious. "How did you get the money to do this? It had to be expensive."

"I just told people that you two were my birth parents and I wanted to give you a nice date night. Everyone was all like *'Aaaaahhhhh, that's so sweet.'* Then, they gave me money."

216

She struggled for something to balance her because this was embarrassing, mortifying. And David should have known . . . . She placed her hands firmly on his shoulders. "This was not the right thing to do."

And that's when it happened. His smile disappeared, turning into a sad bow shape, his eyes lost their sparkle, and his shoulders curled forward.

And Gray felt like crap.

Stacey put a steadying hand on David's arm. His brows tilted up at the inside edges, making him look sorry. And like an angel being scolded for a good deed. His gaze fell to the gym floor. "I just wanted to do something nice for you. I know you never went to a dance when you were in school."

Oh, why had she admitted that to him? She'd done it back when he'd wanted to go to a couples' dance in seventh grade but never got the courage to ask one of the girls. Her eyes looked up for strength because to continue to look at David felt like pouring acid in her system. She was a horrible mother. To her left, she found Miah. A tender smile, a sympathetic hand stretching to take hers. When she moved past the embarrassment, this was the sweetest thing David could have ever done, and it made her want to hug him so hard it would hurt. She pooled her mom-power and squeezed David's shoulder. "You know what?"

Reluctant hope lifted his chin.

"This is an amazing gift. You're right. I needed this dance, this night. David, you're so much smarter than me." She thought of him before the accident, searching the Internet for charm bracelets for Angie. He'd wanted her gift to be perfect. And now he wanted the night to be perfect for Gray.

His smile lit the room. Stacey bumped his shoulder and the two of them headed off in the direction of the table that housed the red velvet cake.

She turned to find Jeremiah with his arms outstretched and waiting. Waiting for her. His massive shoulders were tucked into a suit that made him even more handsome than should be legal. "May I have this dance?" A half smile tilted his cheek.

"This and nine more." As the music began and the lights dimmed, Gray Smith, resident graveyard freak of the town, danced with the man she loved, in the gymnasium of her old high school. She loved him. She knew that. Could even admit it to herself.

But for all of Gray's trying and working and hoping, she was too vulnerable. Miah had inadvertently hurt David. He'd fixed it, sure. And David had forgiven him. But if he hurt *her*, she wasn't sure *she* could forgive him again. She'd handled the fishing situation badly. But hadn't been able to stop those treacherous feelings from rising from that room deep in her heart, hadn't been able to stop them from taking over. And the worst thing of all, if Miah ever took David away, it would kill her. Sure, he had a document explaining that it was Bill and Angie's wishes to involve her, but that wasn't a paper giving her custody, even joint custody.

As long as she and Miah remained friends, there was no risk to David. If something more between her and Miah developed and then blew up in their faces, would he want her around? She'd walked such a careful line with Angela. She could do it again. It was the only way to ensure she'd never lose her son. Regardless of how much she loved Miah, her love for David had to come first.

CHAPTER 14

"Hey," Miah whispered and pulled her closer in his arms. They were on dance six or seven. She'd lost count. Other couples changed partners, but not Miah and Gray. With each passing song, they steadily came closer and closer until their bodies were touching, lost somewhere beneath the glimmer of an old disco ball and a canopy of balloons. "What's wrong?"

She glanced up to find his eyes—midnight sexy—settled on her. How'd he know something was wrong?

"Your muscles tensed."

She swallowed. "Did they?"

He tilted closer until his lips brushed the hair covering her ear. "Yeah," he said, but it was one quick puff of ultraheated air that caused the strands to scatter, leaving her ear exposed. She felt naked there.

Then, there was a brush, gently, lips against the delicate skin of her lobe. All the strength left her body.

"That's better," he purred.

Okay, something had to happen because all her well-thought-out intentions were eroding and collecting at her feet. Her skin was coming alive under his touch and for a quick instant she didn't even care that there was a room full of people watching. She put on her game face and tilted to look at him. "Jeremiah, we need to talk about—"

And then he ruined her plan and ruined her night and possibly her life. In a quick rush, Miah feathered his lips over hers.

She sucked a breath.

His smile had disappeared. There was an intensity reaching toward her that she'd only seen in him a few times in her life. The night. That night in the cabin with their skin still slick and wet from the rain and the hint of a chill in the summer air and Jeremiah in her arms.

And he knew she was thinking about it. Knew it and it made him smile. Not his practiced smile, but something special, something intimate, something reserved for only her.

"You possessed me that night," he said, quite out of the blue, his golden eyes dazzling with a strange light she'd never seen before. Her feet stopped moving on the dance floor.

Miah filled his lungs. "I'd never experienced anything like it. And I haven't since."

What? *What?*

"I kept telling myself it was because it was forbidden. You know, you being my best friend. I shouldn't have felt . . . like that. Nothing's ever come close."

Gray needed to breathe. There was no air in the room. But instead of helping her or giving her mouth-to-mouth or even calling an ambulance, his head dove again to the bare skin of her ear and she wished she'd worn earmuffs. "Gray, promise me one day you'll make good on everything you promised me that night."

What had she promised? He was the one who'd called it a great send-off, not her. She'd wanted . . . she'd wanted him. That night and forever. She'd given him everything because it was all she had and if she'd had more, she'd freely have given that, too, even if it took her life. Because Miah was her forever, and if it couldn't be him, it might as well be no one. Everything she'd been and felt was poured into him that night.

His hand pressed at the small of her back. "I'm not rushing you. Just . . . just promise me one day you'll give yourself to me like that again."

But she couldn't, because back then there was hope and faith and trust that everything would work out. And now she was a realist. She knew things never went as planned. Her hands had fisted into his suit coat.

He grasped a hand with his free one, untwining it, and drew it to his lips. "I know you're scared."

She hadn't said anything. Nothing. But Miah was carrying on an entire conversation as if she were speaking each thought that entered her mind. "I'm scared, too. For David's sake. But I'm willing to try."

She wanted to look away, to find David at the cake table and be reminded that there were more important things than love and lust and having a man to curl up with. "It would destroy him if things didn't work out between us. Gas and fire, remember?"

"You're so certain I will fail you. What if I don't? What if I could be a great dad and a great husband?"

Husband. Whoa there.

"If you could give me a little room to make mistakes. I know you're scared to trust me, and believe me, I understand why, but give me a chance, Gray. Maybe I'll surprise you."

Tears rushed her eyes because she knew, had always known she was balancing on the edge of a sword. One wrong decision, one wrong move and Bill and Angela could have denied her access to David. And now it was Miah holding the hilt. "I've always felt one step away from losing him. How do I know I won't lose him if things don't work out between us?"

Miah's hands cupped her face. "You're not going to lose him. That will *never* happen. I swear on my father's grave."

Tiny spots appeared before her eyes. Gray drew a deep breath and let it out slowly. When she pulled another, there was something there, some strange sensation that trickled over her skin and into her chest. It was freedom. She'd take Jeremiah at his word. His word was golden and if he said he'd never take David away, then it was the truth.

Still, she found herself repeating the words. "You swear?"

The smile was tender. "I swear."

Gray threaded her hands around his neck and stretched right up off her high heels to hug him tighter, harder. A sound, like popcorn in a microwave, caused her to draw back.

Applause. It was applause, and it came from around the entire gymnasium. Embarrassment clawed up her throat and settled on scorching her cheeks. Jeremiah chuckled. "We're quite the spectacle."

"Yeah," she agreed, but her heart was so light and so full of hope, she didn't even mind. "Just imagine if they knew about us kissing in the graveyard."

His gaze narrowed playfully. "Is that what you call that?"

Gray took his face in her hands and planted a peck on his lips. The applause continued, a few catcalls interspersed, and suddenly, David was at their feet. "You guys are totally embarrassing me. Stop it!"

Gray shrugged. "You created this monster, now live with it, Dr. Frankenstein."

David grinned, half his face contorting in an attempt to scowl. He had a bit of red cake crumbs in the corner of his mouth. "Okay, well, PDAs are not allowed on school grounds, so please control yourselves."

David disappeared when the crowd lost interest in Gray and Jeremiah. Stacey and he were back at the cake table. When it was announced that David had raised the most money for the basketball team, a flurry of tall, gawky boys surrounded him in congratulations. It was the perfect night.

Four dances later, with a heart warm and full, Gray fought the voice in her head that told her fairy tales rarely came true and when it seems like everything's perfect, things were likely about to collapse around you.

They drove her home and Jeremiah walked her to the door, his fingers twined around hers, and in his grip, she felt the reluctance to let go. He kissed her. Not as deeply or as completely as she would have liked—they had a twelve-year-old audience, after all. But a tender kiss that promised both a future and a happily ever after.

"I want to see you again this weekend."

Those words raced down her spine, leaving a tingling sensation as they went.

"Sunday night. Dinner with me. David will be at Stacey's. They're working on a project."

Gray chewed her lip and cast a glance at the truck.

"Come on, Smith." Miah stepped into her, trapping her at her front door. "Don't start chickening out now. We agreed to do this."

She huffed. "Well, it's not like I can think straight with you pressed against me like you are. Your son is watching."

"*Our* son. And I don't think it would be horrible for him to know I'm pretty fond of his mother."

She placed her hands on his chest and shoved, but it was like moving a brick wall. "I'll go to dinner with you. Now back off, McKinley, or I'll go get my gun."

He laughed. "Your gun. Right. Did I tell you how incredible you look tonight?"

She continued to push, but it was halfhearted at best. "You might have mentioned it."

"Wear something nice on Sunday night. You're going to love the place I have in mind."

Her brows and the corners of her mouth both tilted up. "Neon Moon?"

"A real date. Dress for it. You won't be disappointed."

"You always did know how to romance the ladies. Fine." She feigned a yawn.

He pressed his chest against hers. "You are one hard-to-impress female."

Her head tipped back innocently. "Or perhaps you're one overconfident male."

One of his brows tilted seductively. "I guess you'll find out."

The shiver ran from her neck down, sending her nerve endings dancing from the tops of her shoulders to the tips of her toes. There was no way she'd sleep tonight.

He kissed the end of her nose. "Stay warm, Mary Grace."

Stay with me, she wanted to say. But that would serve no purpose at all except thoroughly wrecking whatever this was they were trying to build. She placed a hand to his cheek. It was cold from the night's wind and smooth beneath her touch. "Good night, Jeremiah."

He turned to leave and she dropped her weight against the door-jamb to watch him go.

"Oh, wait." She ran inside and brought back the heavy plastic box she'd kept in her hall closet.

He took it. "What is this?"

"It's David's life. Up to now, of course. I thought you'd like to look through it. There are photos, video, his first birthday, his first science fair. Miah, I'm so sorry for all I denied you. Maybe these can . . . can help."

He took the box and handled it like the treasure it was. His eyes were misty. "Thank you, Gray. Thank you so much."

Over the box, she pecked his cheek. "See ya."

He nodded, but she didn't think he trusted his voice to speak. It was a sensation she understood. She waved good-bye to David as Miah returned to his truck. In a moment, father and son were driving away and Gray was realizing maybe things really were going to be all right.

Jeremiah started to place the container in the back of the truck but decided it was too precious to risk. He slid it inside between him and his son.

"That went well," David said, sitting in the passenger seat and propping his elbow on the plastic box. Town was shutting down, the remaining snow glistening at the edges of the roads and melting away in snowplow piles.

Miah winked. "Dangerous little game you played there, son."

David concentrated his attention on the trim running along the door of the truck. His finger trailed it. "I know. It was worth it."

Miah reached over and gave his hand a squeeze. "You won't hear me complain."

"Stacey's brother asked me if I wanted to go with them next weekend."

An invitation from one of the boys in his class. This was good. Ms. Forrester had it right, suggesting David get involved with the fund-raiser. "What's next weekend?"

"Some of the basketball boys are going up to Old Man Carver's hunting cabin for the night. Bonfire, cook hot dogs. You know, do guy stuff." He was trying to be casual, but Miah could see the excitement sifting through every pore of his being. Maybe he'd never gotten an invite like this.

"Is there an adult going?"

"Trey Billing's older brother and his friend are going. They're seniors." David's eyes widened as if *seniors* meant they were utterly adult and fully responsible.

Still, Miah would like some more details. "I don't know, David. Let me talk to Gray."

David scoffed. "Talk to Gray? You're my dad. I live with *you*. Not her."

Miah's collar felt tight. Maybe David was right. There would be a thousand opportunities like this, and Miah had to man up and not go running to Gray every time he was asked permission for something. "And Stacey's brother is going? Their mom and dad said it was okay?"

David sat up straighter. "Yeah. No big deal."

Miah's thumb tapped the steering wheel as he turned the truck onto the long driveway leading home. The trees sparkled with melting snow that dripped when the sunlight hit but refroze over the cold nights. Winter could either give way to spring or it could hit again with a vengeance—no real way to tell, and that was one of the things he loved about Missouri. The uncertainty. That fun of the unknown, however, ended with David. Where his son was concerned, Miah would prefer all absolutes and no surprises. What was the right thing to do here? Finally, he nodded. "Okay. I guess I'm okay with it, but I want you to take my cell phone. Any problems, anything going on that shouldn't be, you call me." And he gave him a stern look for good measure. A dad look.

"I promise." David could barely contain his exuberance.

Probably Miah was worrying for nothing. Boys did stuff like this all the time. He certainly had. He and his brothers had spent plenty of nights out in the woods . . . and without the comfort of a hunting cabin. He started to mention that if the weather was bad, David couldn't go, but, on second thought, opted not to. No parents were going to let their boys go out in a snowstorm or with temperatures below freezing, so the trip would be canceled and Miah wouldn't have to be the one to spoil it. "What's the weather supposed to be like?"

David grinned. "Snow and ice this coming week, but nicer on the weekend. Might warm up to fifty-five on Saturday."

Though he knew he shouldn't, Miah hoped this time the weatherman was wrong.

———

Sunday was cold but not unbearable, and Miah had fretted over what to wear. Not like him. He'd always prided himself on being a man who knew his own mind. Now, every situation he found himself in had him questioning his own judgment. He came down the stairs and found Caleb and Mr. Gruber sitting on the couch. What was Gruber doing there?

Miah greeted him as he entered the living room. There was a fire in the fireplace and it gave a perfect glow to the space. Building fires was good for Caleb, working various muscle groups. Plus, he loved watching the flames chew the wood until only embers remained. Then, Caleb would make a trip to the woodshed and start it all again.

Gruber stood from the couch and whistled. "Must be some lady you're trying to impress."

Miah chuckled. "Yeah, and she doesn't impress easily."

"The boy's mother?" Gruber asked, his pale blue eyes shining.

"Yes, sir."

"I like your sport coat, young man." He pointed to Miah's feet. "Change out of those dress shoes and put on your best cowboy boots. Jeans, not the dress pants."

Miah raised his arms and looked down over his clothing. "It's a fancy place."

Gruber scratched at the days' worth of stubble on his chin. "Boy, you live in Missouri, there's no restaurant within a hundred miles of here that refuses to serve a man in cowboy boots. They'd go under, for sure. You don't want to look like you're trying too hard." He closed one eye and pointed at Miah with a crooked finger. "Gotta keep that air of mystery. Women love a mysterious man."

"All right. I won't argue with experience. Jeans and boots it is."

Gruber gave him a crooked smile. "She'll appreciate that. Guarantee it."

Miah headed back upstairs.

Caleb spoke up. "Thanks for coming, Mr. Gruber. I'll plan to drop by tomorrow?"

At the top of the stairs, Miah paused.

Caleb answered the unspoken question. "Gray said I need more therapy for my right hand. She suggested painting. Gruber's going to give me lessons."

Miah's heart swelled. His brother had made so much progress but still struggled the most with his right hand. "That's great, Caleb. But no naked women; we have a minor in the house now."

Caleb's gaze went to Gruber. "Naked women? Can we paint those?"

Gruber chuckled. "I'm not interested in corrupting a minor, so no. We'll start with still lifes. Bowls of fruit, things like that."

"Naked women sounds better," Caleb grumbled. "But you're the boss."

———

Miah changed into his best jeans while downstairs he heard Caleb telling Gruber good-bye. A minute later, Caleb was at his door. "You look more comfortable; Gruber was right about the clothes."

Miah nodded.

Caleb entered and sat down on Miah's bed. "Got a minute?"

He knew he did. He was ready forty-five minutes early. "Sure."

Caleb put his hands together, the left rubbing the right.

He did that often now, and Miah had to wonder if the right hand felt different than it used to. Instead of asking, he sat down beside him and watched his baby brother.

"I got a call from a guy in my unit. He told me about the accident."

Miah's hand protectively covered his brothers. "When?"

"He called last week."

Miah squeezed, worry crawling over him. "Caleb, why didn't you tell me?"

"You've been busy."

Miah swallowed hard. Between getting the place ready for Isaiah and Gabriel's visit and everything with David, he'd neglected his own brother—a man who still needed him.

"Anyway, he was there. There was . . . there was water, Miah. In the bottom of the ravine. I was underwater when they got to me. Two of the other guys in the Humvee cut me out."

Cold flooded Miah's system. "Water."

"That's why I reacted like I did in the pool." Caleb stood and walked away from him. He came to a stop at the window. "I can't swim now. Isn't that the weirdest thing you've ever heard? I get in the water and I just seize up."

Miah walked to his brother. "It'll come back, Caleb."

He shook his head. "No." It was one of the saddest resolves Miah had ever heard. "It won't. I just wanted to say I'm sorry. I know how hard it was for you to let Grandfather Havinger stake a claim here by doing the pool."

Miah watched a bird tip its wings and land on the winter water below. His room had a nice view, but nothing compared to the room he'd given David. "Actually, I've been thinking about that. Maybe we should invite him over to see the pool now that it's done."

"What?" Caleb faced him.

"These last several weeks have made me realize how important family is. What are we really holding against Grandfather Havinger? The fact that he was watching his daughter die and wanted to help? Doesn't seem like a good enough reason anymore."

"There was a lot more than that, Miah. He hated Dad. Never approved of their relationship, cut her out of the will when she married Dad."

"But he also wrote her back in. I've never understood those kinds of feelings until now. When it's your child, you'll do just about anything to keep them from making the wrong choices. Just think about it, okay?"

Caleb nodded.

When Miah turned, Caleb placed a hand on his shoulder. "Thanks, bro."

"For what?"

"For everything. You took in your crippled, brain-damaged little brother. Didn't have to. I just want you to know I appreciate it."

Miah faced him fully, because it was important, vital that Caleb know this. "I didn't do anything you wouldn't do for me, Caleb. Any one of us brothers would take a bullet to protect the other. And we each know that. No need to say thanks."

Caleb's eyes softened. "Guess I'd save your sorry butt if it came down to it."

"You know you would."

"Will you hate me if I don't attempt the pool anymore?"

The only thing Miah hated was the idea that Caleb was willing to give up on it. "Of course not."

"Will you hate me if I move on to my own property in the summer?"

Miah frowned. "I thought you were happy here."

"I am, Miah, but I've got a pretty cool cabin sitting in the hillside surrounded by hot springs. I'm totally able to live on my own. Besides, your lodge is getting crowded. If you play your cards right, Gray is going to end up being my sister-in-law and there's no way I can listen to her nagging all day and all night."

Miah knew his little brother. Knew him so well. "You want to live on your own, don't you?"

"You're close by. Plus, I'm planning to have you help me renovate it. It's in good shape, but needs to be updated."

Miah understood the spark of excitement in his brother's eyes. He'd had it, back when he talked about fixing up the lodge. "I get it."

"One more thing. This hunting, fishing lodge?"

"Yeah?"

"What if it was something else?"

Now he had no clue what his brother was getting at. "Like what?"

"Still a hunting, fishing lodge, but rehab too."

"Huh?"

"Miah, there are a lot of guys coming home like me. We've got the pool; we've got Gray. You could guide hunting trips and fishing trips. It'd be great for guys who are taking that first step back into civilian life. Hunting is familiar ground for soldiers. It's just something to consider."

Giving injured soldiers a place to begin that long assimilation back into civilian life. It definitely had its merits. But funding something like that would be costly. His lodge was supposed to make money, not drain his trust fund, plus there was David to think about now. Miah needed to make money, at least some. Eventually.

His brother had given him a lot to think about and Miah pivoted to see his own reflection in the bathroom mirror once again.

Caleb grunted. "You look fine. Go have a great night with Gray. If David gets home before you get back, I'll take care of him."

Miah's brows shot up.

"Really. We're good. The science nerd is even starting to grow on me."

Miah pointed. "Don't corrupt him."

"Whatever."

———

Miah picked Gray up with a good supply of nerves jangling in his gut. "We're going to Kensington. There's a restaurant there that sits on the riverbank and used to be a speakeasy in the twenties."

Gray's face lit. "I've heard about it. They renovated it several years back." She clasped her hands together. "I've wanted to go there since I read an article about the place."

Miah reached for her hand. "I thought you'd like it."

She pivoted in the truck seat so she could look at him. "You look really great tonight."

Gruber had it right. "Thanks. Caleb and Gruber dressed me."

This made her nose crinkle and her head tilt.

He laughed. "I was overdressed. Gruber set me straight. You, on the other hand, look perfect."

She wore a dark gray sweater dress that accentuated her curves, hugging her body in all the right places. Tiny diamond-stud earrings made her lobes twinkle and tall black boots covered her calves and feet. "And you look like you just stepped off a fashion show runway." he added.

Her shoulder tilted up. "It's the boots." At that, she raised the edge of her dress to give him a better view of the shining leather and tall heel.

He reached over, grabbed her calf. "Nice."

She squirmed to get away, but giggled when the attempt proved futile. Miah had her in a death grip and was in no hurry to let go. Beneath the leather, he could feel her flesh. It was warm, muscle tightened. He'd like to drag that boot off her . . .

Miah cleared his throat. He'd weighed the options about when it would be appropriate to discuss certain matters. Now seemed as good a time as any. Honestly, he wanted to get it over with because if she bucked—like he expected her to—he'd rather deal with it now. "I need to talk to you about something."

"Okay." She tilted the mirror down and checked her lip gloss. It looked good enough to kiss right off her mouth, but he opted to keep that idea to himself until later.

"Stacey's brother asked David to go camping with them next weekend. He and some boys from the basketball team." Full speed ahead.

Her gaze slipped from the mirror to him. "And?"

"And I told him yes. It was okay to go. Another thing about the trip. No parents going. Two of the senior boys are chaperoning."

One blink. Two. Three more and her mouth opened. A tiny dimple appeared on one side and she clamped her mouth shut. Silence filled the truck.

"Gray?" His eyes left the road. "Gray? Say something."

Her lips pursed.

"Say something, for Pete's sake. Yes? No? Good idea, bad idea?"

Her fingernails clicked together on her lap. "I don't know."

Okay, this wasn't helping. She was the one who was supposed to have the answers.

She ran her fingers through her hair, but it wasn't to smooth the strands, instead it seemed an attempt to shake off her tension. Finally, she turned to face him. "Miah."

And in that one word, his name, there was a desperation borne of too many nights of uncertainty. Jeremiah pulled the truck onto the shoulder of the road and put it in park. He flipped the blinkers on and turned to face her.

Her head shook slowly. "I'm no good at this. I mean, David's growing up. It always seemed like Angela knew exactly what to do. I don't. He's twelve. Caught between child and teen. I know it's not all up to me; he's living with you, so you'll obviously be making more of these kinds of decisions, but I still can't stop hoping I'll know what's right."

His hand cupped her cheek. "You *are* good at this. You don't even know how good. And like right now, we'll be making these decisions together. Maybe Angela seemed sure, but maybe it was just an act. Maybe inside, she was just as scared and uncertain as we are now."

Gray smiled; her hand came up to caress his and hold him there. "Whether she did or didn't, we can tell ourselves that, right?"

Miah nodded. He was learning that parenting wasn't an exact science. "I didn't know what to say to him. In the end, I went with yes, you can go."

Tension entered her features and she dropped her hands to her lap. "We don't really know any of these boys or their families."

"I know." Outside, a few fat snowflakes began to blow in the beam of light before them.

"We don't know what kind of kids they are."

"I know." Snow collected on the windshield.

"We . . ." She glanced down at her hands. They'd fisted. "We have to learn to let go. Okay." She raised her fists to eye level and opened her hands. "I'm letting go."

Miah took her hands in his. "I promise it's going to be okay."

"How can you promise that?"

"We don't know what kind of kids they are. But we know what kind of kid David is."

She moved and gripped his wrists. "You're pretty smart."

He grinned. "I had a great teacher. Let's go to dinner."

She bobbed her head once in agreement. "Let's."

Miah pulled back onto the road. That had gone better than he'd anticipated. With each passing day, Gray was becoming more and more open. She was beginning to see him as actual father material . . . a fact Miah appreciated. Mostly because she was a tough critic, and if *she* believed he could be a good father, *he* could believe it.

A half hour later, they arrived at the restaurant that was already teeming with patrons. Apparently, the encroaching snow wasn't a deterrent for speakeasy lovers. Miah and Gray sat at a table with a picture window overlooking the river. Gray had insisted on touring the entire restaurant before eating. Now, she sat with her sweater sleeves shoved up to her elbows, eyes glistening with all the discovery and magic that made this place special. She scanned a brochure about the building. "Oh, look! Here in that cellar we walked through is the entrance to the cave. They don't let people go inside anymore—unsafe. But they say Jesse James used to hide in there."

Yes, Miah had been along on the tour with her, but she seemed intent on recapping it. "Cool."

"Did you notice the false floor in the kitchen?" she said.

He bit back a smile. "Yes." There was a large section where the oak flooring had been removed. All six people on the tour had seen it.

"That's where they hid the alcohol," Gray whispered, as if the G-men were sitting right beside them.

"Uh-huh."

Gray hugged herself. "I love this place."

Miah's gaze narrowed. "No. You don't."

"What?" she squeaked.

"What you love, Gray, is people. Their history, their stories. You couldn't care less about this building. It's the life inside it that you're interested in."

He watched as her head tipped, thoughtfully considering his words. "I've never thought about it that way."

"That's probably why you like graveyards. You look around them and you see the lives, not the deaths. You're an incredible woman, Gray Smith. The world could learn a lot by watching you."

She chewed her lip. "Well, I'm glad the world isn't watching; I'd undoubtedly trip down the stairs and land on my head."

He laughed. "Can I talk to you about something else?"

She took a sip of her drink. "Sure."

"Caleb wants me to turn the lodge into a place where soldiers can come for rehabilitation."

The gnawing on her bottom lip intensified. "Really?"

"Said we have everything we need. If it's helped him, it could help others."

She leaned forward, resting her forearms on the table. "It's a great idea."

"He also wants to live alone."

Gray reached to take Miah's hand. "How do you feel about that?"

"Sad." His head tilted back and forth. "And happy for him. It's good." He continued to nod, convincing himself and Gray.

"It is good." While they ate, Miah told her the details of Caleb's accident. Firelight flickered on the table, casting a soft glow onto Gray's face.

"That's why he almost drowned in the pool." Gray used the end of her fork to toy with her dessert. He knew she was enjoying the food, but she had lost some interest in it when he started talking about Caleb. She was back in work mode now. He'd need to redirect soon.

Miah nodded. "Guess so. He doesn't want to even try anymore."

"It's okay, Miah. One day he will. Until then, I think we just have to respect his wishes and not push."

But Miah was a soldier. Pushing was what he did best. "Yes ma'am, Dr. Gray."

She giggled. "Try this." She speared a bite of chocolate cake and held it out to him.

Miah's lips closed on her fork. "Mmm."

Gray pushed her sleeves up a bit farther on her arms. "Is it warm in here? I think it's warm in here." It was, and it had nothing to do with the temperature in the restaurant.

They sat a while longer, looking out over the river and enjoying the comfortable silence between them. This was right, Miah decided as he paid the check and tucked an arm around Gray. This was perfect and something he didn't want to ever give up. This was . . . this was what soldiers should get to come home to.

He kept an arm around her as they walked to the truck. The flurries had stopped, but Gray watched the sky as they strolled. "Do you think it looks like we'll get more snow tonight?"

"Yes." Miah didn't know, but the way her head was tipped back, exposing her throat, made him want to keep her examining the heavens.

"You do?" Her chin came down to find him staring at her.

He reached the truck and moved her so that the passenger door was at her back and he was at her front. "I do." The words rolled off his tongue as if carrying some deep, hidden meaning. He'd considered the merits of marrying Gray. Then, they could raise David together. But if Gray thought that was why he wanted her by his side, she'd never go there. She didn't want to be anyone's tagalong. But that's not why Miah wanted her. He wanted every ounce of Gray in every way. And it had nothing to do with the child they shared. It was her laugh, her frown, her scent. It was the sunshine on her hair and the wind across her flesh. She was daylight and dusk and everything in between. "I love you, Gray." It came right out of his mouth. He supposed hiding it anymore would be ridiculous. Surely, she already knew.

Gray sucked a sharp breath. "You . . ."

His lips found hers. Cold, sweet, tinged with chocolate cake and the kind of desire that can only come from a woman like Gray. He nuzzled against her cheek, the smooth skin at her temple. His hands roamed over her hips, her back. "I love you," he said again, just in case she'd missed it the first time.

———

Gray's heart nearly erupted from her chest. Her hands found their way beneath his suit coat and bunched into the material of his shirt. She'd wrinkle it for sure, but she didn't care. This was a fantasy world where she was the princess and Jeremiah was in love with her. She flattened her hands on his chest and pushed him away. When he was at arm's length, she whispered, "Say it again."

The frown from being interrupted disappeared into a warm smile. "I." And he moved in to find the hollow of her throat. She groaned at the kiss he placed there against her throbbing vessel.

"Love." His hands slid down, down, with excruciating slowness, then shot back up like a rocket, clamping over her shoulder blades and pressing her entire body to his. It was a roller coaster she could feel from the inside out.

"You," he whispered against her ear, and every ounce of her soul melted into his hands.

When the silence stretched, he tipped out. "I think this is the part where you say you've fallen in love with me, too." One of his brows peaked, waiting.

So many emotions assaulted her, she wondered if she'd be able to sort and articulate them. She had to try. She had to make Miah understand. "I haven't fallen in love with you, Miah." She started to explain, but was stopped by the sudden fear and tension that entered his gaze. A long breath, ragged and full of hopelessness, drifted from his lips. He looked lost, haunted.

"Wait. You didn't let me finish. How could I fall in love with you if I never stopped loving you?"

His hands became soft on her arms, as if all his strength had gone into staying upright. "Say it again," he whispered, repeating her words.

She moved closer. "I." With her hands roaming over his shoulders, she tipped up to find the hollow of his throat. He growled in response to the kiss she placed there. "Have." Her fingers traipsed over his chest. "Always." Eyes opened and fitted tightly to him, she smiled. "Loved you." For good measure, she mouthed the word "always" again.

His kiss was fast, hard, and left her body screaming for more. When a harsh wind pressed into them, Miah groped for the truck's door handle. He quickly deposited her inside then climbed in himself, but rather than put the car into drive and head home, he turned on the engine, cranked the heat, then returned to her mouth. He kissed her until the windows fogged and the truck's heater became too much.

Finally, Gray dragged herself from him. "Miah," she whispered. "We're making out in a restaurant parking lot like two teenagers."

His grin was quick and wickedly sexy. "So?"

"As much as I'm enjoying this, people are coming out of the restaurant and staring at your truck."

He dropped his forehead to hers. "Let them stare."

She giggled and went right back to kissing him. She loved him, after all. And this was only the beginning.

When his cell phone rang, they both jumped.

Gray straightened her dress and tried to wipe off the lip gloss smeared around the edges of her mouth. Miah held the phone away from his face and mouthed, "It's David. He's just checking on us."

Aw. She reached for the phone. "Hi, honey. Did you and Stacey get plenty of homework done?" As she spoke, Miah's hand landed on the bare flesh of her knee and he squeezed. She kicked and tried to stifle her laugh. She gave him a death look.

David asked if she was all right.

"Yes, I'm fine. Miah is being a brat, but I can handle him."

At that, he leaned over and sank his head into the hollow of her throat, the heat of his mouth burning her flesh.

"I'll see you tomorrow after school, okay?" She tried to squirm away, but a hulking Miah made it difficult. "Good night, David. Sleep tight. Love you big."

She gave Miah his phone and settled under his arm. "Thanks for an amazing evening, Miah."

He toyed with the edge of her sleeve. "It doesn't have to end, you know."

She looked up at him. "I know."

He bent to kiss her temple. "Come back to the lodge with me."

She dragged her knuckles down his cheek, knowing exactly what he meant and wanting it more than she wanted her next breath. She'd stayed at the lodge lots of times. It wouldn't be that strange for David to wake and find her there. But Gray had no poker face, was a terrible liar, and David was way too perceptive for his own good. And staying at the lodge tonight meant an entirely different thing than any time before.

"You won't, will you?" He answered to keep her from having to.

"I don't want to rush." It was all so beautiful and perfect right now, couldn't they just enjoy the status quo for a little longer before they took that next step? Maybe for him, it wasn't any big deal, but for her it was. Huge. Monumental and it was bound to alter everything.

He drew a breath that seemed full of both reluctance and resignation. "I promised you we wouldn't rush. But don't forget *you've* got a promise to keep to me."

Yes, she did, and the very thought sent white-hot lava down into the depths of her being.

He looked over, examined her face closely. "You do know what I'm talking about?"

She thought of earlier in the night when he'd said, "I do." Now, it was her turn. "I do."

Miah planted his hand on the seat between them and leaned over to kiss her. She met his lips willingly, touching, tasting, loving the feel of his hot breath and soft mouth. It was the kind of kiss that meant forever and she drank it in, hoping forever was as real as the feel of his lips on hers, as real as the snowflakes dotting the window, and as real as the earth beneath her feet.

While the flurries continued to fall, Miah and Gray drove back to River Rock. Two people who'd finally learned what it was to not only love their son, but each other.

———

The back wall of the hardware store was dedicated to camping and hunting and offered a good supply of fishing gear. Jeremiah was going to spend a small fortune on the top-of-the-line backpack and a goose-down sleeping bag for David. Earl, the store clerk, had pointed out the merits of the lightweight pack. Miah was just choosing a lantern when Earl returned. "You say it's for a twelve-year-old? He'll grow right into this one." Earl patted the backpack as if Miah needed more confirmation about dropping the hundred bucks on it.

"I think I've got everything." He followed Earl to the front.

Earl took the purchases and placed them on the counter. "One of my employees, he's a senior at River Rock High, just bought this sleeping bag. Going to some hunting cabin this weekend."

Miah stopped digging in his wallet. "Oh yeah?"

"Yeah. Him and his buddy. I overheard them talking. Said they're getting beer on the way." Earl shook his head. "Man, I remember what it was like to be eighteen."

Miah's heart was pounding. Surely it wasn't one of the seniors taking his son. "Just the two of them going? No younger kids?"

Earl pinched the bridge of his nose. "I think he said some of the basketball team was going, but I'm not sure."

Miah's hands were shaking as the nausea unfurled in his stomach. "What's the kid's name? Your employee?"

"Randall. You know him?"

He quickly accessed the details he knew from David. "He have a little brother named Trey?"

Earl shook his head. "No. But his friend does. Markus Billings. The other boy that's going along."

Miah had to close his eyes and count to five before he could say more. There was a white-hot ball of fire in his gut. "I'm pretty sure Randall and Markus are going to Old Man Carver's hunting cabin. And the basketball boys going with them are from the junior high."

Earl's face paled, the smile disappearing. "What?"

Someone yelled from the back corner of the store. "Hey, Earl, I'm here."

Earl threw an angry look in the direction of the camping gear. "I'm having a talk with that boy now."

Miah motioned with his thumb. "That's Randall?"

Earl nodded, but when Miah flew away from him, Earl hollered, "Wait."

But Miah was a soldier on a mission. His target lay somewhere in the back of the store. He rounded a curve so fast, he nearly took out a display of rope. Sound intensified around him. He heard the squeak of tennis shoes and knew he'd almost reached his target. One more corner and there he was. Tall, skinny, wearing a green shirt with the hardware store's logo on the breast pocket. Randall. Target acquired. Miah gave half a glance behind the kid who'd been stacking water bottles on a cardboard display. First, the boy turned in greeting, but when he saw the murderous look on Miah's face, his grin faded quickly.

Miah's fingers dug into the material of the kid's shirt and with one quick shove, the boy was against the wall, feet dangling beneath him. "You were taking alcohol on a camping trip with a bunch of twelve-year-olds?" The words were audible, but only barely, through gritted teeth.

"What? No. No, I swear." The kid clamped his hands over Miah's as if he could pry his way free.

Earl finally caught up to them. "Are you going to Old Man Carver's hunting cabin or not?"

At least Miah had backup. Earl wasn't calling the cops on him.

The boy continued to dangle. "Yeah, but we're not taking—"

Miah shoved him higher on the wall.

Earl stepped closer. "I heard you bragging about it, Randall. I think it's best you come clean; this is a decorated war veteran and I'd guess he knows how to hide a body. His son was one of the boys going."

Randall's eyes had rounded to the point where Miah wondered if they'd pop right out of his skull. The kid shook his head. "I'm sorry. I'm really sorry. The beer was just for me and Markus. We figured no one would be checking up on us, and the kids would all be busy roasting marshmallows and stuff."

Judging by the look on Randall's face, Miah'd made his point. He lowered the kid to the ground. "This is what you're going to do. You're going to call and cancel that trip. You're going to apologize to the parents, and you're never going to offer to take those kids again, you got it?"

Randall nodded furiously and started breathing again when Miah released his hold.

Earl placed a calming hand on Miah's shoulder. "I'll see that he makes the calls."

Miah nodded. "Appreciate it."

Earl guided him back to the front of the store. Earl hadn't tried to stop him, but he obviously didn't want the situation to escalate any further. "He's got a truck to unload and was going to get out of here at six to get ready for the trip. As soon as he's done with the truck, I'll have him sit down and call those parents."

Miah cast a glance at his watch. It was after four now. David was probably home from school and Gray would be leaving the lodge soon to get ready for their date at the Neon Moon.

"You want me to refund your money on the camping gear?" Earl started taking things from the bags.

"Nah. We'll be going soon enough. Once it warms up a little more. I'll keep everything."

Earl replaced the lantern in the sack. "Sorry about this."

"Not your fault." But Miah couldn't help but wonder if this was a harbinger of things to come. He was raising a boy. And boys found trouble. Sometimes, they didn't even mean to, but trouble abounded in the realms of boyhood. David was a tween-ager. It could only get worse from here.

Earl pointed down the aisle in Randall's direction. "He really is a good kid."

Miah chuckled. "Good kid, bad idea."

The two shook hands and Miah left. Now all he had to do was figure out how to tell David his camping trip was canceled.

He drove home in silence without even the radio to keep him company. The weather had warmed to a comfortable forty-five degrees, as if the weatherman were taunting him.

When he pulled into the drive, he spotted Gray, and his stomach did that tightening thing he was becoming more and more used to. She wore jeans, a vintage T-shirt that was too worn to read, and her hair was tucked behind her ears. One hand clamped on the railing at the foot of his porch stairs. She shook the railing back and forth and the motion made her entire body move.

He stopped the truck and watched while she tested the stability of his railing. When she saw him, her smile was bright, full, and just for him. He'd turned her concentration into a beaming grin, and blast it all if he didn't want to do that over and over every day of his life. Take all of Gray's seriousness and turn it upside down. She needed him. As a counterbalance. And he needed her for everything and then some.

She placed a hand to her forehead when the sun hit her. "This needs to be tightened."

His fingers itched to crawl over her skin. Miah moved in closer, snagging her by the waist in one arm. "Is that so?"

Her full concentration left the banister and landed on him.

His body hummed like a race car in response. He'd like to follow this train of consciousness for a while, see where it led, but there were other things that took precedence.

"We need to talk."

She blinked. "What's up?"

He sat down on the stairs and she followed his lead. "David's camping trip."

"He can't wait. He's been asking Caleb all about building a campfire, and he's raided your pantry for marshmallows and graham crackers."

"Gray, there's not going to be a camping trip." Miah filled her in on the situation, his reaction and Earl's response. "Luckily, I'm not banned from the hardware store. I'm also not in jail for assaulting a minor. So, on those fronts, we can call the incident a success."

She dropped her head into her hands, then let her fingers glide through the strands of hair that had fallen forward. She made two fists at the back of her head, holding her hair off her face. "How do we tell him?"

"Tell me what?" David closed the lodge door behind him and stepped out onto the porch.

Miah's mouth hung open. He knew all the words were in there, they just weren't working their way forward. The phone rang, its sound muffled through the door, and David bolted. "I'll get it."

Miah and Gray stood to follow him in. Gray slipped her hand into Miah's as they walked.

David listened as they both watched his face go from young excitement to utter disappointment. Even his posture seemed to curl under the news. When he sat the phone on the kitchen counter, he said, "Trip's canceled." And with that, he sighed and trudged past them. "I'm going up to my room to read."

Caleb stepped into the kitchen. He did a quick scan of Gray and Miah and said, "Who died?"

"Not helping, Caleb."

Caleb shrugged and went to the refrigerator to stare inside.

Gray checked the kitchen doorway to make sure David was gone. "His trip was canceled because Miah found out the older boys were planning to take beer along with them."

Caleb grinned. "Dude, he is so gonna hate you."

Miah braced his hands against the butcher-block counter of the kitchen island. "Not. Helping."

Caleb popped the top on the root beer he'd grabbed from the fridge. "You're not going to tell him, are you?"

Miah looked at Gray, who looked at Miah, then they both looked at Caleb. The younger man shook his head. "Don't admit anything. It's bad enough the trip went south. But for it to be his fault . . ."

Gray shook her head. "It's not David's fault."

Caleb's shoulder tipped up. "Sure it is. His dad is the one who found out."

Miah buried his face in his hands. His fingers smelled like Gray, but he forced the quick, hot image from his mind. Through his digits he muttered, "This is a disaster."

"David will be fine." Caleb drained the drink and spun on his barstool to toss it into the trash. "Let it rest for a day or two. Then, if you have to tell him, do it. But not now; it's all too raw."

Was he actually considering taking parenting advice from his twenty-five-year-old brother? Then again, Caleb was almost as close to David's age as he was to Miah's. Maybe he had a point.

He looked to Gray for her thoughts on the subject, but the blank stare said it all. She was as clueless as he on how to handle this.

Caleb rolled his eyes. "Look, I'll put the phone on silent, so no one can call him tonight. You guys go have your date and I'll hang here with the science geek. I'll corrupt him with the new RPG game I bought."

Gray's eyes narrowed. "Rating?"

Caleb shook his head. "E for everyone."

She did her mom-nod and settled into her seat waiting for Miah to make the call. Man, this stuff was tough.

"That's nice, Caleb, really. And I know you only bought that game because you know it's one David likes, but I think it would be better for him to go out with us tonight."

Gray perked up. "Yes. I agree."

Caleb lifted his hands and dropped them. "Whatever, but he's not going to want to go."

"Then we'll stay here."

"Yeah," Caleb smiled. "Make it worse for him. He's been working like a dog to get you two together."

Miah tapped the counter. "We'll let David decide."

Caleb hunched over a hunting magazine on the counter. "Okay, but when he turns you down, let him know I'm ordering cheeseburger pizza."

Miah stopped at the door and faced his brother. "You're bribing him." Then, his face split into a smile. "Thanks, Caleb. You're the best."

"I know I am."

Thirty minutes later, and after Caleb was exceedingly right about . . . everything, Miah and Gray sat down to dinner at the Neon Moon.

———

Caleb stood motionless, his attentions drifting to the good deed he'd done earlier in the evening by offering to babysit David. They'd eaten an entire pizza and David had slaughtered him at the new video game. He'd be inside right now requesting an opportunity for payback, but he'd been drawn to the front yard when he heard something rustling against the trashcan. A furry little thief entered his line of vision. It was dark, but he easily identified the family of raccoons that had learned a delicious buffet of food awaited them in the trash bins by the side of the house. Caleb spotted one just as it trekked through the yard on the scattered water puddles and remaining snow. Everything had still seemed frozen solid until the sun peeked out in the early afternoon and started melting the world around. He'd take the snowmobile out tomorrow if it was cold. Since they were pushing the end of February, who knew if he'd get another chance. He placed a block on top of the trash and went back into the house.

Just inside the doorway, Caleb stopped. The hair on the back of his neck prickled, and he'd been in combat long enough to know something was off.

He took a couple steps deeper into the lodge where he waited, listening. Could someone have slipped in while he was outside? His eyes scanned the room. If it was an intruder, he'd better have either a big gun or combat training. Though Caleb's right side still wasn't up to par with the rest of him, he would be lethal against an unarmed assailant. Then, he remembered David was upstairs and a new set of scenarios shot through his mind. "David?" he yelled, hoping the kid would hear him and come to the top of the stairs. As he waited, eyes still working the room, he made his way to the fireplace and pretended to poke at the embers while testing the handle of the wrought-iron poker. It was good. Now, he had a weapon. He turned with it in his hand. "Hey, David, come down for a minute." The boy would be safer by Caleb's side.

He counted one second. Two. Three. No answer from upstairs. Fear and adrenaline worked through him, heightening his senses. "David!" This time, it was a stern warning, but still, no answer.

Then, he heard something outside. A deep rumble, then a hum, and he knew there was no intruder in the house. Someone hadn't snuck in; David had snuck out.

Caleb loped to the door and swung it open just as he saw the flash leaving the edge of the property headed for the lake.

———

Gray scooted a little closer in the seat of the truck as Miah pulled out of the Neon Moon. They were holding hands and to Gray it felt like things were beginning to be the way they should have been all evening. It had been a good night. They'd made the best of it knowing they had an upset twelve-year-old at home to deal with. But relationships couldn't be based solely on the one thing that bound them together, and she knew that. They both did, and were working hard at keeping proper perspective. David was the center of her universe. But Miah was the center of her world, and they both needed to take up a certain amount of real estate in her heart. They needed to do this, needed to be a good, solid couple. Because if David was the only thing that brought them together, he could easily rip them apart, and though Gray was no expert in the relationship department, she knew that was an unbalanced path to tread. For all of them. So, she and Miah had gone on their date as planned. She hoped, she *prayed* they hadn't made the wrong decision.

Miah's phone buzzed in his pocket. He'd kept it handy all evening in case Caleb called. He stretched back, pulled the phone from his hip, and answered. "Caleb, calm down. What's going on?"

Miah listened and Gray watched the horror spread across his face. Something was wrong. "Follow him. Take the four-wheeler. We'll find your tracks." Miah hung up and placed the phone in his jacket pocket.

Gray clutched his hand as he pressed his foot onto the gas pedal and the truck leapt forward. She couldn't ask, couldn't even get a coherent thought to form in her mind.

"David took off."

Gray tried to sort the words. "What do you mean? Ran away?"

Miah's eyes were a strange glow in the dashboard lights. "He left on the snowmobile."

Gray's heart stopped and when Miah reached for her, she clung to him.

"Caleb's on the four-wheeler. We'll find him, Gray."

———

Caleb stopped the four-wheeler and cut the engine. Two snowmobile paths stretched before him, and in the dim light, it was impossible to tell which one was fresh. The first led up the hill toward Stacey's house. The second went down to the cove. Caleb closed his eyes and listened. Snow could easily bounce sound around, making it difficult to track, but if he got lucky, he'd be able to tell which way the snowmobile was headed. Above him, an owl howled. The water lapped along the frozen coastline of the lake; wind whispered through the pine trees. And nothing else. He should be hearing the snowmobile's engine. Scenarios shot into his mind. Could David have made it to Stacey's house? Maybe. He wasn't more than four or five minutes behind him. If he was at Stacey's house, he was safe. Caleb hopped back on the four-wheeler and started the engine. He did two donuts in the cove path, making it obvious for Miah which way he'd gone, and opened the throttle to full bore, bouncing and jostling with every hidden rock and root on the trail.

He skated the edge of the lake following what he now knew to be the right tracks. Powder-white snow mixed with mud along the water's edge, where a snowmobile had recently cut into the soft ground. This was fresh; he had to be getting closer. What scared him was that beyond the next turn, there was no more trail to follow. The rocky coastline rose into a hillside that surrounded the cove. The snowmobile would never make a slippery climb like that. Since the four-wheeler sat higher, Caleb had to plow through snow-dusted vegetation. The chill in the wind burned his face as overgrown tree limbs sliced into his cheeks. He dodged as much as possible, trying to keep his eyes focused ahead to catch a glimpse of David or the snowmobile. When he rounded the last turn that opened up to a C-shaped cove—usually one of Caleb's favorite places—he realized things were much worse than he could have imagined.

There was no sign of David or the snowmobile anywhere. And the tracks ended.

He jumped off the four-wheeler and did a quick 360. Nothing. Could he have missed him? He cut the engine and was just deciding to go back up to Stacey's house when he saw that the tracks didn't end. They curved and headed straight out onto the cove.

Caleb ran to the edge of the water. "David?"

A tiny voice met him. "I'm . . . here."

He took two steps out onto the ice and spotted the boy's head. David was in water up to his chest and he was clinging to a broken edge of ice. Between them was a snowmobile-size hole.

"Hang on!" Caleb instructed, forcing his mind to calm, forcing his body to go into survival mode, combat mode. When the ice chunk David was clinging to broke off, Caleb pushed all his training aside. And dived into the frozen lake.

His face hit the cold water first and he had to fight the urge to suck in air at the shock. The water was an unforgiving ice bath, soaking into his clothing, weighing him down. Already, his limbs were burning with a freezing sensation. His face came up out of the water, and he kicked, half expecting his legs to refuse to work. He swam the distance to David, yelling for the boy to hang on. Fear froze David's features. One arm was up out of the water, one shoulder, his head. The rest was beneath. Caleb grabbed him, and just having David in his grasp made the situation better.

"Are you injured?" Caleb said.

David's body was quaking, his ungloved hand red and trying to grip the ice beside him. His fingernails had dug in until they were bleeding.

"N-n-no."

"David, I want you to listen to me." Caleb judged the distance to the other side of the cove, still ice covered, and decided that was their best option. He drilled his fingers into the snow and found the ice beneath it. His left hand clamped down, his right pressed David into the ice at the edge. "I'm going to lift you and I want you to climb out."

"So . . . cold." David was terrified and possibly going into shock.

Caleb needed him to focus. "David!" He fisted his right hand into the jacket David wore. "Do what I said."

David rallied at the stern order. He braced himself against Caleb and tried to climb.

Caleb pushed, but the boy only moved a few inches higher. David had no strength to pull himself up and Caleb was quickly losing his own strength in the frigid water. If only he could hold on to the ice with his right hand and hoist David with his left, but he knew releasing the ice was a dangerous proposition. He had a good grip on the only solid thing around. Plus, he'd have to let go of both David and the ice to make the switch and that didn't seem smart. If David went under again, he wouldn't come back up.

Caleb maneuvered his body until he was lying as prone as possible. "David, use my body like a ladder and climb out onto the ice. Can you do that?"

David nodded, lips pressed together and turning blue. Caleb's eyes had adjusted to the dark, but the terror coming off of David's body was palpable. Caleb had to get him onto solid ground.

When David began to climb, digging his shod foot into Caleb's leg, Caleb bit back the pain. He grunted, trying to shove David up. They were face-to-face and David burrowed his fingers into Caleb's shoulders in a desperate attempt to escape the icy water. But when his foot slipped, he slid off Caleb's body. Hands groped in the air and Caleb lashed out and grabbed him just before he went under.

Caleb held the boy close and realized trying that again might be the end of both of them. David's cheek was cold against his and the boy's shivering was as constant as any drumbeat he'd ever heard.

David tucked his head deeper into Caleb's coat. "I'm so sorry." At that, Caleb felt the boy release his grip.

He tightened his arm around him. "David, we're gonna get out of this. Okay? Your dad's coming. He'll be here any minute. We just have to hang on for a little while." Caleb's body had begun to shake, too, making it more difficult to hold on to both the ice and David.

"I . . . drowned the . . . snowmobile."

In spite of their circumstances, Caleb found the humor in that. "Yeah, you really did."

"Is my . . . dad . . . gonna be mad at me?" Big, round eyes searched his in the moonlight. Caleb was reminded that kids viewed the world through terms of getting into trouble. This was life or death. Getting into trouble or not made little difference. Surviving was what mattered now.

"No. He won't."

David searched his eyes. "You pr-promise?"

"I swear it. He won't get mad at you. I won't let him."

David's head nodded, but the force of his body shaking made it almost imperceptible.

Caleb's limbs were screaming, his legs, constantly in motion beneath them, were getting hard to feel. He might not be able to hold on much longer. Then, an idea struck him. If it got bad enough, if he knew he couldn't make it out, maybe he could use one solid shove to get David onto the ice. It would be a gamble, but if he was going down anyway, it was worth the risk. He just hoped it wouldn't come to that. But just in case, he'd go ahead and position David for it.

"I want you to turn over so that your back is against my chest. Try to keep your lungs as full of air as you can; it will help you float."

Caleb released his grip just enough for David to pivot. "I . . . won't be able to h-hold on."

"That's okay, David. I'll have you."

Once in position, the two were on their backs, heads bobbing in the icy water. David whispered, "Are we gonna d-die?"

Caleb's heart squeezed; it seemed the only heat still left in his body surrounded the muscle that kept blood moving through his blood vessels. "Look up, David."

He felt the boy angle, his neck tipping back.

"You see that bright star that twinkles?"

"Yes."

"My brother Isaiah once told me that star is the Eye of God. And as long as you can look up and see it, He's looking down at you."

When a hard wind slammed against them, David's quaking intensified. A few moments later, he calmed and Caleb got a better grip on the boy. He could feel his body going lax.

"David! Listen to me; I've been in far worse situations than this one. I've been in combat where there was no way out, you hear me?" He shook him a little.

"Y-yes."

But Caleb could hear it in his voice; he was giving up the fight.

"As long as you can look up and see the Eye of God, you're not going to die. Understand?"

No answer.

He shook his shoulders again. "Can you see it?"

David's head tilted. "Yes."

"What's it mean?"

"It means we . . . we're not going to die."

"That's right." Caleb needed to keep him talking. This was quickly getting dire, and if David released his grip on the ice and Caleb was supporting his entire weight, he didn't know how long he would hold out. He was really grateful Gray had been a tyrant about his therapy, though. If he hadn't been working so hard to strengthen his right side, they'd already be dead.

David's body stopped shaking, sending panic through Caleb. "You okay there?" He shook the boy, causing water to come up onto his cheeks. They were riding lower in the cold water. Caleb knew his body was giving out with each sharp pain that shot through his limbs; eventually his body's distress would take over, he'd go numb and that would be the end.

"I . . . can see the star."

"Good, David. You keep looking at it."

There had been other times in his life when he'd considered the possibility of dying. Once, in a firefight gone wrong, he'd made a call to run into a building under fire to get to a guy in his unit who had been shot. He'd made a choice. He'd been at peace with it. If he died, it was to protect another human being. It was to give all he had to make sure someone else came home. He'd thought over his life, most of it spent on foreign soil, and he hadn't been sorry or filled with regret. And he'd supposed that it was an all right time to check out. But this was different.

David wasn't just some kid who deserved a future. David was his own blood, his nephew. His brother's child. If Caleb had to die for him, that'd be better than okay. Caleb looked at the sky. He knew his thoughts were getting cloudy, the icy water of the lake stealing his equilibrium and creating the sensation of needles shoving deeper and deeper into his flesh. Off in the distance, he saw a flash of light. Sounds, muffled, but coming closer. A voice.

Caleb knew he was losing his grip on David. "When I push," he said, "I want you to climb with all you've got, David. We get one shot at this. Don't you dare let me down."

David's breathing increased. He was readying to climb.

"Don't worry. It's all gonna be okay." And with that, Caleb took a deep breath and shoved David up out of the water as his own head went under. Legs and tennis shoes above him scurried onto the glassy white surface. Caleb smiled, his body giving up the last bits of energy it held.

He sank deeper and deeper, the water feeling warm now, not cold, and a peace fell over him unlike anything he'd ever known. The last thing he saw was the Eye of God.

CHAPTER 15

Miah was screaming Caleb's name. Gray'd never heard a more horrified sound. They'd made it to the water's edge and Miah had snagged David just as he was coming up. He deposited David in her hands and ran back, yelling for her to get him into the truck and bring him the rope from the back. She tried to obey, but her thoughts were on David. He was pale, shaking, and soaking wet.

He pushed away from her. "I'm okay. I'm okay, Gray. Go! They need you." And with more strength than her son should have, he shoved her into motion.

Gray grabbed the rope and tied it off on the front of the four-wheeler.

Her hands were shaking, mostly from fear, partly from the icy water that now drenched the front of her clothing where she'd pulled David into her arms. They'd already called an ambulance, but knowing David was in the truck with the heater on helped her to do what Miah needed. She jerked on the rope to test its knot and ran out toward him. He'd stripped from his coat and boots and just as she got the rope in his hands, he disappeared into the water. First she thought he'd fallen or that more of the ice shelf had broken off, but she looked at the boots and coat and realized, this had been his plan.

He came up once, slinging water and pulling a deep lungful of air, then, he was down again.

A dead silence rose from the water where she stared down at the rippling waves, perched on her hands and knees. "Please," she pleaded for them to appear as icy wind smacked the side of her face. From behind her, the truck's headlights cast a yellow-tinged glow on the hole where Miah and Caleb had disappeared.

She searched the water, her body frozen, and breathing white puffs of air that dissolved into the atmosphere. Her shadow darkened one section of the water, so she shifted until her shadow lay across the bumpy snow of the frozen cove and she scanned the black abyss again. When she saw nothing, Gray stretched her body out on the snow-blanketed ice. Should she reach in? Just before she made the decision to, the rope moved. She grabbed it.

This time, two heads came up out of the water. She began frantically pulling the rope that gathered at her feet with each tug. Miah shoved Caleb toward her and she gripped him by the shoulders, digging her fingers into his water-soaked clothing. She pulled with all her strength until she felt something tearing in one shoulder blade. Adrenaline spiked through her system and she clamped her hands deeper into his coat and this time when she pulled, she screamed. The sound bounced off the rocky cliffs and snowcapped hills around them. She squeezed her eyes shut, releasing all her energy, all the power she possessed, into her arms and shoulders. Her back curved and provided an anchor for the task. Her legs spread and she forcefully dug her heels into the ground like two ice picks. When Caleb was on solid ground, she shoved him off her. Miah was still in the water.

She dropped to her knees. Miah shook from the cold and she could tell he was barely hanging on, his hands shaking and trying to maintain their grip on the icy ledge. His flesh was bright red and as she dropped to help him, gripping his body like she had Caleb's, she felt him slip. "No!" she screamed and the sound fortified her strength.

His golden eyes met hers above the blackened water. For a moment, he stayed right there and she had to wonder if the power they needed to get him out was already gone, used up on saving David and Caleb. But something shifted in his gaze and suddenly, he was pulling himself up. Gray grabbed him by the shoulders and jerked. From her periphery, she saw one of his legs, water covered, flop up onto the snow and ice. She readjusted her grip, clamping her hands around his midsection and rolling him up onto the ledge.

He was on his feet in no time. "Go to the truck. Check on David. The ambulance can't make it down here. We have to get back to the house."

It was only then that she realized Caleb hadn't moved. His lifeless body lay on the white snow. Stunned, Gray turned from him, using the headlights as a guide and forcing herself not to focus on the possibilities.

Miah dragged his brother to the edge of the lake and deposited him on the bank. He rolled him onto his back and stripped the coat from his chest.

David opened the truck door for her and she climbed in.

There before them in the yellow glow of the truck's headlights, Miah gave his brother CPR.

———

Gray had watched as a helicopter airlifted Caleb to the hospital. David had been allowed to go in an ambulance so she'd insisted on riding with him. She remained at his side while Miah followed in the truck, still in his soaking wet clothes. She'd had the foresight to grab him a change at the house and had called Charlee and Ian to meet them at the hospital.

Once there, time drifted by slowly, as if in some distorted fun house where mirrors made monsters of normal people. Gray was tired to the bone and knew Miah must be as well. His face was twisted into a frown that seemed as though it would surely stick and remain there for the rest of his life.

Caleb was alive. That's all they'd tell them.

Ian and Charlee met them, and the four of them paced the waiting room while Caleb was being worked on and David was being put into a room. They'd keep him for observation for the night, but the doctor said he thought the boy would be fine.

Gray still felt shell-shocked by the incident and ran the whole thing over and over in her mind as if at some point, she could magically change the outcome. But here they were, once again in a hospital, and this time, they were waiting to hear if Caleb would make it. David would be okay. No permanent damage done, still, she couldn't imagine the psychological ramifications if—God forbid—Caleb didn't pull through.

When the doctor gave the okay, Gray and Miah entered David's room quietly in case he'd fallen asleep.

Gray was breathing hard, and the sound must have roused David. "Is Caleb okay?"

Miah crossed the room and patted his arm. "He'll be fine. Are you okay?"

David closed his eyes. "Yes. I'm sorry."

Gray came around the bed and brushed dark spikes of hair from his face. At least there was color there, on his cheeks, instead of that deathly white he'd been earlier in the evening when she'd watched the paramedics trying to encourage warmth into his stunned system. "It's okay, honey. The only thing that matters is you getting well."

"I lost the snowmobile."

Miah sniffed. "I don't care about that, David."

"Caleb saved me. And half the time, I didn't even think he liked me, but he saved me."

Miah's chin quivered. "He's a real hero, David." She could see that Miah's hands itched to grab David up and hold him in his arms, but Miah restrained his emotions, probably to help keep any panic over the incident at bay.

David nodded. "Are you guys mad at me?"

Miah let a long breath escape from his mouth. "You could have died. You almost died. What was in your head that made you want to go over that water?"

"You said all your friends had done it. If I'm gonna be one of your friends, I just thought . . ."

"David, you don't have to do anything to earn my approval. You're my son. I love you. And driving over the cove was stupid of me but it was when the cove was frozen, not half thawed."

"So, this didn't have anything to do with the camping trip?" Gray asked, because she'd assumed that David had somehow learned the details and was mad at them when he'd left the house.

"Yeah, at first it did. I called Stacey while Caleb was outside and found out why the trip was canceled." He turned away from them. "I figured her brother and the others would blame me. That's okay. I'm used to not having any friends. But I was mad at Miah. Then I was just wanting to prove I wasn't a little kid. Sometimes you guys treat me like I am."

Gray brushed his hair back. He was right. Sometimes they didn't give him the credit he deserved. At twelve, he'd been through more heartache than many people twice his age. "I'll try to be better about that, okay? And you don't ever do something like this again."

His eyes widened, stark against the bed. "I won't."

When his lashes became heavy lines half covering his eyes, he yawned. "Pretty tired."

Gray turned down the light and kissed his forehead. "Get some rest, David. I'll be right here if you need me."

But David didn't answer. A light snore slipped from his mouth and

Gray motioned for Miah to follow her out of his room so they could talk without disturbing him. "I'm going to stay with him tonight," she said.

He nodded.

She waited for him to lean toward her and kiss her cheek, or squeeze her shoulder, but he didn't. Just stared, blankly, as if he wasn't sure what to do or say. "You okay?"

His chin dipped again. "Sure. Listen, Caleb will probably be in for a few days. Could David stay with you? I need to be available in case he needs me."

"Sure." But there was something in Miah's tone she didn't like. She brushed it off. It had been a long night for all of them.

He sank his hands into his pockets. "I'll bring him some clothes over tomorrow morning. I can pick you up here and take you home."

"Okay." But a strange detachment floated in the air, creating a cavern between her and Miah. It was a sensation powerful enough to cause the hair on her neck to prickle. Still, she waited for a touch, a hug, anything. But Miah's shoulders were square, his elbows out, hands firmly planted in his jeans.

He motioned with his elbow behind him. "I'm going to check on Caleb."

She nodded and watched as he walked down the hall. *It's been a long, hard night*, she told herself over and over again. But that didn't settle the apprehension in her stomach. As Jeremiah disappeared around the corner, she had to wonder if tonight had changed everything for them.

———

Miah was at Caleb's side when he first opened his eyes. He got the chance to give his brother's hand a firm squeeze just before a nurse ushered Miah into the hall. "We'll let you know when you can come back in," she'd said.

So Miah waited. His fingers finding their way together, one hand grasping the other, remembering the sensation of holding his brother's hand moments ago. He could have lost him. He almost did lose him.

A lump rose in Miah's throat; his nose tingled. He made his way down the hall to a restroom and ducked inside. Without bothering to turn on the light, he locked the door and anchored his hands on the edges of the sink. He didn't stop the tears from coming. Tears were a release, something he understood from the army. Tears cleared the mind after elevated stress; it was the body's way of rebalancing.

At the lake's edge, he'd held his brother's lifeless body in his hands. He knew that feeling . . . when life left. He'd carried a dead soldier once. Life was so much more than a beating heart. It was more than nerves and neurons, muscles and brain matter. It was a soul and a spirit. It was magical. And once it was gone, it was gone.

Miah's eyes had adjusted to the darkness. He studied himself in the mirror, barely a shard of illumination, but it was enough, the shine on his cheeks catching the light and holding it. Right there, he made a promise. Do whatever he needed to do to protect Caleb. To protect David. Regardless of the number of tears it might cause him.

Miah made his way back to his brother's room. The doctor spoke with him briefly in the hall, then held the door open so Miah could go inside.

Caleb was hooked up to a variety of machines that made strange beeping noises. He played with the end of a piece of surgical tape that held an IV in place. Miah went to him, a half smile on his face, and dropped a hand on Caleb's arm. His skin was pale and to the touch he still felt cold, as if they were having to thaw him from the inside out.

"Doc says you'll be fine." Waves of relief continued over Miah. He supposed that would happen each time he repeated those words.

Caleb nodded. "Yeah. He told me that, too."

"You could have died, Caleb."

Caleb mumbled, "I'm not sure I didn't."

Miah swallowed hard.

Caleb attempted a smile and met his gaze. "I didn't mind the idea of dying. It would have been to save David."

Miah pressed his lips together. The night's disaster had stolen every bit of his own energy. He wanted a long shower—where he could lean an arm against the cold tile and thank God this had turned out the way it had—and he wanted a good night's sleep. But Caleb needed to talk through this. Miah understood, but didn't love reliving it. He did love the fact that his brother was going to be okay.

Caleb had started explaining about finding David and everything that had happened before Miah arrived. "When I got under that water, I saw my future. I saw a life and kids of my own and I . . . I didn't want to die. Suddenly, I had something to live for and it was nothing I'd ever known about or even imagined. I had kids, Miah. A boy and a girl with blond hair and I was watching them through the cabin window on my property. They were by one of the hot springs and they were playing with a frog."

Miah could see the confusion playing across his brother's features, but his eyes were clear and sure. "What are you saying, Caleb? You had a vision?"

"I don't know. Most people see their past flash before them. Not their futures. You remember what Isaiah used to tell us about the Eye of God?"

"Sure." Miah remembered; Caleb had pointed it out to him not long ago when Miah himself had been searching for answers.

Caleb leaned up on the white bed, causing the scent of bleach to surge around them. "I was ready to die, Miah. Ready. Thought it through, was glad to go if it would save David."

Miah tried to swallow the lump in his throat. "Yeah."

"I had no fight because I'd already resolved myself to dying. And then, under the water, I saw light."

"The headlights." Miah drew a metal chair beside Caleb's bed. It was as much to hold on to as it was to sit in.

"Maybe. I saw light and inside it was my future. And suddenly, I wanted to live."

"Good choice." Miah's throat closed. "You saved my son. He would have died if you hadn't been there."

"We're brothers. Any one of us would take a bullet for the other."

Miah smiled at the same words he'd once said to Caleb.

"I didn't do anything you wouldn't have done for me."

Caleb reached his hand out for his brother. Miah closed his hand in his then gripped Caleb by the shoulder. "I love you, Caleb."

"Love you too, bro."

———

Gray climbed into Miah's truck only barely noticing the tarp in the back. It had been a rough night on a vinyl reclining chair in David's hospital room. "He's doing great," she said, through the fog of morning after little sleep. "They're releasing him today, late afternoon."

Miah handed her a steaming cup.

"Cocoa?" she asked, expectantly.

"Coffee. Came from the gas station."

"Oh." She tried to hide her disappointment.

Miah pulled the truck out onto the road and it was then that Gray noticed the stiffness she'd seen last night. It was still there, creating a crust around Jeremiah. She'd hoped whatever it was would be gone, and that warm, touchy Miah would be back. That didn't seem to be the case.

Rather than ask, she cast a sidelong glance at his profile. His chiseled features made a handsome silhouette in the morning sunlight. He suddenly felt far away from her, like a photograph from long ago, something one gazes upon, but something that can't be reached, can't even be touched. "What's going on, McKinley?"

His hands tightened on the wheel, loosened, then tightened again as if he were having a whole internal dialogue that ran rampant through his mind but didn't bother to slip out of his mouth. "I've been doing some thinking about all this."

"What does that mean?" She recognized that detached look. Now, she remembered from where. It was nearly thirteen years ago when he'd called their night together a great send-off. And that was when the first threads of panic set in.

"David. Caleb was right. I shouldn't have taken him away from you. He needs to be with you where he's safe." His voice was smooth, almost practiced.

Cold fire shot into her gut, causing her stomach to roil. She craned her neck and there under the edge of the tarp was David's blanket from his bed. The truck was full of . . . "What's back there?" she snapped.

"Just hear me out. David needs to be somewhere stable. He needs a mom—"

"He needs us both. Don't you even think about ditching us right now. Don't do it, Miah. I swear, you will ruin him." She couldn't breathe. She was going to throw up. Gray pushed the window button and threw the contents of the coffee cup out into the cold morning air.

"You said I couldn't ruin him. You said he was strong."

"He's not strong enough for this. Miah, I'm begging you. This will destroy him. Please." She had to make him understand. David loved him. She loved him. No, no, this wasn't happening. She wouldn't let their future, *David's* future, be ripped from him again.

Miah sailed into her driveway and threw the truck into park. "I almost killed him, Gray."

"That wasn't your fault."

He turned and gripped her shoulder. "Whose fault was it? It's my lodge, my snowmobile. Everywhere I look there is nothing but danger for him."

"Miah, you're not making any sense. He's a kid. Those are all things kids do."

"Not kids like David. You told me yourself that it was all new to him. He's used to museums and the symphony. Those are safe, Gray. All

I can offer him is opportunity to get hurt, and maybe next time we won't get so lucky. Maybe next time—"

His hand bit into the flesh at her shoulder, but it paled by comparison to the despair unleashed in her heart. But she could make him understand; she had to. "David ran off. You couldn't have stopped him. He's going to make choices, and the best we can do is try to be there to help him know which choices to make."

Miah released her. "He's better off with you."

No. The very thought that he could walk away right now caused heat to rush over her from the neck down. Suddenly, she was light-headed, ready to pass out as if his words had stolen the blood and oxygen from her brain. She shook her head to clear the fear from her mind. "I know it scared you. Miah, it scared me, too, but he's your son and he needs you now more than ever. He needs you to do the right thing."

"I am." He stormed out of the truck and slammed the door.

Stubborn McKinley pride. She followed him and gripped his arm as he began untying the tarp. "Miah, don't leave us again." Us. So many years before, on that fateful night, with her clothes still drenched and her heart filled with hope, he'd destroyed everything she'd seen in their future. He'd run a wrecking ball through her heart. This was just the same and as she watched him refuse to even look at her, she knew.

Miah was doing this. Period. There was no stopping him because he was a McKinley and once his mind was made up, that was it. He was leaving them. Leaving her. Once again, Jeremiah was shattering her heart and this time he'd shatter David's as well.

She threw her hands in the air. "Unload his stuff," she ordered, then stomped into her house, trying to outrun the tears and the pain that had stayed dormant for thirteen years. But there was no escaping it. She went into the bathroom and shut the door. There in the mirror was a scared, alone, eighteen-year-old girl with a problem that was bigger than the world. And there was no one to help her through it.

Beyond the bathroom door, she heard him filling her house with David's things. How many nights had she cried back while she was pregnant, and alone, a tiny, innocent child growing in her stomach? A child who would look to her for nourishment, life, hope. Somehow, she'd survived those desperate months. She would survive this. She had to; in just a few hours, she'd have a brokenhearted twelve-year-old boy here and he'd need her to be strong.

When she knew Miah was finished placing David's belongings in her house, she steeled herself and exited the bathroom to find him standing by the front door. Her voice was a rasp when she said, "It's not too late to change your mind, Miah."

"I'll call to check on him later today." Between his fingers, he gripped the stuffed Ninja Turtle.

She pointed at the door. "Then go. If you're not willing to fight for him, you don't deserve him."

He took a step forward and she had to remind herself this was the man who'd broken her heart. His eyes were misty, his mouth tipped into the saddest frown, so sad that if she wasn't so angry, so furious, she could almost be persuaded to invite him to sit down, to talk it through. But the fact remained, Jeremiah was giving up on them.

He placed the stuffed animal gently on the couch as if it might break, then his gaze scanned over the things he'd brought in. A stack of manga books, a video game system, a backpack. Haunted eyes landed on Gray and as he took a step toward her, she put both hands out to stop him.

"Gray," he pleaded, the single word dragging out as if it alone could speak volumes.

"Unless you're willing to take all of this back to the lodge, just go." Her voice was solid, firm, riding on the fury that fueled her. She could collapse once he was gone, but right now, she had to be strong. Especially since he was running away.

He lifted and dropped his hands in a gesture that read utter despair. "I don't know what to do," he whispered, his eyes locked on the floor.

Part of her heart fractured and swirled around in her mind. She knew that feeling, knew it so well, but that couldn't matter because he was taking the easy way out. Instead of stepping toward him, she crossed her arms over her chest and waited for him to go.

A solitary tear dropped from his face and she watched it land on her floor. Miah tilted his head back and stared up at the ceiling. "I'm doing what's right for David."

And now he was an expert? She wanted to scream at him, but he didn't look solid enough to take the abuse. He swayed as he reached for the door.

A tiny part of her wanted to move forward, just go to him, make him see he was wrong about this. David needed him. Needed to be at the lodge. He'd grown in the weeks he'd been there, branching out of his comfort zone and thriving. But she wouldn't. Gray had never had many people she could count on. Her nana, of course, until the stroke when Nana reverted to childlike behavior and Gray had to be the grown-up. That was okay; she'd loved her nana and nothing had ever changed that. She'd been able to count on Angela—as long as Gray didn't reveal David's existence to his birth father. Gray had herself to depend on. She'd thought she had Miah, but just like last time—when she needed him most—he was saying good-bye.

Once again, David was all she had, and this time no one was going to take him away.

———

After two weeks, David had settled into a routine at Gray's house. A routine that included contact with his biological father in snippets of time. Miah would drop by every other day after school and visit, always with a too-bright smile and a too-lax posture. Trying so hard to stitch up some of the wounds he'd caused. She'd watched David carefully in the days since the snowmobile accident. Though he was heartbroken over Miah, he seemed strong. She, on the other hand, was miserable. Heartsick and lonely. Of course, having David there was the biggest blessing she could ever hope for, but still her body ached for Miah. It wasn't natural. It wasn't normal. But what in their relationship had been?

Miah was still larger than life, brighter than the sun and stronger than the granite deep in the Ozark Mountain. And she supposed she'd always love him. But she'd decided to stop wasting her time on a fairy tale with no hope of a happy ending.

She stepped out of the bedroom and held up a dress for David's inspection. "How about this one?"

He rose from the floor in front of the fireplace to lean on his elbow. Volume 49 of his manga book shifted in his hand. One shoulder tipped up. "Eh."

She stared at the floral thing in her hands, seeing it through the eyes of a twelve-year-old. "Kind of hideous, huh?"

"You want to sabotage your night, go with that one."

She dropped the dress and returned to her closet. Earlier in the day, she'd run into the "cat doctor," as David liked to call him. He'd been friendly, genuinely excited to see her, and for some strange reason when he asked her out for a second date, she agreed. She still couldn't quite wrap her mind around why she'd so quickly said yes. After all, he'd bored her to tears on their first date, and the only interesting thing that had happened was her chance encounter with the McKinley clan.

Her fingers reached into the closet and closed around the dress she'd worn on Valentine's night when David had coerced a town into helping him throw his parents together. Her fingers trailed along the soft material as she remembered Miah holding her, his fingertips electric against her skin. He'd sworn to her she'd never lose David. And she hadn't. He was here to stay. What she'd lost was the man she loved. But that wasn't her doing; it was his. She was over the mad part of it. What good did anger do for a person, anyway? It only poisoned the body. No, she wouldn't stay angry with him. He'd jumped into fatherhood head-first, enthusiasm bursting, hope full. But he'd quickly learned that kids didn't come with an instruction manual and bad things could happen at any time. Parenthood was terrifying.

On the floor of her closet were the spike-heeled boots she'd been wearing when they'd rescued David and Caleb. She'd scraped the sides and had broken off one of the heels. Still, she hadn't been able to throw them away. But today, she felt stronger, so she snatched them up and deposited them in the trashcan in the corner of her bedroom. It was a new day. It was time to move on. She'd spent too many years wishing things had been different with Miah. Too many nights wondering what might have happened if he hadn't left for LA back when they were teenagers, when it seemed the whole world stretched before them, ready to be lived and relished.

Now, she just wanted to move on with her life. She *did* have a bright future. His name was David. And David understood, too. Which was miraculous, in Gray's mind. He'd told her he knew Miah loved him, but being a full-time dad was probably scary and he'd tried, but he just . . . wasn't that good at it yet.

Gray shoved the Valentine's dress to the back of her closet and pulled out a simple black one that was cut to fit her body and landed just above the knees.

In the living room, David had returned to his book.

"How about this one?"

He inspected it with narrowed eyes. "Yep."

The smile meant approval and Gray breathed relief. "See? I'm not trying to sabotage it."

"Yeah. Keep telling yourself that."

"Okay, mister. That's enough. Make sure you have your stuff ready, or I'm leaving you here."

"Stacey and Rick are expecting me."

Stacey's brother, Rick, and David had hung out together quite a bit in the last two weeks. Apparently, David's antics on the snowmobile had spawned a sort of idol worship with some of the other boys. Horrible how a near tragedy could do that. At least something good had come out of it. Everyone forgot about the camping trip gone wrong, too busy chattering about being in the cold water, the rescue, how the incident made it on to the Laver news.

David had gathered his backpack and stood at the front door when Gray came out dressed and fumbling with her heels. When she realized she'd forgotten her earrings, she spun. "Two seconds."

He groaned. "Ugh. Women."

Gray clamped a hand on the bedroom door and angled to look at him. "Did you learn that from Jeremiah?"

David grinned in answer. "Yep. He said women's clocks are broken so they're not good with time."

She slipped the small hoops into her ears. "What does that mean?"

His eyes sparkled with mischief. "If a woman says it will take her fifteen minutes to get ready that means thirty at least. If she says she's only going to shop five more minutes, it will be an hour because her watch is broken so no matter how long she shops, five minutes is always five minutes away."

"He's completely corrupted you." Maybe she should stay angry a while longer.

David plopped down on the bench on her front porch as she locked the front door. "I'm sorry about everything, Gray. You know, about you and Miah." His face was smooth, the concentration causing a line between his brows.

She sat, too, and pulled him into a side hug. "It just wasn't meant to be," she said. "But we'll both be here for you. That's what matters. And we both love you." That, she was certain of. That was undeniable. David would have them for the rest of his life. One day, she'd find a good man who could be a good stepdad for David. And she supposed one day, Miah would marry. The thought of him loving another woman bit into her heart. But it was inevitable.

David watched her for several seconds. The sun had set behind them, its last glow throwing an orangey hue onto the yard. He pointed to the sky. "See that star?"

She followed his gaze. "The bright one that twinkles?"

"That's the Eye of God. As long as you can see it, it means He's watching over you. It means everything is going to be okay. It means things are going to work out like they're supposed to."

She squeezed his shoulders. "I'm so proud of you, David. You've been through a lot in the last several months and I'm constantly amazed at your ability to handle all the things thrown your way."

"It's your fault, Gray."

She tilted to look at him.

He smiled, the shine from the streetlight snagging on his dark head. "It's your fault I'm so strong. You've always been there for me. Always. You taught me to never give up. You'll see. Things are gonna work out like they're supposed to."

The image of Miah fanning a billow of smoke in the kitchen at the lodge skittered through her mind. She forced it down into the pit of her stomach where all her sorrows lay in clumps surrounded by the could-have-beens. She smiled through the sorrow, then rested the side of her head on David's, where they could sit for a few minutes and gaze at the Eye of God.

———

Caleb had returned home after four days in the hospital. He'd begged for a couple weeks off from therapy and reluctantly, Miah had agreed. Besides, it hurt too much to see Gray right now, especially here at the lodge. He kept telling himself it would get better, but every time he'd show up at her door, the flu-like pain racked his system anew.

Around the house, things were back to some pseudosense of normalcy even though the house was too quiet without David and Gray lighting up the place. The fact was Miah wanted both of them more than he wanted his next breath. Unfortunately, his knee-jerk reaction had cost him everything. Now he understood why good parents never, ever gave up on their kids. He wanted to be a full-time dad. And would gladly accept all the risk that came with that title. If only it wasn't too late.

Caleb had cooked spaghetti for dinner. Miah was clearing dishes and knew his younger brother's eyes were on him. Finally, Caleb cornered him at the sink. "Dude, you gotta snap out of it."

Water ran in rivulets down the sink, creating a spaghetti-orange miniwhirlpool at the drain. "Huh?"

Caleb slapped a hand on the counter. "That's what I'm talking about. You're lost, dude. Like a brainless robot going through the motions of daily life, but not feeling any of it."

Not feeling any of it? Was he kidding? Miah felt everything, as if his entire system was in hypersensitive mode. Every pain, every memory, every thought. All of them intensified to the point of torture. Two weeks ago, he almost lost his son permanently. Now, he'd lost not only his son but also the woman he loved. In one night, everything had changed. In one night, his whole world had crumbled. But it wasn't anyone's fault but his own. He'd pushed Gray away. He'd made the call to send David to live with her. He carried the full brunt of the decision. And that choice was eating away at him, like acid corroding his body. And that right there was why he'd never get to carry the full-time dad label where David was concerned. Miah had already blown it.

For the first few days, David wouldn't even talk to him, refused to see him, then one day, Miah had shown up and David was cordial, not friendly, but tolerant. He'd tried to make him understand and David had rallied. But there was a deep hurt in Gray's eyes that opened the wounds that she'd sealed twelve years ago. Kids were more forgiving, he supposed. Gray, well, Gray was Gray and she didn't allow people to trouble the deep waters of her heart. But when someone did, she'd close them off completely. He couldn't blame her. He deserved the treatment he got.

He still loved her. Now, he'd have to live with the pain of his actions. He guessed he deserved that, too. He raised his head to find Caleb snapping his fingers under Miah's nose. "You gotta fix this."

He wrung his hands on a dishtowel. "I don't think I can, Caleb."

"No. You don't get it. I'm not making a suggestion. You and Gray deserve this chance."

"I had my chance. I blew it."

"You totally blew it." Caleb sank his hands in his pockets, head shaking. "She's more than you think she is."

"What?"

Caleb slapped him on the back and started to walk out of the kitchen.

Miah stopped him. "What do you mean?"

His younger brother turned, came back slowly. "Do you have any idea how tedious it was for her to watch me do my therapy? Day after day, exercise after exercise. Constant. Over and over. It would have been boring for a snail."

"I'm not following you." But Miah placed the towel by the sink and anchored his hands on the counter so he could hear Caleb out. If there was any way, any hope . . .

"She doesn't give up as easily as you think. Somewhere in her heart, there's the capacity to forgive you . . . again . . . you're such an idiot, but whatever. She can forgive you, Miah. If she can do that, she can give you another chance."

He shook his head. "Not sure I deserve it. David was still in the hospital and I just loaded up his stuff and dumped it all on her."

"You made a mistake. You're not perfect; you just like to think you are." Caleb's mouth quirked. "Besides, if you don't deserve a second chance, then who does?"

"What?"

Caleb leaned forward on the butcher-block counter. "You've spent your life protecting our country. You put your life on the line so families were free to sleep at night. You protected so others wouldn't have to. If you don't deserve a second chance, who does?"

Miah patted Caleb's forearm. "Not sure it works like that."

Caleb leaned away from him. "I just never thought I'd see you run away."

Miah's fingers clamped on to the edge of the counter. No one could make him mad faster than Caleb. "I'm not—"

"Miah. Gray has loved you her whole life. Don't you think *she* deserves this?"

His hands were going sweaty. "She deserves better—"

"Stop it. Man, for a dude who walks around like God's gift, you really have no self-esteem, do you? Who will love her more? Who will take better care of her? Who do you want to grow old with, Miah? And more importantly, who do you want her to grow old with?"

Miah's face was slick with sweat because, for the first time in two weeks, he was convinced he might not have completely ruined his life. Miah swabbed his face with the dish towel. It smelled like spaghetti sauce. His heart pounded against his chest like a drum, thumping away the moments, ushering in the thought that maybe, just maybe, he could actually fix this. But his mind was a blank. Even the idea that he might still have a chance with Gray caused his muscles to seize up.

There was a knock at the door. It took a moment to register the sound and when Miah finally did, Caleb was already making his way there.

Hope and fear fought inside Miah's chest. Could it be Gray?

Caleb pulled the door open to David and Stacey. "Hey, science nerd."

David grinned. "Hey, meathead. Can I talk to Miah?"

Miah stepped into the living room, his heart floating on hope. David was here. This was the first time he'd come to the lodge since the snowmobile incident. "Come in."

Caleb looked at Stacey. "You want some hot cocoa? Miah made it earlier. We can warm it up in the kitchen while these two talk."

She nodded and pulled her jacket off, then followed Caleb.

David walked into the room, shoulders squared and a serious look on his face. "I'm here to talk to you man-to-man."

"Okay." Miah followed him to the couch and David motioned for him to sit down. He obeyed and watched as David paced the floor in front of him, his hands deep in his pockets. "My mom's out on a date."

Miah lurched forward. "A date?" What? It had only been two weeks.

"Yeah, with that plastic-looking cat doctor who smiles too much. I don't even think those teeth are real; I think he stole 'em from a horse."

A date. Flu-like symptoms rushed his body. Again.

"Here's the thing. She's a really great lady. She doesn't like the cat doctor, not really, she just has her heart hurt and she wants to make it better."

Miah dropped his gaze. "David, I've ruined everything."

He moved over to him, patted Miah's shoulder. "It's okay. You can fix it."

He looked up to find his son's face full of hope. "I ruined things with you, too. I made a really stupid mistake. I thought I was doing the right thing having you move in with Gray. I didn't want to see anything bad happen to you."

David dropped onto the couch beside him. "But it did happen. Not the accident, but you. We lost you. We don't want to lose you, Miah. Mom doesn't either, she just . . . she's so used to having to be strong for everyone else. She's sooooo mad at you, but she really, really in her heart loves you."

"It might be too late."

"I listened to her cry herself to sleep for the first week. Now, she's just pretending like we can move on. But we can't move on. Not without you."

Emotions swelled to the point where Miah could no longer contain them. Here his son was exhibiting more strength than he could muster. Here, his son was trying to repair all of their broken hearts. He pivoted and took David's face in his hands. "Do you remember when I screwed up on the fishing trip? You told me that just because you weren't good at it didn't mean you didn't want to try?"

David nodded, causing Miah's hands to bob up and down. "I want to try, David. I'm not very good at being your dad, but I want to try. I'm so sorry I pushed you away." There were tears streaking Miah's face. David reached up, brushed them off.

"You'll always be my dad." And with those few words, Miah broke. He pulled his son into a hug and held him there while the tears fell.

A few minutes later, Caleb and Stacey came out of the kitchen. "So, what's the game plan?" Caleb said.

Miah stood, brushing the last of the tears from his face.

Caleb pointed to Stacey. "She told me why they came. What's your move, Miah?"

He didn't know. All he could think about was the fact that Gray was on a date and that now he felt the tiniest shred of hope that he could correct things. "Tomorrow—"

David groaned. "Tomorrow? She's out there now. With someone else."

Miah clamped his teeth together, fighting off the images shooting through his mind. "You're right."

David raised his hands and dropped them with a clop. "You gotta go. Now. She's at the Neon Moon."

Miah nodded, but sudden fear stole his focus. Black spots appeared before his eyes and the blood in his veins stopped moving. He was aware of Caleb moving in closer and grabbing his arm.

"He's useless." Caleb dragged him to the front door. "I'll drive him to her. You guys wait at Stacey's house. If this thing goes south, he'll need some recoup time. I'll call you in an hour."

Miah was aware of being led toward his truck. What was he going to do when he got there? It wasn't like they hadn't seen each other; it wasn't like he was some white knight riding in on a horse and rescuing her. This was a disaster of his own making. He wasn't the answer to the problem. He *was* the problem.

"You need to breathe, bro."

Miah sucked a deep breath as if it were a foreign thing. "I don't know what I'm going to say."

Caleb pulled the truck onto the main road. "You love her, right?"

"She already knows I do."

"I guess that's as good a place to start as any."

Miah nodded and counted the minutes until they pulled into the parking lot of the Neon Moon.

CHAPTER 16

Blah, blah, blah. She knew the cat doctor was talking, but all she could hear was *blah, blah, blah.* Vince Evers had launched into another story about how he discovered one of his clients was taking the anxiety pills he'd prescribed for her high-strung schnauzer. When a new Blake Shelton song came on, she perked up. "Oh. I love this song."

He paused for half a second then went on with his story as if his voice were the most incredible thing one could hear. Under her breath, she muttered, "Doesn't even come close to Blake's."

The good doctor blinked his bright blue eyes at her. "What?"

Oops. She toyed with her salad. "Oh, nothing. Just saying again how much I like this new song."

"Right." He smiled and kept talking.

She wondered if it were possible to steal teeth from horses. She'd never noticed how long his were until David mentioned it before she started getting ready. Garish, really. Long and blue-white. Unnatural. She glanced down at her watch to find she'd only been there thirty minutes. *Gah.* Gray let her mind trail back to earlier in the night. Women and broken watches and how David's face lit up sharing the insights on women and time and shopping and suddenly, without any warning, her heart hurt.

When the hair on the back of her neck prickled, she stood. "Would you excuse me for a couple minutes?" She'd seek solitude in the bathroom. By David's estimation, a couple minutes could be fifteen in woman-time. Then she could return to the table and maybe only have to endure another five or so, then, she could go home.

"Absolutely. I'll be right here."

That's what I'm afraid of. She turned to go to the restroom and slammed into a chest. Her eyes trailed up, up, up. But she knew that scent. She didn't need to see the face. His hands closed over her upper arms, and instantly her flesh came alive beneath his grasp.

"Gray," he whispered. And in her name, she heard more than a single word should contain. She heard love and hope and a promise. When his body shifted to accommodate her, she felt a thousand tomorrows in his touch. She dared not look up in his eyes. She knew what she'd find. Of course she did; this was Miah and she was Gray and what was between them was as powerful as it was inexplicable. And it was death for her.

"Don't," she whispered back. Why did the contact with his body steal every last bit of energy from hers? It was like grabbing a live wire and then being perplexed by the damage.

He released her with one hand and used it to capture her chin. He lifted her face until their eyes met.

Movement beside them faded into their space. She heard the voice of her date. "Excuse me, but, uh, that's my date. I'm afraid you are over the line here."

Gray's eyes drifted shut; such weakness filled his voice, it would be pathetic if she wasn't a little relieved at the interruption. Miah left her and the spot where he'd been was cold. He got nose to nose with her date, then dared him to come closer. The cat doctor dropped into his seat with a plop. Miah leaned over the table like a grizzly over a meal and stared him down. His voice was low and deadly. "This is the mother of my child and you're going to sit right there with your mouth shut while I talk to her."

Gray actually heard his mouth snap closed. Within a heartbeat, Miah was back and holding her. "Gray, I made a mess of everything. But I'm begging you to give me another chance. David and you are the only things in the world that matter. I don't want to miss him growing up. I want to be there every day. But that's not why I'm here now. I love you, Gray. I don't think I can live without you. I want you in my bed every night and in my arms every morning."

A vise had clamped her heart. It couldn't beat, couldn't send blood through her system. Miah went on, "David said you cried for the first week. He'd hear you late at night."

Panic rushed in. She didn't think he'd known.

"I've caused you enough pain. From now on, I only want to cause you happy tears. Gray, I love you and I want you to marry me."

The room spun. Somewhere off in the distance there was a real world where women went on dates with self-impressed veterinarians. Out there was a world where twelve-year-olds acted their age. But right here, here was the fairy tale. It was she and Miah, and she was useless to fight him because she loved him. Had always loved him. Would always love him. But fear surged into her mind, taking it captive. Miah wasn't perfect, but he'd given up so quickly. Maybe he'd learned and maybe he'd never do that again. But what if he did? What if a year or two or ten down the road, something scared him and just like that, he'd be gone? She couldn't survive it. She needed someone who would fight to the death for her if that's what it took. Her heart screamed yes, but her mind fought back. In a breathy whisper, she uttered, "No."

For being a mountain of a man, it looked like a gust of wind could knock him over. "What?" He drew closer, examining her face.

"I said no." With each word she felt stronger, more powerful. At least if she only depended on herself, she could survive the worst life could throw at her.

His breathing hitched and, for an instant, she wondered if he would pass out.

"I'm sorry, Miah."

He dropped his hands from her. His face had gone white.

Gray swallowed, but her throat was cotton. She drifted away from him and started to slide back into the seat across from her date, but strong hands clamped on her arm and pulled her right back. "And I'm not giving up," he growled. "I won't give up on you, Gray. I'll fight for the rest of my life and if God will let me, I'll fight for you right into the next life. I'm sorry. Maybe that's not fair to you, but I'm just not letting go. Not. Ever. Again."

He was a prince on a white horse, his words sailing right into the deepest part of her heart. They wound around her uncertainty; they liberated her fear. But Gray wasn't some weakened, emaciated princess. In the root of her being, she was strong. She'd meet her man face-to-face, toe-to-toe. If he said he was never giving up, she'd make him prove it. Right now. Gray jerked free from him and clamped her teeth shut. "You're *not* giving up?"

Confusion flickered across his face. "I'm never giving up."

She grabbed his chin. "Look me in the eye and say it again."

A smile threatened to appear on his face, she could see it, toying at the edges of his mouth. And she knew he understood. Because a night, not long before, they'd stood in the parking lot of a speakeasy declaring their love, each one telling the other to "say it again."

He fought the grin no longer. "I'm not ever giving up on you. On us."

It was there, in the Neon Moon with her date beside her and the man she loved captured between her thumb and index finger, that Gray felt the first sensations of what life without fear could offer. She'd been a captive for so long, but now she was free. Her smile was quick. Eyes blinking back the tears she didn't want to cry. "You swear?"

"I do."

Her heart beat with the knowledge of what she was about to do. Enormous in its scope, all-encompassing in its radius. She was Gray and he was Miah and together, they were something more, something beyond human comprehension, something that could span galaxies and live out the fairy tale she'd always dreamed. With plump tears in her eyes, she said, "I do, too." She threw her arms around his neck. "Miah, I love you."

He held her there for a moment then tilted to look at her. "That's it? Now we can move on together?"

"Yes." She shook her head and her hair danced over his arms. "All I ever wanted was for you to fight for me. Knowing you will . . . it gives me everything I need."

When his body melted against her, Gray kissed him, her mouth closing over his, their hearts pounding against one another. And again, she heard the distinct sound of applause.

They glanced around the room to find an audience of captivated dinner guests watching them. The cat doctor scooted from the seat and mumbled something about not paying the check. In a moment, he was gone. The people in the Neon Moon faded away and there was only Gray and Miah. "Let's take a walk," he growled in her ear.

She grabbed her jacket from the seat while he tossed money on the table. "At this time of night?"

"Yeah. I know a great little graveyard right around the corner."

He tucked her beneath his arm as they left the restaurant. "Ooooh. I love graveyards."

EPILOGUE

Gray smiled at her reflection in the mirror—Mrs. Jeremiah McKinley. Miah entered the hotel room with a full ice bucket for the champagne. The wedding had been a quick one because Gray didn't care about things like long white dresses and hundreds of flowers. They'd taken David and Caleb and the whole crew from the artists' retreat and gone to Eureka Springs. Of course, she'd tried to get Miah on board with having the service in the graveyard and she'd failed. The quaint turn-of-the-century hotel provided a perfect backdrop of natural beauty for the service, complete with a rocky waterfall nestled in the beautiful Arkansas Mountains. She had to concede; it was a better choice than leaning headstones and rusty fences.

David had left the hotel with Charlee and Ian and would stay with them for a few days while Gray and Miah had their honeymoon. Caleb would be checking up on David while he did his painting therapy with Mr. Gruber.

Gray'd just pulled a delicate piece of black-lace lingerie from her suitcase, but before she could steal away into the bathroom, Miah caught her in his arms. He ran a finger under the edge of the shoulder strap of her wedding dress, sending her body into orbit. "What's this?" He took the lingerie from her hand, letting it dangle on his finger.

"That should be obvious." She giggled when the strap of her dress slipped right off her shoulder. He lowered the silky black garment and dropped a kiss on the bare spot where her dress strap had been.

"You won't be needing it." He tossed the lingerie back into her suitcase and spun her to face away from him then concentrated his attention on the tiny pearl buttons on the bodice of her gown. "You won't be needing this, either."

Her gaze trailed to the bed, exposing her neck. He dropped a kiss there on the vessel throbbing beneath her jaw while he continued to loosen the gown. His hands moved with the precision of a soldier who could fieldstrip a rifle and reassemble it in total darkness. Gray cleared her throat; it had gone completely dry. The truth was, she was as nervous as . . . well . . . as a virgin on her wedding night. But she was also excited. Because in her mind, she'd played out this fantasy hundreds of times and already *this* was better than any her mind had created. When the top of her dress was loose and she had to use her forearms against her ribs to hold it in place, she pulled one solid, steadying breath. "Miah," she whispered.

He'd gotten lost somewhere with his lips making tiny little kisses down her spine. The sensation was dizzying and if he didn't carry her to the bed, she might faint before making it.

He growled in response to his name while one hand skated down the edge of her long hair and swept it all out of the way, over her shoulder. Goose bumps spread across her arms.

"What if . . ."

He must have registered the concern in her voice because he stopped and angled his body so he could look at her face.

"What if . . ." She cast her gaze to the floor. It was marble, solid. "What if I disappoint you?"

He took her face in his hands. "That's not possible, Gray. This—" and he motioned between them as he said it, "—is just part of who we are. Together. Almost thirteen years ago a young girl rocked my world. That was you. I didn't even know how important you were and still you changed everything for me that night. The real question is, what if I disappoint you?"

"Are you kidding me?" She laughed. "I've waited my whole life for this."

"Well, let's not keep you waiting any longer."

Her arms loosened against her ribs and her eyes drifted shut. His mouth, his lips, they were lethal and she couldn't wait to feel just how many ways he could destroy her, revive her, destroy her again. "You're right. We've waited long enough."

He bent and placed a delicate kiss on her ribs. She'd never realized that part of her flesh was so sensitive. "You have a promise to make good on."

"And I intend to," she purred.

He circled her, placing kisses here and there as he went along, discovering a new taste and a new texture at each spot. Standing behind her, his lips and mouth trailed over her back. She tried to breathe but was lost and floating down the river that was Miah. He lifted her until she was in his arms. He'd carried her across the threshold the same way.

Gray let her hands roam over his chest. "I love you, Jeremiah McKinley."

"I love you, too, Mary Grace McKinley." And with the gentleness of a dove, he deposited her on the king-size bed, where she fulfilled every promise she'd ever made him.

Two hours later and just as the moon began to peek into the bedroom of the honeymoon suite, Gray drifted off to sleep. She woke at the nudge of Miah's ribs against her. His fingers trailed her arm and if bliss were water, she was drowning in the largest ocean on the planet. She looked up at him. "You happy?"

He chuckled. "Only you would ask something like that at a time like this."

She scrunched her face and leaned up on one elbow. Her hair fell in waves around them.

Miah captured some of it in his hands. "Am I happy? I just had the most incredible experience with the most incredible woman in the world."

She smiled, but he'd grown serious. "I'm not kidding, Gray. That night, all those years ago, I said you'd possessed me. Nothing since then had ever even come close. But now, I'm living that moment, that . . . magic all over again. And I can't believe I'm going to live it for the rest of my life."

Magic. Her? No. She was just Gray and he was just Miah. But together, they *were* more. They'd created David. They'd weathered almost losing him. And their future held promise. Because they loved each other beyond measure, and what on this planet could compare to that? As the night settled in, lengthening the shadows around their bed, Gray lay in his arms counting the stars through the window. Just beyond the moon, the Eye of God kept watch over them.

Miah and David walked to the water, as was their weekend habit. They'd been doing that for three months now. Each Saturday morning, they'd go to the lakeside, Miah would start a fire and there, they'd each write a note to the fathers they'd lost. Miah stoked up the blaze. "Did you tell your dad about the fishing competition?" It was a father/son tournament and they'd taken third place.

"No."

David's demeanor was different today. Miah wondered if something had happened at school. They went on, writing in silence, and when

Miah was finished, he tossed the sheet onto the burning logs. David seemed to be struggling a little and Miah wished he knew what it was about, but he wouldn't press.

David brushed his hair from his brow. "Okay, I'm done."

Miah waited for him to silently reread it, then fold it and toss it onto the flame. When David didn't move, he asked, "You want me to give you a few minutes? I can wait for you up at the house."

David's face contorted; he gripped the paper so tightly it wrinkled in his hand. "No. I just . . . I . . ." His lips pressed together in a straight line and he held the paper out to Miah.

He took it, uncertain if David wanted him to wait or lay it on the fire now.

"It's to you."

Miah's fingers tightened on the single page. He lifted it slowly.

> *Dear Dad,*
>
> *There are a lot of things I want to say, but most of all, I want to tell you thanks for finding me. I know I didn't make it easy at first, but you made me want to try harder. Since I've been here, I've gotten to do lots of things and found out some things I really like. Plus, you make great hot cocoa and Gray loves you.*
>
> *I guess what I'm trying to say, Miah, is that I think it's time I start calling you by your real name. Dad. I hope that's okay with you. I already told Bill I was going to do that in a letter in my room. I think he'd like that. I used to think that if I called you Dad, it would be like erasing him. But now I know it's not. You were my dad first. Then Bill. Now you again. I guess I'm lucky that way to have had two great dads.*
>
> *Anyway, I guess that's all I wanted to say.*
> *I love you, Dad.*
>
> *Your son,*
> *David*

Miah fought to keep the tears at bay but knew it was a battle already lost. There was no voice with his words when he said, "Can I keep this one?"

David nodded.

Miah carefully folded the paper and placed it in his pocket. David watched him closely, chewing the inside of his cheek. "Is it okay?"

Miah grabbed him by the shoulders. "It's better than okay, David. You just made me the happiest man on earth."

David released a sigh. "Okay. Good." He landed in his father's arms for a bone-crushing hug. "Hey, Dad?"

Miah kept hold; fact was, he was never letting go. "Yes?"

"Can't breathe."

"Sorry." But he *would* need to loosen his grip now and then.

David nodded up the hill behind them. "We gotta get back. Mom is cooking and now there's black smoke rolling out of the kitchen window."

Miah laughed and turned to see his wife waving a kitchen towel and directing the smoke.

David stopped halfway to the house. "Can we go fishing later, Dad?" He was sampling the new title for Miah, trying it out, seeing how he liked it.

"Yes. But you've got to let me in on your secret to catching those large catfish."

David's mouth twisted in mock concentration. "I'll think about it."

Miah threw an arm around his shoulder. "I can live with that." If dreams were pebbles, he had enough to fill a swimming pool. If love were magic, he could put Houdini to shame. And if life were promises, he'd live to be a ripe old age with the woman he loved and the child they'd created when they were merely kids themselves. He'd once told his dad in a letter that he hoped to be a good father someday. Someday had come in an instant, and though Miah wasn't perfect, he was determined. For the rest of his life, he'd make good on the promises he should have made over a decade ago.

He could do it. He could be a good soldier, a good man, and a good father.

After all, the Eye of God was watching over him.

ACKNOWLEDGMENTS

A special thank-you to Angela Whitener, supervisory coordinator and administrator at James A. Haley Veterans' Hospital in Tampa for her information on Traumatic Brain Injuries.

A giant thanks to my dear friend Julie Palella, a law professional who wrote a Child Protective Plan for my character, David Olson. The information in it was invaluable.

A heartfelt thanks to my editor, Charlotte Herscher, who helped make this story what it is now.

Thanks to my supportive family, who never let me go hungry or without coffee during the long hours of writing and edits.

Ellis Jones, web designer extraordinaire, thank you so much for building my new website. It's incredible, and I will likely be your biggest cheerleader for a very long time!

My deepest gratitude goes to the Johns Creek Veterans Association and the Johns Creek Memorial Walk near Atlanta. I was so honored to have my words become a small part of the memorial for our US veterans. May America never forget what our troops have paid and the hefty price they continue to pay for our freedom. God bless you.

ABOUT THE AUTHOR

Heather Burch writes full time and lives in Florida. Her debut novel was released in 2012 and garnered praise from *USA Today*, *Booklist* magazine, *Romantic Times*, and *Publishers Weekly*. Her epic love story, *One Lavender Ribbon*, was an international bestseller and one of the top 100 books on Amazon Kindle in 2014. *Down the Hidden Path* is the follow-up novel to *Along the Broken Road*, the first book in The Roads to River Rock series. Living in a house where she's the only female, Heather is intrigued by the relationships that form among men, especially soldiers. Her heartbeat is to tell unforgettable stories of love and war, commitment and loss . . . stories that make your heart sigh. Please visit heatherburch-books.com for more about Heather. She loves to hear from readers!